The Equity OF Love

MARCUS LAPIERRE

ISBN (hardcover) 978-1-7389394-0-4
ISBN (paperback) 978-1-7389394-2-8
ISBN (ebook) 978-1-7389394-1-1

CONTENTS

PART THREE: UNDONE

PART FOUR: HEALING

PART FIVE: COUPLING

PART SIX: LOYALTIES

PART SEVEN: LEGACY

PROLOGUE: AMSTERDAM, 2010

WE arrived in Amsterdam two nights ago. At a nice hotel near the rail station, we've set up our base for a few days to wander the streets, see the museums and galleries, and enjoy the bars. Anne Frank House is on the agenda for tomorrow, and a stroll through the Jordaan neighborhood.

I'm getting my clothes for tomorrow from my luggage. There, beneath the shirts, socks, and underwear, tucked away, is an envelope containing a manuscript. A story. It's my secret. My traveling companion knows nothing of it.

Like any amateur writer without a grand idea, I wrote about events in my own life; the only ones that seemed worthy of a story. I wrote about her, my desire, and her continual pull upon me. She is no longer a fire on my soul; she is dormant embers perpetually burning that can be stirred on a moment's notice and ignite an entire forest. She is the reason this book exists. She is the reason why even when I am happy, even when I am content, I am ungrateful and always wondering.

Wondering, thinking—what if? What a horrible state *what if* is.

This manuscript has a destination, a journey's end of its own. It's not an agent or a publisher, but an altar of sorts. There is a place I will leave it, and hopefully, the dreams that spurred it. What-ifs can kill you if you let them, distorting the possibility of complete happiness. They must be burned, forgotten.

And yet, this saddens me even as I touch the envelope and feel its smooth surface. I'm proud of what's here, of the secret labor I've put into this story. And I doubt; I doubt my own determination. I feel the story, the history, its words, and its characters whom I know so well. There's only one character I distrust in all the pages. It's me. I don't know how to write me. And I don't know that I like what I am.

After I've laid out my clothes, I turn to my companion. She's tired and is lying on the bed, peering over a map of one of the guidebooks I have.

She's beautiful. Because of her belief in me, her love for me, I am here.

I lie down beside her and rest my hand on her breast over her heart. She laughs, saying she's too tired, but she has misinterpreted my intent. I want to feel her heartbeat, the organ that pumps her blood. I want to imagine *her* blood flowing.

I pray *she's* safe.

PART ONE: POSTMORTEM

CHAPTER 1

A Visitor (Richard Earning, February 2004)

J UST as Richard Earning flicked ash out of the car window, he saw him: a figure rounding the corner of the single-story red office building. Few people ever trod to this small back parking lot other than the employees of Enigma Solutions. Few people even knew there was another office secreted away behind the accounting firm.

The man was large already, but his frame was further ballooned by a bulky winter jacket that rendered him gigantic. Carrying the lumbering weight of his mass, he walked as delicately as he could on the path toward a brown industrial-steel door, more fit for a warehouse than an office.

He was trying to avoid slipping on the ice. Small, flurried steps were followed by great long strides to the safety of an asphalt patch. But this jerky movement, combined with a cold wind, caused the fedora on top of his head to teeter, as if it might fall off at any moment. He had to rescue it several times by planting his large hand firmly on his crown to pin the hat down. This precarious game of hopscotch, where he risked throwing out his back or breaking his bones, lasted until he reached the door. There, he paused and then pounded on it with his fist. At length, the door opened, and the man was granted entry.

Richard had never seen the man before but knew exactly who he was.

Earlier that morning, his boss, a short, stocky fellow named Bill Spindrall, said to expect an important visitor. Richard, rightly curious, asked who.

"'Sname's David Burlow," Bill said. "One of James Hardich's friends and business partners."

"What does he have to do with Enigma?"

A slight frown passed over Bill's face. "He's James's executor. I knew he'd come calling eventually. Didn't know he'd do it in person, though." He ran his hand through his perpetually disheveled brown hair, pushing back his bangs. But the attempt to keep them at bay failed as they crashed back down upon his forehead.

Richard had worked with Bill long enough to know it was his twitch, his tell when he was troubled. "You're worried. Should we be?"

"Yes, but the matter needs to be sorted. The best scenario would be if we had a million dollars to buy out James's stake. What are the odds of you having a large pile of cash you're sitting on that you can loan me?"

Richard shook his head. "You'd need to raise my salary quite a bit for that to happen."

"And that's never going to happen," Bill said, grinning. Then, more seriously, he added, "All will be well. Hopefully, nothing changes, and we just carry on our way as we always have."

"Do you know him?"

"Burlow? Sort of. Met him at a party at James's house last year, and I've seen him at a couple of events. Obviously saw him at the funeral. Burlow's not a warm fellow, not much of a conversationalist. I know more *of* him than I know him, if that makes sense. He did well by James and was a bit like a friend, a butler, and a secretary all rolled into one. When you see him, you'll know what I mean. He's literally the size of three people!"

"Coming in person doesn't sound good," Richard said.

"Hey. The lucky wife says not to worry. Let's leave it at that. You run the Pit, and I'll manage Burlow."

That was the extent of the discussion before they moved on to other business. And although Richard went about his tasks, he remained curious and uneasy. The prophecies of Bill's wife weren't reassuring.

Now, Richard stubbed his cigarette in the ashtray and rolled up the window. He reached down and grabbed some trays of coffee and a box of doughnuts from the passenger floor, stacked them precariously, and made his own careful journey across the parking lot to the steel door. Once at the door, he gave it two solid, heavy kicks and waited. To the side of the door was a small plastic sign that read, *Enigma Solutions: Innovating Education. 26 Columbia Ave, Suite B, Waterloo, ON.* But below it, a paper sign, taped with layers of duct tape to ensure it stayed in place in the middle of winter, read, *Doorbell broken. Please bang loudly for assistance.*

The door was opened from within by Jeremy, a young man with a Bob Marley T-shirt on, a thick head of dark curls, and a patchy beard that seemed too old for his face.

"That took forever. Pit was getting anxious," Jeremy said, taking the doughnuts and one of the trays of coffee.

"Roads were slippery," Richard said, wiping his dress shoes on the rubber mat that covered a small landing just before a flight of descending stairs.

They went down into the basement offices of Enigma. At the bottom was a hallway running perpendicular to the stairs. Though they veered to the right to enter the Pit, Richard cast a glance in the opposing direction. At the other end of the hall, the door to the boardroom, and Enigma's only meeting room, was closed. Was that where Bill was with David Burlow?

The Pit was a large, unadorned room of some fifteen cubicles. Only half were occupied. The others were vacant, their emptiness alluding to Bill's growth aspirations for Enigma. The occupied cubicles were all on the edges of the wall with access to a sky view from the small windows that were near the ceiling. Below ground level, a seat with a sliver of a view outside could well be considered a perk, even if all the inhabitants saw was the gray, overcast blandness of a winter's day. The only light that touched the faces in the Pit this morning was yellow and stale, from the phosphorescent bulbs in the ceiling.

"Fancy stitches, here, returns bearing gifts," Jeremy announced to the room while pointing at Richard's suit.

"Someone has to look professional," Richard said. "I only look fancy because none of you even try."

The Pit's inhabitants stood up from their desks and computer screens to claim their coffees and grab one of the doughnuts. The crew had all adopted the same casual jean and T-shirt attire as Jeremy, complete with varying stages of facial hair growth.

"Hang on, hang on," Richard said as the small gathering of developers and a lone QA specialist congregated around Richard's cubicle. Eager hands reaching for coffee and food froze in midair.

"Before anyone gets anything," Richard went on, "I want to make sure: is our release going to be ready by the end of the day? I mean QAed and everything. No mess-ups."

"We finished integration testing last night, and everything is good," one of the team said.

"All is on track," Jeremy said, clapping Richard on the back. "You should probably buy us beers for all the late nights we've been doing."

"I can't wait to buy you guys a beer," Richard said. "Just make sure we go live smoothly next week for the university's pilot. They are going to have three new instructors in distance education running our software for connected classrooms. It's a big day."

"It'll work" Jeremy said.

As the Pit lingered around Richard's cubicle, they devoured the doughnuts while bantering briefly about work and plans for the upcoming weekend. Jeremy maneuvered closer to Richard and quietly said, "A small planet entered our orbit. He's in the boardroom with Billy."

Richard nodded. "Yeah, saw him when he was coming in. I'll brief you later."

He looked at the last coffee, still untouched in a tray. It was Bill's.

Richard grabbed it and left the Pit to walk down the lone hallway to the boardroom. The hall walls were white, but nobody could tell if it was a coat of cheap paint or a good primer. Scuff marks and black streaks from errant shoes and banged laptops were everywhere. He passed the storage room, followed by the only office at Enigma, its nameplate reading, *Bill Spindrall, Co-Founder and CEO*. And he passed the only two pieces of artwork in the whole office: framed motivational posters that likely inspired no one, even if someone condescended to notice. One was the picture of a golfer on an empty golf course with the caption *Success—becoming an expert at something is one part luck, and the rest is practice*. The other, a picture of an iceberg floating in the sea, with its immense size captured below the waterline, followed by the words: *The depth of your strength is not measured by what appears on the surface*.

When he reached the boardroom door, Richard knocked and entered.

In the middle of a small and windowless room was a scratched-up rectangular table with eight chairs around it. The synthetic leather on the chairs was either so old or of such shabby material that it slouched on the chair frames.

Two men were seated across from each other. Bill looked perturbed; he was pushing his hair back with his hand spasmodically. The other man, the "planet," had an unreadable expression.

"Oh yeah, my coffee," Bill said distractedly, taking the cup from Richard. He seemed to recollect himself and said to David, "This is Richard—he owns the product, tells the Pit what to develop."

Richard greeted David Burlow, extending his hand.

Burlow took it with dismissive annoyance and grunted. It was both the opening and the termination of their conversation—no pleasantries.

Sensing the two were in the midst of an intense discussion, Richard left as quickly as he had entered.

At his desk in the Pit, he answered some emails while wondering about Bill's visibly agitated behavior in the boardroom. After an hour, he overheard the voices of the men in the hallway, followed by David Burlow's slow, heavy stomp up the stairs. Richard was on the verge of getting up to go to Bill's office to find out what had happened, but he had no need.

Bill came into the Pit and right up to Richard's desk, and abruptly said, "Going to work the rest of the day from home. Run the ship and call if there's an emergency." Then he was gone.

Jeremy must have overheard the conversation, for he came over to Richard's desk. "Did he just leave? What the hell happened?"

"That man who was here was James Hardich's executor. And when I brought Bill his coffee, it looked a little grim."

"Shit. Think we'll be okay?" Jeremy asked.

"I'm sure Bill would say something if we were in a bad way."

"This is where it would have been nice to have voting shares. If our five percent were real, Bill would have to tell us what's happening. This nonvoting share stuff is bullshit; we're at their mercy. The Bourgeoisie are always looking for a reason to exclude the proles, even when they throw us a bone after we bust our asses."

"I'll take the bone. And don't use the proles argument. We're the only two guys in the Pit with the equity, even if it's nonvoting. We're proof some proles are better than others."

"Whatever," Jeremy said, giving him the finger. "I just hope things are all right."

And Richard did too. He spent the rest of his day trying to stay focused on his work.

* * *

That night, Richard sat at the kitchen table in his small apartment in Waterloo, sipping coffee. Caffeine at this time meant he would be up late, but he didn't care. It was Friday, after all.

Though the morning's events had made him anxious, they had also stirred his muses. His Uni-ball pen crossed the page, inking an imagination that embellished his memories.

The immense man stomped across the icy snow in the parking lot, making a crushing sound. He was an unstoppable force, and anyone who bore witness to his coming could see where he had been by a path of large foot-sized indents behind him.

Arriving at a large steel door, he growled a laugh at its presence. It was just another minor obstacle, like the cold, like the snow. He banged on it with such force and for so long and with such frequency, that were it not opened to give him access, he might well have knocked it right off its hinges with the monstrous velocity of his hammering arm. He was a corporate wolf, and he'd blow this place down.

Once inside, he descended some stairs and entered a small office space. He scoffed at the assets of the little company, determining that its worth was at the lower end. He would devour it, as he had so many other fledgling firms before. They were young and tender, defenseless. He would gorge himself on it, then sell off the carcass to ready buyers. That was his way. And he had done well by it, fattening himself on the weak, the meek …

A voice at the back of Richard's mind wondered if Jeremy's political views were influencing his thoughts. But he continued to write, unsure where the paragraphs were going, or if it was even a story. Probably, these scribblings would be added to the hundreds of others he had amassed over the years: half-written beginnings ranging from a few hundred to a few thousand words, incomplete like half-built houses. Still, the moment he saw David Burlow in Enigma's parking lot, he was impatient to write it down. Perhaps, in a mundane life, inspiration must be found in commonplace affairs.

But David Burlow's visit to Enigma had not been commonplace. And Richard had yet to learn the outcome from whatever transpired in the boardroom.

What was clear was that a messenger for a dead business partner had brought news. And judging by Bill's abrupt departure, it had been unfavorable. What was the problem? And what did it mean for him and Enigma?

The death of Enigma's primary investor had caused uncertainty. Richard mulled over the possibilities in the back of his mind as he drank his coffee and distracted himself by starting another scene for yet another story.

CHAPTER 2

The Inheritance *(Xavier Hardich, February 2004)*

O N a fine Saturday morning, the sun's brilliance was amplified by a foot of pristine white snow that had fallen overnight. Xavier Hardich stood at the window in the first-floor office of the Hardich home in Cambridge, overlooking the front yard. Stirring his cappuccino, he watched the sunlight reflect off the snow, little shards of light that seemed to have their own power source in the white powder itself.

In this room, Xavier's father, James, had toiled. He had started businesses, sold them, sat on boards as a director, and invested in the markets. He had built a small fortune. And it was this room Xavier found comfort in as he pondered his options—his next move.

He was eager for news today.

The room looked exactly as James Hardich had left it, right down to the scribbled notes beside a computer on an oak desk and a stack of printed emails. These artifacts lingered despite being over four months old. Xavier's mother, Elinor, had forbidden any disturbance to the room. She wanted nothing of her husband's touched—no book or pen holder or paperweight moved, no drawers opened. The office was a shrine to James. Only in the last few weeks, a concession had been made with his mother where he was permitted to enter and sit in the office as a place of quiet contemplation and guidance.

Xavier would have preferred to claim the space for his own work, but he would indulge his mother's fancy for now. There was no point frustrating her. She needed to grieve in her way.

It had only been two months ago, in December, that James had died. He was buried in the cemetery just a ten-minute walk from the house. The event was still fresh in the minds of the Hardiches, as James's gravestone was fresh in the graveyard, with a certain luster and polish that made it stand out among its weather-worn companions. James might be pleased to know he was outdoing his neighbors at that place of repose.

Xavier's father had not breathed any last words of wisdom before he passed on. There was no profound utterance as Xavier and his family surrounded James in a spacious private hospital room, waiting for a sign of possible recovery, waiting for the man punctured and violated by tubes to regain consciousness from the brain aneurism that had stricken him. The family waited and whispered around James, hoping. They hoped until the hospital equipment gave a high-pitched drone when it no longer had anything to report.

The ending seemed grotesquely unfit to such a loved and respected man in the community. Everyone, including Xavier, had assumed he would get better. "He will recover, he's a strong man," they said. "He's always been lucky, he'll get through." Perhaps he had been too lucky; perhaps his ability to defy the revolutions of Fortune's wheel, to somehow always remain at the zenith of her spin, had frustrated that capricious lady so much that the bitch thought she'd attack not his fortune, but his body.

And now that lady seemed to be tempting Xavier, challenging him, goading him.

He was taking stock of his life, his ambitions, his accomplishments. And he was all too aware that his storeroom was empty. Sure, he had a job as a sales representative for RIM, the maker of Blackberry, but it was a lower-level position in his estimation. As a young man of twenty-six, he was still living at home and hadn't thought much about the future, and life was relatively carefree. Until now.

Everything was different. A torch had been passed to him, a responsibility. Xavier had a sense of a newfound charge—an obligation to preserve the integrity and reputation of the family name. He must assert himself and lead his family through the darkness that his father's death had created.

He went to the desk and sat down in his father's high-backed chair and scanned the business section of the newspaper. What conclusions was he supposed to arrive at, given the news? What action was he to take? There must be some intelligence here that was meaningful. His father had always read the paper, and Xavier hoped that by replicating this ritual, some insight would descend upon him.

The rapid, light tread of footsteps on stairs descending from the second floor caught his ear. It would be his sister, Augusta. Earlier, he had overheard her talking to their mother and knew she was going to the University of Waterloo to do some research. He assumed she would then stay at her boyfriend's for a night or two, which was good news—he wouldn't have to see her for the next couple of days. The side door of the house, which exited to the standalone garage, opened and slammed shut. She was gone.

Xavier tried to focus on the newspaper again, but he didn't read long before he heard a car horn out front. He left the desk and walked to the front window again. Augusta had stopped her Volkswagen Golf as she reversed down the driveway to the street. She was talking through the passenger window to a large man wearing a fedora coming up the walk to the house. They must have exchanged words for a full minute before they broke apart, each resuming their journey.

James Hardich's old dog had finally come.

Xavier went to the front door and opened it just as David Burlow arrived. They exchanged some formal, though not warm, greetings, and he told Burlow to come into the office when he was ready. Xavier waited patiently in his father's old chair, listening to the great sighs, pulls for breath, and shuffling in the hallway as his guest removed his shoes.

When Burlow appeared in the doorway, he didn't enter the room but paused at the threshold. Even when Xavier motioned irritably for the man to take one of the chairs on the opposing side of the desk, Burlow did not budge.

"Does your mother know you're in here?" Burlow asked, with a disapproving look on his visage.

"It doesn't matter. I don't need to ask permission," Xavier replied tersely. "I invited you in here, so come in."

Burlow flashed him a scowl before entering and sitting in one of the chairs. He unzipped his coat, which Xavier had never offered to take, but he never took off his fedora.

"You said you wanted to talk. And you refused to tell me about Bill Spindrall. Did you even meet with him yesterday?" Xavier asked as he stirred his cappuccino again, this time furiously, the spoon making a loud clang.

"That was my errand, wasn't it?" Burlow asked. His eyes locked onto the desk, where the newspaper was spread out. His jowls bunched up either in a smile or grimace.

"You gonna tell me the result? Does he have the money to buy me out?"

"No, he can't buy your father's equity."

"*My* equity," Xavier said curtly.

"Given to you by your father," Burlow said. "And it's also your sister's."

"She'll follow my lead. I have more experience in these matters."

Burlow snorted.

"Why did you want to see me in person?" Xavier asked. "Or was there someone else you were hoping would be here?"

Burlow ignored the question, choosing instead to reach inside his coat to produce a large, folded brown envelope. "I wanted to drop Enigma's accounting off and Spindrall's plan for the company. You should see it and understand what you own equity in." He placed the envelope on the desk. "Has a CD in it too, with other information. Do you want me to explain it all to you?"

"I'll make sense of it."

There was a brief silence before Burlow spoke. "Just let Enigma grow on the side and on its own. Spindrall's an honest man, and he's sticking to the five-year plan. He's on track to have a good little company. If you want to help, help him with the contacts at the schools. He relied on your father for those. Keep your current job and be hands-off with Enigma. It's just a seed that someone else waters and nurtures until it matures. Then you make your money with no effort. You should pursue your own things."

"Enigma *is* my own thing," Xavier declared. "And why are you so concerned about it? It's not like my father included you on the deal when he decided to invest in it. Why was that?"

"He knew I didn't believe in tech companies as a viable investment. And I still don't."

"Or he wanted you to know how irrelevant you were," Xavier said. "My father left Enigma to me so I could do something with it. I won't just sit around and hope it succeeds. Though, I suppose that tactic has served you well. You were always looked after if you clung to my dad."

Burlow let out a humph and leaned back in his chair. "I just rode on his coattails, did I? Think whatever you want. I owe it to your father and your mother to advise you on what's best. I say it's best for you to leave this business alone. What do you know? What makes you qualified to step into any position at Enigma? Your two years of experience? Your MBA?"

"There's younger than me that have built successful companies."

"You're right. They had an idea, sacrificed everything to bring it into fruition, and earned that success," Burlow said. "You're inheriting a position. Let's not mince words about it."

"Ah, there it is: you don't like the fact my dad left me his equity. If you had children, you'd know this is a common occurrence. Were you hoping he'd leave it to you?"

"I don't care about the shares. I am telling you what is best for Enigma and you."

"Whatever candor and advice you gave to my father doesn't extend to me. You're executor of his estate, that's all. It's my business," Xavier responded heatedly. He sipped his cappuccino and eyed Burlow over the rim of his cup.

Burlow leaned forward and seemed ready to engage in the argument. His face was redder now and his jowls were twitching. But whatever tirade he was about to release ceased at the sound of his name pronounced from behind him.

"David! I knew I heard your voice," Elinor Hardich said from the door. She looked down at the threshold with trepidation, and, as if mustering courage, crossed it with a deliberate step to enter the room and approach the men. As soon as she rested her small hand on his large shoulder, Burlow's anger seemed to dissipate, his large mass relaxing back into his chair. Beside Burlow, Xavier's mother looked small and dainty.

Elinor looked at Xavier sitting in her late husband's chair and gave a faint frown. "You haven't touched anything, I hope."

Xavier assured her nothing had been disrupted.

Elinor must have heard the tension in their discussion, for she said to Burlow, "Although I never really understood what you and James talked about in this room, I don't recall many arguments happening. Are you two getting on?"

"I think we're just wrapping up, Mom," Xavier said, before Burlow could answer. Her entrance gave him the opportunity to end the meeting and calm his nerves. "So, your timing's good. I've decided I should make arrangements to meet Bill Spindrall at Enigma."

"Ah, the company!" Elinor smiled. "I think Xavier will be as good as James at this business stuff—don't you, David?"

Burlow chuckled. "Oh yes, he's a quick study."

"I knew he would be! I worry about him, though. He's become very serious of late," she said, smiling at Xavier.

Xavier let out a long breath. "I'm fine, Mom."

"I know you are," she said. Again, to Burlow, she continued, "He's been so good to me, so attentive this last little while. He's started to make it a point of being home for dinner at least once a week now. He was so busy before with clients."

"Clients, eh? I'm glad he respects his dear mother—he's a good son, then," Burlow said flippantly.

Elinor seemed unable to detect Burlow's sarcasm, which made Xavier seethe more.

"I should make you men some eggs and sausages," Elinor said. "Just like the old days, right, David? When you and James would sit in this room and do all your business planning and machinations. You'll stay for brunch, won't you?"

Xavier watched how happy his mother had become at the sight of Burlow. She was pleased to have one of the old guard around—a connection to the past that persisted in the present.

Burlow smiled at Elinor. "I'm not very hungry. But thank you for the offer. As Xavier said, we're wrapping up."

"Nonsense. You must have something." She gave Burlow a pleading look.

"You heard he doesn't want anything," Xavier said, standing up. "We should leave Burlow be so he can get going."

Elinor glared at Xavier. "I'm not going to leave him be."

Xavier saw she was becoming anxious. She could become sad, angry, or flustered with the slightest of triggers since James had passed away. He was trying to think of how to calm her before her emotions escalated to the shedding of tears, when Burlow conceded to her request.

"Perhaps I'm a touch hungry—some brunch never did a man harm. And I do miss the way you make it," he said, bowing his head.

"You see, Xavier? David is hungry. And you offered him nothing. He still has his coat on, for God's sake."

"It's fine, Elinor. I wanted to keep it on. I'll come with you into the kitchen," Burlow said, standing up. He then addressed Xavier flatly. "You have all you need. My duties as executor are done, and this is in your hands now."

Burlow and his mother left the office, leaving him to brood. He heard the faint laughter of his mother in the kitchen. He was glad she could find some moments of joy now. For months she had been solemn, seemingly living in memories. But he wished it wasn't the ogre who was the source of happiness for her.

He didn't know how the man had managed to be so inextricably linked to the family. Like a dog, Burlow seemed to be about all the time, in every room. His parents may laud Burlow as a great friend, but Xavier only saw a beggar living off his father's generosity and achievements.

However, it was the familiarity Burlow had with his mother that Xavier most disliked. The man had always lingered about Elinor at gatherings and events, fawning over her. There was a secret longing lurking in this troll's body. If ever Xavier had doubted it, he couldn't avoid seeing it on full display at his father's funeral. At the front of the church, Burlow sat with them in the pew reserved for family. And Xavier caught Burlow looking for a long time at his mother; he had seen pity there in Burlow's expression but something else too. Was it desire? Joy? Opportunity? Quite possibly, it was all three.

CHAPTER 3

Favors *(Natalie Mitchell, April 2004)*

NATALIE had just come out of the subway at street level when her phone began to chime. She reached into the pocket of her spring jacket, her fingers touching and darting between objects— small wallet, Tylenol, Kleenex pack—until she felt the smooth, closed clamshell of her Razr mobile. Pulling out the sleek, thin, silver device, she looked at the letters that ran across the black screen and flipped the phone open.

"Hey, Granny," she said between breaths.

"Natalie, how are you?" a voice greeted her warmly.

"Good, but I can't talk too long. Got a meeting." She dodged to the left to avoid the large purse of a woman, and then to the right as she almost ended up in the trampling path of a man with his face fixated on his Blackberry screen.

"Oh, you've got an interview?" Granny jubilantly asked.

"Well, no," she said, then paused. "I'm going to meet *him*."

The way she said *him* gave the powerful weight of a proper noun. There was no need to say more, no further description required; it was a single word for a singular representation that could not be confused with any other *him*.

"Oh," Granny's voice lost its energy, its warmth. "Already? I thought you were going to look around a bit more before leaning on him."

"I want to see what he thinks. I'm a little wary of running right back into working for someone else. Who knows, maybe he won't be up for helping me," she said.

"Hmm. It just seems drastic. I still think you should move back in with us to save money. That way you won't need to … you know … need him."

"Granny, we talked about this. That region is hot with startups that could use my skills. And I can be my own boss. He knows people."

"He may know people, but we don't know him; that's for sure."

Natalie bit her tongue. "I have to go, Granny. We'll talk later?"

"Yes, okay. Come by afterwards for tea."

Natalie agreed she would and ended the call. She crossed Bloor Street and entered the vast grounds of Toronto's largest urban park, High Park, and cut off the main road to a well-worn trail going downhill.

The emerging greenery of spring in the park suited her mood and her thoughts. It heralded a new beginning, a new season. The barrenness of winter receded, replaced with the awakening of life that had remained dormant and secluded for months. Trails and paths that had only had infrequent use by committed joggers and walkers when covered by snow and ice now braced for the onslaught of centipede steps and the wheels of humanity. Little feet, large feet, strollers, walkers, wheelchairs, and bicycles would all tread, run, and roll through every swath of pavement, patch of grass, and dirt path. And with humanity came the dogs—digging, running, fetching, and thrashing through bushes, chasing—almost always unsuccessfully—the many smaller animals that called these environs home.

Her trail snaked along the shores of the large Grenadier Pond where birds floated lazily on the breeze-rippled surface. There was a legend, of dubious authenticity, that the pond received its name after British soldiers had fallen through the ice and drowned in the water when conducting a charge against an American position in the War of 1812. And the legend laid the foundation for the ghost stories told to children about spectral hauntings in the park at night—of ghastly, pale, wet men in Grenadier uniforms lurking in the woods and at the water's edge.

When Natalie was a teenager, she and her group of friends would sometimes come to the park at night, using the darkness and trees to conceal them while they experimented with cigarettes and swigged beer or rum borrowed from unsuspecting parents. On more than one occasion, a boy and a girl would hold hands and exchange kisses. Some of her friends ventured greater indiscretions in the darkness behind bushes away from the group.

Just when the ghost stories seemed to be myths created by adults and the teens felt comfortable in the park, a rustle in the bushes, an unexplained flicker of light between the trees would summon the legend of drenched uniformed men to all their imaginations, and they would make excuses to leave, only to return another night with more courage.

For Natalie, High Park was familiar and peaceful. Even now, she found her spirits becoming lighter as the small frets and worries of the day were absorbed by the trees and the air. She left the shoreline of the pond and cut up a gradual but steady hill. At its summit, she entered a small ornamental garden. This was her favorite place in the whole park: three separate fountains and pools of water sunken into the ground. The surrounding wall of hedges that fenced in the pools cloistered the area and gave it a sense of privacy and isolation. Here she had come when her mother died to add her tears to the fountain pools. Here she had come sometime later to sit with him for the first time. In these pools, grief, reflection, and revelations all converged.

She checked her watch; it was still a few minutes to 2 p.m. He was usually punctual, so she opted to sit on a bench overlooking the fountains and wait. There was dampness in the air from a light rainfall a few hours previous. She would occasionally grab a piece of her thick, curly, dark-brown hair to see if it was frizzing.

Seeing movement out of the corner of her eye, she looked over to an adjacent fountain and saw him coming. His beige trench coat was open, revealing a tie and white dress shirt—and his immense girth. He always dressed well, but his size prohibited him from looking well dressed. He wore a flat, brown cap that he raised slightly off his head and tilted toward her in salutation. She smiled and gave a small wave.

"You're looking well," David Burlow said as he reached the bench and sat down beside her. He was out of breath, and small drops of sweat clung to his temples and forehead.

"I hope so; I'm younger than you," she quipped. "How've you been?"

"Good. Busy of course, but good."

"Are you, though?" Natalie asked. She took a more serious tone. "Have you finished all that business of your friend's?"

"Yes," he grunted looking at the fountain. "If you ever want to punish someone, make them your executor."

"I'm glad it's over, then," she said. "I know it was weighing on you the last time we spoke." She put her hand lightly on his arm and gave it a squeeze. He pulled his gaze from the fountain and looked down at her hand as if puzzled. He let her hand linger a moment before slowly pulling his arm away.

He was always this way—guarded, private, distant.

"How's work with that internet stuff?" David asked.

He didn't entirely understand the type of business she was in. She had tried to explain online marketing and user experience to him, but it was a challenge. A couple of times, when she had her computer with her, she showed him some of the projects she was working on, explained the online strategies she created for businesses and how she designed their websites. When she would tell him the price tags of the projects, he was always shocked. He couldn't comprehend that people paid for things they couldn't touch and that didn't exist in the real world.

His question to her remained unanswered for some time. She wasn't sure if she should tell him the news. But wasn't that what she wanted to talk to him about today? Why was she losing her resolve? Perhaps she should just lie and tell him everything was fine. Her granny's phone call played out in her mind.

Acknowledging her hesitation, her silence, he said, without looking at her, "Go on, tell me."

"I left a couple of weeks ago."

As if to absorb this information and its gravity, David craned his head back to look up at the sky and then slowly brought it forward while exhaling a long "Hmm." After a pause, he asked, "Was that your choice? I thought you were getting promoted to a VP or something."

Natalie had told this story often enough to her friends since her departure from the marketing agency she had worked at for four years. She could now recite it succinctly and without emotion. "I was a VP for four weeks. They dangled that carrot, and I chased it. But what I didn't know is that the owners were plotting to sell the company without telling anyone. And they did. They got their money, and everyone else dealt with the fallout. Of course, once the new company came in, there were obvious redundancies. They bought us for our client list, not the people. Another VP and I were cut soon after we trained our replacements. I was packaged off with a few months' severance. Not much of a return for killing myself nights and weekends all these years."

"I see," David said. "I'm sorry to hear that. That's the way of the employee though—always beholden to a master."

"I know, I know," she said. "And I also know the owners of a company can sell it however they like—it's their company."

"Ah, so you have been listening to me. Good. It's not their job to look out for you. It's your job to do that," he lectured, though he hardly needed to.

Over the years, the two of them had frequently discussed business, and she understood his position. As a man who had been an employee and an entrepreneur, David's views were quite clear. If she wanted to control her own destiny, she should have her own business. Otherwise, be an employee dependent on everyone else and don't complain.

"So, what's next?" he asked. "You must be in demand a bit? Got some irons in the fire?"

"I'm still considering my options," Natalie said, looking at him. "People are reaching out. I'd say I'm holding off going to work for someone else so quickly. I want to make sure when I do sign up for something, it's right for me. I was gonna do some contract work for a bit. I don't want to leave the frying pan and jump into the fire."

He nodded at this. She thought she even heard a grunt of approval.

"I know I'm good enough to strike out on my own," Natalie went on. "The nature of the services I provide can be done remotely. I don't need to be on site every day. I have a couple of contacts here, and I've already got a little contract project starting next week. I think I could get more."

"That's a start." David nodded. "Enough to pay your bills?"

"I think so." She paused to collect her thoughts and assemble the sentences carefully. She realized she was nervous. "I also thought you might be able to help me out a bit."

"You need money?"

"No, I don't need your money. I need your help if you're willing to give it."

David looked at her askance. He likely didn't see the difference. Perhaps for him, these were one and the same. After all, history had shown he was partial to providing money as the currency for help.

"I've never asked anything of you," she stated.

David said nothing.

"Have I?" she asked, wanting confirmation to her statement, ensuring that they both recognized the fact.

"No. You haven't."

"You have always offered financial help. And many times, I told you I didn't need it, but you insisted. I've often taken it to satisfy you. But I never asked for it."

David's eyes were narrowing at her. He seemed wary now, as if sensing something was afoot, as if he knew this preamble might reveal a point he didn't like.

"You told me in the past that if I ever wanted help, you'd give it," Natalie continued. "I don't want you to go out of your way or anything. All I'm saying is that you may know people down in Kitchener-Waterloo, people that could be looking for my services on a project or a contract. If you want to help, I'd be grateful for any introductions." She had increased the speed of her sentences as she finally requested this favor.

David was looking at her expectantly, as if still waiting for something more. When she added no additional requests, he seemed taken aback and sought clarity. "You want introductions?"

"Yes. But if you aren't comfortable doing it, I understand."

He stared back at the fountains. She could hear his breathing. She could see his large chest take in air, rise, and then expel it. The wary look he had when she first introduced the idea was vanishing and replaced by what appeared to be relief. There was a slow nod that started out small, then it gained momentum and pronouncement, as if he were coming to an agreement with his own mind.

"I think I can help with that," David stated.

If he was relieved, then she was doubly so. Natalie had been wondering if he would be upset at her petition; if he would see it as leeching off him. The fact is, she didn't know him well enough to know how he'd react.

"However," he added, "you'll need to explain what you do. I can't make sense of it."

She laughed at that. "Deal," she said. "I'll teach you how to represent me in intros and email you some one-page brochures I've made to share with your contacts."

After talking on the bench about her plans, they opted to stroll through the park at a slow pace to a neighborhood called Bloor West Village. There, they grabbed some midafternoon snacks and a drink, though David ordered a steak. Afterward, David declared he should get on the road to drive home. She offered to walk him back to his car in the lot on the other side of the park, but he declined, saying he would just take a cab, as he was too exhausted to walk.

Before she left him on the street to go to the subway, Natalie gave him a quick, awkward hug as she usually did. Despite the many years they had been doing this, he always seemed surprised at her movement. This afternoon, he draped one of his heavy arms around her and patted her back lightly, as if he feared breaking her thin frame.

"You don't mind doing this ... I mean the intro stuff, do you?" Natalie asked him.

David didn't flinch at the question; he merely shook his head. "I can help. I'm in a position to now more than I was in the past." Then, he reached into his trench coat and pulled out a white envelope. "Before you go, take this. Go for dinner or something."

"I don't need it," she protested waving her hands in front of her. "I'm fine. You're doing enough for me."

"Then take it for me. You'll need it with everything that's going on."

This game had been played almost every time they met. He would offer an envelope, she would refuse, he would insist, and eventually she would accept, seeing that it pleased him.

"Thank you. For everything," she said.

Turning to go, she crossed the street. Before rounding the corner into the station, she turned back and saw he was still standing on the corner watching her go. He raised the cap from his head. Natalie gave him a final wave and went into the station.

She knew little about David Burlow; he was an enigma. But she believed she could trust him. At one point, her mother had. So why shouldn't she? For a long time, David had ensured that Natalie and her mother were looked after financially. He might not have been much of a parent, but he tried, in his way, to be useful. Whatever grudges her grandparents held, she chose not to share them.

The only doubt that existed in Natalie's mind was that her mother had ever been attracted to him. That Natalie was the progeny of this immense man was perplexing. She was secretly grateful to have none of his physical characteristics or features. Not for the first time, she wondered if he had always looked as she saw him now. And if so, how could her mother have possibly been charmed by the man?

PART TWO: NEW BEGINNINGS

CHAPTER 4

A Tip *(Xavier Hardich, May 2004)*

L EE Iacocca's autobiography was slow going. In fact, it wasn't going. Over the past three weeks, Xavier had been unable to get past the first fifty pages. Though he recalled his father often speaking of Iacocca in reverential terms, Xavier had to concede there was little he found interesting about the book. Thus, when there was a knock at the door of his father's old office, it was not greeted by him as an irritable distraction, but as a relief—an excuse to put the book down that he was never taking up.

"There's the man," Derek Lam said, striding in. "A real captain of industry now." He unbuttoned the jacket of his navy-blue chalk-stripe suit and took a seat in the chair across from Xavier.

Derek Lam was a man who caught light and reflected it. From gold cufflinks, gold tie pins, gold rings, and a gold Rolex watch, various parts of his body seemed to perpetually shine with the accoutrements of success.

"Here to pick up Augusta?" Xavier asked. If he had to say anything positive about his sister, it was that she had managed to land the most eligible bachelor in the region as her boyfriend. Xavier was keen to strengthen the bond between Derek and the Hardi-ches.

"Yup. Thought I'd take her out for dinner. I was in the area, visiting a client."

"Anyone I know?

"The Kowalskis."

Xavier nodded. The Kowalskis owned a series of Tim Hortons coffee shops. "They giving you more money?" he boldly asked.

"Of course," Derek said, raising his hands questioningly. "Why wouldn't they?"

Xavier laughed. Derek's expertise in investing money was widely acknowledged. And Derek was by no means humble about his re-sults. "I suppose they'd be fools not to."

"I agree with you. So, it really makes me wonder what's wrong with me when people I care about don't take advantage of my skills."

Xavier felt the pointed remark. It was a deep prick followed by a stern look from Derek. "I'm just waiting for the right moment to bring it up with my mother," he said. "Nothing has changed. You and I both agree on what's best."

Derek leaned forward and put his hands on the desk. "Good. I'm glad. I'd like to be of more service to Augusta and you—and your mother, of course. It's always a bit of a bother for me when money is left on the table. Especially when it relates to people I am personally connected with."

"I understand and I'm thankful. Just need a bit more time."

"Of course," Derek said. He fiddled with his gold cufflink. "Brings me to my next point on your latest venture—Enigma. You're really taking this on, eh? That's what Augusta tells me."

"Sure. Why wouldn't I?"

Derek frowned. "A tricky business. We learned in 2000 the perils of that tech stuff. I don't see the real payoff in these small software companies."

Xavier wasn't prepared for Derek's assessment on Enigma. He had never thought Derek would see the company's future in such a poor light. Or, Xavier thought with sullenness, was it Derek's opinion that Xavier couldn't lead the company to be something greater? "Every company has to start somewhere," he mumbled.

Derek must have heard the disappointment in Xavier's voice, for he said, "I'm not saying you won't be able to grow the company or that it will fail or anything. But it's a lot of work with a lot of risk for modest returns. And let's face it, I hear it's not even spinning a profit yet." He paused and spun one of the rings around his finger. "Do you have a plan for Enigma?"

"Build it. Take it to the next level," Xavier replied, mustering what he hoped sounded like confidence.

"Certainly, an option."

"But you don't agree."

"As I said, lots of work," Derek said. "Here's another option. Go in there and make it efficient. Maybe land a couple of deals, but don't get attached to the place. Short game. Get on top of a wave and sell. Don't ride the wave to shore."

"Then what would I do?"

Derek smiled. "Whatever you want. Invest the money, with me for example. I could fetch you a more reliable and higher annual return than that place. Then, if you want to start a new venture, I give you a pile of money back that's grown significantly, and away you go. Life of leisure or life of toil. Your choice—but at least it's a choice."

When Derek left that day, Xavier never bothered trying to read more Lee Iacocca. Rather, he put the book back on the shelf and didn't care to look for a replacement read. Derek's words were gnawing at him. For an hour, he sat alone thinking.

Until that moment, Xavier had been looking forward to his arrival at Enigma. Over the past months and several conversations with Bill Spindrall, the two men had agreed to a date for Xavier to come on board. He resigned from RIM, and his first day at his new company would be next week. And it was his new company, for Augusta had already said she would go along with his decisions, since she had such little interest in it.

Now, he wondered, was he really thinking about this the right way? "Don't get attached," Derek had said. But he had been doing exactly that. Xavier had been visualizing years into the future when Enigma was a global enterprise, and he was at its head. This was going to be his big play, his great achievement. Yet, in one passing conversation, Derek had made him question it all. Only Derek could have done that to him.

Derek Lam's opinion was not one to be discarded without consideration. Immensely successful as an investor and wealth manager, Derek was a star in certain circles of the well-to-do. At parties, he held court over people that listened to everything he said, dissecting his words and inflections, his pauses and silences, in hopes that a small stock tip might be heard.

Xavier had just received a tip. Now he had to decide what to do with it.

CHAPTER 5

A Spring Gathering *(Richard Earning, May 2004)*

I F the Pit could ignore the noise of hammers breaking drywall, of banging and taping, of the fresh smell of paint, maybe it wasn't really happening. Maybe the arrival day of the person these activities all precipitated would never come.

But it was hard to ignore the transformation of the storage room in the hallway leading to the boardroom. It was cleared out, and one of its walls adjacent to Bill's office was knocked down and erected again, greatly reducing Bill's office size, while increasing the size of the former storage room. A new desk and office shelving arrived—unheard of at Enigma, since all the cubicles and desks were second-hand purchases from the accounting office upstairs—and the walls were painted to a deep, rich gray, a lone oasis of contrast in an office where every other wall was a scuffed, bland white.

Xavier Hardich's new office was ready, and change was afoot.

A black BMW became a common sighting in the back parking lot, and Xavier started to attend meetings with Bill, Richard, and Jeremy. His presence was a constant distraction, a break from the casual rhythm of the days that preceded him. At over six feet tall, in fine tailored suits, with a perfectly side-parted haircut and a clean-shaven face, he sat among them in the boardroom with an officious look, bringing a formality Enigma was hardly accustomed to. He would ask questions and take notes but would generally stay quiet. His stern, focused face seemed to be weighing—even judging—what was said and the people who said it.

At other times, Xavier would come in expressly to meet with Bill in his new office. The result of these closed-door chats was unknown to Richard and the Pit, but Bill was always in a sullen mood after the visitations; his usual awkward joviality replaced with a pensive and troubled look.

What the son of the now-deceased owner was going to do at Enigma was anyone's guess, including Bill's. Privately, Bill confided as much in conversations with Richard and Jeremy. "I'm not sure what he's thinking. But he's already decided to draw down a good salary—better than mine! For a man who says the company's payroll is too high, you'd think he'd cut his own wages some."

Xavier's hours were irregular. Sometimes he came in after 10 a.m. and would go directly to his office without ever entering the Pit. If, however, he came in before 9 a.m., he would linger and pace about the Pit, surveying it, as a captain inspects his ship crew. He would approach each person, inquire as to how they were doing, and then ask what was being worked on. If someone was absent during these rollcalls, Xavier would inquire as to his whereabouts. Whatever answer he received, a suspicious frown would contort his mouth as if he had some other information on the matter.

Outside of these small interactions, Xavier remained relatively aloof. On occasion, Richard would get requests for documents or presentations, but once he'd sent them over via email, he would hear nothing back.

"I don't like him," Jeremy said, while standing at Richard's cubicle. "The prick inherited a company. Who gets that?"

"Keep it down," Richard scolded, looking at the Pit entrance. Even if Xavier wasn't just around the corner, he didn't want the Pit hearing of dissent in the ranks.

"What? You like him?"

"I don't know him. But I know he's cutting the checks," Richard said. Trying to be more optimistic, he added, "I'm sure it's hard for him; he's trying to figure things out too. He's gotta ease into it here."

"I haven't seen any ease," Jeremy said.

* * *

Richard worked on his computer, updating a requirements document, when a firm tap on the metal frame of his cubicle entrance broke his train of thought. He turned, expecting to see Jeremy or one of the developers, but was surprised to see Xavier standing before him in a navy pinstripe suit.

"I'd like to take you for lunch, talk some business. You good to go now?" Xavier asked. His manner was casual, as if conversing with a friend.

Richard took a moment to collect himself. "Yeah, I think so," he said, glancing at his computer screen. He had intended to work through lunch to get the document done by end of day, but he didn't think rejecting Xavier's first attempt at connecting with anyone would be wise. It was a positive sign, wasn't it?

If Richard was surprised at the overture, so too was the rest of the team. As he followed Xavier out of the Pit, he saw various eyes peeking over monitors and cubicle walls. Jeremy's eyebrows were raised half in question, half in concern.

Xavier insisted they take his BMW. Despite the sun being out, it was a cool day, but this did not prevent Xavier driving with the windows down and blaring the music on the radio—"Somebody Told Me" by The Killers. The BMW rapidly accelerated out of the parking lot, weaved unnecessarily around some cars on the road, and braked hard at every light that turned red. Conversation was sparse, except for Xavier's occasional banter on the car's performance.

"I love the handling of her. You really feel like you're in control—like you own the road. You ever driven a BMW?"

Richard shook his head.

Xavier grinned. "Oh, man. You have to experience it. I'll let you drive it on the way back to the office. You'll go out and buy one right after."

"Maybe," Richard responded. But he knew that there was no fancy car in his immediate future—he had paid off his Honda Civic and would not be embarking on any new car purchase soon.

Within five minutes, they were at a classic fifties-themed diner called Mel's near the universities. On weekends, the diner was flooded with students recovering from the revelries of the previous night. During the week, it catered to the local business crowd with diner favorites like all-day breakfast, burgers, and Reuben and club sandwiches with good portions.

Sitting across from Xavier at a table, Richard could only watch, with some admiration, Xavier's confident manner. Xavier dominated the conversation, like he did the space around him. His one arm draped over the empty chair beside him, his other arm made sweeping gestures in the air in front of him or slid across and slammed the surface of their table. He spoke of his previous job, of some of the big deals he won, and of how he had opted to help Bill sort out Enigma. "It was a tough decision coming over. But Bill asked me to join. In the end, I felt I needed to look after my investment. Bill's in over his head."

Richard, surprised at this interpretation greatly at odds with what Bill had suggested, only nodded while taking a bite out of his sandwich.

"I'm gonna make some changes. Roll up my sleeves and jump in," Xavier went on. "I want to be included in all the client meetings now. I'll come with you—we'll be joined at the hip. The whole reason we're in the universities is because of Hardich connections, know what I mean?"

"Yeah, sure. I can include you. What about Bill, though? He normally comes too."

"We'll phase him out from this part of the business. It's not his strong suit. To be honest, though he'd never admit it, he's happy I'm taking it on. Which brings me to my next point: we're doing a small reorg."

Richard had not expected that. Was something happening to Bill—was he being pushed out? Richard's face must have betrayed some concern.

"It's not bad!" Xavier told him reassuringly. "It's a good thing—don't worry. Bill wanted to have a big sit-down with you and me and discuss it, but I said that was way too dramatic. Why bother, right?"

"What's happening?"

"We've decided that you'll report to me now. It makes the most sense. When you think about it, we're the only two customer-facing guys at the company. Nothing against anybody else, but you and I dress like professionals. We can't have Jeremy and his band of misfits walking around client sites," Xavier said, expecting agreement.

"Great. Of course. Looking forward to it," Richard said, trying to sound upbeat. He didn't mention that Jeremy had occasionally accompanied him to meetings at the university, and nobody seemed to mind Jeremy's attire.

"Oh, and Bill told me about the VP title change you guys were discussing and a bit of a raise. Obviously, we still want to make that happen in the future, but right now we gotta focus on getting the company aligned. You understand?"

"Yeah," Richard said. But Xavier's future sounded far away, not weeks away.

For the remainder of their lunch, Xavier spoke of some vague "big plans" for Enigma that were broad enough to be applicable to any business. He was going to accelerate the time-to-market of the product, make investments in marketing to help drive Enigma's reputation in the industry, and expand the company's foothold in existing accounts. He continuously emphasized that Enigma had to "up its game" and that he relied on Richard to assist him.

Richard found himself nodding along with Xavier the whole time, not out of explicit agreement, but because he was keenly aware that Xavier held several opinions about Enigma and its people, and he had no desire to be corrected. Bill was "good at getting things started, but couldn't get the firm to the next level," or "the Pit needed to take their jobs more seriously and hold regular office hours," and "salaries were higher than industry standards, and productivity ratios were off."

With their food finished, Xavier paid the bill. Then he slid his car keys across the table. "Ready?"

Richard picked them up, grimacing inwardly. He wondered what it was about Xavier that made him acquiesce, made him go along with things he either didn't agree with or didn't care for.

As they walked toward the car, Xavier patted him on the back. "Hey," he said suddenly, "I'm having a party this weekend. Call it the 'Spring Gathering.' I do it every year. Saturday night. Got plans? Why don't you pop in later in the evening?"

"Is anyone else going from Enigma?"

"I haven't invited anyone else."

"Even Bill or Jeremy?"

"Jeremy wouldn't like it. Not really a place for hippies. My sister is bad enough. Bill … I don't know. My father invited him last year, and he came, but he didn't really fit."

Richard shrugged his shoulders. "You should probably still ask. He's your business partner."

"Yeah, maybe you're right. I'll have a word with him," Xavier said.

* * *

On the night of Xavier's Spring Gathering, Richard parked his car on an old street in Cambridge, just after 9 p.m. He had never been to this area of the city before but knew it was called Galt by locals with long memories and who still divided the city up into the pre-amalgamation names of Galt, Preston, and Hespeler.

He was standing on the sidewalk, breathing in the air, smelling it, feeling it enter his lungs. The neighborhood was the remnant of another century—an old era with old money. Large verandas encircled strong, ornate Victorian and Edwardian houses perched on immense lots set back at a distance from the sidewalk.

He tasted the dampness of the earth and the gathering energy that was bursting and exploding after the repressing winter. Through his nose and mouth, he drank that pent-up aroma and flavor from the trees, gardens, and lawns. Around him, up and down the road, globelike streetlamps emitted a soft yellow glow atop green metal posts.

These lamps seemed in league with the trees, or at least in some respectful collaboration with them, for they never proposed to infringe on each other's space. The trees had grown in sufficient distance from every post (or perhaps the posts were planted in sufficient distance from the trees), and the illumination of the lamp glow touched only the edges of these old, majestic wooden sages, as if to say, "I will let people know you are here, but I will let you sleep too."

Richard had difficulty reading the house numbers from the sidewalk, which is likely the reason Xavier had referred to the Hardich house as being located between this and that street next to the white colonial house. Now, looking head on at the Hardiches', he wondered if Xavier had wanted to underplay the magnificence of the place. The Tudor revival–style home couldn't be missed. The immense, red-bricked structure had three stories and two double-bay window towers flanking a covered porch that led up to a grand double-door entrance. The porch roof, supported by white pillars, also served as a balcony for the second story. Each bay tower was topped by steeply pitched roof gables on the third story and massive dormer windows. The impression it gave was of thick and sturdy rectangles, squares, and triangles. On one side of the house was a detached garage, and on the other, a spacious veranda. He could see figures moving about on the veranda and hear the murmur of conversing voices.

Filled with humility and the sense he was out of place, Richard walked up an interlocking brick path to the front porch. Gazing down at the bottle of wine he had picked up as a gift, he contemplated how insignificant it seemed; perhaps it was better to bring nothing at all than insult his hosts with a modest Chilean red. Reaching the front doors, he heard talking and laughter from within the house.

He had no desire to just walk in; in fact, he was rendered timid as if he were an imposter at such a place. Knocking lightly, and then more forcefully, there was no acknowledgment issuing from inside. He had the sense the door absorbed all the noise and transmitted nothing to the other side.

With uncertainty rising in him, Richard wondered if the lack of response was a sign for him to slink away. Xavier was no friend; the whole reason Richard was here was as a courtesy, a show of respect, an optics game to appease his new boss. Throughout the afternoon, he had thought of skipping the event but determined there was more harm in not showing up at all than in making a brief appearance.

The absurdity of standing alone at the front door with a bottle of red wine in hand and an elaborate party just a few feet away registered with him. He took another look at his single-breasted, two-button suit. It wouldn't hold up to Xavier's wardrobe, but it was the finest Richard could muster.

He pushed the doorbell.

A slow *ding, dong, dung, dumb*, each chime successively lower than the last, sounded out. Then, it was mirrored by the same four chimes rising from the lowest pitch to the highest, *dumb, dung, dong, ding*. He cringed at his arrival being announced—eight times and musically! There was no falter of conversation from within. At last, one of the double doors swung open; a young woman in a knee-length cream-colored dress with red-brown hair greeted him, a glass of wine in her hand.

"Can I help you?" she asked, her eyes narrowing suspiciously, though a playful smile touched her lips.

He had not anticipated being questioned. He assumed that standing on a porch with a bottle of wine in his hand evidence enough that he had come to join the gathering. "I'm here for Xavier Hardich's gathering—is this the right place?"

"Are you asking if this is the Xavier Hardich gathering or the right place?" she inquired.

"Well, both I suppose."

"No to one, and yes to the other."

Richard was disarmed at this point. Confused, he opted to banter more with this cryptic gatekeeper of the party. "May I ask which of my statements was true and which was false?"

"You may."

"Is this Xavier Hardich's gathering?"

"No."

Richard withdrew a step and studied the speaker again. Perhaps he was mild entertainment for this young woman, who seemed content to obstruct him from entering but not send him away. "If it's not Xavier's gathering, but I'm at the right place, I must ask where I am and why you are so interested in confusing me."

She laughed, and her eyes narrowed mischievously. "What is your name, Mr. Guest?"

"Richard."

"Richard what?"

"Richard Earning."

A man's voice from within shouted out, "What are you up to? Who's at the door?"

The young woman turned her head to inform the inquirer she would be back soon and that she was tending to someone selling knives. More conversations and laughter wafted freely through the now-open portal.

"Well, Mr. Earning," she emphasized his last name with playful pomp, "you are, in fact, at the right place. But it is the Hardich gathering. It has been going on for many years every spring for friends and acquaintances of this family. My brother cannot lay claim to it as his. He's rather full of self-import these days, since we inherited some piece of an enigmatic company I'd never heard of until I owned it." She smiled watching him. "You seem so serious that I felt compelled to loosen you up a little. I'm Augusta. I won't say I'm Xavier's sister, but I am the sister." She stepped aside to stop blocking the entrance. Seeing that he hesitated, she giggled and made assurances that she would no longer pick on him. "You are most welcome to join the party."

Richard stepped into a spacious entryway. To his left was a large living room, accessed by closed French doors. Through the glass panes, he could see several groups of conversing guests. To the right was a large, closed wooden door, rendering whatever lay behind a mystery. The entrance hall held benches, sitting chairs, and side tables that sat on thick, wide, wooden floorboards. Shoes, heels, and boots ran the length of the room, under chairs, under benches, or just in the open, but all were paired neatly.

Augusta Hardich received his wine bottle and thanked him, though she never pulled it out of the bag to look at it. As he removed his shoes to add to the army of soles, she continued to study him.

"Are you a friend of Xavier's?" she asked.

"No, more of an employee, actually. From Enigma—the company you are only recently familiar with."

"Oh!" she said, startled. "So, you're one of mine," Augusta laughed. "Are we treating you well at work?"

Richard smiled and nodded, rather speechless at her manner. She spoke with the same casual confidence as her brother, though hers had a peculiar blend of playfulness and indifference.

She put her hand on his arm and lightly ushered him past a large, elaborate wooden staircase that wound to the upper stories. "We'll get you a drink in the kitchen," she said.

The kitchen, like the other rooms in the house, was filled with people talking in small groups. She wove among them, making casual comments, all the while guiding him.

"Richard, relax. You look like a scared tourist. We're not good people, but you're safe. I won't let anything happen to my first employee that I've met."

He was, in fact, in an uncomfortable awe. The opulence of the house and the guests within, all smartly dressed in fashionable clothes, conspired to form a scene entirely foreign to him. And there was the nervousness that Augusta caused in him—her light touch, her smile, her attention.

She had just given him a glass of beer and was on the verge of saying something when a loud "Rich!" came from one end of the kitchen. Turning, he saw Xavier pointing at him and clumsily moving through the crowd, laughing as he jostled his guests.

"You'll be in good company now," Augusta said with a smirk. "Maybe we'll talk later." And she flitted away.

Richard was hard pressed to distribute his gaze between the oncoming Xavier and the departing Augusta.

"Welcome. You finally showed up," Xavier Hardich pronounced loudly, slapping Richard on the back.

"Very kind of you to have me over. It's a wonderful party," Richard complimented. "I understand this yearly gathering has quite a few followers."

"Does indeed. A blend of the old guard and the new. My father began this a long time ago. Many of his friends are here, and I have started to add my own acquaintances to the mix. Over there—you see the woman there in the pink blouse? She runs Stallman's Construction. Took it over from her father when it was in dire straits and turned it around to be a powerhouse. She's a smart one! And over there, the man with the glasses talking to the older guy, a friend of mine from school who's now VP at RIM. That guy there, him, yeah; he's an exec at Manulife. Did you pass through the living room yet? No? You'll see a few faces you'll want to know—some of the brass from the universities are here, including a president."

They were interrupted in Xavier's mapping of the who's who at the gathering by a young blonde woman who came up beside him and slipped her hand in his back pocket. Her green, tight-fitting shirt was unbuttoned low enough to reveal a considerable amount of her bosom.

Xavier's girlfriend, Jocelyn Miller, hardly needed introduction. Jocelyn was a bit of a regional celebrity; every weekday morning, she cohosted a two-hour timeslot on the local television station that focused on community news, events, and people, while also functioning as a sort of talk show. Even Richard, who seldom watched television, knew who she was. Again, he found himself in a strange awe of Xavier, the crowd Xavier moved in, and the women he dated.

But Jocelyn's demeanor tonight resembled nothing of her on-air personality. Her eyes had a bloodshot glaze, and she teetered back and forth as she slurred some words of greeting. Her request—or demand—for more wine was met with a look from Xavier suggesting she had indulged in too many glasses as it was. Under his scrutiny, she slid away, laughing loudly at Xavier's stern look.

"Did Bill come?" Richard asked.

"Bill?"

"Yes, you were going to invite him."

"I was? Bill Spindrall? No. Didn't talk to him." And then his focus was on something behind Richard. "No! Don't have another one! Excuse me, Rich," Xavier said, annoyed, as he strode past him to where Jocelyn was filling up a beer mug with red wine. He clutched her arm forcefully and guided her out of the kitchen.

Finding himself alone, Richard surveyed his surroundings, trying to attune himself to them. Weaving around and between people were black-clad caterers with platters of food and drink. There must have been some seventy guests at the party, and they all seemed to know one another. The only person he might have known was Bill, who had never been invited. Was that really an oversight?

He strolled self-consciously through the rooms populated by the mid-crust bourgeoisie. He found it hard to interject himself into a group. Even when he gathered the courage to do so, he was lacking in contributions to the topics discussed. He was unfamiliar with the exorbitant costs of private schools for young children. He had no referrals for a good nanny or dog walker (the qualities of a good dog walker never really defined, but a universal understanding pervaded that a bad dog walker was a horrid thing). He did not have a personal trainer so could not recommend one, he had no idea where to procure cheaper vitamins and supplements in bulk, he was not upset about rising property taxes on cottages since he didn't have one, and he wasn't considering breaking the lease on an Audi to upgrade to a newer model.

His desire to linger at the gathering was waning. He might well have left already, were it not for one particular silver lining: the occasional glimpse of Augusta Hardich. She flitted between rooms and groups of revelers, always at some distance from him. She would attach herself to threesomes and foursomes with ease and join in whatever topic was being discussed to take center stage. She did not approach him again, but she would occasionally see him and smile or gesture with her head as if to say, "You again."

Richard was close to her at one point. He was talking to a couple who had recently returned from a trip to Australia. When he expressed an interest in travel, they were happily telling him of the places he had to visit there. Although interested in the recount of their experiences, he was only half-listening to them. His ear was trained on a conversation between a group of men and Augusta just feet away.

"The sponsorship scandal will bring down Paul Martin's government," one of the men was saying. "The finance minister turned prime minister doesn't have the simpleton charisma that his predecessor did."

"Mark my words," another man said, "we elected our new conservative leader two months ago, and he'll be the one to watch!"

Augusta Hardich playfully booed this statement. "Are you honestly praising Stephen Harper? The leader of that unholy union of the Progressive Conservatives and Reform Parties?"

"He'll be prime minister someday soon, Augusta," the first man noted. "We finally have a strong right party to counter the liberals."

"I see you've already been programmed by your robotic overlord," Augusta quipped back to some laughter.

"I'm surprised you're still in town," returned another man defensively. "Thought you'd be volunteering down in the States for Ralph Nader—or perhaps trying to convince Chomsky to run for president?"

"Not yet," Augusta snickered. "There's plenty of work to do in my own backyard supporting the resistance."

Richard lost her sound among competing voices. What was it that made her so curious to him? There was something about her confidence, her fearless movement amid the crowd, her directness, that made him want to know her. When he watched her, she was a whirlwind, engaging people on her terms, at her leisure, and withdrawing to strike somewhere else in another room.

At some point, Richard found himself standing off to the side in the corner of a room, surveying the festivities. Soaking in the view, he had the desire to write this scene down. He had never been exposed to a party or social circle quite like this. He made mental notes of the people, of the clothes, of certain mannerisms of some of the guests.

The craving for a cigarette rose within him. He knew the veranda was where this habit was exercised, and he was about to make his way there when he felt a touch on his arm. Augusta Hardich was at his elbow.

"I'm concerned about one of my employees," Augusta said. "He doesn't seem to be having a good time."

"I'm fine," Richard said, trying to sound reassuring.

She eyed him skeptically. "It's a pretentious crowd, I know. I do wonder why Xavier invited you. You're not his usual sort."

"What's his usual sort?"

She pressed her lips together in an amused smile and seemed to not hear his question. "Talk to me about something you like." She was so casual in her demands.

"Politics? Books?" he asked.

"You really know how to pique a woman's interest. I'll take books for a thousand. What are you reading now? Be honest—bet you I've read it."

"Dickens."

"Which one?"

"*Dombey and Son.* Be honest—have you read it?"

She paused, her smile widening. "Shit," she responded. "I've only ever read *Great Expectations* and *A Tale of Two Cities.* You just became a little interesting, Richard Earning."

"Just a little, though?" he asked, feigning insult.

Augusta's eyes lit up. He could see she was hammering a hot and witty remark in the smithy of her mind and cooling it with a mouthful of wine before it was delivered. But just as she opened her mouth, an arm encircled her waist from behind and the face of a clean-shaven man around Richard's age appeared at her ear. "Dear, I can see from across the room you are getting ready to lampoon this poor man for some belief or other."

The man could not see Augusta's face, for if he could, he would see what Richard saw: a wince of displeasure as her upper teeth drove with force into her bottom lip, contorting her face. After a moment, she spoke calmly. "I am merely discussing literature with Richard here. He's fond of the classics. A reader, it would seem—you should take a page from his book. Have the two of you met?"

"No, we haven't. I'm Derek Lam." He unclasped Augusta's waist and shook Richard's hand. "You're new here?"

"First-timer, yes," Richard said trying to conceal his irritation. Was he frustrated at the interruption? Or was it the revelation that Augusta was connected to Derek in some way beyond friendship?

"I hope she's taking it easy on you." He laughed and leaned in to kiss her. She smiled neutrally, only offering Derek some of her cheek and the edge of her lips.

"She's not all that bad," Richard said, looking at her, though he could glean nothing from her expression.

"Nobody goes head to head with her," Derek continued. "She's usually throttling us all with her lefty politics—Marxist stuff, feminist stuff, and whatever else. She indirectly donates money to Ralph Nader, if you can believe it. Whether we agree with her or not—and we usually don't—she knows how to win a debate."

"Really?" Richard said. "She should learn how to win bets then."

Augusta chuckled while Derek stared confusedly at them.

Richard, though disappointed at Augusta's attachment, was curious as to the manner of man Augusta dated and inquired about his profession.

"I manage people's money. I've got a fund that helps generate real wealth," Derek said proudly. "Not that RRSP and mutual fund junk. You'll not get rich on that. Some people here," he waved his hand at the guests, "are my happy clients. You have an investment strategy, Richard? You won't find returns like the ones I can get."

Augusta touched Derek's arm. "Stop, not now," she said.

Derek would likely have pitched his services more, but a woman's voice from behind Richard declared loudly, "Look at you two—how interesting! You're still the best-looking couple I've ever seen!"

The newcomer joined their conversation. She had yellow hair, was in her mid-fifties, and wore a fitted dress that accentuated her artificial enhancements. "Somebody had to say it—we're all thinking it, you know."

Derek Lam laughed. "Augusta carries the two of us, I must admit. But thanks for the compliment, Cassandra."

Cassandra, without regard for the conversation that existed before her entrance, proceeded with her own mandate—to inquire what the young, dashing couple had been up to. She was extremely interested in being interested, even when the topic was rather drab. No matter how banal something may be, Cassandra never ran out of her stock phrase: "Really, that's so interesting!" When Derek remarked that he jogged in Waterloo Park the other evening and was rained upon, it was "very interesting." When Augusta noted that she did not see much of Derek in the last two weeks due to her studies and teaching, it was "really very interesting." The party tonight was "exceedingly interesting."

When Cassandra was exhausted from being interested in things, she turned to Richard. "And who are you?"

Richard introduced himself and explained he worked with Xavier at Enigma.

"Oh yes, his little tech company! How interesting is that? You're one of those computer people. We've been having problems with our computer at home. I'll have my husband, Sam, talk to you later. I'm sure you can help." Cassandra declared.

"Maybe," Richard told her.

She chatted briefly with him, peppering him with questions about working for Xavier before turning her attention back to her favorite couple. She began talking in a low voice about people Richard didn't know, discussing some family dramas of some form or other. "Did you hear about the Wrights? No? Something's off—they're on hard times, I think. Jonathan reached out to Sam about selling their house. Sam just sold it to them a year ago."

Richard excused himself from the group. While moving away, he saw Augusta giving him a smirk while she rolled her eyes as Cassandra chattered away to Derek. Perhaps that was a sign to save her, but Richard couldn't be sure, and he thought it best to leave this happy couple to their gossiping admirer.

At the door leading out to the veranda, there were mats where several pairs of simple rubber sandals of varying sizes were laid out. They were meant for the guests to slip on and go outside instead of fetching their shoes from the front entranceway. Richard shook his head; only at a gathering like this would these little details be considered. He put on a pair of sandals and went outside.

On the veranda, the air was filled with the smell of cigars and cigarette smoke. He paced the length of it, lighting his own cigarette. After a few moments, he recognized the figure of an immense man leaning against the wooden railing, a cigar in his mouth. It was David Burlow.

Beside Burlow, and creating a peculiar juxtaposition, was a petite woman in her fifties with red-brown hair.

Richard approached the two of them. "David, it's Richard. We met at Enigma a few months back," he offered.

David studied Richard and then nodded as if finally placing him in his memory. "Surprised you're here. Did Xavier invite you?" David asked.

"Yes," Richard replied. "I thought Bill would be here too, but I think Xavier forgot to invite him."

"Of course, he did," David said crisply.

"Bill Spindrall? Xavier's partner? Good heavens, it must have slipped his mind," the woman said.

Burlow chortled slightly. He introduced Richard to Elinor Hardich and explained to her that Richard was from Enigma. Immediately, Richard saw Augusta's features in the woman.

Elinor Hardich smiled warmly. "Thank you for coming. How's my son doing? He tells me that he's bringing about some much-needed improvement to the company."

"I think we're all happy to have Xavier come on board."

"He's becoming more like his father of late," Elinor said. "I suppose I shouldn't expect anything else from James's son. I don't need to worry about him. It's the other one that concerns me," she said wryly. "Have you met my Augusta? She's here, you know."

"I've had the pleasure, yes."

David raised his beer mug to Richard. "If you call it a pleasure, she took it easy on you."

Elinor laughed. "Her interests are not those of her brother. She's the academic of the family, doing her PhD. None of us really knows how to take her," Elinor confided. "Even James was confounded by her often enough! Derek's good for her. A good man. James was right—he grounds her."

"He's certainly the first one that has fit in here," David seconded. "Augusta's love interests have always been peculiar. There was that boy from Greenpeace she was dating. She had him here a couple years back. What was his name?"

"I don't remember, but he was quite aloof," Elinor returned.

"Aloof? I think he despised the lot of us! No matter, I didn't think much of him either," David said. "And there was that monolith of a man too—a bouncer at a bar of some sort. Grizzly looking, something out of a movie. That's Augusta. Always had her own mind. I remember when James was conned into putting up a Progressive Conservative sign on the front lawn during an election. The next day Augusta nailed in a New Democratic Party sign, a Green Party sign, and a Marxist-Leninist Party sign all in front of the PC sign! You couldn't see the PC sign, except for a little bit of the blue coloring."

Richard had only just met Augusta, but he had no problem imagining her committing this treasonous act.

"This is a wonderful party, Mrs. Hardich," Richard complimented.

"Thank you," Elinor replied. "Odd to have this gathering without James. I wasn't going to do it, but Xavier pushed me to continue the tradition. Now that it's happening, I can say I'm glad I did it. Nice to see everyone under happier circumstances. James would have been proud; I'm sure of that."

David Burlow nodded.

"Did you bring anyone with you?" Elinor asked Richard.

"No, just me."

"You don't have a girlfriend? No wife?"

"Not at the moment," Richard confessed, entertained at Elinor's direct inquiries. She sounded like his own mother with her undertone of puzzlement that someone his age would not be in a relationship of some sort.

"A good-looking man like you shouldn't be single. If you want to find yourself a girl, may I recommend the Concordia Club at Oktoberfest?" she said, smiling.

"Oh?"

"Yes, that's where James and I met!"

Oktoberfest was a staple celebration in the Kitchener-Waterloo community, where a strong German heritage existed. The city of Kitchener had been called Berlin until 1916, when, during World War I, the rise of anti-German sentiment had triggered a name change.

The city's Oktoberfest parties were popular, especially among the university students, who were ever on the watch for a good reason to drink.

"How long ago was that?" Richard asked.

"My goodness, it was in the early seventies. You two had just started your company, right David?"

"It was 1973," Burlow reported.

"There you have it—1973. Must have been the weekend, a Saturday."

"Was a Friday night," Burlow reported again.

"A Friday then. Me and the girls were out in our dirndl dresses and aprons, having a wonderful time. All the music, all the drink! And then I'm standing alone, looking for my friends, and David here approaches me in full lederhosen. What a sight!"

"I still have those somewhere, but I'm sure they don't fit," David grumbled.

"And he says to me, 'You look lost, let me help you.' He grabbed me by the hand, quite forward of you, David ... but it wasn't David, was it? No, the boys had these silly names for themselves: Ernest and Franz or something—that's Oktoberfest spirit. I don't think I knew your real names until the next time we met. So, David grabs my hand, and we walked about the crowded hall looking for my friends. We found them. But David kept lingering and dancing with us. Drinking too much, I think. He was trying to make conversation with us, but I think you had far too much 'ziggy zaggy oi, oi, oi!' Don't you agree, David? Then James came, also in lederhosen, to collect his friend—he had been searching high and low for David for nearly an hour! James began to talk to me and the girls. I knew then that James was the one. We all started meeting up regularly after that."

"Without the men wearing lederhosen, I hope," Richard jested. He hoped to get a smile out of Burlow at this remark, but the man stared back at him unmoved.

"Definitely not," Elinor said, laughing. "We were all friends for quite some time. We'd go out to the skating rinks and bars.

Eventually, James got enough courage to ask me out. I said yes, of course! And thus began our courtship. We were married in 1976. And David here was the best man!"

"That I was," David confirmed.

"James loved you, David. He trusted you the most out of everyone." Elinor remarked. "You helped make him what he was." And as she spoke, she put both her hands around David and embraced him, her petite frame comically leaning into David's enormousness, and her arms not long enough to encircle half of the man.

A shout issued from the house. "Mom!"

Xavier was hanging out of the door from the house, teetering slightly. "The Donaldsons are leaving. They're looking for you to say goodbye," he said with a slurring briskness. There was undisguised anger in his tone, and he glared at the three of them.

"Ah, I should get in and see some more of the other guests. I've been remiss," Elinor said, squeezing David's arm, and walked off to join her son. David's eyes followed her the entire way as she left him.

There was an uncomfortable silence between Richard and David as they stood beside each other. Richard had the impression David was rather indifferent to conversing with anyone other than Elinor.

"I think I'll be going soon, so I should start to make my exit as well," Richard said, finishing his cigarette. "If I don't see you again, have a good night."

"Good night," David said. It was in the same dismissive tone with which he had spoken to Richard in the boardroom months earlier.

Richard was relieved to be away from Burlow. The man's surliness made him uncomfortable. As he entered the house, he looked back to see Burlow standing alone, relighting his cigar, mingling with none of the other guests on the veranda. Nobody made any attempt to approach him.

Inside, Richard moved through the kitchen and then the dining room. The crowd had thinned slightly as eleven o'clock approached. The guests of more senior years had taken to seats about the rooms, while the younger crowd were still standing and ready to party well past midnight.

He quickly circled the rooms, saying quick goodbyes to some of the people he had met earlier in the night. He saw Augusta, regrettably in conversation with a group of people, and Derek Lam still at her side. There seemed little point in approaching her.

His last task was to seek out his new boss and thank him for his hospitality. He found his host amid a group of friends, teetering backward and forward. Xavier likely would have stumbled and fallen flat on his face on several occasions were it not for his companions, who put their hands up to right him whenever he leaned too far back or too far forward. Jocelyn was nowhere to be seen.

Richard made his way over to Xavier and stood in front of him. "Thank you for having me over," he said. "I had a great time."

"Going?" Xavier asked as his head rolled back. "No, have something else to drink. Get this man a beer," Xavier slurred commandingly to one of the caterers. A beer was subsequently brought over, but by the time it was in Richard's hand, Xavier had wandered over to sit in a chair and started trying to converse with someone else.

It couldn't have worked better as far as Richard was concerned. They had barely spoken at all that night, and it was easy to resist these drunken overtures of camaraderie. He left Xavier and entered the kitchen area, where he left his full beer on the counter before continuing down to the entrance hallway.

He had some ideas in his head from the gathering, and he was eager to get home to pen some of them down. His mood was turning contemplative, and there were enough incidents tonight that he had the ingredients to begin yet another story.

He found his shoes neatly arranged in one of the rows of soles and began to slip them on.

"Mr. Richard Earning, I gather you're leaving without saying goodbye," a pronouncement came from behind him. Turning, he met the eyes of Augusta. She was alone and holding a glass of wine in one hand and a can of beer in the other.

"I'm afraid I must be going, but I had a wonderful evening. I'm sorry we weren't able to talk more."

"Don't be sorry; we can start now," she smiled.

"But I'm leaving," Richard said, but he was already thinking he might stay.

"You haven't left. We can go outside where we won't be bothered. I noticed you're a smoker, and I need to get one from you. It must all be done secretly, since it's very much frowned upon by my family."

Though he had started to look forward to his night of writing, Augusta was here, asking him to stay—or telling him to. He was pleased by her attention, pleased that she must have been watching him to know he was leaving.

"Are you drinking wine and beer?" Richard asked.

"The beer is for you," she said. "Now get the door for me. My hands are full."

Richard swung the door open to let Augusta go out. He glanced back in the hallway to the kitchen. He was grateful nobody was watching them, nobody was coming, nobody would follow. Alone to steal a few brief moments in private with her.

Augusta walked past him, closely, more so than was necessary. And she paused, her shoulder touching his chest. He could smell her perfume—an airy and light, zesty smell with a lemony undertone.

"You're all right to drive, I assume?" she asked.

"Yes, I've only had the one you gave me earlier. I'm fine."

"Good. But it doesn't really matter. If you get pulled over or anything happens, just call me. The local police are on our payroll. I'll make sure you're set free."

"Oh," Richard said, surprised. Was that possible? Were the Hardiches that powerful?

"I'm joking, Richard. Jesus, I said you were too serious."

Outside, Richard shut the door behind them. The noise of conversation continued to drift over from the veranda, but it was more subdued now that the night was later. Augusta led him behind the detached garage just to the side of the house. Once there, she pulled the tab on the beer can to the sound of a short and decisive *sfff.*

"We'll be safe here," Augusta said, handing him the open beer. "Get your cigarettes out."

"Won't people be looking for you?" Richard queried as he pulled out his pack and handed her one. "Maybe your brother? Or Derek?"

"Let them look," she said, while putting the cigarette in her mouth and signaling that she needed a light.

Richard flicked his lighter and cupped the flame to protect it from any breeze. He brought it to the end of Augusta's cigarette, so that she need only lean its tip into the flame. But she made no attempt to do so. He looked up at her eyes to see why she was delaying. She, in turn, was staring directly back at him, considering him, seemingly every aspect of him.

"What?" he asked.

"Why do you suppose my brother invited you to the party?"

Richard shook his head. "To be nice?"

"Oh, Richard," she said with condescension, as if speaking to a naïve fool. "That's not the type of people we are. You shouldn't have accepted. We're not good for you."

"Does *we* include you?" Richard asked, surprised.

"I'm the worst of the lot." She winced momentarily, then gave him a throaty laugh. At last, she leaned in to light her cigarette, taking a long drag followed by an emphatic exhale of smoke that hung about, stationary in the damp air, lingering like a thick fog before breaking apart and dissipating on a light breeze.

Again, he was captivated by her manner, and he tried to decipher her mysterious meaning. He felt there was more significance in her casual comment than he was able to tease out. He lit a cigarette for himself.

"Tell me about yourself, Richard," Augusta said.

CHAPTER 6

Images of You *(Natalie Mitchell, June 2004)*

THERE was no denying the value of a good introduction and referral.

That thought was foremost in Natalie's mind as her meeting ended in the law offices of Miller and Associates in Kitchener. The established firm was growing, and like so many other traditional businesses, was behind the curve in its online marketing and website. She knew she could help. This would be the first of a couple of meetings. From here, there would be a proposal and, hopefully, a signed contract.

Bart Miller had attended the meeting himself, along with one of his associates and some administrative staff.

"I'll walk Ms. Mitchell out," Miller said to everyone as she packed up her laptop and notes. He was a tranquil-looking man in his early sixties with a full head of salted brown hair. He watched her, closely thrumming his fingers on the table.

As the others left the room, Natalie thanked Bart again for his time, feeling the need to break the silence and hopefully stop him from staring at her.

"No bother, really," he replied. "Burlow's been good to my firm over the years. Pushed plenty of business my way. Glad I can return the favor."

"I hope you're doing this because you need to, though—not just as a favor to David. I'd like to think my services are relevant regardless of my connection to him."

"Of course." Bart gave a faint laugh. "I like your confidence. Interesting to see you all grown up now—turned into quite the woman."

Natalie, taken aback, looked at him. "Have we met?" she fumbled.

"Once. Many years ago, when you were very young. I met your mother and grandparents too. You remind me of your mom quite a bit. My condolences on her passing, though I know they are quite belated."

"Thanks," Natalie said, still confused. After a moment, trying to find her bearings, she asked, "When did you meet her? Us?"

"I set up the trust fund for you and your mother at Burlow's request. I was the one that drove down to Toronto and met with your mother to have her sign the papers." He stood up from his chair and gestured for her to follow him as he walked out of the room and down the hallway toward the office reception. "I suppose you'll be popping into Burlow's now?"

"Yes, we're going to connect," Natalie said. She was supposed to call him when she was done. "He wants me to let him know how it went."

"You can tell him it was splendid," Bart returned with enthusiasm. "I'll call him later to report as much myself." They had just walked out of reception, and his finger lingered above the elevator button but did not push it. "How's he doing—really?"

The question surprised her. It was as if Bart presumed she had more knowledge of David than he did. "He seems fine. He hasn't mentioned anything to me. But then," she paused to measure her words, "I don't know him really well. You think there's something wrong?"

"Just wondering how he was managing after James's death. Did you know his old partner?"

"No. I never met him, but David told me about him. David was his executor."

"Yes. They were very close. Anybody who knew James knew Burlow was his loyal man. So, I wondered how he was coping. Saw him at the party, the Hardich Spring Gathering, a few weeks back, but he kept to himself. Nothing unusual in that, I suppose; he's always been a bit removed from all of us. You weren't there."

"He never mentioned it to me."

Bart nodded slowly, as if puzzling over this point. "Well, perhaps next year." He pushed the button at last to summon the elevator for her. "I look forward to doing business with you, Ms. Mitchell. I'm glad Burlow has finally decided to introduce you to us."

Only when she was in the elevator going down did the idea strike her. In fact, it had been put in her mind by Bart Miller himself. He had presumed she was going over to David's house now. And why should she not? She was supposed to call him, but would a visit not be better? The problem—she had no address. David always met her out at places.

As soon as the elevator reached the ground floor, she pushed the button to go back up to the fifth floor and entered the law office reception again. The receptionist smiled, asking if Natalie had forgotten something.

"May I have a quick word with Bart, please?"

Bart Miller would have David's address.

A slight fib, yes, but harmless. She had no ill intent. She would just say she couldn't find David's address, and that his phone was going through to voicemail.

* * *

Her motive was beyond just seeing him—she wanted to see his place, how he lived. In all the years she had known him, she had never once been to his house. David had never invited her. He was still a stranger in so many ways. Perhaps he would be upset at her audacity in just dropping by, but she felt she tiptoed enough around him. If randomly popping in to visit friends and family was a sin, then she was all for committing it.

Entering the address Bart had given her into the GPS, she saw that David lived a mere seven-minute drive from the law office. When she pulled up to the front of his house to park on the street, she thought the place wonderfully quaint. A small two-story, red-bricked house with a high, dark-brown peaked roof. The house fronted a large park with a small lake, much like Grenadier Pond in High Park, just a short walk away. She could make out a little island on the water connected to land by a footbridge. There were great weeping willows on the banks of the pond, their long branches draping into the water.

Natalie had wondered about the type of place David would live in. She imagined he might live in an old mansion of some sort, large and imposing, like him. So, she was surprised at seeing the house now: a century home, modest, but well kept.

She called him from her phone.

"How did it go?" he answered without any greeting.

"Good—I thought I would pop by for a coffee to tell you about it."

There was a brief silence. "I can meet you somewhere. Where are you now?"

"Out front of your house."

Another silence. The front door opened, and David came out onto the porch wearing navy-blue dress pants with a white dress shirt. Natalie got out of the car and walked to the foot of the porch, smiling at him. David bore neither a smile nor a scowl, just an expressionless and unreadable face.

"Nice day!" she remarked.

"I wasn't expecting company," he said gruffly. "How do you know where I live?"

"It'll be quick. I need to get on the road," she said, sidestepping his question while stepping up to the top of the porch. "We can stay out here if you'd like. Or walk in the park."

"No. I'd rather sit in the cool house," David said grudgingly. There were no chairs or tables on the porch. It was swept clean of dust and furniture alike. He took a deep breath and went inside, swinging the door wide so that she might follow.

Natalie entered, stepping onto a deep-brown hardwood floor. David closed a wooden door to his right, which she glimpsed was his office space. To her left was a living room populated with what looked like old but sturdy furniture. A brick fireplace, giving the room a feeling of coziness, rested disused in the summer. The wall color was a uniform burgundy throughout the living room and hall-way, complemented by thick white crown molding.

Aside from a coffee table and large wall unit, everything was perfectly ordered with neither superfluous décor nor an ounce of clutter;

no little extra shelves, side tables, or console tables bearing trinkets or photos. The hallways and the rooms were designed for free and easy movement around—no obstructions, nothing to get snagged on, nothing to be mindful of.

"It's a very nice place," Natalie complimented.

"It's a home," David dismissively replied. 'Have a seat there." He pointed to the couch in the living room. "I'll get the coffee ready."

"I'll help if y—"

"No, I'm fine." And he walked down the hallway to the back of the house where the kitchen was.

Natalie entered the living room to take a seat on the sofa, which was so free of the slightest wrinkle or blemish, she thought she might be the first person to have ever graced it with her weight. Opposite her was a large leather chair, heavily creased with use. She assumed that was David's place of repose. Some newspapers and magazines were stacked on a coffee table in front of her.

She waited, listening to some noises from David in the kitchen. She glanced again at the wall unit at the back of the room: an old, ornate structure of a deep-brown wood, over five feet tall. There were solid cabinet doors on the bottom, an exposed main ledge with some liquor bottles on it, and three shelves that lay behind some protected glass doors. The doors and sides of the unit had an intricate pattern of branches carved into them that climbed and laced up the cabinet to a steeple top.

Curiosity took hold of her; she stood up and lightly stepped over to the cabinet. She didn't want David to know she was moving about his house. The cabinet was an anomaly, the only decorative piece in a house that was minimalist and utilitarian.

"Bart Miller seemed like a nice man," she called out. She could still hear movement issuing from the back of the house. Spoons were clanging. "He knew me—remembered me, actually."

David did not respond.

Looking past the intricate detailing of the cabinet, peering through the thin branches and the glass onto the shelves themselves, she saw neatly framed photographs. She wanted to open the doors and look at them, but she felt she would be invading too much of David's world all at once. She had already done one underhanded thing today. Sneaking peeks into David's private life without his knowledge crossed some moral line with her, especially since it was clear he was not entirely pleased with her surprise visit. She suppressed her curiosity and returned to the sofa in the front of the room to wait again.

"He asked if you were okay. He seemed concerned about you," she went on. "I thought it was nice of him."

Still no response from the kitchen.

"He said to say hello. He mentioned he saw you at some party."

"Do you take sugar or milk?" David queried loudly.

Natalie thought about it for a moment. She would have preferred a latte or tea, but didn't want to disrupt what was in motion. "Two sugars and lots of milk."

At length, she heard David's heavy footfalls coming down the hallway before he appeared carrying two cups in his hand. He placed them both on the coffee table and sat down in his leather chair.

"Does he have something for you?" he asked, folding his arms in front of him.

"Bart? Yes. It will take a couple more meetings, though. That's three for three," she said, referring to the other two meetings David had arranged for her. She was already contracted with one company, a manufacturer in Cambridge, to create their website. And she was drawing up a contract with a national insurance company in Waterloo for some general online marketing consulting. These opportunities, combined with some projects she had in Toronto, meant she had enough to keep her busy for a few months. "So, what was the party?" she asked. David didn't strike her as a man who went to parties.

David snorted, "A tedious affair with a pretentious lot."

"But you still went."

"To support James's widow, Elinor."

Natalie had always known David was sparse on words, but today he seemed remarkably so. Was he pouting at her surprise visit? She floundered about for another comment, a new topic, and they fell into a valley of silence. She began to drink her coffee. It tasted horrible—it was instant.

"That's a beautiful cabinet there," she remarked, nodding to the wall unit she had superficially explored earlier. "Where did you get it?"

"Antique store," he said, not elaborating further.

"Are those photographs in it?" she asked, craning her neck as if just seeing them for the first time. "May I look at them?" She stood up to walk over but kept her eyes on David.

David sipped his coffee. "Is that why you came by?" he retorted with irritation. "Did you want to see what I'm about?"

His words stung her, and she was caught off guard. Should she leave at that rebuke? She puzzled over it for a good moment before arriving at her answer. No, she was indebted to him for what he had done recently. And she was guilty for coming upon him when he wasn't prepared. That was the real problem here. She wouldn't do it again.

"David," she said, trying to sound calm, "I'm not asking something out of the ordinary. People typically look at photographs when they are on display in someone's house. If it bothers you, I won't do it."

David's lower lip pushed up into his upper one; the pout of his face exacerbated by his sagging cheeks. He looked away from her and took another sip of his coffee. She didn't move; she just continued to stare at him. Perhaps, feeling that he'd rather have her look at pictures than at him, he waved his hand as if to say, *"Fine then, do as you will."*

Natalie walked closely past him and rested her hand on his shoulder for a moment. He glanced at it and cleared his throat but made no other movement.

Moving on, she approached the cabinet with a careful respect, as if she were nearing a tabernacle or shrine. Her hand moved to the small pulls, shaped like acorns, and she proceeded to swing open the doors. There were three shelves, with two photographs apiece.

On the top shelf were two older black-and-white pictures. The first of a young family, two adults and two children, with a small house in the background. The man was severe looking—tall and wiry, while the woman had a much more welcoming look with a large smile revealing her teeth. The boy of the two children, less than ten years old, was slightly thick compared to the older lanky girl beside him. The other picture was just of the two adults, each maintaining their expressions: he, grave in a soldier's uniform with a tilted angular cap; she, in a dress, smiling so wide as if to compensate for the austerity of her partner.

Natalie's gaze moved to the next shelf; two young men standing outside of an industrial building. She could tell the shorter of the men was David; though stocky, he was by no means obese as now. The taller of the men had height and a proud stance. She assumed it was James Hardich. Next, a wedding day photo with a young woman, flanked by James on one side and David on the other.

Now, on looking at the lowest shelf, her breath caught. She hadn't expected to see this—it was so out of place here, in a house she had never been to until this day. She clasped the silver frame and lifted it close to her face. She felt sadness, longing. She remembered this picture; she had boxed it away long ago, displeased with the memory and the time it revived.

Her mom, Ayisha, had dragged her to one of the department stores to have a professional photograph taken. She loathed the idea, but Ayisha was adamant it needed to be done. Natalie was sixteen; the unruly curls of her hair were puffing out wildly, and her face was overshadowed by her own locks. She remembered despising how she looked in her teens—she had been completely insecure in herself. In the picture, although her mother smiled, Natalie looked morbid and sullen; indeed, she looked like she was conducting this entire exercise under duress. A revolt in still life—a daughter ruining a picture for her mother to make a statement.

"It's a nice photo of you and your mother."

She turned to look at David, surprised. Some part of her had heard him come behind her (he could do nothing stealthily), but she had not registered it. She had to reorient herself to him, to the room, to David's house.

"Of her," Natalie corrected him. She had discovered a year after the photo was taken that her mother had been diagnosed with cancer and was in a fight for her life. Ayisha Mitchell had known her face and body would change; this was the family portrait before the decline—except that Natalie had put quite a blemish on it.

"She didn't tell me why she wanted it. Had I known, I would have been more ... accommodating," Natalie said. "I can't believe she sent you ... I'm ... surprised." As she spoke, she felt an unease within her. This man, who had been absent all her childhood, had in his possession deeply personal memories of her.

Of course, she knew there were communications between her mother and him. That was, after all, part of the arrangement between this once-nameless and faceless man and her mom. That was the string attached to the financial support: Ayisha gave information and David gave money. But what was the depth of the information provided?

"Is this the only picture she ever sent?" she asked.

"No, but it was the last."

"If she had stopped writing to you, would you have stopped supporting us?" Natalie asked, turning to look at David head on.

David stared straight back at her, frowning. "What do you think?"

She felt sheepish and ashamed for asking the question. Why should she interrogate this man who had supported her over the years? Where did this resentment in her come from? Was it the picture of her mom that he had displayed on a shelf, despite never bothering to see her? Was it that he had the presumption to dictate any conditions to her mother, even if he never intended to exact a consequence? Was it that between Bart Miller and now David, she was feeling like people all had some knowledge of her and she had none of anybody?

Enough conversation about her mother for now, she decided. "I'm sorry," she said to him, putting the picture back on the shelf. She needed to calm herself; this was an odd day of jarring incidents for her. "Your father was in the army?" she asked, pointing to the black-and-white photo of the man in the uniform on the top shelf.

"Royal Canadian Air Force. World War Two. But he didn't stay in after the war."

"You've never mentioned him before."

David's eyes stared hard at the picture. His mouth opened, and he started to say something, stopped, then resumed. "My father was a hard man. Not much else to say. I think my mother was the real soldier. The war lasted a few years for my father; it lasted over fifty years for her being married to him."

She felt a quick chill run through her by his statement, a slight turn of the stomach. The vagueness of it alluded to some suffering, something violent, but she didn't want more details. It was the first glimpse of a past David had ever given to her, and she didn't want to know more.

Something had been loosened in David, however; a rock covering up the well of conversation dislodged. For once, he had offered up more information without being questioned. "And that was my sister," he said, pointing to the young girl in the picture on the top shelf.

"Where is she?"

"Not sure. We lost touch a long time ago. She went off with a man none too good for her—I guess she thought men like my father were the ideal." David smirked at the photo momentarily and then dropped his attention to the next shelf.

"That's James and I after we started up our first business together," he said, pointing to the second shelf. "And that's James and his wife, Elinor. I was the best man," he added.

"And is that his family there?" she asked, looking on the last shelf. She had overlooked that photo entirely the first time when she had seen the picture of her mother.

"Yes. James, Elinor, and their children—Xavier and Augusta."

"They're a good-looking family," she observed. She meant it. The picture could have been the stock card that accompanies a frame when purchased at a store. Elinor had an oval-like face, her hair gathered in a bun. Augusta was a captivating young woman, her hair pulled back in a partial ponytail on top, with the rest draping elegantly on either side of her face. Xavier had shoulder-length, dark-brown hair that was slicked back, showing high cheekbones and eyes she could only describe as determined.

"I suppose they are, in their way," David said, shutting the cabinet doors. The interlude of show-and-tell was over. They returned to their seats to finish their coffee. The rock was relodged in David's conversation well, and he became quiet again. This time, Natalie didn't mind; she had her own thoughts to mull over.

It had been a strange day. She had experienced, for the first time, David opening up, even just a little. Perhaps this was the start of something new in their relationship.

When she left him, he did not seem as standoffish. His pouting had ceased, and he was more amicable. She noted that he didn't press an envelope onto her at her departure. He had not been prepared for her this time. How could he be? For once, *he* had not determined the terms of the meeting.

Driving back to Toronto, her mind turned over the events of the day, and of David Burlow.

* * *

Natalie had been nineteen, filled with grief, anger, and confusion. She had reached out to him, looking for some connection to fill an emptiness that had been left by the departure of her mother. Her grandparents had been wary, even counseled against the meeting, but she had demanded it.

Her mother had told her to see him if the chance presented itself. Ayisha Mitchell, always forgiving, never holding a grudge, blamed him for nothing—she was even grateful to him. "He's provided a good life for us," she said. "See him. Thank him." Ayisha never once considered he was obliged to help, that any man with a moral compass would. Never once did her mother reflect that he had left her to raise a child on her own.

On a day in May, she met him. It was simultaneously profound and uneventful. Via a phone call, they arranged to see each other in High Park at the tomb of John Howard. All she knew is that he would have a trench coat and umbrella, and that he had mentioned he was rather difficult to overlook.

Armed with this vague description, she came upon the meeting point and saw he was there first. She studied the back of him as she approached. He was heavyset, even gigantic, wearing a black trench coat that hugged his body too snug in some places and too loose in others. He had close-cut, fading brown hair that went over a large roll on his upper neck before ending in a perfect horizontal line above the collar of his trench coat. Extending from his hand, and poking into the ground, was an umbrella.

His back was to her as he stared at the tomb, motionless. The monument holding his gaze was more than twice his size, the upper part composed of a decorative pedestal topped by a Maltese cross. In front of the monument was the old tombstone of John Howard and his wife, Jemima Francis, who had bequeathed these park lands to the city in the nineteenth century. The tomb was set in among trees and protected by a tall, black iron fence.

Moving closer, thinking about how to command his attention and introduce herself, Natalie settled on approaching the fence a few paces away from his position. She put her hands around the iron posts, taking in the tomb and thinking of what her first words ought to be. He had not noticed her yet, either because his mind was elsewhere or he had chosen to disregard her presence.

She recalled a quip her teacher had said when they visited this monument in elementary school and now used it to break the ice. "Someone was really counting the days of their life, weren't they?" she stated. She was referring to the inscription of John and Jemima Howard. After each of their birth and death dates were engraved precise calculations of their age at the time of death: Jemima was seventy-five years and fourteen days, while John was eighty-six years, six months, and twenty-seven days.

"What's that?" David broke from his thoughts and stared at her. She wasn't sure if he registered the joke first or her. "Yes, quite specific," he said, nodding in comprehension. "I guess it was a competition and he won. You must be Natalie."

"I am."

"You have your mother's look in you."

Natalie let go of the iron bars and walked closer to him. She studied his face: plump cheeks, somewhat droopy eyelids, and light-blue eyes that seemed to be pushed back in his head. She thought of her own image in the mirror before she left her house and compared it to his: her delicate oval face, high cheeks and dark-brown eyes. She was ashamed by the gratitude she felt for having no resemblance to this man.

"David Burlow," he said, extending his hand.

"Natalie," she responded, receiving his hand somewhat meekly. He didn't let go of hers.

"Firm your grip up, girl. Don't be timid about it," David chastised her. His hands were large and fat and had almost devoured her slender fingers and palm. She did her best to rearrange her grip to clutch his massive hand and squeeze. Once she had done so, he nodded at her as if to say *that's better.*

They stood looking at each other for some time, absorbing the silence between them, each contemplating the other. A breeze wafted through the trees, a crow cawed, and the movement of a small animal rustled bushes off in the forest in a brief, frenetic burst of energy. Still, Natalie could only wonder at the man. She felt that this was a moment of resolution, of conclusion, yet she could not structure a thought as to why. She neither felt happy nor sad, only satisfied. When David suggested they take a stroll through the park, she agreed. What else could she say?

They talked about many things that day but were also silent on many others. In retrospect, Natalie wondered if her desire was really to talk to him or just be near him, to identify this missing piece of her life. She had no plan as to what she wanted to achieve. Such unfocused foresight could only beget long stretches where the sound of their feet walking on the paved paths was the only communion they shared. Natalie struggled with her feelings; she could not make any of them out, but she distinctly remembered being in some dream state. There was no sense of time, no sense of hunger, though she hadn't eaten all day, no sense of fatigue, though she had a restless sleep, and no sense of responsibility or life outside of the park at that moment.

They came upon three fountains fenced in by hedges at the top of the hill overlooking Grenadier Pond. He asked to rest on the benches. She was moved to tell him about her mother, about how wonderful Ayisha had been and how much Natalie missed her. There was a therapeutic joy in describing her mother to a stranger, to one who knew so little of Ayisha. David listened while staring into the turquoise-painted basins filled with water.

"Do you regret not coming to the funeral?" she asked him.

He didn't answer.

"I think you should have. For your own closure," she said.

"It wasn't my place," was all he said.

She supposed he meant that he had moved on. That whatever had existed between Ayisha and him was long gone. The only thing that kept him even partially connected to events was Natalie.

When they parted that day at the north end of the park, near the subway, he pulled out an envelope from his breast pocket and handed it to her. "Just a little something. Maybe you can take your grandparents out for dinner," he said.

"Sure, thank you." Natalie took the envelope. She didn't open it in front of him. "Are we going to see each other again?"

David paused and then shrugged. "We can make arrangements from time to time if you like. You know how to get a hold of me." This was an indication to Natalie that she would be the one who would have to reach out to him.

On the subway ride home, she opened the envelope to see numerous hundred-dollar bills—some twenty of them. Astonished, she became suddenly suspicious of the people around her; everyone looked like a potential thief. As soon as the train reached Pape Station in Greektown, she sprinted home to her grandparents, fearing she was being followed the whole way.

CHAPTER 7

A Casual Meeting *(Richard Earning, June 2004)*

A FTER the Spring Gathering, Richard thought about Augusta every day. Indeed, elements of his interaction with her made their way into the opening paragraphs of a new story he began writing the moment he got home from the gathering.

There was something gloriously secretive about the two of them slinking off from the other guests to be alone, with him supplying her with cigarettes to feed an illicit habit. For almost an hour behind the garage, they talked of books, movies, and the people at the party. They were occasionally forced to lower their voices as guests would leave from the front door to walk to their cars.

When Augusta felt obliged to return to the gathering, Richard knew he needed to act. With uncharacteristic boldness, he joked with her saying, "I still don't have my insurance policy."

"What do you mean?"

Richard pulled out his phone. "In the event that the police take me. How will I get in contact with you?"

Augusta smiled. "You might regret this, Richard," she said. She took the phone from his hand and entered her contact information.

Now, he just needed to do something with it.

On the Thursday night after the gathering, his desire to see her was all-consuming. He had hoped to hold out a couple of weeks and then drop her a casual note, as if he had just remembered her. But he succumbed to his own urgency, and he texted her asking if she'd be open to meet for a coffee over the next few days.

As each minute passed with no response, he began to doubt if there had been any connection between them. Perhaps their private moment was unremarkable to a woman like Augusta. She seemed to have everything together; she was so confident, so alluring—so commanding. He would merely be added to a long list of people who carried her number in their phone, remembering her, but whom she would never call or recall.

At 8:30 p.m., Richard was mobilized into action when a text lit up his screen. *At William's studying. Come at 9:30.*

William's Coffee House was as much a part of the Waterloo University fabric as a library or campus pub. It was always open, and thousands of assignments had been completed there by countless students. As a gathering place for academic insomniacs, the solution to more than one world problem had been started and never finished. For the pseudo-intelligentsia lost their caffeine-powered trains of thought in mid-debate and derailed themselves in their own arguments.

Amid the coffee grinding, the hissing of steam and frothing milk, the ceaseless chatter of patrons, and clicking keyboards, he found her. She had managed to secure a booth. Her papers and books were spread out across the table, and she was sipping a coffee while she read. Her attire was nothing close to that of her peers, who sought casual and comfortable clothing, conducive for sitting in classes and lounging in study rooms or libraries. Augusta could easily be confused with an established professional, with her beige Burberry spring coat thrown casually on the bench beside her, her hair elegantly feathered, and wearing a crisp white blouse with a black collar. She could have floated into a job interview or a chic club with equal ease.

When he sat down opposite her, Augusta didn't look up. She continued the perusal of her text. For a few minutes, he waited, saying nothing, and watched as the highlighter in her hand traversed the length of a page, then made some additional little blips of movement before she closed the book and capped her marker with a solid click. She looked at him, entirely unaffected, made no apology, and gave him a slight smile.

"You can go on if I've interrupted," he said.

"No, I'm done now." She stacked her books and papers and moved them off to the side. "It's nice to see you again. I'm glad you could make the time work. Were you bored or craving my company?"

He smiled at her, hoping it concealed his panic. What was he supposed to say to that? How did she know? Of course, he had been craving her company. He was thrilled when her name had lit up his phone. From the time he had texted her until now, he had been agitated, eagerly awaiting this meeting.

Richard snatched one of the books she had been reading from the pile. "What's all this about?" he asked, evading her question while flipping through the pages. He came across some notes in the margins, presumably Augusta's writing: *Interesting study. Review source*, and further down, *Builds on Bandura's theory, but misses latest research*.

While he was reading her notes, four fingers with red painted nails covered the letters on the open page. He looked up to see Augusta shaking her head.

"No," she said, pulling the book out of his hands. "If we talk about that, I'll be doing all the talking."

"What makes you so sure I don't know all about Bandura and his theories?"

"I'm as sure of that as I knew you'd come tonight when I texted you back."

Again, her directness checked him. The confidence with which she spoke stifled any retort he might make. She was so certain about things—like her brother.

"You're right, I don't know much past Psychology 101. I'm an English lit grad," he said. "What do you want to talk about, then?" He hoped they would be able to find some common ground. He hoped their interaction at the Hardich gathering had been more than a one-night affair of interesting dialogue.

"The last bet we had, I chose books and lost. I choose current events and politics tonight," she said.

"This might not be good for me. I've heard about your political leanings," he remarked.

She laughed. "Did the ultra-privileged conservative crowd tell you I was a raging communist?"

"David Burlow and your own mother betrayed you."

She smirked and gave a mild shake of her head, as if she expected nothing less. "A good humanities education made me a bad bourgeois."

"I'm not sure you make a good communist either," Richard countered. "Your clothes are far from the simple proletariat attire your comrades would consider acceptable."

"Is my attire not to your liking?"

Richard couldn't suppress a laugh. "Don't get me wrong. I think your look is great—"

"Thank you," she interrupted.

"Right, yes, but it's all designer stuff. Well beyond the means of most of the working class. You and your brother both seem to have a fetish for expensive clothes."

"So? Are you suggesting my communist leanings are insincere because of my fashion sense?"

"You don't see the conflict?"

"I never said I was a commie," Augusta said, rolling her bottom lip into her mouth and biting it gently with her incisors. "Those are all the myths surrounding me from my parents' polite society because I call them out on their bullshit. Admittedly, I had a phase in undergrad where I latched on to Marxist theories and became a bit of a terror for my parents. I believed in the theories, preached all about class oppression and exploitation, but I moved past all that. As you rightly pointed out, it would be very hard for me to hold those convictions when I have such a penchant for the finer things in life."

Intrigued by her honest admission, he pressed on. "And your new convictions?"

She was quiet for a long time before she answered. "I think I chose politics and current events as our topic. Not me." And she abruptly got up and approached a lone table with a newspaper on it. She grabbed it and returned. "Now we have our agenda," she said.

Her game was simple: they would scan the headlines and debate the snippets of news. They talked and argued late into the night. She was opinionated and well spoken, often sounding older than her appearance, which he guessed to be twenty-four or twenty-five. Her eyes had an intensity as she stared at him, always with a bit of an amused smile.

There was an intellectualism in their banter, a sparring for which Richard was hungry. His mind was stirring, as if a dusty blanket had been removed from furniture in a summerhouse as residents returned after years of neglect. He was out of practice with such discussions; corporate life in an office had dulled his ability and awareness of anything other than budgets, project timelines, status, and product requirements. But with her, he felt like he was back in university—like a young student again.

She always made him state his opinion first, as if she needed to hear it first so she could offer an entirely contrarian view. When talking about an article on the military intervention in Afghanistan, Richard suggested that the Canadian troops were being trapped in a quagmire and they would likely achieve no lasting impact. Augusta responded by saying that "isolationist attitudes have no place in a global world" and everyone needed to "help build free democracies." If he referenced an article on long wait times in hospitals and the need for more funding in healthcare, she would say that "privatization was the only answer to a system that was broken and grossly mismanaged by an ineffectual government monopoly." If he supported higher taxes to provide services to the less fortunate, she would say "taxation is destroying the middle class, and it's unreasonable for them to bear the burden for the nation."

Her stance on everything was the opposing side, and he could never reconcile what her worldview was—it seemed entirely devoid of a consistent philosophy or political leaning.

When he remarked this point to her, she shrugged her shoulders. "They taught me to think critically. So, I became a critic of everything. What's the point in having an opinion? It's all relative anyway."

The night rolled past, and at two o'clock in the morning, Richard grudgingly conceded he needed to get some sleep before work. When he left her that night, she gave him a light embrace and told him she would reach out for another coffee sometime.

For two days, he waited expectantly. He checked his phone repeatedly. He would call it, reboot it, have members of the Pit text him to ensure his phone was working properly. There were even times he started to compose some silly trite messages like "hey, hope things are good." But he would never send them, realizing how desperate they sounded. All he was able to do was infect his writing with her.

On first glance, he would have dismissed any interest in her. Not because her features or her look weren't appealing—indeed, the opposite—but rather, because she was so striking. He would have projected onto her a personality type, one of arrogance and entitlement. How strange, then, to actually know her more and learn that his assessment of her type was correct, but that he was seduced by it. The criteria he had set up to classify a person as undesirable suddenly became the characteristics that aroused his curiosity further.

Three days after their coffee meeting, he got what he wanted.

A simple text: *Meet me.*

CHAPTER 8

Portrait of a Family (Xavier Hardich, June 2004)

XAVIER set the tray of fresh salmon and bowl of mashed potatoes down in the center of the dining room table. He was very pleased with the food he had helped his mother create.

The time was just shy of 6:30 p.m., and Augusta had still not come down. Xavier grabbed two small candles from a cabinet and placed them on the table. He was lighting them as his mother entered with a bowl of vegetables.

"This is a real treat!" Elinor said, surveying the scene and ensuring everything was in place. "Now we just need Augusta."

Xavier walked to the foot of the stairs leading to the second level and called up, "Augusta! Dinner!" Then he returned to the dining room and stood behind the chair at the head of the table. His mother waited patiently on his left, and Augusta's place was set to his right. He gripped the back of the chair tightly.

"She'll be down in a moment," Elinor said, reaching out and patting one of his white clenched hands. "You'll spoil your evening if you let these little things bother you."

At last, he heard the fast and light step of Augusta coming down the stairs. When she entered the dining room, she stopped and furrowed her brow.

"So formal?" she asked suspiciously, staring at Xavier.

"Come along, Augusta, we're waiting for you," Elinor said.

Augusta slowly made her way to the chair on Xavier's right and opposite her mother. "Should I be looking forward to these dinners regularly?" She didn't sound pleased at the prospect.

"Yes," Xavier said, taking his seat, while Elinor and Augusta did likewise. He looked deliberately at Augusta. "I'm hoping you'll join Mom and I more often than you have. All three of us should be making time to eat together."

"I see," Augusta said, giving him a quick, narrow-eyed look. Then she glanced at their mother, as if looking for confirmation that this was all rather an odd spectacle, but she found none in Elinor's smiling face. Elinor seemed filled with an uncontained pleasure to be dining with both her children.

They served themselves, while their mother spoke excitedly about her upcoming fundraisers for the universities and her volunteer work with a local theatre company and the public library. There were dinners and lecture series, small galas and events with silent auctions and raffles, and every other kind of activity to raise money for institutions, organizations, and causes.

The Hardiches owed their good philanthropic name in the community chiefly to Elinor's endeavors. Anyone who wanted money raised would recruit her. When she mobilized her army of well-to-do friends, a fundraiser's success was assured, and if there was a shortfall in the financial goal sought, Elinor was happy to discreetly top it up with her own money to make everything whole. She was the perpetual public relations arm of the family. Even the idea and the organization of the Spring Gathering had been hers.

"If you need help with anything, Mom, you let us know," Xavier said as he served himself another piece of fish. "Augusta and I will do whatever we can. Maybe Enigma can make a small donation to one of your causes." He emphasized *small*.

Xavier saw Augusta looking at him, one eyebrow slightly raised with her amused smile—the one that irritated him, made him wary. It was as if she knew something nobody else did, as if she heard words and meanings of which people were ignorant. When she looked at him that way, he felt like someone unaware of pun he had just spoken. All he could think was that she was mocking him, maybe even the whole world.

"How are things with Enigma?" Elinor asked him.

Xavier shrugged. "I'm making some necessary changes—slowly getting things back on track. But it's challenging with Bill."

He explained he had hoped for a more amicable relationship with his business partner, but Bill Spindrall seemed to take issue with everything he was doing. Bill argued against Xavier taking over the client relationships, argued against the new reporting structure Xavier imposed, and found Xavier's calls for financial prudence shortsighted. Their most recent spat was over Bill's desire to hire more developers. Where Bill was adamant the core team of the Pit should be expanded with invested employees, Xavier only saw the bloating of payroll. Taking Derek Lam's tip on keeping costs contained, Xavier opted to pursue affordable contractors that could be eliminated or replaced on a moment's notice. About the only thing the two partners could agree on was that the company needed a new website. But even here, they differed on the executional plan. Bill had received proposals from marketing and communication firms that were overpriced in Xavier's estimation. Thus, Xavier had rejected them all. Ultimately, Bill was furious that a plan previously approved by James Hardich was now up for revision. Xavier saw it as Bill being finally held to account.

"Your father obviously saw some merit in him," Elinor remarked. "Speaking of Bill, that reminds me. You never invited him to the gathering this year. He's your partner, and you should have."

Xavier laughed. "He was an embarrassment last year. He kept rehashing that story of his lucky wife to anyone that would listen. Behaved like an awkward ass!"

Elinor frowned at him. "Don't be so unkind," she scolded.

A chuckle rose from Augusta's throat. He watched as her eyes lit up with a knowing satisfaction. "But you invited someone else from Enigma," Augusta observed. "Richard, I think, was his name. Perhaps you used him to spite Bill? Bill would surely discover that Richard had come and wonder why he was excluded. An interesting shot to fire over Bill's bow to show your displeasure."

"Not at all," Xavier retorted defensively. "Richard reports to me. He's one of the minor equity holders. We work together, and I was just being friendly."

But the truth was that Augusta had him. She had disassembled his intentions quickly and surmised his game easily with the scantest of details. He was frustrated by that about her—her knowing. She chose not to hound him further; perhaps, for that, he should have been thankful.

They ate in silence for some minutes, Elinor's eyes bouncing between the children, probably hoping all the conversation was not done.

"How's school going?" Xavier enquired of Augusta.

Augusta's fork, with a speared piece of fish on the end of it, froze in midair on its journey to her mouth. She now gave him a puzzled look. "Good," she replied. "They've asked me to teach an introductory psychology class in the fall semester. Between that, doing my coursework, and planning my dissertation, I'm busy."

"You're coming home from university so late at times," Elinor piped in. "It must be early morning—maybe even three or four? I don't like you driving at those ungodly times. What's keeping you?"

"Why don't you just crash at Derek's? It would save you a drive home," Xavier added.

Augusta shrugged. "Derek doesn't like being woken at three in the morning by my entrance."

"Hopefully things will calm down for you," Xavier said. He was trying to be polite with her, but he felt like he was having a conversation with a stranger and floundering for common ground.

"Hopefully," she replied with a breathy laugh.

Xavier could only wonder at his sister. In the house, they could pass days without saying a word and entirely miss each other's comings and goings. She was busy with her teaching and her studies at the university and spent nights up in Waterloo at Derek's condo. Xavier's own social life meant he did not always come home at night either. The siblings lived separate lives. He tended to learn what Augusta was up to from his mother, or even, at times, from Derek.

When they were growing up, they had each pursued their own friends and social spheres independent of the other. They had their run-ins, their arguments, their occasional peace treaties to combat imagined parental tyranny, but they never really confided in one another. The only time he had ever experienced a closeness with her was on a family trip to Italy some years back—a vacation he remembered with fondness and a tinge of melancholy. He was twenty-one and she was eighteen—the perfect ages to experience the culture of Venice, Florence, and Rome. And the perfect ages to experience the modern nightlife of ancient cities.

Early in the trip, the siblings revolted against the cultural-educational day tours their parents had organized. They preferred their own curriculum of late-night city wanderings fueled by excessive consumption of wine, beer, and shots, escalating over the course of the holiday to binge status.

They had received a stern lecture from their mother midway through the trip when Augusta threw up on the wall of the great Florence Duomo. To the consternation and embarrassment of their parents, Augusta quipped she was conducting a restoration, which was true insofar as the substance purged from her stomach was nearly the same greenish hue as the granite blocks of the church. This was a small setback in their education, and they spent some nights recuperating before getting their studies back on track in Rome, where they pursued their examinations of the bars, cafes, and clubs with renewed vigor.

Only on that trip did Xavier realize that Augusta was a desirable object for men. She was frequently looked at, catcalled, and talked to by travelers and locals alike. How many times had she managed to spend an entire evening out without paying for one drink? How many times had she gotten them into crowded, over-capacity places without ever paying a cover? He had watched her kiss men to jump a line, and let them touch her to get free drinks, but the moment she had achieved her objective, the men were discarded and ignored. He had learned, with some shock, how resourceful she could be with her sexuality.

That brief and fleeting bond with her was short-lived. The laughs they shared, the mishaps, the camaraderie of travel and their adventures couldn't last upon their return home. They fell into their old patterns quickly enough. She became a stranger to him. His mother had told him a couple of years earlier that Augusta was on a cocktail of antidepressants and anti-anxiety pills, and he wondered what that was doing to her. Is that what made her extroverted and aloof at the same time? Pleasant and simultaneously derisive?

"Do you know what you're going to write about for your dissertation?" Xavier asked. He didn't particularly care; he just needed to connect with her on some level.

"Where's all this coming from, Xavier? Are you worried about me?" Augusta's voice had a tinge of annoyance in it.

"I'm just asking."

"But what does it matter to you?" She must have surmised something was amiss, out of the ordinary. "You've never taken much interest in me before, and you probably shouldn't bother now. I believe you organized this dinner for some specific purpose. I would rather we speak about that."

"Augusta," Elinor reproached her, "is it so wrong for us to ask about one another? Can we not enjoy one another's company? Have a dinner together?"

Augusta flinched under Elinor's scolding and looked momentarily abashed. The table went quiet except for the scratching of a knife on a plate as it cut through fish, a clang of cutlery set upon the plate rim.

In the silence, Xavier quelled his frustration with his sister. And he also saw an opportunity to broker peace and lead into his true intent. "It's not Augusta's fault," he said to his mother. "We aren't used to talking together as a family. We're a little out of practice, but I'm confident we'll get better."

Elinor nodded. "I agree, and I'm proud of your effort."

He resumed, "I think we can all agree that since Dad passed, we haven't had any discussions about our ... position. About the legacy Dad left us and what we need to do to ensure it grows."

"You sound like you want to propose something," Augusta remarked.

"I have some ideas. I'm doing what I can with Enigma," Xavier said.

"I'm already going along with whatever your plans are there," Augusta reminded him. "That support gives you majority decision making."

"That's important, yes," Xavier said. He needed to proceed carefully now. Gently. "There are other things we should consider too. I've been talking to Derek, and he has some good ideas about where we can invest our money and grow it—get a great return. People are making a killing with him. And he's open to giving us a reduction in his fees."

"I wasn't aware you had anything to invest with Derek," Augusta returned. "He doesn't touch much below a million."

"This isn't about me or you." Xavier turned to look at Elinor. "Mom has considerable investments that are all currently managed by Burlow."

Augusta exhaled sharply through her nose. "Ah, I see. Now we have it out."

If Elinor had been following the conversation, she had not yet fully digested Xavier's intent.

"I've been doing a lot of thinking," Xavier said to his mother. "We should consider moving your money over to Derek."

"David's looking after it. It's fine," Elinor said confusedly.

"Mom, Burlow doesn't have access to the investment vehicles that Derek does. Derek's returns are going to be way more than anything Burlow can fetch. They are astronomical. People I know are doing very well by him. I think Dad only meant to have the money with Burlow until we figured out what to do with it—where to put it."

"I've never been done wrong by David, honey. I'm happy with how my affairs are being conducted. I've nothing against Derek at all, but I don't see the need for change."

"We can't let old friendships impede us," Xavier said, annoyed with her unwavering stance. "We need … you need … to be thinking about Dad's legacy—how to ensure it lasts."

His mother looked perturbed by the conversation. She sat back in her chair and seemed to lose her appetite.

"Mom, I'm thinking of the family now," he said. "You know that. This is nothing against David. I want us—"

"This whole legacy thing is yours," Augusta interrupted. "Pursue it with your own money if it's so important to you. I don't see any reason why Derek should have it. Mom's comfortable with David handling it, so why not leave it be." She stood up from the table and started to gather plates. "I suggest we not talk about money at the next family supper."

As Augusta carried dishes to the kitchen, Xavier sat with his mother in silence. Elinor extended her hand to him, which he took. She squeezed his tightly.

"We love Derek, honey, but this is all a little sudden," Elinor said.

"Dad's been gone for over six months," Xavier countered.

"I don't want to talk about it."

The family disbanded to their private lives and private thoughts; Augusta upstairs to her studies, and Elinor to read in the living room. Xavier, irritated, removed himself to his father's office with the remnants of the wine from dinner. The complacency of his family gnawed at him.

His first major effort to steer Elinor's money to Lam Investments had failed. Both his mother and sister seemed content to rely on tired old friendships to steward the family's money to mediocre performance. He was ashamed at what Derek might perceive as his inability to corral the family to achieve such a simple task. Xavier appeared powerless and inept, unable to exert even the slightest influence over his mother or Augusta.

And at Enigma, Bill sparred and resisted him.

Everyone was second-guessing him and doubting his ability.

As the wine went to Xavier's head, he sat in his father's chair, asking the books, and the spirit of his father, for guidance.

CHAPTER 9

A Romance in Secrecy *(Richard Earning, July 2004)*

RICHARD parked his car in a small lot off the main street in Waterloo. Misty rain deposited fine drops on his windshield. Tonight, he would see her again, but this was the first time she had suggested a place other than their coffeehouse rendezvous.

For over a month, they had been meeting regularly. Each time, they talked into the early morning. Augusta now dominated his mind; there was an ever-present eagerness to see her, an unseen cord that tugged and pulled on him, drawing him to her.

He felt foolish in his yearnings. Every day, Richard swore he would show more discipline, more restraint, and avoid Augusta for a week or two so he could get his sanity back. But Augusta was like a cigarette. Every night, his commitment to quit her, even for a short time, was undone upon waking in the morning when the craving began anew. He submitted to it. *Good morning* ... he would text her. And if his resolve managed to last through his morning routine, and he stifled his cravings and withdrawal, it evaporated the moment she beckoned him with a text: *Coffee tonight, meet me.* If more than a few hours passed by without any message from her, he wandered in a state of agitation, checking his phone frequently, often experiencing ghost vibrations in his pocket or hearing imaginary rings and pings.

But doubts began to grow in his mind about this odd relationship. Was it purely a social distraction for her? Did she really just enjoy their conversation? Augusta had never indicated that this was more than a casual friendship. Yet, he believed she felt something for him— the way she looked at him, the way she would study him, the way she would touch his arm or smile. He hoped she felt something, even if it was just a mere fraction of the turmoil she was causing in him.

He got out of the car and walked the short distance to the bar-restaurant and entered. The establishment possessed a peculiar personality. It had an eclectic amalgamation of grunge with a retro-indie ambience; 1970s-style plastic kitchen chairs were paired with simple tables that flickered with slivers of silver from a small disco ball spinning on the ceiling. Dimly lit, shadows created silos of intimacy between the tables. Unlike some of the surrounding university watering holes, this bar was more subdued and frequented by those who preferred the rhythm of quiet conversation, spurred on by lounge music in the background.

The crowd was thin tonight, and he easily spotted Augusta, dressed smartly as usual. She was sitting at a table in the corner with a book in one hand and a notepad in front of her. The other hand held a pen that would be idle one moment, then spasmodically start writing feverishly on the pad. A half-consumed glass of wine was at her elbow. He could tell she was slightly straining to read, for in addition to the candle that was meant for her table, she had added another from the table beside her. Her red-brown hair was pulled back into a ponytail, allowing the candlelight to dance upon her face. It gave her features a warm orange glow when she hunched over to write.

As Richard approached the table, Augusta spied him, smiled, and stood up. She put her arms around his neck to embrace him, more fully than he could ever recall her doing before. She'd never greeted him this warmly.

Richard returned her embrace. As his arms enveloped her, his hands registered the feel of her back, the small abutment of her spine, and they slowly slid to her waist and rested on her hip bones. She seemed to sense his lingering, but instead of pulling away, she afforded him the chance to enjoy it by continuing her embrace of him. When she finally released him, she did not step away, but only arched her back slightly to look into his eyes. For a fleeting moment, he saw an unreadable expression, maybe sadness, before it was replaced with a smile. She then kissed him quickly on the cheek, seemed almost puzzled with herself, and took her seat.

A waitress came over, and without asking him what he wanted, deposited a pint of his favorite beer on the table. He looked at Augusta questioningly, and she remarked, "I know what you like."

He took a sip from the glass. "This is different than our usual coffee meets," he said. "Have we graduated to drinks now?"

"Yes, you passed the test."

"I'm glad. What was the test?"

Augusta bit her lower lip. "To see if you could hold my interest this long."

Richard was elated at her frank admission. Holding her interest seemed like a remarkable achievement.

They started as they usually did—providing summary updates to one another since the last time they had met. Richard was brief in his account, since he never felt the drudgery at Enigma was in any way interesting compared to Augusta's university life. She would tell him of the topics she covered as a lecturer or of interesting journal articles she read. Then they would effortlessly stumble into another debate about whatever was prominent in the news.

Later in the night, as Augusta nursed her second glass of wine, she leaned forward and put her elbows on the table. "You're an odd one to be working at my company," she said. "Bit of a scholar, certainly a reader, and apparently a writer—though I've had no evidence of the latter. I wonder, do you really enjoy working at Enigma?"

Richard smiled. "Not sure I can be honest with this question."

"Try me. Think of me like the resident psychologist."

He pondered how much he ought to reveal before answering. "I don't love my job, if that's what you're asking. But it's helping me lay the foundation so I can pursue my passions. I have equity in the company. If Enigma makes it big, my money comes in, and I can get off this hamster wheel. That's why it's so important to me that Enigma succeeds. It's why I bust my ass—equity will drive a man to do strange things."

"And when all the money comes in, what will you do?"

"You know, the writing traveler thing. Seeing the world and writing about my experiences or finally getting a novel done."

"Ah yes, your little bohemian dream you described to me. You'd make a good wanderer, I think," Augusta mused. "But why haven't you done it? Why work at Enigma at all? The future you want is modest enough that you could start it next year if you really wanted."

"I need to work, you know," Richard said, shaking his head in surprise. Was Augusta that oblivious to her own station? To his? She didn't have the same pressures he did—that's what affluence alleviated. "There's rent to pay, food to buy, gas, insurance, retirement … I'm trying to save for a house too."

She shook her head. "Those are all things you need if you're not traveling and writing—but you'd need none of that if you were actually doing what you wanted to do."

"People need stability. Most of us can't actually live like nomads," he commented with mild frustration. "That's why they're called dreams. You can't live them; you have responsibilities, obligations, and all that. If I came from money like …" He trailed off, not finishing his thought, thinking it might be perceived as a slight.

But she knew what he was alluding to. "If you came from money like me, you mean?"

"I didn't say that," he said, ashamed.

She laughed. "We all want what other people have. That's just one of our many problems."

"And what do *you* want? You've never talked about your dreams. What are they?"

Augusta leaned back, and she swished wine about in her mouth. She was quiet for a long moment before answering. "To know less. To believe more in people, in everything."

He studied her, wondering if she was playing with him in jest or revealing something. "Why can't you?"

She shrugged. "I've a nihilistic view of life and a low opinion of humanity. How's that?"

Richard went quiet, trying to interpret her meaning. At a conversational crossroads, he wasn't sure if he should delve more into the topic or wait for her to expand on it.

Augusta appeared to sense the impasse of his thoughts, for she smiled. "You once asked me about my convictions," Augusta went on. "I don't know that I have any. I just have a belief that we're base creatures. We're self-interested. I see how we all use each other for our own ends, our own gains. In the end, there's not much meaning in this life. And as far as I can tell, what meaning there is comes from ensuring we have as many of our wants and desires satisfied as possible."

"That's a rather cynical view of things," Richard said, surprised at her admission.

"Horrible, isn't it? It's like Dorian Gray was on to something."

Richard pondered her allusion to Oscar Wilde's famous hedonistic villain. This conversation was so different from their other ones, as if the coffee, now replaced by wine and beer, made Augusta comfortable enough to share some confessions and inner turmoil in her.

"I'm not sure I agree with your perspective," he said at last. And then, some part of him that he could hardly control offered up more of his own feeling. "In fact, I think you're entirely wrong. The truth is, I like being here with you. And I'm not using you for anything."

This time she gave him a knowing laugh. "Yes. You are. We're both using each other."

"How?" he asked incredulously.

Augusta chewed the inside of her mouth, her eyes narrowed. "Do you really want to know?"

"Yeah, I do. How am I using you?" he asked again.

She scrutinized him for a full minute before she spoke. "You like our conversations—you like me. I see it in your eyes, in the way you look at me. In the way you always respond to my little summonses. I give you something, Richard—you're stimulated by me. Intellectually, yes, but in other ways. I suspect you've been thinking about me—imagining me, what I'd be like to have. On my knees looking up at you? On top looking down at you? I know I'm pretty, Richard. I know I'm desirable. And I know you want to fuck me. Those are all the little thoughts in your head you try to repress, but they're there. That's how you'd use me. An object of desire is always meant to be used."

Richard, stunned at her brazenness, sat back in his chair and crossed his arms. He avoided looking at her. Was she blunt, crass, arrogant or all of them combined? He didn't think she was merely adopting some affectation to shock him. Her words reduced the things he felt for her, the unique connection he thought he shared with her, into something base and self-serving.

And yet, despite the distaste for what she had said and the vulgar way she had said it, he was drawn to the sensual allusion it created in his mind. He had thought of her often in that way, imagined her flesh underneath her clothing.

Her singular conviction was correct, and it frustrated him further.

The silence in the air between them was heavy as it gained the weight of awkwardness. Augusta tilted her head slightly to look at him, then turned and tilted her head the other way, as if that turning and twisting would pry open a door for a good look at the contents within him.

"You're bothered by what I said," Augusta remarked to break the quiet. "I usually keep those thoughts in my head. I don't normally provide my assessment of what's going on in the other person. I guess I thought, given the rest of our discussion, I could tell you. And I did ask, to be sure you were ready to hear it. I'm sorry if I embarrassed you."

"No," he said. "You didn't embarrass me. But I think you reduce things ... motives, even good ones, into something sinister and animalistic."

Augusta frowned. A slight touch of redness flushed her cheeks, though Richard couldn't be sure it wasn't a trick of the candlelight.

"I know. It's the problem I have. Maybe that's why I'm in psychology. Trying to figure out how to make this better," she said, tapping her forehead. She gave a weak smile, but it was one of discomfort.

Despite his desire to dissipate the strange tension between them, he could think of no words to restore the easy flow of their conversation.

Augusta swirled the wine in her glass and broke the silence. "I like being with you too," she said. "I think about you. I want us to keep seeing each other."

She held up her glass to him to make peace. He touched it gently with a soft clink of his own pint. And with that cheers, Richard felt they were able to move past their troublesome state. The distance between them faded and the thrill of being in her company was renewed, even more strongly.

Now he knew Augusta felt something for him. He crossed a threshold that night, embraced his longing for her.

"You look very pleased and contented, Richard," Augusta said, cupping one of the candles on the table in her hands so that the light glowed about her face.

"I am," he said. He grabbed the other candle and cupped it as she had.

It was the beginning of a strange séance, where instead of communicating with the dead, they quietly communicated their desires to each other. Richard was able to feel her craving for him. He didn't want to fuck her; he wanted to love her.

Later that night, outside of the bar, he leaned against the wall of the building while she leaned into him, kissing him fully. He felt the mysterious contours of her body through her clothes as if he were trying to read braille with a thin gauze material over the words and the meanings they contained. Whatever Augusta's paradoxes, he loved her—he lusted for her.

CHAPTER 10

Dinners (*Xavier Hardich, August 2004*)

"So, what does Bill do now?" Derek Lam asked, taking another mouthful of wine.

Xavier had met up with Derek for dinner at a restaurant in Waterloo after leaving the office. It was an upscale establishment with a higher-priced menu, prohibitive to university students and young revelers who sought value and large portions over a fine culinary experience.

"He's purely operational. Pretty much administration," Xavier said. "I don't let him handle any external relationships. And I've got a tight hand on the finances. Crushed his dreams more than once."

"I'll bet he's not happy about that."

Xavier laughed. "He's not, but I don't care. I'm about getting this product done as efficiently as possible and getting the company into the black. All Bill does is cite the old business plan my father had agreed to. That doesn't matter much anymore, does it? He kept barking at me about hiring three more developers and how it was agreed to. I just brought in a few cheap contractors to get us over a hump."

Xavier was taking the necessary steps to strip Bill Spindrall of his influence and decision-making power. The tension between Enigma's two active partners was barely concealed in meetings, even when their employees were present. They would take deep exasperated breaths as the other spoke; they would criticize each other's ideas or recommendations and talk over one another while Richard or Jeremy, or any other unfortunate soul present, was left to stare silently at a notebook or computer. Outside of meetings, they avoided interaction and frequently used Richard Earning as a proxy to communicate between one another. Despite their offices being separated by one thin wall, they might as well have been on separate continents.

Derek approved. "Sounds like you're getting a handle on things. That's good. Rein in those costs. Do you want me to put some feelers out to see who might be interested in scooping Enigma up?"

Xavier shook his head. "Too early for that, I think. Feel like we'd be undervalued at the moment."

"At this juncture, something is better than nothing," Derek remarked. "Money in hand now is a certainty compared to the possibility of money in the future. Enigma's IP might fetch a reasonable price, even if undervalued. That's what makes it appealing for buyers, after all."

Xavier could feel himself squirming a bit. He wasn't ready to rush into something yet. He had just taken the reins at Enigma. Wouldn't selling it off so quickly be an admission of failure? As much as he valued Derek's advice, it seemed premature to flip the firm. Besides, he enjoyed holding the reins of Enigma; he had never before felt the importance of his role and responsibilities.

"Let's hold off for now, but thanks," Xavier said.

Derek shrugged. "Your call. But plan your exit. Give yourself a time. Otherwise, you'll be at it for five years, and you'll have missed every opportunity." Derek leaned forward. "What's your date?"

"I don't know, a year?"

"A year. Long time. Hopefully, we can sell for something then. I have an obligation to look after Augusta's share in that business too, you know."

When Xavier said nothing, Derek leaned back. "How's your mom's money doing?"

Xavier picked up the wine bottle and poured the remnants of it into Derek's glass. "I'm still working on her. She's loyal to old Burlow, but I know I can get the money moved over to you eventually. I just need a little more time." He felt sheepish having to justify this to Derek.

Derek gave a slight frown. "Your family is losing out. We probably could have increased what she had by twenty percent if she had given it to me last year. The markets are good if you know where to invest."

They were interrupted by a man in a beige suit who came to their table and rested his hand lightly on Derek's shoulder.

"Derek my friend, good to see you."

Derek looked up. "Ravi!"

"Enjoying a night out, are we? Good. Good. You need your breaks to keep you sharp. Need that leisure, eh?"

"I'm always sharp," Derek said.

"I know it. I know it." Ravi lowered his voice. "I need to get in your calendar. Want to give you a little more. Loving the performance."

"Always happy to be of service for a man like you," Derek said. "Email my admin. I'll tell her to keep an eye out for your note. Give you priority."

As Ravi and Derek talked, Xavier sat quietly watching his friend. This was the second time they had been interrupted tonight by one of Derek's clients. He wasn't so much annoyed by the attentions Derek received as he was humbled by them; this is what it was like to be at the top of the ladder where everyone sought you out. Not for the first time, Xavier felt a sense of pride that he was attached to Derek and called him a friend. They were friends, weren't they?

When Derek Lam had come to Waterloo a few years ago, he had trumpeted his arrival by attending all the right business events, wining and dining at all the right restaurants, and securing invitations to all the right parties. Despite being only in his early thirties, he had done stints in boutique private equity firms in Silicon Valley, New York, and Toronto. It didn't take long for him or the fund he managed to catch the attention of a few people with money who felt cheated by average returns. His impeccable eye for reading the market got him noticed. But, like any money manager, he needed more capital to give his fund increased clout and charge higher management fees.

As Ravi departed, Derek turned back to Xavier. "Sorry about that. Another happy client ... wish I could say your mother was one of them."

Xavier smirked. "I know, I know. We're on the same page. Mom's just not seeing things clearly right now. Unfortunately, your girlfriend hasn't exactly been supportive of my cause." He gave Derek a level look. "Since Augusta doesn't listen to me, you might push her a bit to encourage my mom."

"Talking to Augusta about that stuff will just cause an argument. You're the older brother—you should make this happen," Derek said, wagging his finger. "You know Augusta is good at devouring money—she just doesn't know where it comes from."

"Don't get me started," Xavier lamented.

"On the topic of Augusta, wanted to ask you about something," Derek said, looking uncomfortable. "I don't like doing this. I mean, it's awkward with you being her brother and all ..." Derek's voice becoming lower, as if someone in the restaurant would hear what he was saying and care immensely about the subject of his inquiry. "But I wanted to ask if anything was wrong with her?"

The sincerity with which Derek asked his question obliged Xavier to stifle a laugh. His immediate response would have been that Derek ought to know better than him. But he didn't want to seem dismissive. Derek had never asked him a question like this before; the universal prohibition among men to never talk about just what one did with another's sister was respected.

"She seems okay to me. Why, is something up?" Xavier asked, wondering if Derek was finally recognizing Augusta's peculiarities.

Derek sipped the wine, as if buying time to think about what he wanted to say. "Distant, not coming over much. Says she's busy a lot. Didn't even want to come to Toronto this weekend with me. She's always up for a shop, you know? It's odd."

Why was his sister irritating Derek, of all people? In his haste to assure Derek that nothing was out of the ordinary, he found himself making excuses for her. "She's just stressed. You gotta remember she's never held down a real job, so school seems overwhelming. She's not like us, toughing it out in the real world," Xavier quipped, trying to lighten the mood and defuse Derek's scrutiny. "Welcome to women."

Derek gave a slow nod, then smiled. "Good. Just wanted to be sure."

But Xavier wasn't sure. He made a mental note to check in on Augusta and see if there was something else causing her to strain such a vital connection. Derek was, without a doubt, her first sensible pick of a boyfriend.

After the bill was requested, Xavier flipped the conversation back to Enigma to avoid further conversation about Augusta. He liked Derek's advice and observations on the company; in fact, he saw Derek as more of a partner in the business than Bill or Augusta. But while he was speaking, Xavier noticed Derek's eyes shift away and look at something behind him.

"What is it?" Xavier asked.

Derek used his head as a pointer. "Burlow's here. He just walked in with a girl."

Xavier turned around and saw David Burlow led to a table by a server. With him was a young woman with a mass of thick, dark curls on either side of her face and light-brown skin.

"What's she doing with that fat miser? You think she's an escort or something?" Xavier jibed.

"Don't know," Derek said, chuckling. Then he seemed to recall something. "Oh, I wonder if she's the one we've been hearing about—"

"Yes, yes," Xavier interrupted, feeling a piece of a puzzle slide into place along with his friend.

They had both heard through the grapevine of a young woman Burlow was introducing around town. Burlow had never been known to have any close friends or family; he kept to himself like a troll under a bridge. When he surfaced in society with a pretty young woman, there were bound to be some raised eyebrows and rumors. Some people suggested he was grooming a protégée who would inherit his money, while others hinted that she was the child of some prostitute Burlow secretly visited. Still others said he was getting philanthropic after the death of James Hardich and that the girl was the daughter of someone Burlow knew and wanted to help.

The woman seemed comfortable with him, smiling as they were seated. Burlow, for his part, looked happy and engaged in their conversation, which struck Xavier as unusual. The only time the dog looked that animated and pleased was when he was stalking and clinging to Xavier's mother.

"We'll have to say goodbye to them when we leave and find out what we can about this girl," Xavier said. Derek nodded in agreement.

When their drinks were done and the bill paid, Xavier led the way through the restaurant and between tables to approach the couple.

"Burlow, nice to see you," Xavier said, extending his hand.

His father's old friend looked up. The mirth that had played on his face slipped away while he reluctantly took Xavier's hand. And Xavier saw, emanating from Burlow's eyes, back in the depths of his thick face, a piercing look easy to read. *What are you up to? Why would you even bother to say hello?* his expression said.

Despite the exchange of pleasantries, Burlow made no attempt to introduce his companion. Finally, the woman, staring at the three men the whole time, raised her eyebrows slightly at Burlow, signaling to him he was omitting something rather significant.

"This is ... this is Natalie Mitchell," Burlow fumbled at last, with slight irritation.

"A pleasure," Xavier said, shaking her hand. Her eyebrows were thin and her cheekbones high, which accentuated her prominent brown eyes. "And how do you know Burlow?"

"David is kindly helping me find some clients for my consulting services," she said.

"Oh! And what services are those?" Xavier prodded.

"Design, online marketing, UX. You know about it?"

"Of course, this is a tech town, and I own a tech company," Xavier replied. "Do your services include websites then?"

"Absolutely."

Xavier turned to address Burlow. "Have you told Natalie about us?"

Burlow glared at him. "No. Didn't see the need to. Wasn't worth it."

Xavier put his hand behind his back and squeezed it hard into a fist to maintain calm. Like hot water simmering on the stove, small bubbles rising, Xavier was controlling himself from hitting full boil. That was quite a swipe by Burlow. Was that how he felt about Enigma? That it wasn't worth mentioning now that Xavier ran it? And to do it in front of Derek ...

"Are you all right?" Natalie cocked her head to one side, her forehead crinkling in concern. Derek was looking at him too. They were all looking at him.

"Yes. Yes," Xavier repeated himself. "I was thinking I should give you my card, though." He reached into the inside pocket of his sports coat. "Maybe I can help you out. I've been wanting to redo our website. It's a bit of a disaster, in my mind. I need someone to come in and translate my vision into something real. And when we meet, I'll fill in all the blanks left out by Burlow here about what we do."

Natalie took the business card and thanked him, assuring him she would be in touch. Then, she let out an "Ah!" and quickly rummaged through her purse. "I just realized I picked up my cards the other day. I haven't given any out yet—you'll be my first!" She handed Xavier a single thick, black business card with a feltlike strip running on the bottom. The letters on it were a bright silver: *NextGen Marketing and Design*.

Xavier thumbed the corner of it, pressing down, but the card didn't bend. "Nice card. You could hurt someone with this."

"I like to think it's memorable. More durable than that flimsy little thing you gave me," she said with a mischievous smile. "At the very least, I'm sure I can help you with your business cards."

Though Xavier laughed, he didn't see much humor in the jab. He immediately cursed Bill Spindrall for the poor quality of the Enigma cards, since he was the one responsible for ordering them. Just another example of his partner's poor business decisions.

Upon Derek's suggestion, they left Natalie and Burlow to their dinner and walked outside into the warm night.

Derek chuckled. "Burlow's pissed. Happy to see the back of us."

"He gave me a good glare or two. I think the only thing that saved him from telling me to fuck off was that Natalie was there."

Derek agreed. "So that's the mysterious girl. And now you want to hire her?"

"I've heard she's good. Jocelyn's dad is using her," Xavier said. "We do need a better website. She'll be cheaper than the agencies Bill wanted to hire. If she can help, I'll take her. I like her confidence."

"Burlow isn't going to like that."

"No, he won't. That's also a beautiful thing."

CHAPTER 11

A New Client *(Natalie Mitchell, August 2004)*

Prior to the death of Natalie's mother, David Burlow had never factored much into family conversations. He was a non-topic, largely because he had no real role in Natalie's life, and he had quietly lurked ("like a shamed dog," her grandfather would say) in the periphery of it, easily forgotten except for the money he provided.

But when Ayisha died and Natalie opted to see this strange benefactor, David became an object of discussion, even when he wasn't being discussed. That Natalie had sought a relationship with him was a point of confusion and frustration for her grandparents. They held an unwavering suspicion of him; an assessment that was natural given he had abandoned their pregnant daughter. To them, David's redeeming quality of having sent money for many years was valid as long as he was polite enough to not interfere or meddle in Natalie's life.

"Why would you want to have anything to do with that man?" her grandpa once asked. "You are perfectly capable of getting on without him."

She wondered, at times, if her grandfather was somehow threatened by David. To all intents and purposes, Grandpa had been the person she identified as a father. From her infancy, he had always been about, taking her to the park, bike riding with her, pulling her on a sled, or whatever the season permitted. Grandpa was also the looming figure of masculine discipline in her teens, when both her mother's and Granny's methods were insufficient. He seemed unwilling to allow any other man to share that burden, responsibility, or privilege.

Natalie couldn't argue with Grandpa Mitchell's assessment. She was capable of making it without any more assistance from David Burlow. By the time her mother died, she was getting through school, and the family was self-sufficient. They didn't need help. Nevertheless,

Natalie could not explain to herself, let alone her grandparents, her curiosity to meet this man. Even when he had been absent for all those years, she still wanted to know the other half of her origins. Her mother understood this when she encouraged Natalie to have a connection with him if the opportunity arose.

Despite their many meetings over the years, she had learned little of David. This became abundantly clear when she answered the interrogations of her grandparents. "Yes, he's nice in a reserved way, but not affectionate. No, he doesn't have a regular job, but he sits on boards and invests in companies. Yes, like a trader, I guess. No, no family really, at least that he talks about. No, he doesn't really talk about Mom. No, I never asked why he 'abandoned' her; it doesn't come up in conversation. Apologize? No, he hasn't apologized. No, he never asked to meet you."

Earlier this year, when her grandparents discovered she had asked him for assistance, they had the same concerns they always did. "Something's not quite right about him," Grandpa Mitchell declared. And his comment was not unwarranted; David Burlow was a mystery, a man who kept to himself enough to make one wonder what he was hiding.

Her decision to ask for help from David was by no means out of necessity. Natalie was easily capable of finding other work. And even when she opted to pursue contract work as a break from employee serfdom, she might well have been able to make ends meet entirely with a Toronto client base, though it would have taken longer and been harder.

The truth was she approached David to see how much he might do for her—to see if he would, and could, deliver on old promises. She hoped that he would rise to the occasion, because it would give her the opportunity to know more of the man her mother had, at one time, been fond of. But her plan had gone wayward. For though David honored his commitments, Natalie had been unable to learn much more about him.

David was still a mystery. The only time he ever revealed anything of himself was when she had stopped by his house unannounced months ago. Since then, little else was disclosed about his personal life. Despite her trips out to Kitchener-Waterloo to see the contacts and clients he had connected her with, she still only saw him in scheduled time segments and locations that he stipulated. When he invited her to his house, she never made it past the living room, past the pictures in the elaborate wall unit. Like their scheduled meeting times, and where they met, David Burlow determined the course of conversation.

The topics of conversation he willfully engaged in were either about Natalie or her business. Though she resented that he passively avoided speaking with her on any other matter, she had to admit she did enjoy talking about business with him. She had never had a professional mentor before, and David seemed more than willing to take up this role. If she would ever say that he was tender and kind, it was when he guided her in the matters of entrepreneurial bureaucracy. He taught her how to set up her accounting, bill her clients, organize her expenses for tax purposes, and assisted writing up her contracts. But most of all, he gave her access to his network.

If David was skeptical about whether Natalie could prove value to his network, he was surely corrected in his notion now. Every company David had introduced her to had become a client. They were smaller website projects, but paid reasonable money. When she had converted the fourth prospect to a client a week ago, Natalie had wanted to thank David by taking him out for a dinner. It was on this outing that Xavier Hardich had come to their table to introduce himself.

She had been surprised by David's ill-concealed dislike for "the boy," as he disparagingly referred to Xavier. Should not some bond or affinity exist between David and the son of his best friend and business partner? At the very least, they should have been amicable with one another. There were pictures of Xavier in David's living room, for God's sake.

"I wouldn't bother getting mixed up with that company. That boy will run it into the ground," David had growled shortly after the men had left them at the restaurant.

What injustice had David suffered at the hands of Xavier Hardich? As far as Natalie could tell, Xavier had been more than civil to him. "The boy" had even offered the possibility of doing business with her. Again, Natalie was left to wonder about David and his private life. The only friend he seemed to have was dead.

Natalie understood him enough by now to know that if she pressed him on his behavior toward Xavier, he would either terminate the conversation or switch topics. So, she adopted a different approach. "What does his company do?" she asked

"It's not his company, though he walks around telling everyone that," David countered curtly. "He's just learning to be an entrepreneur with other people's money."

"But what does it do?"

Their food arrived, and David was quiet until the waiter was done dropping off their dinner and had left.

"Software for educational organizations—Learning Portals, as I've heard it described," David said as he began devouring his beef tenderloin. "Brings teaching and classrooms to the internet. All a bit foolish to me. Can't imagine it will ever get really big, but seems they have a niche. All the brainchild of a man named Bill Spindrall. But Bill needed two things to get it going: money and connections. Enter James—he had both." David gave a grimace and a slight shake of his head. "I suppose the money was burning a hole in his pocket. James always thought everyone was making out like a bandit in tech. He would have bought into whatever came his way, as long as it had something to do with a computer."

"So, they partnered and started Enigma," Natalie said.

"Correct. Bill put in a few hundred thousand and James put in almost triple that. Bill essentially ran the company, and James just used his influence at the local universities to get the software in." Between mouthfuls, he muttered, "A strange business model. Never seen the like. The initial clients become partners and get everything at a discount in return for providing feedback on the software. When the product's done, Enigma will go and sell it to other schools with references in hand and some case studies. That's what Bill says will happen, at least."

"Xavier got the job because of James then?" Natalie asked.

David snorted. "Yes, but only when James died," he said. "Xavier, along with his sister, inherited their ownership—thirty percent equity each. Bill's a lame duck owner with another thirty percent. The remaining ten percent is divvied up between a couple of employees, but those are nonvoting shares. Xavier quit his sales job at RIM and appointed himself an officer of Enigma. Fancies himself a big boy now," David remarked with such irritation that he seemed to struggle swallowing a bite of his food. He reached for his glass of water and downed it in one gulp. He took a few breaths before resuming. "Guess he felt the company would benefit from the little he had to offer. Bill tells me the boy's throwing his weight around now, and he can because Augusta goes along with him. Don't think she cares about any of it. The partnership agreement dictates that the will of the majority rules, except if the company or its equity is sold, in which case all three of them need to agree. That's the only time Bill will have any meaningful say again. For now, the poor bastard's impotent."

David's assessment of Enigma's toxic partner politics, coupled with his obvious intolerance of Xavier, stifled Natalie's usual excitement when she met a prospect. Though she had been intrigued in Enigma, she decided not to follow up.

By all accounts, it should have been left at that.

* * *

Natalie was working in her small apartment in Toronto when her cell phone rang. The number wasn't in her contacts, and she didn't recognize it.

"Hello?"

"Is this Natalie?" a man's voice asked.

"Yes."

"Natalie. It's Xavier Hardich. We met at the restaurant week ago. Couldn't remember who was to call whom. Thought I'd take the initiative and get this ball rolling."

"Oh right, yes," she said, trying to sound as if she was in the midst of recollecting him and their conversation. But she knew exactly who he was and what he was referring to. "Were we supposed to connect?" She winced, thinking she sounded flaky even to herself.

"I think we were," Xavier sounded upbeat. "I've some work for you. You're taking on clients, right? I mean, you gave me a business card after I told you about wanting to redo my website. Or did you give me your card so I wouldn't call you?"

"No, this is great," Natalie said, a small knot forming in her stomach. "I've got a lot on the go, but always happy to see if I can help. What were you thinking? Even if I'm not the right fit, I know plenty of people that can support you," she added, though it pained her to say it. She would hate to pass up work because of a spat between Xavier and David.

"I'm sure you'll be fine. Chatted with Bart Miller, and he says you're the one."

Natalie's heart skipped a beat. This was getting messy. Other clients were referring her. In any other situation, this would have been perfectly ideal.

"When are you in town next?" Xavier went on. "You can come by the office for an informal chat, and I can tell you what my vision is."

When the date was set and she got off the phone, Natalie felt anxious: *what would David think?*

Natalie gave herself a pep talk. There was no harm in having a meeting to discuss an opportunity. No commitments were made. She took some mild comfort in the fact that she had not pursued Enigma, not instigated the meeting. Surely, David would understand that she couldn't reject a conversation because of his personal prejudices. Besides, her other clients were referring her now.

Yet, she couldn't shake the gnawing sense of guilt she felt. How could David have this effect on her? How was he exacting this shame from her?

She decided that she would tell David only if anything came of the meeting. There was no sense in making an issue out of something that might not even proceed beyond a "chat."

* * *

On the day of Natalie's meeting, and after some confusion finding the office, she left the sunshine of a beautiful summer's day at the end of August to descend into the inhospitable subterranean cavern of Enigma.

She was guided into a boardroom that no sunlight ever touched, by a man named Richard in a gray suit. He informed her that Xavier was running late for the meeting, so she spent the first ten minutes making conversation with Richard alone. His hair was brown and cut short, but the top was long enough to style in a messy orderliness. He sat across from her at the boardroom table with an affable presence, his intense blue eyes studying her. She found herself becoming self-conscious of her own little habits—the way she brushed stray strands of hair that had come loose from her ponytail, the way she leaned backward or forward in the chair, the way she rubbed her forehead when she laughed.

He was about her age and was soft spoken with a calming voice. He didn't adopt the formality the suit suggested; he slouched in his chair with his legs crossed. The questions he asked were not the traditional time-killers; they were friendlier, more personal. "Where have you traveled?" and "What's the next place you want to visit? Why?" and "What are you reading right now? Is that what makes up most of your word diet?"

"I feel like we're speed dating!" she said to him.

He shrugged his shoulders and then grinned. "Fortunately, you have a while longer to redeem yourself. Quite a strike against you when you said all you read are business books."

"Any recommendations of what else I should read?"

"Since you're in town, go to Words Worth—best bookstore around here. They'll hook you up with something."

With Xavier's entrance to the boardroom, the mood changed. He was emphatic in his pleasantries and made all the idle and mundane chitchat that Richard had avoided.

"Great to see you again, Natalie. Thanks for coming!" he said loudly with a wide smile. "A nice day out there, isn't it?" he guffawed. "Great weather! Will be cold in another few months, so we should enjoy this, right? It rained quite a bit last week—horrible. Much traffic on the drive in?"

Was it David's doing that she was scrutinizing Xavier more than she might have? Was it really that Xavier seemed dominating and insincere in his conversation, or was that just who he was? Was he almost theatrical the way he projected his voice while waving his arms about with wide, sweeping gestures, or was she just being overly critical? She wished she could judge him from a cleaner lens, but David's comments at dinner had made her hyperalert.

Richard became quiet the moment Xavier entered the room. The casual posture he had adopted when alone with her was replaced with a formal straight-back pose with both arms in front of him on the table and his hands clasped together. He said little while Xavier spoke about the need for a "slick website," that could "sell and get prospects and investors calling."

"When I was an executive sales rep at RIM," Xavier went on, "people called us all the time. The website generated leads. Everybody wanted to partner with us. That's what I want. Every university and college in North America should be calling Enigma! That's what I'm looking for you to do." And he painted his vision for an online presence that sounded like he wanted RIM's website reproduced and the word "Blackberry" changed to "Enigma." Natalie nodded and listened, made notes, and even walked the men through her portfolio. The meeting lasted an hour. At the end, Xavier asked her to send along a quote for her services before running off to take a call in his office.

The moment Xavier left, Richard reverted to his casual demeanor, like he had been set free from some leash that had constrained him. He walked her out, but not before giving her a brief tour of the Pit and explaining more of the company's software. The employees were all young, either her age or a few years her junior. She immediately felt the quirky energy peculiar to startups: the chaotic avant-garde industriousness, the uncouth banter over cubicle walls, the raging epithets against keyboards or monitors displaying lines of code, and the casual insults exchanged between the team all amounted to grotesque HR violations. Yet nobody seemed to mind. Natalie felt the vibe of the place and thought how it was Xavier who was the misfit in his polished talk and shoes, in his tailored suit, and with his clean-cut, perfectly parted hair.

As Richard went to walk her up the stairs back to the sunlight, a man came out of one of the offices in the hallway. He was older than everyone else, perhaps in his forties. He pushed his hair back from his forehead with his hand and looked at Natalie with suspicion before questioning Richard.

"Who's this? Another contractor?" He put his hands on his hips, bracing for an answer he decided would displease him.

"This is Natalie," Richard said. "Xavier asked her to come in to talk about our website."

"Ah," he smirked. "So, the meeting happened, and Xavier didn't invite me?"

"He said he would pull you in when the time was right," Richard said.

Bill rolled his eyes. "Of course, he did!" He pushed his bangs back from his forehead again. "Why should I be involved at all? I don't know anything about what we're doing anyway." And with a brief flashing frown at Natalie, he went back into his office and closed the door.

Richard guided Natalie up the stairs and into the parking lot. "That's Bill Spindrall, another owner in the company," he said. "He's just having a tough day. He's not normally like that. I apologize."

When Natalie left the basement office, she had conflicting emotions. Enigma would be an interesting client, and she relished working with an innovating company of predominantly young people. She already had some ideas running through her mind. The work would be a refreshing change from the traditional websites she was building for law firms and manufacturing companies. She could be more experimental and add some slick Flash animations.

Her run-in with Bill Spindrall, however, and her inability to read Xavier, made her cautious. There was also, lingering more strongly now in her mind, the matter of David and what he would think.

Uncertain of whether she should take work from Xavier and his company or not, she played the game that many entrepreneurs do when confronted with such indecision: she let some other power decide. Over the next few nights, she assembled a quote and padded her costs to the point where they might very well be prohibitive to Enigma Solutions. She was charging almost 50 percent more than she normally would; it was a pure cash grab for the personal complications that may arise if Xavier accepted the contract.

The quote went out, and she heard nothing for a few days. Natalie took the silence as a sign from the universe. The grape died on the vine.

Until Xavier emailed her back a signed contract, asking when she could start.

Natalie was simultaneously ecstatic and filled with dread. There was good money in this for her. But what would David say?

Unlike the other contracts she had countersigned with her clients, which were happy and triumphant occasions, this contract was filled with thorns. For a full hour, she sat at the table in her little apartment in Toronto, her pen hovering over the signature line above her printed name. Then she would stand up, pace around the room, and return again to the table. At last, she decided she could not operate, in fear of David's grudges. This was a good thing—she would just need to tell David why.

The careful neat letters of her name were scrawled on the paper in blue pen. Natalie scanned the document and sent it back to Xavier. Enigma Solutions was now a client.

CHAPTER 12

Under Watch *(Xavier Hardich, September 2004)*

SOMETIME after 9:30 a.m., Xavier walked into the kitchen in his housecoat. He poured himself a coffee from the pot to try to revive himself. There was no way he would get to work this morning. He had already sent a note to Bill and Richard, telling them he was sick and would not be in until the afternoon, if at all.

Last night was a late one with friends and far too much to drink. He was fighting a headache and nausea. But he wouldn't undo any of his decisions. Derek had been out with him and had a great time. The two were seeing each other more on friendly terms, which was important for Xavier.

The television was on in the other room. He assumed it was his mother, but then he noticed Augusta's Samsung phone on the island counter and her backpack on one of the island barstools. He walked over to Augusta's things, glanced quickly around, and then snatched the phone to flip it open. She had never enabled a passcode, so he could access the main features, including her messages and call logs.

Nothing. It was the same as the other couple of times he had stolen a glance—everything was empty. No history of texts or calls.

Since his dinner with Derek a few weeks ago, Xavier had been keeping an eye on her comings and goings. Derek's inquiries about Augusta worried him, and he feared his sister's capricious nature might undo the alliance the Hardiches had with an important figure in the city. So far, there was no evidence that Augusta was up to her old tricks. If she was, she was thorough in ensuring the phone held no information.

He placed the phone back exactly as he had found it, then walked over to the living room where the television noise was coming from. Both his mother and sister were watching the news. The same story that had been playing nonstop for two days—the Beslan school siege in Russia. On the screen, he saw a blown-out building, and he knew there must have been a new development from yesterday.

His mother's hand covered her mouth, and her thumb kept rubbing, prodding, and grinding into her cheek to make one side of her face completely red.

"God, it's horrible," Elinor said to him when she turned away from the television. "Can you believe it? They stormed the school. They fear that many of the children are dead."

Xavier watched the television for a few minutes, watched the footage and the translated interviews from eyewitnesses. He felt his anger rising in him, his disgust. "Innocent kids … hope they catch every one of those bastards. We need to be more forceful and aggressive to take on these terrorists."

There was silence from his mother, but Augusta seemed itching to pipe in. "I completely agree. We need another war with atrocities to stop all these evils. And when the bombing is done, we can establish humane institutions like Abu Ghraib and Guantanamo Bay. They go a long way to mending fences."

"What's your solution?" Xavier turned on her. "Russia does nothing? Nobody does anything? Tell people it's okay, nothing wrong, just an isolated incident?"

"Being really committed to a solution requires looking at an entire system that uses people all around the world as pawns to benefit the few—it means looking at root causes," Augusta told him with academic pretension. "You'd need to look at how military and economic imperialism, and most certainly how capitalism, oppresses nations and people to bring out the absolute worst in humanity. I'm not sure you're up to speed enough on all that to have this conversation with me."

"Oh, hell," Xavier sneered. He saw his mother out of the corner of her eye cross her arms in frustration, but he could not let Augusta go unchecked. "I'm not sure you're up to speed enough on the privileged position you hold in that system to be commenting on it at all. That capitalism that you despise helps fund your little marshmallow world at the university. I'm not going to mention that my hands are getting dirty increasing the value of our stake in Enigma while you pursue your fairy-tale life in academia. Hell, I won't even talk about the life provided to you by Dad, who was in that dirty world of business. And I won't talk about Mom's fundraising from all those big-bad corporations to fund projects at the universities—often enough, the one you attend. And we certainly won't discuss how Derek's job in that messy world helps pay for those little vacations and your designer clothes."

Augusta bore his onslaught with calm indifference. Midway through his chastisement, much to his frustration and anger, he could see the faint smile starting to show on her face. But it looked more bitter today. "For someone who wasn't going to mention or talk about any of *that*, you've said quite a bit," she said. "But I know ..." she went on, turning to the television. "I know we're part of the problem."

"Whatever the hell that means," Xavier said. He would have pursued her more, but their mother had reached her limit.

"Stop it, the two of you," Elinor scolded. "I don't want to hear any more. Look—look what's happening!" Her arms flailed about in the air at the television.

For a few minutes more, everyone was silent, then Augusta got up. "I need to get to my class, Mom. I'll be staying up in Waterloo tonight," she said. She gave Elinor a light peck on the top of her head and walked out of the room, passing Xavier with no acknowledgment.

She grabbed her bag and her phone and made to leave, but Xavier asked, "You staying at Derek's tonight?"

"No. Friends."

He had never known Augusta to have real friends, and certainly not the kind where she repeatedly went out with them. He had never once met any of her girlfriends from university, though she had a few from high school that still came by from time to time. Still, she could hardly be considered close with anyone.

"You're spending lots of time with these friends. Why don't you have them over sometime?" Xavier asked.

She left, never answering.

CHAPTER 13

Breaks for Coffee *(Richard Earning, September 2004)*

R ICHARD's thoughts were all focused into the end of his pen meandering across the paper.

Her legs were crossed, and her topmost thigh was nearly exposed right to her hip from under her black skirt. A slender calf swung up and down in a steady kick-rock motion, like a pendulum keeping time. Her white shirt, three buttons undone, revealed the beginning of the small valley between her breasts.

He had not been writing his little scribbles as much lately. He found he was more inclined to daydream when he was alone. But tonight, he was stirred to describe her, and make her the central character of a scene. It was his way of being with Augusta, even when she was with someone else.

But when the phone rang, and her name appeared on the screen, he answered it quickly.

"Change of plans," she said. "*He* had to go to Toronto. Won't be back until tomorrow."

"You want to meet for a drink?"

There was a pause. "No, I'm coming over."

Augusta had never been to his place. They had never met anywhere other than bars and cafes around town. "Do you even know where I live?"

"You once told me which building you were in, but never the apartment number. I'm almost there."

"What? Shit, I need time to clean, Augusta. What are we going to do? I'm not ready for you."

He could hear her breathy laugh. "You have five minutes," she said.

Richard's abode was not a complete mess, but it was far from the orderly state he would have preferred she see it in. He ran about, tidying up areas to make it as presentable as possible. Unfortunately, what became apparent was that no amount of housework could redeem the modest apartment.

Never before had the place bothered him, but it seemed base and inadequate to host her. Cleaning could not hide mismatched hand-me-down furniture from his family and friends, his artsy pictures from IKEA, the cheap yellow linoleum flooring in the kitchen and bathroom, and the hideous brown carpeting that concealed the stains of many tenants. It was all beneath Augusta.

When she arrived, he was waiting in the apartment lobby to greet her. By personally escorting her to his unit, he hoped to make reasonable excuses for why he lived there and prepare her for the disappointment she would experience upon entering his unit.

"The rent's reasonable, and I'm able to save money," he said as they rode the elevator up to his floor. Another man was on it, staring at Augusta, leering at her in her tight black jeans and a transparent sheer white shirt that covered what was either a black bikini top or a bra.

Getting off at his floor, they walked down the hallway to his apartment. "The building's a little rough around the edges," he said, "but I've never had a problem with anyone. My neighbors are quite nice." The smell of cigarette smoke and the odors of hundreds of meals cooked every night for thirty years meshed and melded, filling the air with a ubiquitous but unidentifiable scent. "In the winter, they all have their heat blasting, and I think my place is warmed as a consequence. I don't have much of a heating bill at all."

Augusta walked beside him, her arm linked in his, smiling at him the whole time. But it was her eyes that were most peculiar. She was observing him with an expression he couldn't read and had never seen from her before.

When they entered his unit, she did not turn and run or breathe a sigh of disgust. She strode around the place, as if to take it all in, before sitting on the living room couch. She accepted his offer of a beer in the absence of wine, saying, "You should have some on hand for me, or any other girl you may have over."

But she was surprisingly quiet tonight and seemed to be focused more on watching him than talking to him.

"Are you all right?" he asked her.

"Yaaah." She drew out the word to suggest it was a ridiculous question.

He put some music on and sat down on the couch, but he did not cozy up beside her. A few feet separated them. Despite the intimacy, the kissing, and the handholding they had done recently in shadows and around corners in bars and cafes, he felt strangely unsure of how to behave with her now that they were completely alone with no fear of being spotted by anyone.

Worse still, he was fighting his emotional and physical response to her. His heart, his entire body was surging, craving her, aroused by her. She was divinely beautiful to him. Like the man on the elevator, he kept trying to peer through her translucent shirt and discern what was beneath. He was trying so hard to repress his thoughts, to not think of her on her knees looking up at him, on her back looking down at him, that he became the worst conversationalist imaginable.

He bumbled about for something to say. "I started reading a book by Carlos Ruiz Zafon but went down the rabbit hole researching the Spanish Civil War. Have you read *The Shadow of the Wind*?"

"No. Tell me about it," she said, looking down at the space between them. Her pursed lips curled the sides of her mouth.

He started to talk about Francisco Franco, in an attempt to restore some coherence and intelligence to his ramblings. Though Augusta remained entirely attentive to him, she continued to remain contently silent.

Then, without warning, she leaned forward and interrupted him. "Richard."

That's all Augusta said when she closed the space between them, her face hovered nearer, her eyes locked on his. Whether she had timed it to be thus, or by some fluke, the album they were listening to was in concert with her will, "In Your Eyes" by Peter Gabriel was playing.

Her tongue darted out to lick just the edges of his lips, and she pulled back. Then she drew near again, licking his lips before putting her tongue inside his mouth.

The lid he had put on the container of his desires blew off. He returned her kiss fiercely, and the moan that he heard from within her throat told him to continue, to not stop, to do more. Then he was lightly running his hands over her body, tasting her neck and the bitter sourness of her perfume. He undid the buttons on her see-through shirt, continuing to work his mouth down onto her breasts while he fumbled to undo her pants and slide them off. At last, he would see all of her, feel all of her.

A desirous thought came to him: maybe he should be the one on his knees, looking up at her.

* * *

Richard Earning stirred his coffee. Flipping through the main section of the newspaper, he tried to focus his attention on the news of the world: the catastrophes, the wars, the political scandals. Yet, they all seemed distant from him today. He was detached from the words that alluded to corruption, injustice, death, and misery. His own private world consumed him. Today was so much more glorious than yesterday. The light tapping water on the skylights above did not suggest dreariness or sadness, but rather the opportunity to relish the safety of the dry and cozy indoors while looking out at the rain-drenched street.

It was half past twelve in the afternoon. Richard was sitting upstairs, outside a coffee shop in the common area of a small, two-story retail complex known as The Atrium in downtown Waterloo. When he had entered from the back, he passed a well-known British pub before climbing the stairs to where the cafe was. The pub enticed him, as it did any passersby, with the promise of beer and laughter. A beer might have served him well—it would have been an antidote to calm the excitement and thrill he was feeling.

Today, especially, the very thought of her stimulated him—distracted him. He hadn't been able to focus at work all morning. Nothing would be accomplished until he looked at her, heard her speak, touched her. She had sent a text an hour ago telling him to meet her here so they could talk.

So many things lingered in the realm of the unsaid when she left his apartment early this morning—just a brief kiss on the lips (so fleeting), and a promise to contact him. She had stayed over last night, slept in his bed, slept with him.

Last night.

Now, the rain above thudded loudly on the skylights for a few minutes before subsiding again. Richard sipped his coffee and looked at his watch. He was getting anxious. Even if he only met her for thirty minutes, it would be worthwhile. He had ordered her a latte, and the cup stood opposite him on the table, its foam subsiding. He took a long breath and exhaled to calm himself.

"Was that sigh for me?" he heard a voice say from behind him, and he felt hands gently squeeze the back of his neck, then slide down to lightly massage his shoulders. Her face then appeared close to his cheek as he received a kiss.

"Thanks for coming. I know it was short notice," Augusta whispered in his ear. She walked out from behind him and sat in the chair across from him. Her hair and jacket were wet. She cupped her hands around the latte and looked down at it. She was uncharacteristically quiet.

"Are you okay?" Richard asked leaning forward.

"Yeah, I'm great!" Augusta responded with uncommon alacrity. But her moment of excitement subsided. "Are you?"

"Of course. Busy day; can't stay past one. Meeting back at the office at one thirty," Richard said apologetically.

Perhaps the topic that hovered above them was too big to confront. After a brief silence, they slipped into some light conversation. At that moment, everything that wasn't about last night was fair game.

"Oh," Richard said, recalling a rare piece of news that would warrant his referencing Enigma. "Remember that marketing consultant from Toronto I told you about?"

"Burlow's girl? Natalie, right?"

"Yeah. She apparently signed a contract with us. She'll be coming in next week."

Augusta bit the inside of her lower lip, contemplating this intelligence and musing aloud, "Hmm. What's Xavier up to with that one? Is he trying to get on Burlow's good side or irritate him? Probably the latter."

"Why would Burlow be bothered by it—isn't it a good thing?"

"Burlow and Xavier aren't fond of each other. Supposedly it was Burlow that convinced my father to make Xavier get his own job after school, no favors. Remember, my father had enough clout that he could have had my brother placed in a management gig at several companies. I think Xavier was expecting that. And when Dad started talking about Enigma, Xavier also assumed he would be picked to oversee the investment. Not so. Who knows if Burlow actually influenced my father? But that is how it was presented to Xavier." Augusta laughed. "He was furious. My poor brother had to apply for jobs like everyone else. But I think my dad still pulled in a favor to get him in at RIM.

"That could foster some bad blood," Richard agreed. "Do you get along with Burlow?"

"I don't think anyone really 'gets along' with him personally, except my mother. Well, my dad did. I like him. He's interesting to me—bit of a mystery. He's always been very good to my mom," Augusta said with a reticent grin.

Richard peeked at his watch. Time was running out. He wanted more time with her, especially after last night.

She saw him fidget. "Stay a while longer. Just tell them you're at a lunch with a client," she told him.

"I organized the meeting. I can't miss it."

"Tell them you ate something that made you sick."

Richard shook his head, but he already felt the pull of her will making his determination to go back to the office falter.

"There's a pub below," she reminded him mischievously. "Would you rather be at Enigma this afternoon or with me in a quiet corner having a pint? You know I can't see you for a few days after this."

He was so close to succumbing to her entreaty, but Augusta had unknowingly triggered his resistance and altered his mood. A surge of jealousy flashed through Richard, and he looked away from Augusta. She never said she would be with Derek for the next few days, but it was implied. Her boyfriend had wormed his way into their conversation, into their time. Derek was a shadow on the two of them.

She reached out to his clenched fist and put her hand on it. "Are you upset about last night? You don't regret it, do you?"

"No," he said quietly.

"Does that mean you'll have me back sometime? I shouldn't have to beg to come over, you know."

He knew what she was doing; it had often played out this way, and it would again today. There would be a reminder of her circumstances that would drive him into a sullenness. And she would distract him, change the topic, pull him from the muddy pit that he traveled to in his mind whenever he was presented with her other relationship. "I told you: I just wish my place was nicer," Richard mumbled. "I know you're used to fancier things."

"I am," she said casually. "But I didn't come over to judge your place—I came to be with you. I know you're saving your money to buy a place."

"Even when I do, it won't be anywhere as nice as Derek's," he said.

There was a slight flinch in Augusta's cheek as she registered his verbal bite. She was quiet while she took his hand and ran one of her fingers over the hills and valleys of his knuckles. "Let's go away together," she said. "You want to travel and yet have never been anywhere. We'll take a vacation."

He was surprised at the abrupt change of topic. "What?"

"A vacation—let's take one."

"Like, where?" he asked, still annoyed.

"Paris."

Richard watched her for some line in her face, some curve of her mouth that would betray a joke, but could see no sign of humor afoot. "You're serious? You mean France?"

"I sure don't mean Paris, Ontario!"

"How?" he asked in disbelief. The resistance inside him was immediate and without thought or control.

"It's not that complicated," she replied dismissively. "We buy plane tickets, we book a hotel, and we go. When did the academic become the practical one?" She caressed the back of his hand, drawing little circles on it with her finger.

"Setting aside the financial concerns, what about Derek?"

"I'm twenty-four. I do my own thing. I'll just say there's a conference or I need to do some research. As if anyone is checking up on me. We could go when my class is done in mid-December. And if you need me to buy your ticket, I will." She smiled and nodded, as if encouraging him to give the answer that she wanted to hear—the one he wanted to give.

"I'll have to think about it," he said at last, overwhelmed at the conflict in his mind. "I can't just make a decision of this magnitude quickly. There's the money, and work. And ..." he trailed off. Paris? Of course, he wanted to go. He wanted to be with her. But was it possible?

Above them, the tap of the rain on the skylights eased and stopped. The cafe was filled with a new light as her hand turned on the table, palm up, inviting him to clasp it. The call of her flesh, her slender fingers that had touched him tenderly last night, was irresistible. Before he knew it, his hand, as if being controlled by a marionette string, lay on hers, clutched hers.

"Just say yes," she said with a smile. She did not plead; she compelled. She commanded.

"Yes, then," he said at last, uncertain if he even had a choice.

Augusta's smile was triumphant. "Now that that's settled, you need to go," she said, releasing his hand. "Unless you've decided to stay for a while longer?"

Seeing the time, he cursed; the clock read 1:15 p.m. He wanted to stay, but he couldn't. Besides, he needed to show he could resist her in something. Standing up, he draped his rain jacket over his arm. He pushed the chair in to tuck it under the table. Then began a series of horrible delaying tactics: he switched the arm holding the jacket as if something weren't right, and he pulled the chair out again to realign it so it that it slid in more precisely under the table.

Augusta watched all the while with a smile.

He blurted it out, the question that demanded a response. It had been caught like a knot in his body somewhere between his heart and throat. "What is this, Augusta?"

Her brow crinkled slightly. "What?"

"This!" he said emphatically, taking his hand and gesturing in a circular motion between the two of them, by which indication he was trying to communicate an indescribable feeling, an ethereal essence, a connection that existed between the two of them when the freshness of passion drove rash decisions. All of that was implied in the wave of his arm, but he didn't know how to say any of it. He wanted her to resolve his doubts, to acknowledge the sublime gravity of what they were doing, to speak in reverie of what was consummated last night.

She stood up. A flicker of pensiveness—or was it sadness?—crossed her face and she came close to him. They were nearly the same height. She licked her lips to moisten them while her fingers clasped his lapel.

"You're going to be way late instead of just late," she whispered as her lips pressed against his and her tongue darted into his mouth. He closed his eyes and felt the warmth of her organ, with its milky-coffee taste, as it played his soul. He felt her body, the heat exuding from it passing through his suit and dress shirt. When his eyes opened, he saw she had never closed hers.

She pulled back, and her amused smile was there. "We'll set something up for next week. I'll text you."

Putting on her jacket, Augusta grabbed her purse and walked out the front doors of the building, never turning back.

Richard watched her go; his chance to be with her longer had slipped away. He walked down the stairs to the parking lot at the back, past the pub that invited him to drink. They could have been there together, nestled in a corner booth, alone, passing the afternoon away.

Resisting her preferences was always a double-edged sword. Though there was momentary pride at his strength for not succumbing to her every wish, he always felt like he was punishing himself afterward. For in his heart, he wanted to go along with everything she proposed.

Outside was damp and humid. He stared across the lot, over the hoods of cars, to a five-story condominium building in the distance known as the Seagram Lofts just a short walk away. Derek lived there, and Augusta would be with him later tonight. She needed to perform her titular duties as girlfriend. He wondered what those duties entailed, and for a moment his imagination went to a dark, carnal place, stirring a raging jealousy.

He had to share Augusta for now. But only for now.

CHAPTER 14

Unforeseen Complications *(David Burlow, October 2004)*

IN late October, David Burlow sat in his home office. A small pile of neatly stacked folders was in front of him, with the topmost one open. A short letter, handwritten, stared up at him, and he looked down at it. Dated February 24, 1994, this was the last letter that the trust fund ever received; it was the final communication to an anonymous benefactor.

To whom it may concern,

It has been a while since you last got a letter from us. Not sure if you know, but my mother was very sick, and she passed away a few months ago.

I know you supported me and my mother. With your help, I think I have done well for myself. I am in my second year of graphic design at college. Maybe my mother told you that already. I don't know what she tells you. It's strange to have someone know about me, while I know almost nothing about them. I don't think I'm comfortable with this.

I don't mean to sound ungrateful for your help, but it isn't required anymore. I hold down a part-time job at a restaurant to support myself and I still live with my grandparents while in school. I don't see the point in keeping this letter thing going. Do you read the letters that are sent to you? Will you read this?

Please find enclosed the forms you sent. I have not signed them.

I would like to meet you. If you are interested in seeing me, then please write to me with contact information so that we can make plans. I'd much rather that than telling a stranger about my life and taking his money.

If this is of no interest to you, I understand. Thank you for your assistance over the years and goodbye.

Natalie Mitchell

David remembered thinking, even then, that the girl had a certain amount of courage to refuse his financial aid. Money was money, and if she had to hold down a part-time job while in school, she was hardly in a position to disregard her good fortune. She was foolhardy. Why couldn't she just keep the system in play that had worked so well over the years? And to issue him an ultimatum—that took some nerve!

The letter had triggered their first meeting in High Park. And from that moment, their peculiar, yet cordial, relationship began. He would journey a few times a year to Toronto for a casual stroll and dinner with Natalie, always on his terms. He contained their relationship, kept her separate from his life in Kitchener-Waterloo, isolated her to a city a hundred kilometers away—a banished secret.

Only this year had he violated his own boundaries. She had asked him for a favor. It must have seemed so harmless to her, such a simple request—but not without complications for him. Now, Natalie was breaking the containment walls he had confined her to for all these years. And she was overflowing, like a breached dam, into his life here.

David closed the lid of the folder back on the letter. He bundled the folders together with a thick, blue elastic band and placed them in the filing cabinet drawer with his other documents. He looked up from his desk to stare through the window that fronted the park. It was a cool, sunny day.

Natalie would be stopping in later in the afternoon for a coffee before driving back to Toronto. She always called him to meet whenever she was in town for one of her clients. He made himself available to her, though he always greeted these rendezvous with a mix of annoyance and pleasure.

A man who has been alone for so long tends to fill his time with a series of habits that give structure to days, weeks, months, and years. Eventually, these habits become rituals, then unbreakable laws. David had a set time for getting up and having his coffee, a set time for walking to the gazebo on the small island in the park across the street from his house (and back), a set time for eating, a set time for working in his office, a set time for reading, and a set time for bed. He knew it was irrational, almost silly, but his daily organization had kept him sane for decades.

It's what solitary people do. These habits helped give comfort to a man who was alone and had, by necessity, grown fond of being alone.

And each time Natalie called him, wanting to meet, she broke these routines of his.

Despite the disruption, David increasingly looked forward to seeing her. He liked talking to her about her work. He liked her drive, her intelligence. She had upended a few long-held beliefs of his: that the generations after him were entitled, coddled, and indolent; that they were too self-absorbed to be good workers or employers; and that they took everything for granted. His primary data point for such an assertion was, of course, the Hardich children and those who moved in their sphere. He understood his small sample group might have skewed the results.

And what was it that he felt when some of his professional acquaintances called him up to praise Natalie after she had done work for them? "She's quite talented," and "very bright, your Natalie is," or "she's a mover," they would tell him. He had never known what it was to feel pride in another's accomplishments, but that must be what he experienced. Pride.

However, Natalie's introduction to his network also presented problems. There were rumors. Elinor had told him as much at a September fundraiser when he shadowed her. "Who is she? How come we've never heard of her until now? Is she your protégée? There are some pernicious whisperings, but I won't utter them!"

To these questions and statements, David gave his rehearsed lines that Natalie was the daughter of a deceased friend. Unfortunately, this did not stop the gossip; everyone knew that David didn't have friends. And though he was accustomed to society's perception of him and indifferent to whatever malicious comments might be made—for they had said worse of him over the years—he was suitably irate that Elinor Hardich was being exposed to them. This was the biggest complication of all.

The two worlds David had kept separated for so long were starting to meld. He was struggling with how to ensure they did not disrupt and distort one another. For David Burlow had a singular purpose, and the one thing he had never accounted for was that in rendering assistance to Natalie, he might jeopardize his intentions with Elinor Hardich.

Tonight's visit with Natalie would be brief. There was a fundraiser at the Cambridge Library and Art Gallery organized by Elinor that he wanted to attend. Since James's death, these were the only times he was able to see her. He couldn't recall what he was supporting by his money or his attendance; all that mattered is that Elinor would be there.

When Natalie arrived at his front door, she was dressed in a gray suit with a laptop bag slung over her shoulder. In her hands were two coffee cups, one of which she handed to him.

"I could have saved you the money and made some here for a lot cheaper," he remarked.

"I didn't feel like instant today."

He snorted and led Natalie into the living room, where she seated herself on the couch as he sat opposite her in his leather chair.

"Where was your meeting today?" he asked.

"Enigma," she said, trying to sound as if it were nothing out of the ordinary, but it was. "Final presentation of the website concepts and the online marketing strategy."

He thought she might say more, but she was looking down at her coffee. She knew his opinion on that contract. "How did it go?"

"Great. Better than I expected," she said, smiling. He could see she was excited. Even though she knew he was displeased, she couldn't contain the glow of victory, of success. "I'll show you the concepts later if you're interested." She patted her laptop bag.

"It's all done with them, then? They're happy?"

Here, Natalie took a deep breath. "They've offered me another contract," she told him, almost as if she were confessing a sin.

"Oh?" It came out like a grunt. He was trying to sound indifferent, but he knew he could hardly mask it. "I suppose you'll take it despite my previous advice and any that I would serve you today." He would have preferred she loathe that place, its people—Xavier.

"You gave no justification for your advice. You merely told me to avoid the company," she said firmly as she elevated her chin. "You haven't given me any reason why taking a contract there is detrimental to me or you."

There it was, that boldness, that challenging attitude. Just like the letter he had read this afternoon. He admired this side of her while also finding it irritating, like optical-illusion artwork. A chalice or two faces? A duck or a rabbit? Both existed in the same image, just as both feelings existed in him.

"I would rather you not keep company with Xavier," he said.

"He's not my friend," she responded. "He's a client. He's paying me money."

This was unfolding the same way their conversation had a month ago when she had told him she was first doing the project at Enigma. He could feel the agitation rising in him. Why wouldn't she just listen to him? Just respect his preferences? When he had owned a company, people obeyed him; at board meetings, people listened to his guidance and executed on it. He shouldn't have to explain himself.

He took a sip of his coffee to try to temper himself. "How's Bill doing?"

Natalie smirked and blew air out of her compressed lips. "You already know. He and Xavier are at odds. But I was able to get some time with Bill when I conducted interviews. It's too bad Xavier doesn't leverage his skills more; he's quite knowledgeable. Xavier didn't even want him involved, but I told him if he wanted a good deliverable to let me do my thing."

"I'm surprised the boy didn't throw a tantrum and terminate the contract."

"I know how to manage people. Besides, I think there are bigger problems than their little rivalry at the moment."

She went on to explain that the Pit was working late hours. Apparently, Xavier had made a series of foolish promises and timeline commitments to the university clients without consulting anyone. Now the Pit was frantically trying to deliver enhancements and new features. To make matters worse, Xavier had brought in contractors to "help," but they had only caused more problems. Clients were upset.

"So, why do you want another contract with that place?" David asked. "It's mayhem there."

"I like the people. And they've asked me to try and redesign their product interface," Natalie said. "Richard, the product manager, suggested to Xavier that I do the same type of workshops with the university partners that I did for Enigma's website. It would help improve the user experience. But it will really be a distraction to the client and buy the Pit time to clean up bugs in the software from previous releases. That's how Richard hopes it will go over anyway. I haven't used my approach on a product before, so it's a good learning opportunity for me. Good for my portfolio."

David snorted and shook his head. "Sounds like you're taking the next contract."

Natalie stared at him. "If you really don't want me to, then I won't. But I hope you would at least explain to me why I shouldn't."

He didn't want to explain; that was the point. He changed tack suddenly. "How much do you talk to Xavier?"

Lines of confusion wrinkled her forehead. "I talk to him—to get my job done. Is that what you mean?"

"Nothing else?"

"No."

"Has he ever asked you anything? Said anything unusual?"

"Like what?"

He knew what he was fishing for, but to remain discreet, he couldn't articulate it plainly. "About you or me? Any offhand remark?"

She gave him a sad smile. "No, I know my lines. You're a friend of my mother's and all that. Is that what you're worried about?"

He didn't answer her question. Based on her puzzlement about his inquiry, he decided there was no cause for alarm. "I don't know why you need to do this at Enigma. There must be other companies you can work with," he stated.

She spread her hands out as if in acceptance of a situation she could not control or avoid. "I like it there. It has a certain energy. It's un-corporate."

David shrugged his shoulders. "Do as you will then. I suppose if you're learning something new, it's a good thing." He said it as if she was seeking his approval, but they both knew she would do whatever she liked.

More relaxed now, Natalie easily slid into some casual conversation about Enigma and the people in the Pit. She told him of Jeremy, the communist in Che Guevara shirts and tattered jeans, who believed computer programmers everywhere were exploited for their skills at creating the new digital world. Then there was Richard, quick and intelligent, who was gentle but forceful as he corralled the Pit around tasks and projects. The other members of the team all had little characteristics that she was amused by. "It's a motley crew, but they pull off some good work," she said.

When his coffee was done, David told Natalie he had to leave for his event. He stood up to indicate she should take her leave. She had been talking so much that she was not done with her own drink. Perhaps he was being rude, but he had promised Elinor he would be at the gallery the moment it opened.

As he ushered Natalie to the door, she hesitated before going outside. "You mentioned an art exhibit tonight?" she said.

"Yes, a charity event."

"I like seeing art. I could come for a bit before I drive home," Natalie suggested, looking at him expectantly, hopefully.

They had never attended any public event together.

David, surprised, shook his head. Why did she put him in this position? Elinor would be there tonight; he couldn't risk it, didn't want his attentions divided, didn't want these worlds coming together. "I don't think it will work tonight," he said, even though he knew it would hurt her.

Her face fell, the disappointment obvious. "I see," she said, giving him a weak smile. "I hope you have a good time then."

Their goodbye was strained. She was dejected, though she put on a brave face. And David wondered, not for the first time, if what he was doing was right. More importantly, he wondered why she put up with him.

CHAPTER 15

Suitors Calling *(Xavier Hardich, October 2004)*

ONLY once or twice a month did all three members of the Hardich family sit down together for dinner. These occasions were always organized by Xavier, the self-appointed head of the household. He had believed these gatherings were vital to ensure some semblance of what might be called familial camaraderie. Nevertheless, over time he began to wonder what the point was, for the family members had long ago run out of conversational topics.

Elinor was pleased enough to go over the same ground again and again, repeat and replay conversations for a third and fourth time, ask the same stock questions and receive the same rehearsed answers for a fifth and sixth time, all in the name of family bonding. For her benefit and satisfaction alone, these painful dinners persisted.

Perhaps, in an act of selfish desperation, Xavier determined he would add new people to either revitalize the dinners, or if they were going to be a morbid affair, he would have other people suffer with him. And so, he suggested broadening the guest list for the next occasion. Thus, Jocelyn and Derek were invited.

Elinor, Xavier, and Augusta were in the kitchen together, preparing the food. The room was spacious enough that Xavier never had to be too close to his sister. They were always on opposite sides of the island counter, chopping up vegetables or mixing a salad. Augusta was chatty with their mother, and he detected none of her double-entendres, subtle mockery, or cynicism. Xavier would almost say she was in good spirits. That must be Derek's influence, for he alone seemed to have the ability to restore a balance in her.

"And what about that Natalie Mitchell?" Elinor asked him, while she pulled some chicken out of the oven.

There was always considerable interest in Natalie. When Xavier had told his family that he had met Natalie and subsequently contracted her to do some work, she became a curious obsession for his mother. Elinor had made it her duty to be a form of ward for this woman she had never met, and she frequently told Xavier to "look after that girl—make sure she's happy."

"She's doing fine," Xavier responded. "She's signed another contract with us. I'm giving her some more work based on how well she did with the new website."

"Good, I'm glad. David will be pleased," Elinor said.

He hardly cared about that. He rather hoped Burlow was furious that his little ward was feeding off Xavier's generosity.

"Has Natalie said anything to you about Burlow? How her mother met him?" Augusta asked as she paused her chopping.

It was a rare event for her to direct a question at him. Xavier shook his head. "Nothing more than what everyone seems to know," he replied. Rumors continued to swirl about David and Natalie. He hadn't known Augusta's curiosity had also been aroused.

Xavier was slightly nervous having Jocelyn in an intimate setting near his sister. He felt he might need to protect his girlfriend from Augusta's barbs. When he had first started dating Jocelyn, his sister had made one of her passing comments that Jocelyn was the perfect twenty-first-century sheep—erudite on the superficial and dumb to everything else. His retort, which surprisingly silenced Augusta, was that Jocelyn seemed a lot happier with her life than Augusta did.

Jocelyn, the daughter of Bart Miller, was stunningly beautiful and the antithesis to Augusta. She was uninterested in, almost surprisingly ignorant of, global events and politics. She preferred, or rather was almost obsessed with, television, movies, fashion, and exercise. Her in-depth knowledge of these fields served her well in her profession. On the morning show she co-hosted, she was master of light conversation, particularly the celebrity gossip beat.

When the guests arrived, the dinner commenced in the dining room. Xavier forfeited the seat at the head of the table to his mother. Derek and Augusta sat on one side of Elinor, and Jocelyn and Xavier sat on the other.

The added company at the dinner signaled a positive development. Elinor demonstrated her ability to host a gathering by building inclusion, asking questions of Derek and then Jocelyn on their respective jobs and families. Everyone was on good behavior, and Xavier would be inclined to suggest things were progressing well.

It wasn't long, however, before politics entered the meal by some comment of Derek's. The United States election was less than a month away, and Republican George W. Bush was attempting his second term. Jobs and the economy, as always, were an election issue, but it was balanced equally with terrorism and the fallout from the Iraq War.

"The Democrats under Kerry seem to be having a tough go capitalizing on all the negative Iraq coverage," Derek remarked. "I would have thought he'd pull ahead by now."

"I think the world's gonna get another four years of George W," Xavier agreed.

"Regardless, we sure know there won't be a Ralph Nader at the helm," Derek quipped, putting his arm around Augusta, as if to say he was sorry for a joke at her expense.

That's when Xavier saw it, the look on his sister's face: a twitch, a turning of the lip in contempt before she smiled. "I know that neither the Republicans nor the Democrats are ready to entertain universal healthcare, getting out of Iraq, or real environmental discussions in any meaningful way. The Democrats don't even want Nader on the ballot. Nader's fighting the established system of the two-party tyrants."

"What do you make of the election, Jocelyn?" Elinor asked. "These three will go on about it forever if we let them, so get your opinions in now!"

Jocelyn gave a shrug, and Xavier tensed. "I don't follow any of it. It's such a waste of time. Nothing ever changes, and all politicians care about is themselves," Jocelyn replied. "I hate when they make me talk about it on the show."

Xavier eyed Augusta, fearing that she would voice some condescending remark. But Augusta raised her glass and said, "I'll drink to that. True insight. And one that can be applied to more than just politicians."

Jocelyn, likewise, raised her glass and giggled. The rest of the dinner guests followed suit, obliged to clink glasses for a toast that was hardly a tribute, but rather an indictment on the poor state of international affairs. As Xavier watched Augusta, he saw her lips form that bitter smile he had seen often, one that alluded to some amused torment inside her. But still, Augusta said nothing. She was holding her comments back.

After dinner, the party moved into the living room for some drinks. Derek and Xavier sat together. Derek was extolling the merits of Enigma offshoring development and QA to India.

"I have an acquaintance named Sanjay you have to talk to," Derek said. "He helps companies like Enigma build their offshore arm. Offshore is vital to reducing overhead. You'll make yourself very attractive for acquisition if you can show lower costs with higher throughput."

Xavier's attention was divided, however. He was listening to Derek while trying to hear the conversation of the women. Elinor, Augusta, and Jocelyn sat on a long couch on the other side of the room. Jocelyn was on her third glass of wine, and he was worried she would speak too freely, not knowing that Augusta might pounce at any time to ridicule her.

Jocelyn, perhaps emboldened by her well-received comment at dinner, was casually briefing Augusta on all that was happening in Hollywood. She was dismayed at Britney Spears's marriage to some dancer, shocked at the marriage of Jennifer Lopez to some other singer after her breakup with Ben Affleck, and perplexed at the selection of "Apple" as the name of some child. Augusta sat listening to all this profound news with a neutral expression.

"Is that a yes?" Derek asked.

"Sorry, distracted listening to the girls. What was that?"

"You mean distracted looking at your girl," Derek joked, giving a nod to Jocelyn, as if to say it was something that could be forgiven. His voice went low. "I was saying I wanted to take you and your mom out for dinner in the next week or two. Just the three of us—without Augusta knowing," he added.

"Yeah, sure. We can arrange something. Everything okay?"

"Absolutely. Can we aim for next Tuesday? Just let me know if your mom is good with the date. We'll go out to a restaurant here in downtown Cambridge."

The dinner party disbanded at ten o'clock. Jocelyn left to get her sleep, since she needed to be at the studio for 6 a.m. Augusta, surprisingly, opted to stay at home and get work done instead of returning with Derek to Waterloo to spend the night.

"Isn't your class early tomorrow morning?" Derek quizzed her. "Would make sense if you stayed at my place."

"Then I wouldn't get any work done," Augusta said. "I'll come by tomorrow night. We should do dinner too."

"Sure. I'll make reservations," Derek said before kissing her. But he gave her at least one narrow-eyed glance as if to imply he still didn't understand her reasoning. Then he gave Xavier a firm handshake. "Until next time—just let me know when," Derek said, alluding to their earlier conversation.

Xavier retired to his father's office, where he had another glass of wine alone. He was planning, in his mind, how he would decorate the office when he assumed ownership. He had told his mother he wanted to make it his personal work area, and she was softening on her rules. She said they could discuss the matter more after Christmas.

One glass of wine turned into the rest of the bottle. And sometime before midnight, Xavier made his way upstairs to bed. Reaching the landing on the second floor, he started to walk to his room and saw Augusta's light on. He heard her voice through the door, laughing. Not a mocking laugh, not embittered, but pleasant, like she found something sincerely funny or joyous.

Xavier drew closer to the door to hear better. His suspicions born by Derek's comments months ago, and even her curious behavior tonight took hold of his thoughts. She was talking on the phone, he assumed. He realized how foolish he must be standing outside his sister's bedroom, slightly drunk and eavesdropping.

"You like it then? We can go the day after Christmas. I've never done New Year's in Paris ... I know it will be beautiful ... We can go there, but what your guidebook hasn't told you about is the hordes of tourists, long lines for that. Might be different in winter though. You'll love the cafes and walking the streets. Bring your books. We'll read together ... No, I'm not going to say that, you fool! I'll just tell him I'm going with some girlfriends. Are you going to say anything to anyone? You better get it off work. If I'm there alone on New Year's, I can't say what horrible things I'll get up to."

Xavier's mind, rendered unclear by the wine, took a moment to register and compute what he heard. Had she not rejected going to Derek's place tonight so she could work? And here she was, chatting away on the phone, and certainly not talking to Derek. In fact, he did not think she was talking to another woman. Knowledge of some deception taking place filled him with anger and indignation. He knocked three times firmly and quickly and then opened the door and stepped into Augusta's room.

He immediately regretted it.

Augusta was standing in a silky, short housecoat in front of a full-length mirror at her closet door. The housecoat was open at the front, and she was staring at her nakedness. Her hair was wrapped up in a towel like a turban. Her head was kinked to the side so that the phone could be pinched by her ear and shoulder blade. When he entered, she turned in shock and quickly grabbed the edges of her housecoat to cover herself.

"Jesus Christ! What the fuck are you doing!" she shrieked.

"Who are you talking to?"

"Get out!"

He took another step toward her. "Who is it?" His voice strained. Fury and wine mixed together in his blood. But he also saw the rage in her eyes.

Augusta pulled the phone from her ear, ended the call, and shut the clamshell face. She clutched it in her fist.

"Get out! You're sick! How dare you—out!" she yelled, and he knew that was more than enough to wake his mother. He subsequently heard Elinor's door open and her quick pace coming to the room.

"What are you two doing?"

"Xavier just walked into my room while I was naked—apparently there's no privacy in this house," Augusta shouted.

Elinor looked at Xavier angrily.

"I heard her talking on the phone with some guy. Making plans for a trip—New Year's in Paris! And it wasn't Derek!"

"No, it was my friend Jessica. Sorry you missed that part. Must have happened before you started listening in like a snoop. You goddamn stalker."

"Lord, give me strength," Elinor declared, exasperated. "Adult children at home, and this is what goes on? After the peaceful night we had, I thought things were getting better between you two. Does it ever end?" Elinor's voice was rising in strain. She drew closer to Xavier and looked at him in the eye. "You're drunk, I can see it in you; I can smell it on you. Get out of her room—now!"

The alcohol had compromised his position in his mother's eyes. Nevertheless, Xavier knew what he had heard. He stormed out of the room, but not before a good look at Augusta, whom he wagged his finger at. "I know what you're about," he nearly spat at her.

When he awoke the next morning, he recalled everything with clarity. He replayed the conversation he had overhead, and his understanding of it remained unchanged. His sister was up to her old tricks, but at the expense of Derek Lam. The calamity was that he didn't want to, he couldn't, tell Derek anything. It wasn't his place. Was that it? Or was it that he couldn't risk the friendship or the connection?

* * *

The following week, on Tuesday evening, Elinor and Xavier met Derek at a restored nineteenth-century mill that had been converted to an upscale restaurant. It had long been one of the more formal eating establishments in the city of Cambridge and functioned as the celebratory venue for many weddings and special occasions. Its defining characteristic was its perch above the Grand River, where the restaurant overlooked a dam that separated a calm, tranquil river on one side, and a cascading falls and rapids on the other. Xavier and Elinor arrived first and were seated at a reserved table in a small conservatory with a view of the river.

Elinor was half giddy, sensing that tonight was special. She had an inkling of what was to transpire, as did Xavier. Each had the foresight to anticipate the question that would be asked of them. For Elinor, it was a great day, one that she wished her husband could have been present for. Xavier was more subdued. The events of the previous week with Augusta cast a shadow on what should have been a joyous event.

When Derek came in, he was wearing a traditional blue suit, but he had given it some flair with a red tie. He carried with him a bouquet of chrysanthemum and carnation flowers, which he presented to Elinor with some reverence and a generous smile.

Everything happened when the first drink was served and before the dinner was even ordered. Derek Lam, conducting himself as the perfect gentleman, said that although he would have been honored to ask James Hardich for his daughter's hand in marriage, events that were well known to all rendered such a procedure a sad impossibility.

He was equally honored, however, to request the blessing of Xavier and Elinor before he would ask Augusta to be his wife.

"I intend to propose to her at the end of November if you give me your blessing," Derek said.

Elinor embraced Derek, saying, "You are the perfect man for Augusta. When you are around, she's entirely different, she is a better person and a happier one. And you had James's approval when he was alive—I know that." She was happier than he had seen her in nearly a year.

Xavier readily consented and congratulated Derek. The advantages of being linked to this man were numerous. With Derek's influence rising, the match was perfect—it cemented the friendship of the two men. He only wished the couple could be married tomorrow, to ensure his sister did nothing to sabotage it.

When Elinor left to visit a mirror in the ladies' room to ensure joyful tears had not marred her makeup, Xavier said to Derek, "Really happy you'll be in the family. Soon it will be official."

"Absolutely," Derek said cheerily. His voice dropped a little, but he kept a good-natured smile on his face the whole time when he added, "And you should know that given my now-intimate connection with the Hardiches, I expect your family's money to move over to me. Anything else calls into question my capability publicly. You understand?"

"I'm sure it will happen soon. Like I said, Mom and Burlow—"

Derek cut him off. "How do you think it looks when my fiancé's family chooses to keep their money where it gets shitty returns over investing it with their son-in-law, who can make them richer?"

It took a moment for Xavier to answer. This side of Derek was new to him. "Optically, not great."

"Optically, it's shit," Derek barked. "Now the only question is do I need to talk to your mom and get this family in order or are you going to?"

CHAPTER 16

A Warning *(Richard Earning, October 2004)*

THROUGHOUT the summer and into the fall, Richard's relationship with Augusta continued to evolve. He was entirely enthralled with her. They were spending as much time together as they could, without regard for the secrecy their relationship should entail. Where once they chose corner tables in quiet bars at night, they shed caution as sun worshippers shed clothes to expose skin to the glorious rays of sun. Now, they met even during the day on Saturdays and Sundays and whenever Augusta could free herself from Derek and her dissertation and studies.

But she was still with Derek. This menacing awareness, this cloud that occasionally blotted out his sun, unsettled Richard. He knew it was pointless to talk to Augusta about it. She would only dismiss it. "We're finally alone together, and you want to talk about that?" she'd say accusatorily, as if he were either untoward or wasting time fixating on a drab subject. Yet, she knew he needed appeasement for his jealousy, and she always delivered it. She soothed him and redirected his thoughts by showing him tenderness and affection. It was as if his quiet hurt and anger triggered her love.

Only when alone, in the privacy of his apartment, could he brood and give some release to the agony he felt. His mind was filled with dark images of what happened in that other half of Augusta's life— in the spaces when he was not with her, and she was with Derek. He remembered the week she had gone with Derek to a cottage in the Muskoka region. She had downplayed her time there, saying it was quite a bore, but occasionally a story, a passing memory would emerge about the beauty of the cottage overlooking the lake, the tranquility of canoeing at sunrise, the sight of the millions of stars at night while sitting in a hot tub.

Did she not know how heartless she could be? Did she not know how she made his mind visit dark places? If she was in a hot tub at night, was Derek beside her, touching her? Kissing her? Did she awake beside Derek before that tranquil canoe ride in the morning? What of the nights she spent at Derek's—what did she do with him? How did she keep that relationship *going*? She never discussed the details, and Richard filled in all the blanks and silences.

One night, Richard began to write a story. He never could plan when his inspiration came, but when it did, he would allow it to flow through him. He channeled his half-tortured thoughts onto the pages: a breakup—a woman falling out of love with a man and leaving him for the one she was destined to be with. Different names, different places, but all with subtle hooks and links to his own confounding position. After a week, he set it aside, as he did with all his beginnings. But it was, like some therapy, enough to instill in Richard a renewed sense of hope, of faith.

Faith, a belief in a religion, in a grand narrative, where despite any empirical evidence, some comprehension or understanding of a higher power or purpose prevails. Richard had faith and belief. Augusta would leave Derek; she would be with him. Somehow, everything would be resolved favorably. Like a religion, this knowledge became his compass, a safeguard against doubts.

He could never fully understand what Augusta's pull was on him—how she had infested his mind with only one singular thought: herself. She was as mysterious and enigmatic as the day he had first met her. So full of contradictions, her philosophy and thoughts were immune to categorization, even definition. How could he interpret someone who intelligently laments the ills of global capitalism, of a greedy elite that exploits and uses the less fortunate to further themselves, and then follows it up with a conversation on her latest outfits purchased on a shopping expedition in Toronto?

"Do you have some disdain for me, Richard?" she asked, laughing one time. She seemed amused by this possibility, almost invigorated that he might feel scorn toward her. They were walking hand-in-hand along a trail that circumnavigated a large pond in Waterloo's main park on a Sunday afternoon. Derek was in Toronto for a couple of days.

"It's not disdain. It's confusion. You speak knowledgeably and passionately about all these world problems," he said watching her eyes squint back at him. "But if you were truly interested about fixing them, shouldn't you do something?"

"Knowing about it doesn't mean I'm passionate about it. I'm only passionate about the things I want," she said, stopping and pulling his hand so that he turned to face her. Leaning over and kissing him, she asked, "What would you have me do anyway? Work for the UN or something?"

He shrugged his shoulders. "Join a group or a cause. Volunteer your time somewhere. Get involved with some organization. Maybe it is the UN. Your parents know all about this stuff. Your mom and dad were big into philanthropy, into using their influence to change things for the better."

Augusta was entertained by his suggestion. "Don't kid yourself. You were never at my house when mother got it in her head to 'get involved.' My dad detested those events. Mom convinced him it was good PR. There was no altruism behind it—it served a specific purpose. Everything was done to further Dad's reputation and profile."

"Good came out of it nonetheless."

"If good comes out of a selfish endeavor, is it still good? If bad comes out of an altruistic intention, is it still bad?"

"This is trending toward a philosophical argument. Some sort of 'tree falling in the forest' debate, and you're missing the point," Richard said a little crossly. Her amused smile was inappropriate at times. "Why take the time to know of all the injustices in the world if you don't care to do anything about them?"

She said nothing but pulled his arm to show she was inclined to recommence their walk along the trail. "I could join some bullshit organization," she finally said, answering his question. "But why bother? That's a feel-good penance people adopt to purge guilt. They don't effect any real change." She spoke with contemptuous confidence. "Should I run off and build a house in some poverty-stricken country for a couple weeks and then return here to carry on in my nice bubble? Maybe I could hand out food to those little black kids with the flies crawling all over them. Just a drop of charity in an ocean of despair. If I was really committed to the betterment of the world, I would need to sacrifice and forgo everything I have. Otherwise, I'm just a hypocrite. I would need to remove myself from the system, the machinery that our civilization is built on, that every civilization has been built on, and I'm too weak to do that. I've tried to be someone different, someone better, but I'm not."

Richard eyed her. "You're being cynical again," he said.

"I'm not. I'm being honest with myself. And most people aren't," she returned heatedly. "I like what I have; I like my life of privilege. And I guess that means I'm stepping on everyone below me. I guess that means I support every war that keeps people oppressed to give me this life. I guess it means I support sweat shops somewhere. I guess it means I support companies exploiting the environment. And you do too, Richard, because you live here. As beneficiaries of the system, we hardly have moral credibility to talk about how it should change. Because we aren't ready to take the real steps to fix it."

Richard was perplexed by the contradictions of her intelligence; she prevented herself from achieving her own enlightenment. She demonstrated empathy and accountability, but where it should have moved her to action, she opted to shrug her shoulders and accept it as a necessary system. There was an inner conflict in her that ran deep; it filled her with self-revulsion and despondency.

Whatever her flaws, Richard needed to be in her company. He was no longer ashamed of his place, and she came by frequently, sometimes spending the night. When they lay in bed together after their lovemaking, he would fall asleep to her tracing imaginary lines on his face or caressing his head and rubbing his shoulders. He never really knew when Augusta went to sleep, if at all, for she was always up before him in the morning. And if he awoke in the middle of the night, he would open his eyes and, if he turned to look at her, she was always staring back at him, studying him, with a sort of melancholic smile. When he inquired why she wasn't resting, she would tell him she was "just thinking." Then, she would once again rub his chest or draw lines on his face until darkness took him.

One night, when he awoke, she was sitting slouched with her face buried in her hands. He sat upright and asked what was troubling her.

"I didn't intend to spend the night," she said with sudden urgency. She jumped out of the bed, moving rapidly gathering her things and stuffing them in a bag. She was frantic. Despite his protestations that it was 3 a.m., she insisted on leaving immediately. The next time they saw each other, she dismissed the event, saying she was "having a moment," and told him not to talk about it again.

She never lost a certain commanding tone with him. Her requests and preferences were always stated presumptuously. Richard had even succumbed to her casual demand to see some of his writing. He didn't believe he would ever share it with anyone, rightly viewing it as incomplete. But when Augusta attached a "please" and a smile to her petition, he gave in.

She would read through whatever few pages he had written on any given story and reflect upon them. To his various scenes, she would sometimes make suggestions about where he could take a plot or recommend possible future chapters. He would listen, because he loved her ideas, loved hearing how her mind worked.

"This is interesting," she once said, handing him a sheet of his many beginnings. It was the piece he had written after Burlow had come to the office for the first time. "But you're trying to make too much of a point. I feel you judging him as you write. Be kinder to your characters—they'll offer you more secrets when you do."

Richard contemplated her words, thinking it was such a strange thing for her to say. Was she alluding to something else? Was it her?

When he said nothing, she asked if he would continue to write the story.

"I don't decide whether it continues or not," he answered. "The muses do. When the moment comes, if it comes, I'll keep going. Or I'll start something new—which is usually the case."

She laughed at this. "Seems like you're waiting on other people to write for you," she remarked. "You need to decide to keep going. What's the point in starting if you don't finish? Don't wait on the muse. You have some talent."

"I have a full-time job too," he reminded her. "I'm trying to make you and your brother rich."

Augusta would roll her eyes whenever he brought up Enigma. "You're such a good employee, Richard. A very respected cog in the machine, I'm sure. But you should be doing more of this," she said holding up the pages of his half-scribbled scene. Then she sighed. "You need to stop doing what is safe."

They would talk about books they each were reading and would sometimes read aloud to one another, he in his boxers and she sipping a coffee or wine while lying on his bed in seductive underwear. He learned of Augusta's particular zeal and affection for Oscar Wilde, and together they made their way through a variety of his plays and stories. Those moments with her, reciting words and hearing her return the words as another character in the play were somehow wonderfully intimate.

She was capricious. She was beautiful. She was tender. She was unfaithful. She aroused a passion in him he could not suppress. This was Augusta Hardich.

* * *

They were sitting at his simple kitchen table. She was distracted, however, pensive even. Though she normally bummed cigarettes off of him when she was drinking, tonight she was sober and had her own pack. She was going out to the balcony regularly to smoke. She didn't seem to want to talk, so he watched her quietly and made them coffee in a large French press.

Finally, he brought up the phone call from the previous night.

"What happened last night was bad. I'm glad you're okay. But I think it's a good kick in the ass to both of us," Richard said.

She nodded in agreement. "We need to be more careful; well, I do at least."

That wasn't what he meant. Richard had hoped that the event would be a catalyst for Augusta. It was time for both of them to stop this surreptitious romance. It was time Augusta start to make a break from her present situation—that she trigger a breakup.

They sipped their coffees. "I'm not wearing a wig to Paris so that you can say I'm one of your girlfriends," he told her meaningfully.

Augusta frowned. She reached out and took his hand. "I'm sorry, Richard. I know we were planning our getaway, but I just don't see it happening right now. We'll need to wait a few months. I feel like Xavier will look into things—he's suspicious. He might start connecting dots."

Richard could feel a mix of anger and hurt inside him. He pulled his hand away. He had been planning their trip for over a month now. Augusta had bought him a Pauline Frommer's Guidebook to the city. He became engrossed in building an itinerary of what they would see and do. To go to Paris was akin to embarking on a fantastic voyage. His imagination was so taken by the descriptions of the landmarks and sites in the book that he was traveling to them regularly in his mind. He surveyed Paris streets from the top of the Arc de Triomphe, he gazed up at the Eiffel Tower while fireworks flashed in the sky and changed the colors of the graceful ironwork; he sat in cozy cafes while reading a book; and he walked the galleries of the Louvre, seeing masterpieces. It was all going to be beautiful and perfect. He was there, and she with him—out in the open.

Now the anticipated event was slipping away from him, like a story in an author's mind never written, never realized. Was she really proposing a postponement?

And to make matters worse, she was suggesting they resort to ongoing secrecy in their relationship. Why wasn't she compelled to take action for him?

"Why are we hiding this? Why are we acting as if we're ashamed?" Richard asked her. "We've been carrying on this façade for months. It needs to stop."

She stared at him and then looked away, shaking her head. There was a sorrow-tinged smile. "What we've done, what we've been doing, is beautiful, Richard. But don't confuse our desires with something that's right. It was never right."

"What do you mean?"

"You're not thinking of the consequences."

"I'm not worried about the consequences. Everyone will come around in the end. It will turn out right."

"You're wrong. You've worked hard to get where you are, remember? You have your equity in the company. You're climbing the ladder. You're going to get to the top, save some money, and do your travel and writing. What happened to all of that?"

He laughed sarcastically. "First you tell me I should leave Enigma and follow my dream; now you're telling me I should stay and follow my original plan? I'll manage, don't worry." After a pause in which she refused to look at him, he added, "I want you, Augusta. You are what matters." It was his declaration to her. Once he said it, he knew it was true. It was all that mattered. He would weather any storm if being with her was the result.

"What about me, then? Have you considered all of the consequences for me—all of my plans?" she asked, her voice breaking slightly.

"What plans?" he asked, shocked. He had never known her to have any outside of pursuing her PhD. And he only realized now that they never spoke of what she imagined for her own future.

Augusta said nothing in response, but instead got up and went out on his balcony for another cigarette. He joined her in the cool night and watched with feigned interest as cars pulled in and out of the parking lot below or sped on to the main roads. They smoked in silence on either end of the balcony, their exhaled fumes not even intermingling.

When they returned inside and sat down at the kitchen table, he pressed her again. "Do you not want to be with me?"

"Have I given you joy? Have I made you happy this whole time we've been together?" she asked timidly. She exhibited none of her haughty confidence and sureness to which he was accustomed. He felt guilty for trying to push her down a certain course that she was resisting.

He pulled his chair close to hers and rubbed her back. "Of course, you do—the joy you give me is the whole reason I want you. We're going to get through this, but we need to stop being scared," he said. He could feel the constant yearning for her that always lingered beneath his skin, beginning to bubble.

Whether she sensed his lustful stirring or whether she was filled with her own, he couldn't say, but she stood up and straddled his lap. She pulled his head back and kissed him, her teeth gently clamping down on his tongue.

Her mouth caressed his ear and she whispered, with a lust-filled confidence, "I can't stay too much longer. Let's stop talking and enjoy each other."

CHAPTER 17

Revealed *(Xavier Hardich, November 2004)*

"THIS is so good. You should have some," Natalie told him. Xavier watched as she swirled the spice-coated fried bananas in the rum butter mixture to get as much of it as she could on her spoon before bringing it to her mouth. She raised her eyes to heaven in thanks.

He had taken her out for dinner to one of his favorite restaurants with Indonesian-inspired cuisine. They had spent most of their night talking about Enigma and its clients. She had a good business mind, and he enjoyed hearing her perspective on some of the challenges the company faced.

Natalie had helped him out of a jam. One of the university clients had not been pleased with a series of broken commitments Xavier had made. An executive sponsor from the university had gone as far as to suggest Bill should be put back on the project, since a certain attention to detail seemed to be missing. At this slight on his pride and reputation, Xavier blamed the Pit. Not for the first time, he believed the Pit was trying to thwart him. In the midst of this client satisfaction fiasco, he had sent Natalie in to work her magic. Things went better than expected.

The client was impressed with her design approach and the initial user interface concepts she had created for the product. They were considerably more usable and better looking, and the project sponsors at the university suggested that if the new designs could be implemented, they would go a long way in alleviating some current frustrations. The good news was this bought the Pit more time to fix the quality issues that had plagued the new releases of the software. The bad news, if it could be called as such, was that the client now had an expectation of Natalie's ongoing involvement.

For once, Bill and Xavier seemed aligned in a course of action. Bill had given voice to a thought that was already bouncing about in Xavier's head. "Natalie's not the type of person we should just let walk out the door. She's talented, and it would be good to get her on full time. She's great in front of customers, and even the Pit likes her. She and Richard make a formidable force. She's exponentially better than the contractors you hired and got nothing from."

Though Xavier disputed Spindrall's comment on the value of the contractors, he was in agreement on the other points. Natalie would be good for Enigma.

Her hair was down tonight, thick curls framing her face in a succession of layered arcs. She had a black suit jacket on with an ivory-colored shirt underneath. At various times throughout the evening, he could smell a pleasant but heavily spiced perfume emanating from her.

When he had first seen her months ago, he thought her cute. But having spent some time with her tonight, he recognized her subtle and alluring sexuality. She was not like Jocelyn, who immediately triggered lust with her flesh on display to be devoured. No, Natalie was reserved, discreet. He saw it even in the way only one button was undone in her shirt: she would reveal little about her physical qualities.

"So, you're interviewing then," he said, sipping his drink.

"Yes, but I'm not rushing it." She smiled. "I'm enjoying the contractor life. Don't worry, no matter what, I'll finish my work by end of year."

"What kind of gigs are you going for?"

She paused before answering. "Actually," she said slowly, "thanks to Enigma, I've decided I want to be in a small company with a good startup vibe. Looking for a senior position, maybe even a managing director role or something. Why do you ask?"

Xavier had never taken the time to speak with Natalie about her personal or professional ambitions. She must have felt his line of questioning peculiar compared to their normal interactions; indeed, she probably felt the invite out for dinner more than a little odd.

"I wanted to know where your head was at," he said. "We could use someone like you at Enigma."

"I already work with you."

"As a contractor."

"Are you offering me a full-time job?" she asked, surprised.

He smiled at her, a new thought occurring in his mind. "What would Burlow say about that, I wonder? What does he say about you working at Enigma at all?"

Natalie gave a slight frown at the question. "He's skeptical."

"About Enigma or me?"

"I know you two are oil and water," she said, pushing her finished dessert plate off to the side with a decisiveness that told Xavier she was both done with dessert and the topic of Burlow.

But Xavier was not ready to relent. "He told you we are at odds?"

"It's pretty plain. I figured it out when I first met you at the restaurant. You two give off some aggressive vibrations when you stand near each other. If you don't know that, you should. I thought it strange, given how close he was to your father. He's got pictures of your whole family in his living room."

He gave her a skewed smile. "I suspect my mother has prominence in those photos."

Though she gave him an inquisitive look, she said nothing more about Burlow.

Reminding himself of his purpose this evening, he continued with his questioning. "Entirely theoretical, but if you were offered a position at Enigma, would you take it?"

"In this pretend world, what's in it for me? Do I just become an employee?"

"Probably, we could think of an appropriate title. One that suits your ambitions. I didn't think I'd be hiring more employees anytime soon, but I'd make an exception with you. There would be good compensation, salary, and bonus for performance. And you'd get to be a part of a startup."

"I wouldn't do it for salary and bonuses. I'm looking for equity now."

"Not surprised, everyone wants a piece!" Xavier said. "I suppose you wouldn't be willing to buy in?"

"No money to buy in, sorry," Natalie said, shrugging her shoulders. "It would be vested to me, of course." She took a sip of her wine and then breathed out a long "hmm" thinking sound as something occurred to her. "Do you think you'd still value what I do if I were your employee?"

"Of course, why wouldn't I?"

"You should think more about that answer—even though it's an abstract discussion, it's an important question," she said.

"Here's what I think: Enigma's clients need the right people on the job. Currently they aren't satisfied because of the Pit. I need someone I can work with and get us back on track. Thinking about outsourcing, you know? India. Lots of cheap talent that could help us increase output affordably. I need to make this work—it's my inheritance. If I can't, Enigma goes bust. This is everything to me." After a brief pause, he added, "And to my sister and Bill too."

"You think I can solve all of that?" she said, smiling and biting her lip. He was reminded of Augusta.

"We do, yes."

"I'd need to see what a theoretical offer looked like. Hard for me to imagine all of this."

When the waiter passed, Xavier was partial to ordering another drink for both of them, but Natalie blurted out a request for the bill before he could speak.

"You're done with me tonight?" he playfully remarked, but he was a little offended. Things hadn't gone bad, had they?

"I've got a lot to do tomorrow. Remember, I have to drive back to Toronto tonight. I'll get this one, though," she said.

"Are you going to expense it back to me?"

She chuckled. "No. It's a write-off."

They finished up, and as they were walking toward the door to leave, Xavier felt someone clasp his bicep. Surprised and irritated, he turned around quickly to see the overly smiling face of Cassandra Martin.

"Isn't this interesting seeing you here!" Cassandra remarked loudly. She opened her arms and stared at him expectantly. He gave her a lukewarm hug. She was always one for show, and he felt this embrace was her way of getting the restaurant to behold her.

"I was watching you and this young woman for some time, trying to get your attention to come over. But the two of you were quite in your own world," Cassandra scolded.

"It's a business dinner," he assured her.

"Business? Really interesting." Cassandra said in a tone that implied suspicion. She looked at Natalie with a wide smile and looked back questioningly at Xavier.

"This is Natalie. She's doing some work for Enigma," Xavier said, introducing her.

"Oh. Oh! Natalie!" Cassandra stated with renewed interest. "You're the Natalie we've heard about. Burlow's girl. The smart, savvy businesswoman doing the marketing and websites. Sam! Sam! Come here quickly. I must introduce the two of you—Sam was going to reach out to you. We heard how good you are." She clasped Natalie's hand so that flight was impossible. Then loudly, so that all the patrons of the restaurant might hear, she declared, "Sam is one of the top real estate agents in the area, you know?"

Cassandra proceeded to tell Natalie how much she liked her "lovely curls" and her "beautiful eyes." Under the compliments, Natalie became bashful and gave Xavier a mildly panicked look. She wanted to leave.

"Can you stay for a drink? Sam is right there," Cassandra said, pointing at her husband, who was getting up from a table to approach them.

"I'm sorry, we can't—we have to get going. Natalie is driving back to Toronto, and I have a meeting tomorrow morning," Xavier said.

"You must! It would have been so nice to have another couple with us. Ah, I see that look. You didn't deny it when I said *a couple*." She laughed loudly and gently hit his arm. "Does Jocelyn know you're working late with pretty girls?"

Sam joined them, giving an embarrassed, weak smile. Xavier, and everyone else familiar with these two, were aware that Sam's success came from Cassandra. He hardly needed billboard ads at bus stops; he only needed to send out his wife for groceries, and he was assured of her coming back with leads. Although most people ended up using Sam as an agent, whose services were neither bad nor good, they largely chose him in the hopes of receiving respite from his wife. As Sam and Natalie found themselves thrown into a strained conversation, Cassandra turned back to Xavier.

"So interesting that I run into you and your sister within a few weeks of each other. When it rains Hardiches, it pours, I guess! Tell me," she said, lowering her voice, "is she still with Derek?"

"Yes." Xavier responded briskly to the question. He didn't mention Derek was planning to propose to Augusta this week.

"I thought so. I was surprised to see her in the park with that young man—very close to each other. I even thought I saw them holding hands, and I wondered ... actually, I was worried! Had something happened to my favorite couple? They were walking away from me, so I never got a chance to say hello. I'm so glad she's still with Derek. I would hate it if that dashing couple broke up—they're so good together."

"I'm sure it was just one of her friends from school or something," Xavier said, looking past Cassandra to see how Natalie was faring with Sam. She had her professional face on and was reaching into her purse, from which she produced a business card. The thick, black ones that had impressed him so much when he had first met her.

"Oh, no. It was that young man from your party. Rick?"

"From my party? Could be," he said distractedly. He disliked Cassandra's gossipy tone, especially when it was about his family.

"Wasn't he one of your friends? From your company?"

"Rick?" Xavier pulled his eyes from Natalie. For Cassandra to stop going on about this, he would have to help her solve this petty mystery. "This year's party?"

"Yes, of course. Brown hair, you know? Nice looking boy. Richard! That's it."

"Richard?"

"Yes!"

He felt a jolt register in him, though he didn't know if it was in his head or his heart. But Cassandra was watching him, watching for an expression, waiting for a comment. She wanted a story, a rumor, a scandal. Despite his surprise, he ensured that he remained composed and let no outward sign of his inner turmoil show.

"Yeah, Richard. I guess they meet for coffee sometimes," he said as confidently as he could. But there was anger rising in him—rage. *Is that who it is?*

Cassandra seemed to lose some steam when her shocking revelation lost momentum and petered out—the story of a clandestine tryst was disqualified from her arsenal.

Xavier walked past Cassandra and politely told Natalie that they needed to be on their way. Natalie nodded emphatically, and the two bid Cassandra and Sam a good evening. Natalie, however, had to swear to call Sam the next day—a price Cassandra extracted to let them leave.

Outside, Xavier walked Natalie to her car and wished her a good night. She began her journey to Toronto, and he to Cambridge.

When he returned home, he found a bottle of wine and went to his father's office. He was not one to pray or to seek wisdom from the dead, but in his own way, he tried to tap into the world of spirits. He hoped his father would give a sign as to what should be done about his wayward daughter.

The full weight of Cassandra's intelligence was upon him. The more he drank, the more he flitted between anger and confusion. Focusing on the problem seemed impossible. The depth of Augusta's betrayal to his friend, and of Richard's part in it, enraged him. He knew his sister was upstairs in her bedroom and he resisted the urge to barge in and confront her again. No, he needed to be careful. Too much was at stake for his friend and his family—too much set in motion.

What was he to do with Augusta? With Richard? With this entire situation? He stayed up all night trying to answer these questions.

Whether it was James Hardich communicating from the other side of life or entirely his own planning, Xavier saw a course to follow by the time the gray dawn began to alight the office.

Somehow, in his drunken state, he sent an email to Bill stating that he was not feeling well and wouldn't be in the office for some of their scheduled meetings. But he followed it with a meeting request for the following day.

The subject of the email was "Personnel changes."

PART THREE: UNDONE

CHAPTER 18

The Breaking Point (Natalie Mitchell, November 2004)

For the next two days after her dinner with Xavier, Natalie worked from her apartment in Toronto. She had meetings in the city with some clients, and with the beginning of a new month, there were invoices and expenses to prepare. Not until mid-morning Thursday did she get in her car to begin the nearly two-hour drive into Waterloo to regroup with the team at Enigma.

As she sat in traffic on the highway, her cellphone rang. It was Xavier.

"Are you on your way in?" he asked.

"Yeah, slowly," she said. "Am I missing a meeting or something?"

"No, no. Where are you? Past Cambridge yet?"

"Nope, at least a half hour from there."

"Good! I want you to stop by my house for a chat," he told her. His voice was upbeat. "Bill's here too. We're waiting! I'll flip you a text with the address." He revealed nothing more about what necessitated this stop at his house.

When the text came through, Natalie, intrigued, entered the address into the GPS. When she arrived at the revised destination around eleven in the morning, she got out of her car and surveyed the old homes of Cambridge's West Galt. Whatever these houses cost in Cambridge, they would be quadruple the value in Toronto. And even amid all the great houses, the Hardich house was particularly grand.

For some time, she had thought it odd that Xavier would choose to live at home, given his age. She had moved out to have her own place and privacy as soon as she could. But if her grandparents had a residence this size, she would have stayed at home too. Only three people lived here? It could have been subdivided into at least five or six spacious apartments and rented out.

She walked up to the door of the large, red-bricked Victorian house and rang the doorbell. She waited while a series of bells chimed down and then up again. Before the bells had stopped, the door was opened, and a woman she had seen pictures of stood with a beaming smile—Elinor Hardich. Her reddish-brown hair was perfectly styled, and she possessed a dignified beauty in her later years.

"Natalie Mitchell! Finally, we meet," Elinor said as if a mystery had been solved. She ushered Natalie into the entrance hall and gave her an appraising look. "It has taken too long for you to reveal yourself to us! I blame David entirely. You know that David was James's best friend? And in all that time, we never heard a peep about his friends in Toronto, or a beautiful thing like you. But from what I hear, maybe he was right to keep you a secret. Xavier says you're very talented; he thinks so highly of you." Elinor spoke quickly and excitedly. She took Natalie's jacket and hung it on one of the hooks in the entranceway.

"The men are in James's office here," Elinor continued, pointing to a large wooden door. "But let me get you something before I send you in there. The office is such a serious place. David and James spent so much time in there …" She trailed off, lost in a momentary thought. Then she took Natalie by the arm and guided her past a great staircase going to the upper floors. They entered a large, spacious kitchen.

More fit for a restaurant, the kitchen's size created a sense of awe in Natalie. It was larger than her entire apartment and tastefully modernized to fit within the old-world refinement of the home. A large island in the middle was adorned with a massive vase of flowers.

Thoughts and questions were tumbling out of Elinor, and Natalie fumbled to give answers quickly enough before another volley was directed at her.

"Was the drive in okay? Such a long commute. We're a little way out here in Galt, but James and I love this neighborhood. Is David being good to you? Has he shown you around? I'm not sure he's the one to do that. Maybe I should take you out someday. If you need a friend, I'm here. We both know Burlow's a little bit of a hermit. I suppose Augusta could take you out sometime. She'd be good for showing you the more stylish restaurants or bars in Waterloo."

Natalie smiled and readily accepted Elinor's overtures of friendship, although she wasn't sure when they would find time to see one another. When Elinor queried for a second time on how David Burlow was treating her, Natalie said he was very kind but confirmed some of Elinor's suspicions by stating that he was "a recluse."

Elinor shook her head. "That's David—the man will not be changed." Then, after a pause, she asked, "Your mother passed away when you were younger, is that right?" There was sympathy in her voice.

"Yes, when I was eighteen."

"I'm very sorry," Elinor responded softly. "We know here what it is to lose ones close to us."

"Your loss is recent. I know about your husband, James, through David. I'm sorry for you too. David always describes him as a great man," Natalie said in return.

Elinor gave a sad smile and a nod of thanks.

Elinor offered to make Natalie eggs, sausages, bacon, or anything she might desire, but Natalie insisted a coffee would suffice. A fresh pot was put on.

"You are not alone in Toronto, I hope," Elinor stated. "You have family there?"

"Yes, my grandparents. They live in Greektown. And I have my friends, of course."

"And your father?"

Natalie paused, considering the question, the confessions that could be made, and the damage she could do. She liked this woman, wanted to be honest with her. But she opted, as she always did, to protect David. "Don't know him; he's never presented himself yet. Maybe someday," Natalie finally said.

"Not knowing you is his loss," Elinor said with a sureness suggesting she had no doubt on that point. "Some men run from parenting. Not all of them were made to nurture, you know?"

During their conversation, as the smell of fresh-brewed coffee filled the kitchen, a figure appeared at the entrance to the dining room. Natalie turned to look and beheld a woman about her own age. She knew instantly it was Augusta Hardich.

Augusta's arms were crossed as she leaned against the doorframe. Her reddish-brown hair was freefalling down to her shoulders. She wore black jeans and a fitted white wool turtleneck that accentuated her slim figure and outlined her small breasts. Even this casual pose could not conceal a haughtiness in her manner. She was undeniably pretty, but her stance also made her seem aloof. Augusta's face was unreadable while she eyed Natalie with a piercing stare. Was it hostility or a deep studiousness?

When Elinor saw her daughter, her happiness and enthusiasm tapered slightly.

"Oh! This is Augusta," Elinor declared. "My daughter, but you probably heard of her from David. Augusta is at the University of Waterloo, working on her PhD in psychology." And then to Augusta, she said, "This is the Natalie Mitchell we've heard of!"

"It's nice to meet you." Augusta smiled and walked over, extending her hand, her eyes never leaving Natalie's face. "You're a bit of an enigma," she said with a subtle, mysterious inflection of her voice, as if teasing out something in her mind or maybe just teasing Natalie. The smile that formed from the compression of her lips curled one side of her mouth up into a half-grin of amusement.

Natalie received Augusta's hand, unsettled by the lack of warmth she felt from the woman. Elinor and Augusta were opposites: one was sincerity and tenderness, while the other was cool and evaluating.

"I'm getting ready to leave for the university. Sorry I won't be able to stay and talk," Augusta said. "But I'm sure you have business to discuss with my brother. He probably never mentioned it, but I'm also an owner in Enigma. Can I rely upon you to ensure that we women are represented in whatever dealings he's conjuring?"

"Of course. I'll keep his scheming in check."

"I'd like that," Augusta said. "Perhaps we'll catch up another time." She walked over to her mother and gave Elinor a light embrace before leaving the kitchen.

Whether Elinor sensed Natalie's unsettled state or she always felt she had to smooth wrinkles after anyone encountered Augusta, she drew close to Natalie and quietly said, "I love her dearly, but she's a peculiar one—as I'm sure David has told you." Cocking her head to listen as Augusta's step ascended the stairs to the next level, she lowered her voice to a near whisper. "We're expecting some glorious news shortly pertaining to her. She's going for dinner with her boyfriend tonight, and he's going to propose."

"Does she have any idea?" Natalie asked, surprised to be a confidante in this family secret.

"I don't think so." Elinor shook her head. "Both Xavier and I are very pleased with the match. Have you ever met Xavier's friend Derek? No? Oh, he's quite a catch."

When the coffee was ready, Elinor poured Natalie a cup. "I suspect the men are wondering where you are, since they would have heard you come in. I'll take you to them."

They walked back the way Natalie had come in, to the wooden door just off the entrance hall. Elinor knocked and entered with Natalie following. Inside the office, Bill was sitting at a small circular table by a window overlooking the front street, while Xavier was sitting behind a large desk at the other end of the room. Both men were working on laptops in silence. The physical space between them mirrored the distance between their opinions on Enigma and how it should be run.

Bill looked relieved as soon as she came in, as if her arrival signaled the end of a long shift and he could pack up and go home. He did not want to be here; that much was clear. Something Xavier had done had conned him into this.

"We thought my mother had adopted you and taken you upstairs to your new bedroom or something," Xavier said. Both men stood up.

"We were just getting to know one another," Elinor told him. "You must bring Natalie around again." Then to Natalie, she said, "Do you need anything else, or shall I leave you here with these two?"

"I'll be fine; they're harmless," Natalie said. "I'm quite interested to learn the mystery behind this meeting."

"All will be revealed!" Xavier declared.

As Elinor was leaving, she laughed and said, "Well, this is a first. I used to say, 'I'll leave you men to it' when James and David would sit in here conducting their business. But now I have to say that I'll leave you men and women to it. Times are changing!" And with that she shut the door.

"Grab a seat, Natalie," Xavier said, gesturing his hand to the chairs in front of the desk. "We're sorry about the surprises today, but we wanted to have a good talk with you about your future at Enigma. Bill and I have prepared an offer that we hope you'll like ... and accept."

* * *

Natalie walked briskly up the driveway and onto the front porch. She was filled with both excitement and trepidation. His car was here; he was here. She needed his guidance.

She had canceled her meetings for the afternoon at Enigma—this was much more important. At his front door, she let out a long, nervous breath and watched it mist away on the cold day. She knocked.

She heard his heavy step coming, the slow unbolting of the lock, and then the door swung open. He stood there in black dress pants and a white dress shirt. David Burlow's face looked irritated.

"I needed to see you," Natalie said with urgency. She was holding in her hand the documents Xavier and Bill had given her.

He recognized none of her anxiousness. "I thought we agreed you wouldn't just show up."

"It's important."

"We are meeting for dinner at six tonight. Couldn't it wait?"

Could he stop being difficult? Why did he always make her feel she was forcing herself on him? He made nothing convenient for her, nothing easy. Now her excitement was mingling with annoyance at him. This hurt had been growing in her over the last month, but now it was turning to anger, and she had to check it, lest it spill into the discussion she needed to have with him.

"David, they've made me an offer. They are even giving me some equity in the company."

He stared at her a moment before grudgingly standing aside to let her in. She went into the small greeting hallway.

"I was with Xavier and Bill," she began. "They called me this morning to arrange a surprise meeting. Xavier told me to come by his house. They wanted to meet—"

His manner changed almost instantly. "In Cambridge?" he asked incredulously, interrupting her.

"Yes," she said, surprised at his now-flushing cheeks.

"What were you doing there?" he demanded. He looked panicked. His large chest took great, short, loud gulps of air. "Was Elinor there?" His eyes were wide, wild.

"Yes, she was."

"You shouldn't have gone. Why didn't you check with me beforehand? I would've stopped you." His voice was tight, as if his words needed to squeeze through the cords in his throat.

Natalie had never seen him so ruffled. His large hands were shaking. "They asked me to come over. I hardly knew this would be such a concern of yours."

"What did Elinor say?" he asked.

"I came to talk about the offer they made me, but if you would rather discuss Elinor, we can," Natalie said with an aggression that surprised even her. What was this obsession with Elinor? She recalled Xavier's comment the other night about David displaying pictures of Elinor. Was there something specific Xavier was alluding to—something unhealthy?

"Answer the question." David's voice cracked under the strain.

What did he want to hear? A breakdown word for word of an innocent conversation? No, there was something specific he was interested in, but what? David was watching her, waiting to parse in his mind whatever she told him.

Then came the sudden clarity for her: this was about Elinor and what she might think if she knew what David was.

The anger Natalie had checked earlier now oozed through the cracks of containment. The offer from Enigma vanished from her mind. Perhaps this was the best time to have it out with him then, maybe the only time, the last time. Too long had she shied away from this conversation. She had forgiven him for his absence, but she was increasingly hurt by his refusal to accept what he had done, what he was—and what she was.

"She asked about my father," Natalie bitingly said. "Is that what you wanted to know?"

His jaws clenched. Yes, that was what he was most interested in, she could tell. David said nothing waiting for her to continue. She considered making him ask for her to divulge more, he was so desirous of the intelligence. Were she inclined toward malevolence, she could dole it out in little drops, like water to a man dying of thirst. But toying with him was far from her thoughts when anger was storming in her heart, lightening wanting to lash out.

"Don't worry, I lied for you again," she said. "I wouldn't expose you like that. I wouldn't want you to be put out by me." What was it Elinor said? It's his loss. Yes, it would be.

He was jolted by her statement and frowned. "Stop it."

"Stop what? Lying for you? Why is it so important for you that I'm a secret? Am I a disappointment?" The lie she had uttered to Elinor earlier was in her mouth, as were all the times she denied who she was, and what she was, for him. She was a lie. "I've forgiven you for what you've done. I've never shown you anger or animosity—I have tried to understand your position. But I can't forgive what you're doing now! Why can't I be what I am?" Her voice was cracking; she could hear it.

David's hands made fists, and his breath was ragged. "Forgiven me? For what?" he asked sharply.

"Holy shit! Are you really asking me? How about leaving Mom! How about the whole game with the trust fund so that you could buy off your responsibilities?" She lost all her composure. These thoughts had long been building inside her. Now that she began to give them utterance, they were flowing from her mouth as she could feel her eyes watering.

"I didn't need to do anything," David growled. "I chose to support you and your mother. And I've never regretted that choice, but I do regret introducing you to people here. It turned out to be more than I bargained for."

"You did what you should have done. Between leaving Mom destitute or honoring your obligations, I suppose you had a choice, but only one of them was right. Although I'm grateful, it's hardly commendable," Natalie said. She wiped her eyes to try to stop the blurring. "You're right about me coming here. A part of me thought that we might become closer, that we might have something beyond this superficial and ambivalent thing we've grown accustomed to over the years. But I see that's a fantasy. I protect your secrets, your indiscretions, at the expense of who I am. Do you know that I fought for you, David? I fought to know you when my grandparents told me not to bother with you. They thought it best I never know you. But I wanted to see you, to give you a chance. That's what Mom wanted too. And we're just … I'm done …" she couldn't finish what she was saying; she didn't even know what she was trying to say. A new feeling was surfacing inside her, confusing her.

"Natalie," David said firmly. There was a look of sadness on his face. His eyes were no longer wild. He took a step forward, but stopped, shaking his head.

Defeat. That was the feeling that was confounding her. Natalie was admitting defeat. Whatever she wanted this thing to be with David, it wasn't. Maybe it was her fault—maybe her expectations were too high. Perhaps he had no paternal bone in his body; that he had rightly pegged himself as a man who provided financial support alone and was incapable of deeper relationships and feelings. But if she granted him that, she had to wonder what her mother had seen in him. At some point, many years ago, David Burlow must have been sentient, must have been worthy of love and gave it in return, even if for a brief time. Where was the man who had captivated Ayisha Mitchell?

She turned and left, glad that she hadn't taken her shoes or jacket off. She wanted to be in her car, driving—away from David Burlow, his old mistakes, and her new ones.

He was following her outside, and he called her name again. She didn't turn around. She was in a trancelike state, in a void, as she walked to the car. She only felt now how cool the air was as it bit the lines of her cheeks where some tears had run down. Reaching her car, he called her again.

"What?" she asked, looking at him. He had come out to the driveway. Should she give him one last word? Should she heed anything he said? Was there an apology coming?

"You should take it," he grumbled. "I know what's in the contract. I negotiated it for you when Bill Spindrall called me to ask what you'd accept. I don't think much of you working there, but I know you like it. I got you the best I could."

She heard his words but couldn't process them. Is that what he had to say? She got in the car and drove.

How she made it back to Toronto, she didn't know. She was unaware of the streets she was on or of the intersections she passed through; unaware of the highway and its stopping and starting traffic. Some unknown part of her mind had taken over the task of driving so that she could drive the roadways of her thoughts, which were filled with the traffic of sorrow, regret, and confusion.

CHAPTER 19

A Call to Action *(David Burlow, November 2004)*

DAVID had rebuffed Natalie one too many times; he knew that. The fragile tightrope he had been walking with her gave way under the weight of a history he couldn't share. He couldn't blame her, for she had been fearless in her attempts to broker some meaningful relationship with him that he did not deserve. Her spirit had been seemingly unbreakable, until yesterday.

Early on Friday morning, David sat in his large leather reading chair, staring at the words of the local paper. He could hardly focus; the letters refused to form into comprehensible words and meanings. He was thinking how distraught Natalie had been when she drove away. He, in turn, hadn't slept a wink all night, as guilt rattled his mind. He should never have brought her to the city. He should have just given her money, financial support, as he had always done, and kept her at arm's length in Toronto. She expected little of him when they used to meet at the park, and she never encroached on his well-ordered life.

He wanted to call her, but he was afraid she would reproach him or even reject him. What was more, he couldn't say the only thing that would alleviate any of her anger and pain. He was not prepared to make an admission or confession—yet.

Confessions and admissions were at the forefront of David's mind. Standing up, he walked to the wall unit and stared at Elinor Hardich's wedding picture. She looked beautiful—then and now.

By means of a death, David found himself in a position where he had a second chance with her. A second chance at happiness and fulfillment. But when should the chance be seized? It was a matter of timing. When was the right time?

Nearly a year had passed since James Hardich's demise. And although David was a patient and constant man (what is a year to one who has waited and loved from afar for a quarter of a century?), he also felt the need to move, to act. After all, inaction had been his undoing the first time; a bitter lesson to learn, and one he needed no reinstruction on. He believed the meeting between Elinor and Natalie yesterday was a sign. It was Fortune telling him he was losing control of the situation, that he was becoming passive. Who waits for Fortune? Her wheel turns infinitely; it is for man to determine when to get on and get off. And she was turning up and away.

The first time David had seen Elinor Collins was at a makeshift beer hall in 1973. The place was crowded with bellicose young men and giddy women adorned with the smatterings of chintzy German garb to celebrate Oktoberfest. At the time, he thought it was destiny that so many swinging, dancing, teetering bodies had parted at the exact moment when he had turned his head so that his eyes would rest upon a lone young woman. She looked frustrated, even panicked, amid a forest of human trunks. David had never been drawn to a woman so much as at that moment; never felt more compelled to act as he had that night.

He had walked through the forest of people toward her while she spun in a circle, searching for someone. When David reached her, he touched her arm gently and asked if she was lost.

That was how David had met Elinor.

He often thought of that night and Elinor's beauty, how her distress called out to him. He remembered clearly how he interpreted so many signs by a higher power that turned out to be nothing more than his own fancy. He discovered a year later, in a blow delivered from Elinor's lips, that she read the signs very differently than he did.

For a year after that meeting, David pursued Elinor in the most subtle and discreet manner. They would go out for dinners or desserts and have picnics in a park. He anticipated Elinor's needs before she articulated them. If she needed a ride somewhere, he would offer before she needed to ask; if she needed to run an errand, he would do it for her; and when she wanted to talk about her long day working at the hospital, he would listen attentively. He adored her, and he served her, which was the only way he understood to show interest in a woman, to love a woman.

On many weekends, Elinor and her friends would meet up with David, James, and an ever-growing band of James's friends and acquaintances. They would all drink and dance into the early morning, except David. David was an observer of the festivities; his sole concern was to ensure Elinor had a good time, to ensure she was safe. He would almost always drive Elinor home after these outings, and it was no small frustration to him that he often had to drive other inebriates home as well. He would drop these people off first during a route not optimized for efficiency, but to have Elinor be the last passenger in the car. He wanted to be alone with her.

David, entirely unfamiliar with romance and relationships, didn't know how to broach his feelings to her. But he convinced himself that he should not be direct or blunt. After all, those traits had seldom served him well socially in the past. He would not force the destiny of their ultimate coupling onto her—she would come to that realization in her own time. David just needed to be there when she experienced her epiphany.

On more than one occasion, James Hardich had questioned David about his intentions with Elinor. And although James was dear to him, David concealed his true feelings and said they were good friends. He felt he would cheapen or soil the remarkable uniqueness of his relationship with Elinor if he spoke of it to anyone.

Too late, David learned that serving the woman he was destined to be with did not lead to the glorious coupling he envisioned. One Saturday night at a bar, David slipped into his habitual quiet observation and aloofness while James, Elinor, and their friends danced and drank. He could only watch with increasing panic as the woman he loved and the friend he adored forged a new connection before him. They had always been friendly with one another, but as he watched them on the dance floor, watched them laugh and smile at one another, watched their hands linger on each other's arms and waists, and at last, toward the end of the evening, watched them kiss, David questioned the higher powers that had foretold him of a different fate.

As the night ended and everyone dispersed, James made his own way home, and David did not fail in his duty to drive Elinor home. He had hoped that she would admit, once alone with him, that she was drunk and regretted her behavior. But she didn't. She spoke incessantly about James and how she had always secretly liked him from the first time she had met him at Oktoberfest. Elinor was completely happy—almost to the point of giddiness—as she told David how wonderful the night was, how perfect the kiss had been. She mused that it was "some strange destiny" that David had befriended her and ultimately brought James into her life. Everything had been a series of ordained events leading to this night.

James and Elinor were dating within a week of that kiss and were engaged some nine months later. James asked David to be his best man, a role he accepted with the appropriate outward enthusiasm and inward torment. His initial anger toward Elinor and James gradually receded into a private spite of himself—a misery and disgust he would feed on over the years until his own body showed how much he gorged on it. And as he became more grotesque to himself, he solidified that portion of his destiny that he would never be with anyone other than Elinor Collins. So, he admired Elinor from afar and was content to linger by her and James, be of use if he could, and offer assistance to the two people who meant the most to him in the world. His belief, however, in any divine plan for his life was shattered.

Until now.

James's death presented a second chance. David had only misinterpreted Destiny's timing. He had loved James Hardich, and he believed that nobody would love James's widow better than himself. He had resolved at the very funeral of his best friend to pursue Elinor again, to speak to her of his long ache. This crippling, deforming love, harbored so long in his own mind and heart, caged, like his soul, in the confines of an enormous mass of flesh, would be set free, exhaled, released.

When? The answer he arrived at this morning—now. If he was to make amends with Natalie, he would first need to make his confession to Elinor. They were opposite sides of the coin that needed to be reconciled.

It was nearing ten o'clock in the morning. David assumed Xavier and Augusta would be out of Elinor's house by now. He picked up the cordless phone, and his chest constricted. He started to push digits on the phone, and his breathing became short and irregular as his heart raced. Putting the phone back down, he rubbed his hands together. They were damp with sweat. He stood up and paced, walked around the entire first floor of the house, into every room and every corner, before returning to the living room to stare at the phone. How could a little black device look like a snake and salvation all at once? Again, he picked up the phone and dialed. He heard the ringing on the other end of the line.

"Hello?" Elinor answered.

"Hello Elinor, it's David," he said, his voice shaking slightly.

Elinor casually conversed with him, and he began to feel more comfortable. She was talkative, and he would almost say she was pleased to hear from him. She insisted he come over for a brunch sometime, "like the old days," so that they could sit and talk.

"I wanted to let you know I'll be coming to your Christmas charity gala for the theatre. I didn't respond to your invite, but I'll be there," he said.

Elinor laughed. "You never send invites back. But I knew I could count on you. You'll love it this year. We have a wonderful dinner lined up, a silent auction with some great prizes, and we even have an acrobat doing a performance!"

David acknowledged that this sounded quite splendid and confirmed that he could be relied upon for his usual financial donation.

"I know you're not one to talk on the phone, David, but I must speak with you about that charming girl of yours," Elinor said. "I met her yesterday. I was actually going to call you about it. She's remarkable. And Xavier tells me she's quite a businesswoman."

"We should talk about that," David said, his nervousness increasing again. This was the moment. "But I was wondering ... I thought ... well, I was hoping we might have dinner soon. I mean before the charity event. The two of us for dinner, I mean."

"Oh!" she said, surprised. "Yes, yes, I'd like that. Let's do it."

"Really?" David replied. He could hardly believe how easy it had been—she had agreed!

They made arrangements to meet the following week. He would pick her up at her house. When he hung up the phone, he exhaled deeply. A thrill raced through him—events were in motion now. He would not suffer the same mistake as before. He would not be passive.

He wiped his forehead; he had been perspiring, and his underarms were damp. Though still morning, he poured a small glass of scotch and toasted himself before tilting the spirit down into his throat. It warmed him, calmed him, and he felt like he was on the brink of solving a great problem. In point of fact, he was.

CHAPTER 20

A Misunderstanding *(Richard Earning, November 2004)*

A T the end of the workday on Friday, Richard stared at his computer screen, distracted. He was slowly making headway on his work, but his mind continued to wander to Augusta. She was supposed to come over the previous night after a dinner with Derek, but she never showed up. Even more surprisingly, she had not sent him a word of explanation. Today, after texting her twice, followed by two phone calls, he had still heard nothing.

There was some surprise when Xavier came into the Pit in especially good cheer, giving a greeting to everyone. He seldom stayed past five o'clock, so his presence at the office was an anomaly. Normally, it was Bill who stayed later, but he had not come in today. Xavier approached Richard's cubicle, his eyes scanning the desk and Richard's computer screen.

"Can we meet in ten minutes in my office when the others are gone?" Xavier asked. But it sounded more like a command. When Richard nodded, Xavier added, "Bring your computer too, we'll need that."

Richard was puzzled at the request, but even more astonished when Xavier turned and addressed the rest of the Pit.

"You guys have been working hard, and it's been noted," Xavier said. "I want you to get a good start to the weekend. On me! Jeremy, take the guys out to the pub for some drinks and a dinner. Hand in the receipt on Monday, and I'll reimburse you." Then he left the Pit.

Richard looked at Jeremy, who appeared skeptical. But like everyone else, Jeremy must have felt the opportunity to leave the office and have a night out paid for by Enigma was worthy of immediate action. He stood up, locked his computer screen, and told the Pit to finish up. Some jokes were exchanged among the developers about Xavier "getting laid" tonight, and how fortuitous it was for them all.

"We're leaving before he changes his mind," Jeremy said to Richard. "We'll see you after your meeting—I'll text you what pub we're at."

"Sounds good," Richard said, He watched the others pack up and leave. There was a panic stirring in him. Xavier's unusual benevolence to the Pit was too suspicious to be passed off as the blissful anticipation of sexual release. Augusta's warning some weeks back that her brother suspected something amiss was at the forefront of Richard's mind.

Walking down the hallway to Xavier's office, he peeked inside and tapped lightly at the door.

"Come in," Xavier said from behind his desk.

Richard did as instructed and sat down in the chair opposite his boss. Xavier finished some typing on his computer, sat back in his chair, crossed his hands behind his head, and stared intently at Richard.

"They all gone?" Xavier asked.

"Yeah. What's up? Everything okay?"

"Not really. You seem oblivious as to why we're talking. And you shouldn't be. Let's start with a name: Augusta."

Richard felt an immediate and sharp throb inside his head. Within seconds, it passed through his chest and arms. His heart stopped momentarily, jumped, and frantically pumped while his stomach turned over. In that moment, with head a swirl, he muttered her name, Augusta, in a confused, questioning manner, as if he did not understand its meaning.

"Yes, Augusta; my sister who you have been working on behind my back," Xavier said, his face growing red. "Are you going to own up to any of it?"

"Own up to what? We're just talking. Is that a problem?" Richard asked quietly. He had thought this day would come somehow, and in his private musings, he had been defiant and courageous. But now, under Xavier's scrutiny and blunt inquisition, he felt traces of guilt.

"Just talking? No, it's been a little more than that, I think," Xavier sneered. "You've been carrying on quite a deceit behind my back. I'm not going to let Augusta throw a good relationship away with a better man than you. Let me be clear—this ends now."

Richard heard the words and revolted against them. "I don't think any of this is your decision. Or your business." He could feel his own anger beginning to rise. How presumptuous Xavier was to think he could prohibit a friendship with his sister. But it wasn't a friendship—it was much more than that.

"Wrong. It's entirely my business. My sister is with my friend, Derek," Xavier said. "Let me ask, has Augusta spoken with you in the last twenty-four hours? No? Why do you suppose that is?"

Richard was already perturbed by this, and he made no answer to Xavier's query.

Xavier gave a scornful laugh. "I'll help you out," he said. "You haven't heard from her because you're just one more of her little dalliances. Don't kid yourself, that line is looong. You are what Augusta does when she wants to rebel against the world. You're no different than the parade of fools she's had her flings with over the years. She does it to piss people off; she does it to see if she can. It's all meaningless for her in the end. I had hoped this stopped when she started dating Derek, but I guess you were the last dying gasp of the old Augusta. Do you think you're different than the others? The bouncers, the bartenders, the yoga instructors, they're all just Augusta's little flavor for a time. I gather that was you planning the Paris trip with her on the phone that night. You should thank me. I saved you some money. She went on vacations with the others too, and then it just falls apart shortly after. The only one who was ever able to rein her in is Derek. And you won't be disrupting that anymore."

Richard felt Xavier's repeated stabs. He had heard of some of these previous boyfriends, but he had never known there were so many, or that she had gone away with them. Augusta never mentioned that. Was Xavier lying?

Xavier seemed to become emboldened by the silence. "So now, down to business, Richard. We have a big problem. I don't trust you, and I don't want you in my business. It's pretty challenging for you to work for me under these circumstances."

Richard sat forward in the chair, alarmed at what he was hearing and the direction Xavier was taking the discussion.

"This has nothing to do with Enigma or my work here. They are entirely different things," Richard returned heatedly.

"It's about character. I can't separate them."

"I'm working like a fucking dog for Enigma!" Richard said. He had never been so confrontational, never spoken so angrily at work like this. "You're mixing up Augusta with my work. That's bullshit. My relationship with her has nothing to do with what goes on here."

"You're an opportunist. It's time you and Enigma part ways."

"You can't get rid of me—I own equity in this company! You can't just fire people because you don't like them!"

"I'm not firing you—I'm letting you go. The company has changed direction, and your position is no longer required. You're being packaged out with a three-month salary, which no Labor Board will dispute. You can thank Bill for that. I would have given you much less, but Bill fought tooth and nail for you. The company will buy back your equity position at a fair value, of course."

Richard felt dizzy, like there was either too much or not enough blood in his head. He could feel his heart beating wildly in protest; looking down at his dress shirt, the thought he could see it flutter from those palpitations. His right hand was trembling. Confusion was mounting in him, and he couldn't determine if he was angry or afraid. He wanted one clear emotion to guide him, but with his feelings all mixing together, clarity was inconceivable. Seconds, minutes, must have passed. He wasn't sure. He just kept staring at Xavier, not at all focusing on the man, just his cold decree.

"I'm going to see a lawyer," Richard finally said. It was some form of defiance, a way of letting Xavier know that this was an injustice, that this wasn't over.

"You're welcome to do that. I've prepared the paperwork here," he said. He picked up an empty box and handed it to Richard. Inside was a sealed envelope. "The box is for your personal belongings—the envelope is your severance. You should get to your desk and clear out."

He had been fired by Xavier, the same man he had defended to the Pit. He was turfed from a company that he had sacrificed countless hours working for. Everything he had done, everything he had achieved, was unraveling. Because of Augusta.

Yet, the thought of her was the only thing holding him together. After the warning she had given him, he had told her Enigma didn't matter. In fact, it did matter, but Augusta was more important.

He needed to see her.

Xavier took Richard's laptop. Dazed, and in silence, Richard walked to his cubicle so he could pack his personal belongings. It turned out to be pointless. What need had he for any of the silly trinkets he had acquired over the last two years? Who needed a smiley face stress ball or a coffee mug that held ten pens?

What would the Pit say when they found out about this? Would they unite and quit in protest to teach Xavier a lesson? Yes, maybe that's what they would do. This would be the moment of reckoning for Xavier Hardich.

Xavier was never more than a few feet away from Richard the whole time, stoically supervising with his arms crossed. Richard reached in and grabbed his severance envelope from the box. Then he pulled his keychain out from his pocket, removed the key to the office door, and threw it inside the box.

"Done?" Xavier asked crisply.

"Yup," Richard said trying to sound as if he didn't care.

"I'll walk you out then."

At the top of the stairs, Richard forcefully swung the door open. The air was fresh compared to the stale oxygen in Enigma's cavernous office. He didn't say any parting words to Xavier; he was worried that in his current state of agitation, something might be said or done that was irreversibly wrong. He walked to his car, and just before he got in, he heard Xavier give a parting shot.

"Are you going to call Augusta to cry about this? Don't bother; she's busy."

There was nothing to say to Xavier. In fact, above everything else that had just happened to Richard, he started to feel a new fear. Xavier seemed confident in his complete triumph over Richard, as if he had put him in a grinding machine and rendered him a powerless powder. Why was Xavier so certain Augusta would accept this, or that Richard's relationship with her was done?

He pulled out of the parking lot under Xavier's watch. It was too dark to see his face, but Richard imagined the man grinning. The moment he drove onto the street, he called Augusta again, but she didn't answer. What had Xavier said about her casual relationships? No, he was not just an amusement for her.

Further down the street, as he drove, he placed another call. Finally, Augusta picked up, though she greeted him with uncharacteristic coolness.

"Why haven't you called me back? Where are you?" he demanded. He hadn't intended to sound angry, but so many feelings were bubbling up.

"Busy. I'm at the school," Augusta said defensively. "I've been marking papers all day. Sorry."

"We need to meet. I need to talk to you. I've had a run-in with your brother."

"What did he tell you?" she queried, her voice soft.

"I'll tell you what happened when I see you. Good news in a bad way. I'll meet you at the Psychology Building and text you when I'm there," he said.

There was a long pause. Then, she agreed.

* * *

Richard parked his car at one of the four religious colleges affiliated with the University of Waterloo. The colleges were separated from the main campus by a creek that served as the physical and metaphorical divide between the institutions that looked back to the God of the Bible for truth, and the main campus that looked forward to the gods of science, engineering, and quantum computing for salvation.

The evening was surprisingly cold as he walked on a well-lit path over the parkland behind the colleges to the main campus. With no cover and mostly open space, a rising wind bit at the openings in his lightweight jacket. Winter was starting to make itself known. He briskly walked over the bridge that crossed the creek and continued down the main ring road that encircled the university until he reached the Psychology Building.

The Psychology, Anthropology, and Sociology Building, known as PAS, was a nuclear-bunkerlike structure with no clear entrance. Richard recalled his frosh week tour guide many years previously referring to its inner layout as a lab experiment. "We're all rats here, and the faculty study us to see if we can make it out." The comment was apt, for the mazelike layout inside the building was littered with confusing intersections that confounded any first-time visitor. Tonight, it confused Richard.

He was still grappling with his emotions. As if he were in the ocean, its water up to his shoulders, but with periodic waves cresting over his head every few seconds. Each wave, each submergence, gave rise to a new feeling and a new perspective. He was furious and relieved. He was depressed and happy. He was betrayed and set free. Cultivated dreams had been destroyed before he could harvest them, but there was a new crop to be planted, a new life. Yet, all his optimism hinged on Augusta, on being with her.

He was navigating his way through the maze of hallways and stairs to Augusta's office on the third floor that she shared with another PhD student, when he remembered he was supposed to text her. It was pointless now; he was almost there. Because it was a Friday evening, the building was nearly empty of people. There were no night classes. Richard hoped she was alone.

Reaching Augusta's office, he moved quietly and peeked in through the half-open door. There were a few desks in the room, though all were empty of occupants save one. *Good*, he thought, *she's alone.*

Her phone and papers were on the desk before her. Yet she wasn't looking at any of it. Instead, she was almost hunched over, looking at something in her lap that he couldn't see. Her hair was pulled back in a ponytail, and she was wearing a gray hoodie, uncharacteristic attire for her.

He gave a light knock and pushed the door open. She looked up startled and stared at him for a full few seconds before a flicker of recognition and then anxiousness crossed her face. She looked tired, with dark shadows under her eyes.

"Thought you were going to text me when you got here," she said softly, distantly.

"Slipped my mind. I just came up; I didn't think it would be a problem."

He advanced into the office and toward her. She stood up quickly. Her right hand folded neatly over her left in a strange posture, as if she were walking solemnly down the aisle of a church.

"What did my brother say to you?"

"A lot, but the net result is he found out about us, and I don't have a job anymore." He smiled, trying to appear calm to her. "I think Paris is back on. I suspect Derek will know soon enough."

She closed her eyes and took a deep breath. "I warned you about this—about him. Shit! I can fix it. Let me talk to him. I'll get you your job back. I have my own threats I can use." She began to pace back and forth behind her desk, still in her ceremonial stance, one hand folded over the other.

"No, fuck him. I don't want it back!" Richard declared. He needed to show her he was strong, that he could manage this—that what they had done was right. "This is a good thing. We've talked about it. We've been maintaining a façade because of me at Enigma and you with Derek. We've severed one chain, now let's cut through the other and be done with it."

"Did he say anything else?" she asked, probing him with her eyes.

Her manner was so foreign to him—this strange worry or agitation in her.

"He said some things about you, your past relationships, that weren't flattering. But it doesn't matter." He wanted to stop her frantic movement, so he went to her and placed his hands lightly on her hips.

She tilted her head awkwardly to the side so as not to look at him. "Not here," she said. And then she gently stepped back, pulling away from him until her back was against the wall.

"What's the matter with you?" he asked. "I'm kinda freaking out right now. I just got fired, and you aren't exactly calming me down or putting me at ease."

"You shouldn't have come. I shouldn't have answered the phone," she said as if to reproach herself. She crossed her arms and looked down at the floor.

Richard leaned on the lip of one of the desks. What was happening? He had imagined this meeting to be so different. His expectations about her reaction to the news were so far from what he was now experiencing that he was beginning to numb.

"What's wrong? This is what we wanted," he said.

She turned on him then, with a fury of condescension. "We got what we wanted, Richard. It's in the past. We gave something to each other, we used each other, and now it's done."

Her words left him speechless. Had Xavier spoken true? Had she now wearied of him? He stared at her trying to find that amused look he knew so well. Was she mocking him? Was this some test of hers?

"Don't look at me. Not like that. You knew what we were doing. I promised you nothing, and you took what you wanted," she said. Her voice was cracking, in either rage or a hysterical sorrow, he couldn't tell.

Too much was happening to Richard. "You're not making sense," he whispered. "I don't understand what you're saying!"

"Derek proposed to me last night. And I accepted," Augusta said, finding a newfound calmness that was still strained by an anger Richard couldn't explain. She held up her hand, now, that had been concealed throughout their entire conversation. A glimmering ring, radiating light, encircled one of her fingers.

Seeing it on her finger sucked out any light or hope that Richard had inside him. He was drained and suddenly felt grateful the edge of the desk was propping him up.

"But I'll get you your job back," she added.

"What the fuck? I don't want the job!"

"Don't be a fool. I know how hard you've worked for it."

"I wanted *you*!" Richard shouted. "You're what mattered. I risked everything for you!"

"Don't make it like you didn't know this was how it was going to end," she fired back.

How long he looked at her, how long he was nonplussed, dumb-struck, he couldn't say. But there were no more words exchanged. He was leaving the office. He was walking down a corridor, direction-less. The maze, the wandering, and finally the exit door. Everything was out of place—everything he thought was true had become false. Outside, the cold air on his face, in his lungs, froze the despair inside him.

How had he misread everything?

* * *

Throughout the weekend, Richard sat in his apartment in wretched misery and a growing sense of hopelessness. He cursed Augusta, was enraged at her deceit, but more than that, he cursed his own foolishness.

For the past six months, he had imbued a relationship with so much meaning, staked so much on it, only to discover he had comprehended it so little. It had torn up the map of the life he had planned, made him question everything he had thought he wanted, and then had cost him everything he had. Never had he known an intensity of feeling like what he had for Augusta. No relationship in his past had prepared him for the consuming nature of it. And no relationship in his past had prepared him for the starvation, deprivation, resentment, and emptiness that followed the demise of something so powerful.

He didn't sleep. The future was frightfully unclear. He would be starting over, but at what? Doing what? And for what purpose? The weekend was agony.

Although reason told him he should be preparing a résumé, he was incapable of applying his mind to any task requiring focus. The only thing he managed to do on Saturday was buy beer, even though he knew it was a horrible idea. From noon on Saturday right through to Monday morning, he drank. The alcohol would numb him in intermittent waves.

He sat on his cheap leather couch and surveyed his apartment. He hated the place, every inch of it: the mismatched furniture, the permanent dirt shadow in the carpet along the edges of the room near the baseboards, the cream color of the laminate countertops in the kitchen. All of it showed him he had achieved very little in the material world, given his labor. The only thing he had was a small sum of money saved. What had he been saving for? A house? Is that what he wanted? Is that what mattered?

When Monday morning came around, he moped about the house with a complete loss of purpose, still intoxicated from his heavy drinking the night before. He wasn't needed anywhere. Where should he go?

Despite repeated checks, Augusta had never texted or called him. The last communication on his phone was a text from Jeremy informing him of the pub the Pit went to on Friday night.

He turned on his home computer to see if he could access his work email through VPN—his credentials still worked. Xavier had not told the team to cut him off yet. What would the Pit say when they discovered he was no longer at Enigma?

By 9:30 a.m., Jeremy texted him again, asking if Richard was okay and if he was coming into the office. Still, Richard did not respond.

At 10 a.m., an unusual email came through: a message from Xavier directed to all staff. It was bold and optimistic, littered with the verbiage of how well the company was doing thanks to the efforts of the employees, of how Enigma was becoming a leader in the marketplace, of how the times were very exciting in the evolution of the company, and various other claims and statements designed to instill a collective sense of accomplishment. But the closing paragraph was the real meat. It contained the likely *raison d'etre* for the email in the first place:

We are pleased to announce that Natalie Mitchell has officially joined Enigma Solutions. She will commence work full time effective January 3, 2005. You have all had the pleasure of working with Natalie over the past few months. Natalie brings extensive experience in the areas of Business Management, Leadership, Marketing, and Design. We are excited to welcome her to the family and see her as influential in Enigma's transformation and growth. This will change some of the team reporting structures, but these changes are all designed to make Enigma more efficient and more customer responsive. Welcome aboard, Natalie!

Xavier Hardich
CEO, Enigma Solutions

There had never been such fanfare for anyone hired at Enigma before, and Richard fumed. After all his work, he had never been heralded or lauded in any email with such a grand compliment. His efforts had never been worthy of a corporatewide communication—he had done what he needed to do without complaint and without recognition.

The next email was a critical blow. It was a reply to Xavier's email directed at All Staff.

Hello Team Enigma!

First, thank you, Xavier and Bill, for the warm introduction. These are exciting times for Enigma. I have had the great pleasure of working with you all and know how committed you are to the success of the company. The caliber of professionals we have here is truly amazing. We have some big goals ahead of us, and we will all need to work together to achieve them.

I look forward to working with all of you as we make the Enigma product the best it can be. And it's time to celebrate some of the hard work we've been putting in. Please put Thursday night (December 9) in your calendar. The executive team would like to host you for dinner and drinks at the pub. Details to follow. I'm excited to kick the year off with you in 2005!

Natalie Mitchell
Vice President, Enigma Solutions

Richard could feel himself becoming clammy, a slight wetness on his brow. Anger, rage, all boiled inside him until he felt pincers tightening in around his temple.

In his fatigued and still intoxicated state, he considered answering these emails. Wouldn't it be fitting to reply back to everyone? He could unleash some verbal abuse at Xavier: words, tirades, were demanding to be let out. But he couldn't think coherently enough to write anything.

By 11 a.m., there was another text from Jeremy on his phone: *Dude—what's going on? Where are you? Crazy stuff! I was just told to cut your credentials and VPN. Also told to get you off phone plan. Call me!*

Shortly after Jeremy's message, his email connection to work was severed. For hours, until well into the afternoon, he had imaginary arguments and fights with people in his mind. He yelled at Bill and Xavier, but also Natalie Mitchell.

Somehow, Natalie had been a part of this. That snake now held the role he had been promised long ago. When he picked up his phone, he sent out a terse two-word text. And although it was sent to Natalie, it was meant for all of them: Xavier, Bill, Natalie, the Pit, and most of all, Augusta.

Fuck you.

CHAPTER 21

Unspoken (*David Burlow, December 2004*)

THE hours and days in David Burlow's routine passed slowly leading up to the appointed dinner with Elinor Hardich. And yet, when the day finally arrived, it seemed to have come all too quickly; the long, drawn-out anticipation of waiting was now replaced with anxiety that it was happening now—today, this day.

David's normal rituals were thrown out the window. He did not read the newspaper; he pondered and paced. He did not walk to the pavilion in the park; he sat on the couch reflecting. It was lunchtime before he realized he had missed breakfast. Hours of thought and study were given to turns of phrase, declarations, analogies, metaphors, and numerous rhetorical methods for how he would declare his love for Elinor, how he would tell her things he should have said decades ago.

Though the dinner was at the forefront of his mind, there was another thought lurking about its periphery, one he had been trying to suppress for a couple of weeks now. It was the looming shadow of unresolved conflict. There had been no communication with Natalie since the day she had angrily driven off. This gave David discord, disquiet, and more than a little shame.

How, David wondered, when he had received his second chance, when the event that he had wished for on so many occasions was so close at hand, could he begin to doubt his own plan and methods? Why did this disagreement happen now, distracting him, when he needed to be singularly focused on Elinor? He would have preferred to be at peace before his dinner.

When he called Natalie in the early afternoon, her phone went through to voicemail, and he hung up immediately. Was she screening him? After a few minutes of thought, he called her back. Her voicemail again asked for a message, and this time he left one.

"Natalie, it's David," he said. "I wanted to see how you were ..." And then he hung up, not knowing what else to say. There was more to say, he well knew. But he couldn't confess to the things she wanted to hear, the apologies he needed to make. Not yet, at least.

He was beginning to understand something he had been oblivious to until now: just how much he was taking Natalie for granted. Like a sponge, he had received and absorbed Natalie's earnest efforts of friendship and kindness while giving her so little in return. Now, in the absence of her company, without her insistent overtures to meet for coffee or dinner, he felt a loss.

David made a commitment to himself that afternoon. He swore that when he achieved his purpose at the dinner with Elinor, when he had fulfilled his ambition, he would do better with Natalie. He would try harder with her—if anyone deserved it, it was her.

But right now, Elinor needed his attention.

When David surveyed his wardrobe, he became discouraged. His suits were all grays and blacks, his dress shirts were all white, and his ties were bland single colors. He would look too conservative, too plain, and too professional for the occasion tonight. He put on one of his gray suits and promptly went out to a menswear shop.

At the store, he sought assistance from a young sales associate named Gaurav, who showed him every color of shirt to go with his suit before David settled on a pink one—which, coincidentally, was the same color Gaurav was wearing. A tie with pink, blue, and gray lines was also matched with the shirt and pulled the entire outfit together nicely. If David could look as fashionable as this young man, he would be quite pleased! And off he went to the changing room.

Nervously emerging from the small changing closet, uncertain if his foray into the world of color was too bold, he was greeted by a thumbs-up from Gaurav, who said he was "born for pink." But as he looked at himself in the mirror, he felt something was off, not right. After a minute, he realized it wasn't the shirt or tie; it was his hair. He was just horrified at the prevalence of the gray in it. When had all that come? How had he not noticed? Something must be done quickly.

Gaurav, a true professional, secured David an appointment at a salon five minutes up the street. The price of a basic trim-and-dye job was exorbitant in his mind, and he had never in his life spent that kind of money on vanity. When it was done, however, he felt like a new man. He was ready for dinner with Elinor Hardich.

Just as dusk was falling over the neighborhood in Cambridge's West Galt, David pulled into the driveway of Elinor's house. He was relieved that neither Xavier's nor Augusta's car was there. Getting out of his vehicle, he approached the front door. Though he had walked this driveway a thousand times, everything was different today. The house was more beautiful, more splendid, than he ever remembered it. A Christmas wreath on the door was warm and inviting, and electric candles lit in one of the front windows gave hope and comfort. He looked up and down the street. Were not all the houses quite pleasant and welcoming here? There were so many Christmas lights. Had they been there every Christmas, or was there just more participation in the holiday this year?

He knocked on the door. In a few moments, it opened, and Elinor stood in the entranceway with a beaming smile. She was in a black pencil skirt that went below her knees with black pantyhose. A silky white shirt was topped with a fashionable long black scarf wound around her neck, concealing her throat. She invited him in while she put her jacket and shoes on.

When he stepped into the full light of the entrance hallway, Elinor called out in surprise, "David! My goodness, you've dyed your hair."

He was speechless for a moment, embarrassed. "I just felt like something different," he said, trying to sound as if variations in his appearance were commonplace.

She stared at him for some time in disbelief. Then, seeing that his coat was unbuttoned, she spied his shirt. "I've never seen you wear a pink shirt. What's gotten into you? Is your Natalie helping you modernize?"

"No," he replied more defensively than he intended, "I dressed myself."

She laughed. "Well, you look very nice." She put on her coat, gloves, and shoes. "Shall we?" She smiled, and David Burlow felt like he was twenty-one again.

They made the short drive to the Old Mill restaurant overlooking the Grand River. Once seated at a candlelit table, Elinor remarked she had come here very recently under happy circumstances.

"You know, the news hasn't made its way around our circle yet, but I'll tell you. Derek proposed to Augusta, and she accepted," Elinor proudly declared. "Derek was a complete gentleman. He asked permission of Xavier and me just over there," she said, pointing to another table. "Of course, we said yes. We're very happy, and I know James would have been too."

"Congratulations, then," David said. "That's very good news. I'm glad she found someone she likes." He was, however, puzzled by this information. He couldn't see Augusta with anyone—she seemed to walk in another world. Was she in love with Derek Lam? Perhaps for Augusta, it didn't matter. But David saw the engagement news as fortuitous: one of Elinor's children would be leaving the nest. Now, if only Xavier would pack up and depart ...

"The man has patience, and he'll need it." Elinor shook her head. "She's such a strange girl, you know? I don't know what in her childhood ever made her so jaded. She had a wonderful upbringing, but she's so ... confrontational at times."

"She's different, I'll grant you, but she's clever," David noted. "You only need to talk to her for a few minutes and you see that. Sometimes, I think she's smarter than all the rest of us put together."

"What's the point in being smart if you turn out so cynical?" Elinor huffed. "She's popping all those pills for her depression. Hopefully that will all stop with Derek. I mean to have a word with him about it all. If anyone can get her off them, it'll be him. He's done so much already."

As they ate their meal, Elinor briefed David on the upcoming fundraiser. She spoke of the planning, the dinner arrangements, and the attendees. Their appetizers came and went, as did their main course, and David was entranced, listening to the woman he had loved for years. She was still strikingly beautiful and animated. Age had touched her, of course, the crow's feet around the edges of her eyes, the occasional age spot on her skin, but it all contributed to making her more refined somehow. He felt entirely blessed to be with her alone at dinner—just the two of them.

So much was he enjoying the time with her, David wondered if he should press his cause tonight. Why spoil this? Why risk a difficult conversation when she was so happy?

Be bold! he reminded himself. David Burlow had learned from the regrets of silence—had suffered the effects of it daily, mentally and physically. He must not waver as he had done so long ago.

"I'm talking so much, David. I fear I'm boring you," Elinor said. "But I don't see you as often as I once did. You must come for brunch, like the good old days."

He wanted to declare that he loved the idea, that it would make his days better, that he would come over anytime she would have him. But he seemed unable to muster any of these enthusiastic expressions and could only say, "I would like that."

David had been avoiding his true purpose all night. When dessert was served, he became aware of time; it was passing by, running out. Looking at her, leaning so comfortably close and looking at him, he felt the need to strike. All of the grace, the verbal setup he had practiced earlier was discarded in his excitement and need to urgently let out what had been locked inside him for decades.

In a directness he had never used with her, David spoke. "Elinor, I have long thought about our friendship. You have been a special person in my life, since those early days when we first met at Oktoberfest."

"I know. How often did we go out for picnics and dinners? I'm reminded of those times now. Is that what you're feeling too?"

"It is. And I've often believed we were happy with one another. I certainly was in those times."

"We both were," Elinor said patting his arm. "You were a true friend, and you never stopped being one. James and I always considered you family—you know that."

"I'm grateful for that," David said. He was dismayed that James's name had been mentioned. The man was gone, yet still he intruded here, butting into an idyllic evening. David needed to steer her back to her pre-James life—the one where it was David and her. "But before you married James, those days when we spent so much time together, were they very special to you?"

"Of course, they were. Why wouldn't they be?" she asked with a laugh.

Now is the moment, David thought. "They were the best days for me, Elinor. When I look back over all my life, the year I am most fond of is that one we had together—when it was the two of us. I was very happy then … I think … I was happiest then," he said, watching her.

"Oh," Elinor said. Her eyebrows raised with surprise. "I'm glad that you were. I was too. That was …" she paused searching for words, "so very long ago."

"There is something you should know, something that I have wanted you to know," David continued. "I have long had a hope."

"Yes?" Elinor asked, leaning back in her chair away from the table slightly. There was caution in her question.

"I hope that we might relive those times—relive them regularly. That we might be like we were then. You must know how fond of you I am, how fond of you I have always been. I adore you, Elinor, and I may not be much to look at; I don't cut a fine figure, but my heart is devoted to you. I swear it. I am faithful and loyal to you alone." As he spoke, he watched Elinor's hands fidget, and then she rubbed them together. There was a look of confused alarm on her face. Had he been too blunt? Had he been too direct?

"I don't entirely understand you, David," she said quietly. She began looking around the restaurant, looking at anything but him. "We'll always be very good friends." She then quickened her speech. "Are you done with your dessert? Are you getting anything else?"

David shook his head at her attempt to change the course of the conversation. He was committed to this now. "Could we be more than friends? If your friend is all I may ever be, then I will accept it and be grateful. But I must know if you would ever view me as anything other than a friend. I wish us to be more."

"You're not yourself tonight, David," she said, looking at him warily. "Perhaps the wine has gone to your head—let's not speak any more of this."

"Don't suggest my feelings are the result of the wine. They have been in me for many years."

Elinor leaned fully back in her chair, creating as much space between the two of them as she could while still being at the same table. She picked up her cloth serviette and began to fidget it in her hands.

"Please," she said, "this isn't appropriate, David. You're making me uncomfortable. I have always viewed you as a dear friend. And James did too. You were his best friend, our best friend. That's why he always looked after you—it was the least he could do to someone so kind and loyal. What you speak of is a betrayal to him." Her eyes were watering, and her voice cracked. "I have no desire to be with anyone else. I love and respect you. I have always been honored by your companionship. And I hope we might remain friends for the rest of our lives. Can you accept this?"

She leaned forward and appeared as if she may place her slender hand on his but then stopped. Instead, her eyes implored him to receive her verdict.

David was silent for a long time. Had he acted too soon? Had there ever been any chance? Had she always been beyond him? He fumbled for something to say.

It all seemed a disastrous ending to something he thought so glorious. He thought things would go differently, that she would be open to what he had to offer. And more importantly, that she would be in a state to listen to him unburden himself about Natalie Mitchell. He could yet say something more, something that might turn the course of her decision, but should he? Should he reduce himself to that out of spite?

"David, I'm sorry. Please understand," she pleaded. "Please."

"I would never want to make you uncomfortable," he said.

Elinor brushed imaginary crumbs from the table in front of her. After an awkward silence, she made a comment that it was getting late. But it was only 8 p.m. David sensed she was uneasy; she avoided looking at him. He settled their bill and refused to split it with her despite several protestations.

They drove to her house in yet more silence. Once in the driveway, David made to get out of the car and escort her to the front door, but she checked him.

"No, David, I'm fine. There's no need for you to get cold." She didn't embrace him as she normally did. She only patted his arm. "I enjoyed our time together. Thank you for the wonderful dinner. I'll see you at the fundraiser?"

Embarrassed, he grunted a yes. He noted that she made no allusion to any brunch they might have together. He wanted to apologize to her; he wanted to take everything back he had said. He watched her go to the door, wave briefly, and enter the house.

When Elinor shut the door, David felt that something had closed definitively on his life and dreams. The premise he had governed his days by was that it had been inaction, a lack of confidence, and poor timing that had cost him this woman. But it wasn't. She had never loved him and never would. And now he had exposed himself recklessly.

By the time David arrived back home, he was deeply troubled. He wondered if he could be by her side the rest of his life as a friend. He had said he could accept this possibility, but he had never considered how unbearable it might be, especially now that she knew his true feelings. Where had he gone wrong? Why had he ever thought she was within reach?

Taking off his garments, he saw himself in the mirror in the bathroom. David was revolted to see how his hair looked, as if dye could conceal how hideous he was. And he was disgusted to see the pink shirt on himself, as if donning colors like a peacock would hide the mounds and rolls of fat that weighed him down so heavily to the earth. He ripped it off and threw it in the garbage.

Pacing about the house for an hour, he finally settled into his reading chair with a bottle of scotch and a cigar. Sometimes, he got up to look at the wedding picture of Elinor, only to be overcome by a sense of hopelessness that would drive him back to the chair, where he'd pour another glass of spirits. Late, at an unknown time, he succumbed to a drunken weariness and nodded off in the living room. His sleep was restless. Despite the unsuitability of the chair for sleeping, he lacked the will, and maybe even the coordination, to mount the stairs to go to his bed. Whenever he awoke, the world demoralized him, crushed him, so he tried continuously to run back into the unconscious state of dreams.

The ringing of a cordless phone on the table mid-morning forced him to stir. A pool of saliva had formed on his chest where his chin and head had last rested. He was inclined to let the phone go through to voicemail, but a thought entered his mind that it might be Natalie. He reached over, cleared his throat, and answered.

It was Elinor.

"You sound groggy, David, are you well?" she asked.

"Yes, I'm fine," he said, his mind trying to catch up to what was happening. Had she a change of heart from last night?

"Good. I wanted to thank you for last night. And I didn't mention it, it didn't seem right, but I did want to talk to you about something," she said.

David grunted, which she took as a cue to go on.

"I know you have been looking after the estate and James's money for me. You've been so good, and I'm very thankful. I'm grateful. But it must be very taxing on your time, and I don't want you to worry about it. It seems unfair that you should have to do that," she continued, then paused, as if wanting him to agree.

"It's been no trouble," he said. "I enjoy helping you."

"Yes, you're very good at helping," she chimed back. "But we've had some discussions here and, given we will be welcoming Derek to the family, we want to show … we want him to know … we think it's right that we transfer the money over to him to look after. You understand? This is nothing about you, David. It's more about showing solidarity—helping out the children."

David said nothing.

"Are you there?" Elinor's nervous voice asked.

"Yes."

"Ah, I thought I lost you. Anyway, I don't want you to trouble yourself anymore with my investments. I hardly understand them. But Derek will take it from here. If I put him in contact with you, could you work with him?"

"If that's what you would like."

"I think it's best. James shouldn't have burdened you with it. And I was selfish not to question it until now," she said. "I'll give him your number. Do you have plans for the day?"

He knew she was trying to make small talk to deflect from her message. So, he spared them both the charade. "I'm actually feeling a little ill. I think I should go."

David hung up and poured another scotch.

PART FOUR: HEALING

CHAPTER 22

Wounded *(Natalie Mitchell, January 2005)*

In the second week of January, Natalie sat in her cubicle at the Enigma office. At 5 p.m., it was dark outside. Worse, the snow was continuing to fall. The weather report had predicted some snow, but the great dumping of the white fluff from the skies had taken everyone by surprise. This was an unexpected storm.

She still needed to drive back home to Toronto, and she began to fear the roads. On a night like this, the one-way trip could take well over three hours, more if there were accidents. She should have left hours ago, but an important client meeting required her to stay, and, at that time, nobody had foreseen this storm. When it started to get bad, both Bill and Xavier had left.

Though Natalie had resolved to move to Waterloo when she took the employment offer from Enigma, she had not yet managed to find anything she liked. Maintaining the commute from Toronto was untenable with a three- to four-hour round trip in the car every day. Already, she felt like she had broken her rhythm. Her mealtimes were off from getting home so late at night, and she was picking up more fast food. On some nights, after a particularly long drive, she was so exhausted that she went straight to bed the moment she arrived home. Living in Waterloo would change all that, but it would also instigate a conversation with her grandparents. They would take the news hard.

If she was going to work these hours, there was no choice. There was so much to do with Richard gone.

Natalie still felt odd sitting at his former desk. She had the sense she didn't belong in it, that she was squatting. The desk still hadn't been cleaned out; she hadn't felt right going through the files in detail. There were trinkets lying about, papers, documents, and notes in the drawers. It had been just over a month since she had come into the office on a Monday morning in December for the great announcement of her joining Enigma.

But she also discovered that Richard had been let go.

She knew there was something more to it than the partners were letting on. When she approached Bill to talk to him about it, he became agitated and short with her. Though he said nothing about what happened, he explicitly stated it wasn't his doing or choice.

Only Xavier provided some vague justifications, though he implied that both Bill and he were unanimous in their decision.

"We've restructured with you coming on," Xavier had said. "Unfortunately, the organization had to part ways with Richard."

"Why didn't you tell me that was your intent?" she demanded, frustrated. "You should have consulted with me. If you want me to run the teams and be accountable for projects and the product, I should know when there is a reorganization and if someone is let go."

"In most instances, that would be true," Xavier replied, sitting in his office behind the desk. His hands were folded behind his head. "But this particular event required immediate action from us. There have been performance issues that we could no longer ignore. They predate you, but we acted in the best interest of the company."

When she asked for clarification, he dismissed the matter but segued to some alternate reasoning. "There's overlap in your skill sets, but we feel the long-term nature of the role is better served by you," Xavier said. "Besides, we had to give you an offer you would accept. Bill and I don't want further dilution of our equity. The company had to buy back Richard's shares—at no small expense—so that we could offer it to you. That's how much we're banking on you."

Natalie now perceived a link between her coming to Enigma and Richard leaving it. The feeling that she had taken something from someone, that an untoward act was done in her name, was clearly shared by Richard. He had sent her a vicious two-word text on the day he was laid off. There was anger in those words, bitterness, a sense of betrayal, and she felt it all in his message. She never responded to it, having just found out herself what had happened to him. What could she say? Call me and we can talk it out? It was well past that stage. She felt guilty without ever having committed a crime.

If Richard knew how much she was working to fill his shoes, she thought he might be sadistically satisfied. Early starts, long drives home—and then the same schedule tomorrow.

Now, at 5:30 p.m., Jeremy and the developers gathered their coats to leave, and she opted to head out of the office with them. Those who had cars started them up and began the arduous process of wiping and scraping windows. They helped each other to make the task a little more enjoyable.

"You should find a place to stay," Jeremy said in a muffled voice as he spoke through the collar of his jacket that he had pulled up around his mouth and nose. "I have a couch if you need it, but the place isn't the cleanest."

"That's really nice of you," Natalie told him. "But I think I'm going to try to make it. Sometimes the main roads are cleared."

He was skeptical, and rightly so, as it turned out. She drove slowly behind snowplows on the slick roads of Waterloo's expressway, listening to the radio. The traffic reports described endless lines of cars rolling along at ten or twenty kilometers an hour. Many cars were in ditches, and the authorities were asking people to stay indoors and off the roads unless it was essential travel. Natalie knew, then, it was hopeless. She wouldn't arrive home until midnight at this rate, if she made it home at all without an accident. She wished she had looked for hotels when she was still at work, connected to the internet. Reaching the ramp exits for Kitchener, Natalie pulled off the expressway.

At a gas station with a payphone, she obtained the names and numbers of some hotels from a phonebook. Using her cell phone to call around, she found a reasonably priced room at a respectable hotel in downtown Kitchener. After making a reservation, she slowly drove the slippery and mostly empty city streets to her impromptu place of refuge for the night. As soon as she arrived, she recognized the area from the time she visited Bart Miller at his office.

A less-than-ten-minute drive to the west was David Burlow's house on the Park.

She hadn't spoken to him for over a month. He had called her once, before Christmas. She hadn't picked up and never returned his call. She had almost called him during the holidays, but her confusion and hurt were still ruling her. She wanted him to suffer, to know what it was like to feel unacknowledged, unimportant, unworthy. That was the root of her anger, that he was incapable of seeing how much disavowing their connection wounded her.

Perhaps she was being too hard on him. For there was another side to David Burlow. He was not always insensitive. There were times when his gruff façade would crack, and kindness would shine through. The fact that he had supported her mother and her for so long suggested he had a sense of what was right, a notion of responsibility. He was correct in saying it was his choice to do so. He could have disappeared altogether, as some men do when pregnancies are unplanned. And the one time she had asked him for help, he delivered.

And what about the matter of Enigma—what had he said? "I know what's in the contract ... I negotiated it for you ..."

In the hotel room, Natalie sat on the edge of the bed, reflecting on David. Perhaps his proximity unnaturally stirred thoughts of him in her mind. It was nearing 7 p.m., and she needed to have dinner. Should she call him and see if she could swing by for a coffee? He would be at home on a night like this. Or even better, they could just have a short chat on the phone and plan to meet another night —best not to rush into things.

Finally, after weighing the pros and cons, she flipped open her phone and found his name in her contacts. She pushed the button to call him, and before she could second-guess herself, the ringing began. No hanging up now.

The line rang repeatedly, and she thought it would go through to voicemail until there was a sudden connection. She heard a crackle, movement, something beeping, and a woman's voice in the background. Finally, there was David.

"Natalie," he said, his voice raspy. He was breathing heavily, his inhales and exhales pronounced as if her were overexerting himself.

Befuddled, uncertain of what was happening, she stammered out a sentence, "Hey, sounds like you're busy. Should we chat some other time?" Was he with a woman?

There was a long delay. She heard coughing and more heavy breathing. The woman's voice in the background was clearer now. "Is that a friend of yours? I can talk to them and tell them where you are."

"David?" Natalie asked.

The sound of fumbling on the other end and then the woman's voice speaking clearly into the phone. "Hi. I'm Irene, a nurse at St. Mary's Hospital. Do you know David?"

Natalie went numb with confusion. "Yes. Yes! What's wrong? Has something happened?"

"Everything's okay, but David's sick. Pneumonia actually. Are you in the area?"

"I'm in Kitchener! I'm close. I'll be there in ten minutes!"

Irene tried to discourage her from coming to the hospital, given the late hour and weather, but Natalie insisted. When she arrived at the hospital, she parked and darted in, making her way to intensive care, where she was told David was. Approaching a counter, she waited with more patience than she had in her until a nurse appeared at the counter. Her nametag read "Irene."

"Ah, you're Natalie. Try to calm down. Everything is going to be fine," she said in a firm tone. Irene explained that David had been admitted the previous day, found half-conscious in Kitchener's Victoria Park. An ambulance had brought him to the hospital. "His pneumonia is quite severe, and he already has some respiratory problems. We had to put him on oxygen and give him an IV. He didn't have any emergency contact, and when we pressed him about someone to call, he told us there was nobody."

Irene spoke matter-of-factly, somewhat detached. There was no judgment in her tone, but her eyes suggested she thought this last point interesting. "Since he pulled off the mask to answer your call, I assume he wanted to speak to you."

"I'm here now," Natalie said defensively. "Can you tell me where he is?"

"Yes, down the hall in 304. He's the one closest to the window. Don't try to make him talk too much, and mind the other man in the room trying to sleep. Visiting hours are over in twenty minutes."

Natalie went to the room and entered. The lights were dim. She moved quietly past the first patient, who had his eyes closed and was snoring lightly. On the other side of a curtain divide running down the middle of the room was David. He lay on the bed with his eyes open, staring upward.

She had been ignoring it before, but the smell of hospital was making her nauseous, a stale, thick air filled with the odor of chemical disinfectants. The sounds of machinery and their incessant noises filled her ears: oxygen pumping, carts rolling down halls, high-pitched beeps signifying temporary stability, hope, life. All of the sights, sounds, and smells flooded her senses, grated on them. She hadn't been in a hospital since her mother had died. Memories and sadness were intermingling in her mind.

She moved forward and walked around David's bed to an empty chair beside him. He turned his head and looked at her. His face was pale and had a bluish tinge. He nodded but said nothing.

For some five minutes, they sat in silence. She was thinking of her mother as much as David. The past and the present were colliding, and she rested her hand on David's large fingers. Although his eyes looked at her, they lacked the steely penetration she was accustomed to. She was struggling with how to open their conversation under these circumstances.

"It's been a while," she said quietly. Not much of an opening line, but something.

He snorted.

"I'm sorry I didn't call you sooner."

He coughed, breathed, and wheezed, and patted her hand.

"Why did you tell them you had nobody?" she asked.

He looked at the ceiling of the room. After working up some strength, he only said, "Thank you for coming."

* * *

For the next few days, until David was discharged, Natalie would visit him after work before her commute home. He would watch television in the room or read a magazine, while she tapped away on her laptop beside him. He didn't talk much, but for the first time, Natalie felt like he was pleased to have her around.

As reliance on oxygen subsided, Natalie was told he would be sent home with medication and instructions to rest. On the appointed day, she came after work to get him.

The nurse, Irene, was working. She nodded to Natalie and gave her a business smile. "So, you're a friend of David's?" she inquired.

Natalie suffered a moment's reflection. She was caught again between admitting the truth that David did not accept or the lie that made everything easy. "Family," she said at last.

Irene's eyes widened slightly, but her face remained deadpan. Likely, years of seeing and hearing many family dramas unfold around the sick and dying helped a person keep their composure in all situations.

"I see," Irene said. "He needs rest and good meals. It will take a bit for him to get his appetite back, but it will return. Are you going to be checking in on him at home? Good. There's another thing though. I don't get the sense he looks after himself too well. When we asked him about a family doctor, he said he didn't have one. He should. With his weight, there are often complications. Maybe you could help him on that front."

Natalie agreed to try. Whether David would listen to her or not was another matter, and she told Irene as much.

When Natalie brought him home, David was still fatigued and with a lingering cough. He plopped himself down in his reading chair by the fireplace, tired from getting in and out of the car. He needed to "catch his breath," he said. He was quickly weakened with the slightest activity.

"I want to go upstairs and make your bed. Where do you keep fresh sheets?" she asked.

He protested, "I can do it. You've done more than enough. You have a long drive home."

"No, I'll do it. You either tell me where the sheets are, or I'll open every cupboard and door there is to find them."

David planted his hands on the side of the chair as if to try and erect himself. But he seemed to abandon his efforts within moments. Natalie took this as a sign to pursue her initial suggestion and didn't wait for further objections. She moved to the staircase to go to the upper level. David called her name, but she didn't stop, and reached the landing at the top of the stairs. She had never been to the second story of the house; indeed, she had never been past the living room.

Loneliness, and a sense of emptiness. That's what she felt upstairs. The sensation was confirmed by two vacant rooms in addition to David's bedroom. At one time, these spare rooms would have been for children. The wallpaper in one had a series of old ships on it, but it was peeling back in several places. In the corner, with boxes placed on top and beside it, was a twin bed, but the bedspread was old and looked as if it had formed to the mattress. Nobody had slept there in years, if ever.

The other room was wallpapered with faded jungle animals—monkeys, tigers, and elephants. The space was stacked with cardboard boxes. Most of the boxes were labeled with what appeared to be company names, followed by dates. A couple of boxes, however, held the remnants of old computers, antique devices looking like something from an old B-grade science-fiction film. That was it; no dressers or night tables, no decorative paintings or shelves, just boxes.

A door in the hallway just outside David's master bedroom turned out to be a linen closet. Several sheets and pillowcases were neatly ordered on the shelves, all white except the pillowcase borders. She grabbed a set of linens and entered David's bedroom.

David's room overlooked the front of the house. There were a few dressers, a closet, a chair, and one bare night table. In the middle, a large king-sized bed. Though David kept it tidy and simple, he must have started to slip from his routine when he became sick. Some clothes were piled in the corner of the room, and the bedsheets were in disarray.

She began to strip the sheets and put the new ones on. Midway through the chore, she heard David's heavy, lumbering step up the stairs. He came into the room and, weary from his climb upward, sat in the chair in the corner with a frown.

Natalie, inclined to laugh at his grumpy look, said, "You'll thank me when it's done, and you can lay in it."

He watched her quietly.

As she was putting on the pillowcases, he stopped her. "Not those ones."

"Why? They fit fine."

"Time for the ones with the burgundy edge," he said. He gulped more air. "Last one had the blue edge. You're putting on the brown one. It comes after the burgundy one on the next change."

She stared at him wondering if he was joking with her. "It's a pillowcase."

"If you want to help, then help right—follow the system," he said, before his agitation made him cough.

She went back to the linen closet in frustration and grabbed the pillowcases with the burgundy edge. Returning, she slid the pillows inside them. David grunted approval with a curt nod.

When she started to gather up the dirty clothes and bring everything to the laundry, David began to argue again. But he could hardly put up much of a fight and his talking turned into a coughing spell. Picking up one of his shirts, Natalie saw that a picture frame was underneath it lying on the floor. Clasping the frame, she turned it around.

The glass protector was cracked, as if the picture had been knocked over. Natalie had never seen this picture before—its home was not the wall unit downstairs. The image in the frame was of Elinor and David, taken when they were probably about ten years younger. The background suggested it was an event of some sort, probably one of Elinor's fundraisers. What struck her was how pleased David looked, how broad his smile was. She had never seen him look like that. Again, Natalie recalled Xavier's question one night. "Does my mother feature prominently in those pictures?" She let out a deep exhale; she was beginning to understand something.

"I'll have to get you a new frame," she said to David, holding the picture up.

"It's not necessary."

"But it's broken."

"Then throw it out."

When she left that night, David was propped up on his pillows in bed with a sweatshirt and track pants on; those were his pajamas. At her request, David gave her a key in the event of an emergency. She promised to see him the next day and bring some groceries.

As she was leaving, she put the broken picture of Elinor and David in his wall unit beside the other Hardich photographs. Perhaps he wanted it still.

CHAPTER 23

A Restoration *(Xavier Hardich, January 2005)*

XAVIER was happy to see his mother's state improving. Augusta's engagement seemed to unstick Elinor from the past and push her into a consideration of the future. His mother seemed to accept the absence of her husband and the possibility of a life past his death. Though Augusta decided the wedding would not be until June the following year, almost a year and a half away, Elinor was in full planning mode, getting intelligence on venues, dresses, and wedding planners. Indeed, she was planning so far into the future that she was alluding to grandchildren.

And as his mother looked forward, she began to sever her connections to the past. Elinor decreed that the office of her late husband could be purged of its artifacts. Xavier would be able to claim it as his own, to adorn as he pleased. Drawers and cabinets that had been sealed for over a year by Elinor's command would be opened and cleaned. But his mother wanted the dismantling of the shrine to be a ceremony involving all members of the family. Together, they would sift through the papers and history to organize it before boxing it or shredding it. Tonight, Xavier and Augusta would make nice to appease their mother and create a counterfeit family, give the deception of sibling unity.

Three weeks into the new year, Xavier opened the door of his father's old office and walked into the darkness carrying some empty boxes. Placing the boxes on the floor, he was going to turn on the lights when his eyes were drawn to the window overlooking the front street. The curtains were open, and a soft yellow light from the streetlamps outside poured in. On the round table below the window was an open bottle of wine. Had he left that here from a few nights ago?

He approached the table to inspect the bottle; it was half-full.

"It's mine," a voice behind him said.

He turned, startled, and peered into the shadows at the back of the office. Once his eyes adjusted, he could make out the flesh of Augusta's pale face while she sat in their father's old chair behind the desk. Her eyes were in shadows, but he could feel their hostility.

Xavier didn't say anything to her; there wasn't much point. Walking back to the doorway, he flipped the lights on, hoping his mother would be down soon.

But he stole another quick glance at Augusta. She was holding a glass of wine up so the rim was just below her chin. She wore the expression he knew she'd have, one that was reserved entirely for him—contempt. Lately, she had lost her mischievous smile, as if she was no longer privy to the ongoing joke that she alone had been able to hear for so long. Nothing had been the same between them since the night he barged into her bedroom.

They ignored one another now. If they were forced to be in a room together, or share the same company, such as when Derek, Elinor, or Jocelyn was around, they spoke only briefly out of a general sense of decorum, to maintain the façade of harmony. Although he tried to be neutral with her, even kind so as not to antagonize her, his efforts were not matched. Her words, spoken by anyone else, would be complimentary; but he knew her, knew her tones and inflections. Her overt pleasantness and politeness were intended to mock him.

Never close, they were now entirely at odds. She was his nemesis, or he hers.

He had played a strong hand in the deterioration of their relations, he knew. But he was justified. What would motivate Augusta to jeopardize everything with Derek? It was criminal in his mind, an affront to both Derek and him. Still, Augusta seemed indifferent to all that was at stake or refused to comprehend it. She had no concept of the connection, of the benefit, someone like Derek could bring the family. In one self-indulgent rebellion, Augusta had nearly thrown it all away for some ass at Enigma. Of course, Xavier would attempt to stop her madness.

When Xavier ousted Richard from the company, he waited for Augusta to confront him. He hoped she would, so he could unburden his own grievances to her—speak his mind, unpack his anger. To his surprise, however, she said nothing; made no allusion to Richard. At first, he suspected she might well be indifferent to Richard's banishment. But then he saw the change in her.

Augusta had been more shaken by the whole event than he thought possible. Throughout December, she looked haggard, as if she hadn't slept or eaten. The previous care she had put into her appearance vanished, and she avoided everyone. Elinor and Derek blamed the usual suspects—stress from school, anxiety, depression. Only Xavier had an eye on the true suspect: Richard Earning.

Sometime near Christmas, Xavier heard Elinor in Augusta's room, lecturing her on how many of her pills she was taking. The exchange ended with Elinor departing the room exasperated. "I've never understood you. You have everything you could possibly want, and your mind makes you miserable! I hope to God you aren't like this with Derek!"

Xavier hoped the same.

He was surprised, then, when she addressed him tonight. For over a month, the only thing he was worthy of was her silence, the ceaseless sneer she eyed him with, which was more of a rebuke than anything she might have said.

"Do you think sitting in Daddy's office will make you successful?" Augusta asked.

"Sitting here will make us more successful than you sitting in a lecture hall," he replied.

"Us? Oh yes, I forgot, you're doing all this out of duty to the family," she said, sipping her wine. "Very noble and self-sacrificing."

Before he could fire anything back at her, their mother entered. She was carrying a saucer and cup with a teabag string dangling over the side. She had a look of determination on her face but still smiled when she saw her children in the room together. She made her way to the table near the window.

He knew his mother felt like it was a betrayal to her husband to move on, to pack him up, to box and shelve him. But wasn't that what they had done with James when they boxed him in a coffin?

"Don't worry, Mom. We'll be done in no time. It's just a room. We're cleaning out a room," Xavier said.

Elinor mustered her resolve and nodded. "Still," she added, "children always move on quicker."

Thus, they began the great purge of the office. Manila folders were pulled out and sifted through to determine their worth and relevance. Meanwhile, the picture frames, plaques, and awards were gathered up from the desk by Elinor.

As his mother cleaned, she would impart little stories around the mementos to her children. "Look, Xavier. This is when your father won the Community Leader Award at the Rotary Club. He raised money for a CT scan machine at the Cambridge Hospital. Good thing he won. I arranged so many fundraising dinners and events that your father told me if he didn't get the award, he would drop his membership." On another occasion, she hailed Augusta to tell her of a plaque James received from Doug Wright, president of the University of Waterloo. "Dr. Wright spent an hour chatting with your father at an awards dinner one night. Quite flattering for your father, really. Your father knew how to impress people."

Xavier played along with Elinor when she carefully boxed these items and suggested the children would want them later. He wasn't convinced the boxes would be opened once stored away. The main items he took an interest in were the books that his dad adorned his shelves with. Those, he would read—eventually. Besides, they looked good in the office.

Going through the documents was a slow process. Xavier couldn't help but scan what he was sorting, even though much of it was bound for the shredder pile. They were mostly the business dealings of James Hardich over the years. There were financial statements from companies that his father either partially owned or was a board member of. There were tax filings, investment statements, annual reports, internal memos, and hundreds of printed emails.

Xavier worked his way backward through time in paper. The further back he went, the more paper there seemed to be. Dot-matrix-printed documents, then standard typewritten papers, even some carbon-copy forms. But a disturbing trend was emerging the more he read. There was a thing, a person, pervasive throughout all these pages and notes: a man, constantly writing and injecting himself in messy scribbles on meeting minutes or in short emails or notes to his father—David Burlow.

Burlow was everywhere. His emails and gloss in the margins of reports espoused opinions or suggested things for James to do. "I will be voting against the proposal, and you should do likewise," or "Call Wayne to see where his head's at, and let me know so I can decide what to do," and "You should not have missed the meeting; the board expected you to present the motion I prepared." Sometimes, Burlow's notes summarized information from a report succinctly, and at other times they extrapolated conclusions from seemingly formal and meaningless meeting minutes.

Augusta must have been stumbling across the same intrusive notes from the old dog. "Have you spoken to David lately, Mom?" she asked their mother without taking her eyes off a piece of paper she was reading. "You haven't mentioned him in a while. He didn't even make it to your Christmas charity gala."

"No," Elinor said. "No, he didn't."

"That's odd," Augusta remarked. "Did he say why he didn't come?"

Elinor went and sat down at the window. She took a sip of her tea. "I'm afraid I've offended him," she confessed, "and he won't return my calls."

"What do you mean?" Xavier asked. "What could you have possibly done to him? You're the only friend he's got, for God's sake."

Elinor hunched over the table. "I think he saw the transfer of my finances over to Derek as me questioning his capabilities," she said slowly. "I think he feels betrayed."

"He's being childish," Xavier remarked heatedly. "He needs to grow up. He's just upset you're finally not beholden to him for your own money."

"Stop it, Xavier," Elinor scolded.

Xavier looked over at Augusta and immediately realized the problem created by Elinor's confession. Augusta was looking at them with squinted eyes from the back of the room.

"You transferred your money to Derek? Why?" Augusta demanded.

Elinor looked at Xavier. "Well …" she began but stumbled into silence. "We decided that …" She floundered again, unable to finish.

"Really, Augusta?" Xavier promptly interceded. "We did it to support your fiancé. That should be obvious." He knew she would be doubly furious that Derek had never mentioned it to her, but there was client confidentiality.

"We? I didn't know *we* had decided that. We. Us. It's not your money, Xavier. It's Mom's. And Derek doesn't need her money. He's doing well enough without our help."

"Fine, then," he said. "I wanted to support Derek. I wanted to show him loyalty, although I'm not sure you understand that," he added with a look. "But above all, I wanted Mom's money to be looked after properly by a professional who knows what he's doing."

"David seems to know quite a bit about what he's doing, judging by what I'm reading," Augusta retorted.

Elinor stepped in. "Xavier and I talked about it and decided it was the right move. Derek's a professional, honey. He knows how to do this. He's managing the money of important people. We thought it best. I thought it best."

Augusta smirked and shook her head to indicate she, for one, did not see this as best. "If I were David, I'd be upset too." She resumed pulling out papers and folders.

Thankfully, Augusta made no further comment. Their mother was having enough of a struggle tonight, and if the ceremony of cleaning out the office could not be done with cheer, at least it could be done without an argument. Though they continued their task, Elinor had taken a sullen turn and sat watching her children.

Gradually, a heap of papers amassed on a space on the floor, all destined for destruction. Augusta was moving slower through her filing cabinets, reading everything before discarding it. Meanwhile, Xavier had increased speed and finished his assignment of drawers. He set up the home shredder, and before long, the sound of grinding paper and history filled the room. Although he encouraged Elinor to join in and help, she only watched him with unease as whole batches of pages went into the machine to be split up by blades and cut into hundreds of strips. When the shredder bin became full, Xavier would remove it, empty its contents into a garbage bag, and put the bin back in the machine to continue. Occasionally, Augusta would walk over with folders and add them to the shredder pile.

Just as Xavier was finishing up all his shredding, Augusta added a last batch of items to the pile. Then, still with a series of folders under her arm, she joined their mother at the small table. She shared the contents of these files with Elinor, who quickly lost her melancholic expression and began smiling. Even Augusta seemed happier. Xavier went over to inspect what was preoccupying the women.

His sister must have come across a drawer where James kept sundry items of his life, not as a businessman, but as a father and husband. Mixed between Father's Day and birthday cards given to him by his family were rudimentary art projects: horrendous looking cars and planes, smiling blobs with sticks protruding out of them for arms, and multicolored misspelled captions. Xavier never remembered drawing any of those things; yet, there was his name, crudely written on the corner of the paper.

There were endless school pictures; Elinor and James seemingly always ordered too many. Another folder contained loose photographs of the family at various times, the most recent being from the family trip to Italy some years ago. In one of those, James was in the center with his arms curling over the shoulders of Xavier and Augusta on either side of him, with the crumbling majesty of the Colosseum in the background. All three of them were smiling, were happy.

They *were* all happy then, weren't they?

Elinor seemed inclined to want to cherish this moment of rare unity. "Why don't you two get a drink, and we'll sit together."

Though Xavier was on the verge of agreeing, Augusta was unable to cling to the truce.

"I should get upstairs," Augusta said abruptly. "I have some assignments to get done for tomorrow."

"What's another hour?" their mother pressed her.

"Sorry, Mom; I can't. But I'm sure Xavier will stay for a bit."

Augusta started to walk out of the room. In her hand, held closely to her, were a couple of file folders. She must have decided on some keepsakes from the office. Xavier wondered what memories from the past Augusta cherished.

At the door, Augusta stopped and turned to address him. "How is Natalie Mitchell these days?" she asked him in a voice that did not hold the bitter contempt it usually did.

"Good," he answered carefully, wondering if there was a trap being laid. "Why?"

"Will you have her over again sometime?"

Xavier was trying to tease out her sudden interest in Natalie. "Maybe. I suspect I'll invite her to the Spring Gathering."

"Good," she said. And then she left. Momentarily, he heard her climbing the stairs to the upper level of the house.

He sat down at the table with his mother. "Why do you suppose she asked about Natalie?" he queried, puzzled.

"I'm not sure. Maybe she wants to get to know her?" Elinor said.

Xavier shrugged, slightly unsettled.

For what he did notice was the subtle change in Augusta when she left the room. Her old look had resurfaced briefly, and he saw the amused smile play upon her lips, the one where she knew something nobody else did.

CHAPTER 24

Moving On *(Richard Earning, February 2005)*

IT was nice to have a day off—especially an unexpected one. Richard's friend and now employer, Robbie, had called late last night to say that the cabinetry materials had not been delivered to the house they were renovating. No cabinets meant no work. Maybe they'd show up tomorrow.

Since he no longer needed to get up early, Richard read a book late into the early morning hours, listening to the water thudding against the roof of his parents' house as it flowed in and across the troughs and down the spouts. It was a cold winter rain that would turn to ice by early morning.

He was pulling out of his despondency. The loss of his job and Augusta's betrayal had shaken his world and shattered so many things he held to be true. Though he would not refer to himself as healed or better, he would say things were improving. He could wake up in the morning without the haze of sadness dampening his mind and thoughts. He could get through the day without sudden jolts of anger or anxiety. No, these intense feelings had subsided, though they lived in him like chained beasts that could unaccountably be unleashed when triggered by some event or thought.

For the first month after Augusta, after being forced out of Enigma, Richard drank unceasingly, passing out every night into numbness. He would wake up to the sensation of feeling, to the dagger of Augusta's betrayal, so he would begin to drink again to bring on the numbing comfort. Days and weeks passed in this state until some part of him, looking in on himself with growing unease, intervened. Whatever that second self was, whether another consciousness or some higher power, it had warned him: The road he was going down was a dangerous one. Only more misery would befall him if he proceeded.

Out of fear, Richard had listened to that other self. He needed a drastic change. By early January, he had given notice at his apartment building and moved most of his things into storage. This was followed by a return to the nest. He moved back in with his parents to the house he had grown up in—a small 1970s-style backsplit on the east side of Kitchener. He took up his old bedroom, the same one he used until he graduated from university. Very little had changed. The dressers, bed, and duvet were all the same, and the bland taupe colors had never been painted over after he left. The family photographs hanging on the walls, highlighting the milestones of his life like proms and graduations, remained fixed.

A man returning to the nest after being on his own is a strange business. Home-cooked meals and the care of a concerned mother are pleasant at first, but eventually the same questions that were asked of him during his high school days were asked of him now. His father had given him a respectful space initially, but one night while they drank a beer together in the kitchen, he began to prod Richard. "What are you going to do now? Work for Robbie the rest of your life? You went to university to get a good job, not do general labor like me. You should have an office job."

His father had spent his life on shift work at one of the local factories and possessed a peculiar notion of "an office job." He held the appropriate amount of reverential disdain for it; office jobs were for smart people with degrees who dressed up, took breaks whenever they wanted, made good money, and didn't work too hard. To his father, who had a high-school diploma, a desk job was nothing short of a golden ticket to the good life.

Richard had given his father the only answer he could. "I'm just taking a break to sort some things out and save some money."

His mother knew he was troubled but also accepted that she couldn't extract something out of her adult son if he didn't want to talk. The only thing Richard had revealed to his parents was that things hadn't worked out at Enigma.

He was by no means pressed financially. He could have lived on in his apartment in Waterloo for at least a year without employment if he tightened his belt. The down payment he had saved for a house still sat in his bank account, plus he had his modest equity payout from Enigma and most of his severance package. But he didn't want to touch these, yet. He was still trying to orient himself post Enigma—post Augusta.

The truth that Richard was coming to terms with was that he had no desire to return to the path he had been on. Though there were enough startups and midsized tech firms in the region that could use his skillset, Richard couldn't bring himself to pursue any of them. That would be a mistake; he had never found real fulfillment doing that work—only monetary reward.

So, he worked for his friend Robbie, who owned a general contracting business doing renovations. Richard wasn't "handy," but he was dependable and reliable, and over several weeks, he learned how to use the saws to cut crown molding and baseboards, learned to lay laminate and hardwood floors, and a series of other general skills that were useful to Robbie. Robbie only had one other employee, and he was busy enough that an extra hand was valuable, especially if the extra hand was willing to do it for a low wage. The whole arrangement turned out to be favorable to both parties.

There was something about the physicalness, the realness of the renovation work that Richard liked; it was so different from what he had known in the tech field. He could see his efforts materialize in the real world over the course of hours, days, and weeks. Where once there was an old kitchen, a blank space would appear after demolition. Then the new kitchen would take form as tiles were laid, cabinets installed, doors hinged, countertops placed, sinks hooked up, handles attached, and lighting put in.

But what he really enjoyed most was that he could get lost in thought while he worked. While he fell into the repetitive rhythm of laying another tile or plank, and the radio played the current pop songs, his mind could wander and contemplate his situation. What was his long-term plan?

There was a restlessness stirring in him. For although Augusta Hardich had robbed him of meaning, she had also instilled in him a possibility, a new way of thinking. He wasn't sure how absurd it was or if it was just a flight of fancy, but a vision was forming in his mind of what he might do.

* * *

On a Thursday after work, Richard went to meet his old colleague, Jeremy, at a British pub. He didn't have a chance to go home and change, so he showed up in his working clothes from the jobsite. Arriving earlier than expected, he took a seat at the bar and ordered a beer, grabbed the newspaper, and started to read it. He tried to focus his thoughts away from what was above him: a coffee shop where he had met Augusta the day after she stayed over the first time.

Jeremy had texted Richard a couple of times to meet since the new year began, but Richard had always been too tired; at least, that's what he told himself. He was aware of another factor at play. He wanted to be on his feet, to be moving forward before he met anybody from his old life. He didn't want it getting back to anyone at Enigma that he was angry, stuck, or in a rut.

"Oh buddy, look at you! A proper working man—a proper prole," Jeremy said as he sat on the stool beside him and signaled to the bartender his beer selection. "Fuck, I never thought I'd dress better than Richard Earning."

Richard smiled. "The times are a-changing."

"When you texted you were doing general labor, I was shocked, man. But you were serious."

As Richard studied his old work companion, he too noticed some differences in attire. Jeremy had on his jeans that he never took off, ratting at the heel, but it was his white-check sport shirt that caught his eye.

"What the hell is this?" Richard asked. "What happened to Che and Bob?" He pinched the seams of Jeremy's sport shirt and gave it a tug.

Jeremy looked down and chuckled. "Uh, you know. On client site and stuff."

"What? When did clients ever make you change? What client is this?"

"Not the client, more Natalie. Her preference if we're going into meetings with them."

"Really? You'd never have been in a dress shirt for my meetings," Richard said.

"You never bought me one."

"She's really busting your balls, eh?"

"Nah," Jeremy said. "She's good. All good. Not like fuck-face Xavier."

And there it was, a moment of awareness between them, a knowledge that things were different, that maybe Richard had moved on, but so had the Pit. Whatever injustices had been perpetrated, however much Che Guevara himself might disagree with the treatment of one of the Pit, life goes on, and cogs can be replaced. Did Richard ever really expect the Pit to rise up in union with his persecution? To abandon their work until Richard was mollified? In the end, everyone needs to look after themselves; that's what Augusta would have said.

Maybe Jeremy sensed the undercurrent of his words, for he said, "It's not the same without you. Could really use you. Nobody can do what you did." Then, holding up his glass, "To the old Pit."

"To the old Pit," Richard said in cheers. "And the new bourgeoisie."

CHAPTER 25

Acknowledged (*Natalie Mitchell, February 2005*)

As the sun dipped, Natalie stood in David's kitchen, making a stew. After David's discharge from the hospital, she was appalled to learn that his diet consisted mostly of microwave dinners and ordering in—usually unhealthy food. The man seemed to have a diet devoid of real homemade nutrition.

David's health had improved gradually. With the help of medication and rest, his breathing had returned to normal, and he was slowly getting back into his usual routine. Only a persistent lingering cough remained.

But the greatest improvement in David was how he had changed in his behavior toward her. He was more open to having her around, and he even appeared pleased when she came over to his house, which was more regularly now.

Once or twice a week, Natalie would make David a healthy dinner after work before driving back to Toronto. She took pleasure in being able to do something for him, to help him, and was glad that he let her do it. Secretly, she thought his becoming ill was a good thing all around.

In the dining room, just off the kitchen, David sat flipping through a business magazine. He offered to help prepare dinner, but she found him clumsy in the kitchen. She knew how to cook well, had her way of doing things, and David just got in the way.

"Are Bill and Xavier treating you well?" David asked.

She shrugged while cutting some bread. "Yeah, it's good so far. We'll see in the long run."

"You skeptical?"

"I just wonder about Xavier sometimes. I still think about that stuff with Richard. His fall from grace was fast," she said. She had told David about Richard's surprise dismissal. "I wonder what really happened. He was good, smart, well liked. Sometimes I feel like I've stolen from him. Like he deserved what I have now. In fact, he had the equity I have, but it was taken from him and given to me."

"Your accomplishments are by your own merits," David replied. "Don't blame yourself for his fall. He'll need to learn from it. Not your problem."

"I tell myself that. Still seems wrong, though. Can you imagine how you'd feel if James Hardich cut you out of his business?"

David chortled and then coughed for half a minute before catching his breath. "No. James wouldn't do that—couldn't do that."

"Well, his son would," Natalie said. The stew was ready. She poured two bowls and brought them into the dining room. She would let the leftovers in the pot cool before putting them in microwave containers so that David had food for a few days.

Taking a seat opposite David, she asked, "How did you and James meet and become partners anyway?"

David stirred his stew with his spoon, played with it a bit, as if he were stalling to answer her question. "You may be surprised to learn that I have never had many close friends," he said sardonically and then took a spoonful of food.

She feigned astonishment, and she thought she saw a slight grin at the corners of David's mouth.

He went on. "I met James in the early seventies. We were in our twenties. We both worked in the office of a manufacturer that provided parts to automotive companies—Big Three and all that. I was in operations and had been working there before James showed up. He was hired on in the sales department."

David took another slurp of his stew before resuming.

"When James was brought on, he was loved by everyone instantly. Remarkable how some people have that gift. He was the type of man you were immediately drawn to; witty and always knows what to say to make you feel good. Made people want to help him, even me, which is saying something, I should think. I'm sure his good looks helped him. He made quite an impression all around, including with the young ladies at the office."

Natalie nodded. She had seen the photos. James did have a good look to him. She supposed his son, Xavier, inherited those looks as well.

"I think I was a bit in wonder of him," David said, his eyes looking straight ahead of him, as if staring into the past. "I was never at ease with people the way he was. That was his talent—and a true one at that. I never knew what to say to anyone other than the cold facts and truth of a matter. I've never been able to sugarcoat things, and I'm not very diplomatic. That doesn't get you very far socially." He snorted. "Didn't get me far at that company either. People only talked to me out of necessity. I didn't have James's social graces."

"I'm sure you had your merits," Natalie said with a measure of forced cheerfulness. She was feeling some pity for David; his praise of James seemed to be highlighting all his own deficiencies.

"Not in that company's eyes," David responded glibly. "I did great work for them, knew more than anyone there, saved them more money than they could count, and averted countless disasters. All the while, I watched incompetents get promoted, watched many a star rise—all but my own. I plodded along at the same job—operations manager or something trite.

"Yet, despite my seeming irrelevance, James took the time to know me, even after he became a VP. He talked to me about the company. Unlike everyone else, I think he saw I knew 'what was what,' as they say. I told him once that I would like to strike out on my own. I remember thinking he might laugh at me. He didn't; he thought it a splendid idea. He would talk to me at great lengths about it. He believed such a thing was possible, believed that I could do it.

"I felt honored to be associated with him. Not sure when, but I remember feeling like I was inadequate to be his acquaintance. I even confronted him about it. Do you know what he said? He said, 'Burlow, you have no artifice whatsoever, and you don't mince words; it's completely refreshing.' I suppose he was the only person who saw my directness as a value.

"Ultimately, being my only real friend, I partnered with him. We left that company together to be owners of our own destiny in our first business. After we handed in our resignations, our last workday was a Friday. There was a big to-do about James leaving, and people threw him a surprise goodbye lunch at the office. They had cake and sandwiches in the cafeteria. Strangely, nobody told me about it or invited me. When James realized I wasn't at the little gathering, he came up to my desk and implored me to come down to the lunchroom. I didn't want to go. I suppose I was resentful, but he insisted, saying, 'You come with me or I don't go.' I never liked to see him disappointed, and James had a way of getting what he wants from people. So, I went down to have some cucumber sandwiches and cake. I remember all those faces turning questioningly to us when we walked into the cafeteria together. I think people only found out later it was my last day too. I can't have a cucumber sandwich without thinking of that incident."

Natalie felt sadness for David, discomfort. She didn't like to hear him speak of a perverse masochistic adoration for a man now dead. She had thought by enquiring about David's start as an entrepreneur, she would receive a motivational tale, one of triumph over adversity and the rewards of perseverance. But it wasn't that at all. She heard only of one man's reverie for another. There was gratitude in his tone, but Natalie also thought there was envy too. For the man who inspired David, had even recognized the good in David, was the same man who reminded him of all his failings.

"Obviously, your new business was successful," Natalie commented, trying to find something pleasant to say. "You two showed your old company what was what. You put them out of business, if I recall from another one of your stories."

A snort, a nod, the slightest smile. "Yes," he said. "I showed them."

They talked casually as they ate the rest of their dinner. When they were done, David gathered the plates and started to load the dishes into the dishwasher.

Natalie was more tired than usual tonight and still needed to drive back to Toronto. The roads were fine and well salted, but weariness had set in the instant she had her last spoonful of stew. When she mentioned she should get on the road, David asked her to stay a while longer.

"Relax in the living room, and I'll make some tea. I had someone come in to clean the chimney and drop some wood off. I'd like to get a fire going," he said.

He had never asked her to stay longer before, so she agreed, despite her fatigue. And the prospect of a fire seemed thrilling—she hadn't been in a house with a real fireplace for a long time.

In the living room, they started building a little tipi of kindling and paper, to which they added some thin, halved wooden logs. David was more supervisory than hands-on while he sat in his leather chair giving instructions—not all of which Natalie listened to. Was it only a few months ago he would have been pleased to have his private time and happily send her on her way? She smiled at this new David that had thawed since his sickness. Yet another indication that his comfort with her was increasing.

After lighting the fire and blowing on it to get it going, she stood up as the small flames licked logs. She didn't want to sit down yet in case the fire needed a few more pokes to catch.

Natalie glanced over at the wall unit, the ornate beauty that had struck her on her first visit. It was almost too feminine to live in the house of a lone bachelor who had a utilitarian taste in everything else. What a strange mixture of feelings were locked in that case—caged, protected. There was love, nurturing, loss, authority and abuse, envy, covetousness. All the women in David's life resided there, past and present: his mother, his sister, Ayisha, Natalie … and Elinor.

That's when she noticed she couldn't see the photo, the broken one from David's bedroom she had placed there. Approaching the cabinet, she confirmed it was gone. But the photo had been there a week ago; she was certain of it.

"Did you get a new frame for that picture?" she asked him as he stared at the fire.

"Which one?"

"The broken one. Of Elinor."

"No."

"Is it upstairs?"

"No."

"You didn't throw it out, did you?"

"Of course, I did."

He left it at that; nothing more. She didn't press him further. He could slide into the old David quick enough when he chose to, especially when he didn't want to talk about something.

When they were both confident that the fire was catching well, David put a screen in front and told her to relax while he finished tidying up in the kitchen.

Natalie sat on the small couch. She placed her face on the armrest near the fire and closed her eyes. She just needed a quick rest. Soon, the heat from the fire bathed her skin with a massage-like warmth. She listened to the small crackles and pops of the wood. There was so much work to do. The drive home would be so long.

She needed an apartment here. Yes, more viewings scheduled next week. Maybe she needed to be less picky—just take one.

She drifted off into half-sleep, but aware of movements around her. The fire was still there. She heard David come into the room. There was the sound of him placing something on the table in front of her. There was the sound of the leather moaning, groaning, as he sat in his chair opposite her. Tea and drive. If she didn't leave soon, she never would.

She opened her eyes and sat up quickly. David was reading a magazine across from her. He looked over when she stirred.

"What time is it?" she asked, alarmed.

"It's eight thirty. Enigma is working you too hard. You should take a break," he said.

"Later, when there's time."

"Never time," he snorted. "Remember, you're killing yourself for someone else. Amazing what a sliver of equity does to people."

"It's all I've got. And I think I can grow it. I can grow Enigma too."

He eyed her thoughtfully and shook his head. "Perhaps Xavier is smarter than I give him credit for. He might not know what he's doing, but he had enough sense to hire you," he remarked.

She shrugged. "We'll see."

She reached for the tea David had placed for her on the table. There was a small velvety box beside it.

"What's this?" she queried, picking it up.

"I wanted to give you something."

"Oh?" she said, puzzled.

The box looked like something jewelry would normally go in. David nodded at her encouragingly to proceed. Gently and slowly, she flipped the lid of the box up and looked down at a simple, polished gold ring.

Natalie looked at him, trying to understand. "Did you get this for me?"

"It was my mother's wedding ring," he said softly.

Natalie pulled the ring out of its resting place and held it between her thumb and index finger.

"She gave it to me just before she died," he added.

She was so surprised at the gift, she could say nothing. David was giving her this remnant, this memory, of his mother? The simplicity of the ring concealed the depth of his gesture.

"David, are you sure?" she whispered, still astonished.

"Very sure. Your heart is like my mother's. I think of her sometimes when I watch you. It should be passed down to you." He smiled at her. He so seldom smiled.

"God, David ... thank you." Should she get up? Should she hug him?

His next words shook her. They were subtle, but they were filled with so much meaning. "I want it to stay in the family. I'm glad it's yours now. It has taken me a long time to tell you. I know."

Acknowledged—finally! Her eyes began to water. There was no great emotional gush. Just happiness, closure, resolution. She had known all along, and so had he. But now he finally accepted it.

CHAPTER 26

Reacquainting *(Richard Earning, May 2005)*

ON a late Saturday afternoon in May, when his day ended on the site, Richard drove to one of his favorite bookstores in Waterloo to peruse some titles. Still in his dusty workpants and steel-toed boots, a grease-stained shirt and a few days' stubble on his face, he walked into the store, uncaring of his appearance.

Words Worth Books had long been the preferred destination for book lovers before the big-box book chains emerged. It didn't have the breadth of selection that the box stores had, but it had a community feel, and the owners knew their stock intimately. It still did a good business with a faithful customer base.

Richard was reading a few hours every day now, not just to be escapist, but as a form and method of study. He was interested in story structures, in character voices, in the turns of phrases that authors used, how plots were hatched. He was writing a little more too, trying to finish the little snippets of short stories and scenes he began. No great manuscript in progress—or even the thought of one—just a desire to practice and complete something, anything.

Today's trip, however, was not to stock up on fiction. Richard had another purpose for being here—a different set of books in mind. Over the past couple of months, as each day passed, then each week, an idea burrowed itself deep into his brain until he knew it needed to be acted upon and explored in further detail.

In the travel section, he claimed a chair adjacent to the shelves that held all manner of guidebooks for every corner of the world. He targeted the European guides, since he had already resolved that his first journey out of Canada would be to the Old World. Grabbing a series of books from Rick Steves and Lonely Planet to Frommer's and Let's Go, he sat in the chair and scanned itineraries, trying to plot a possible route a traveler might take if he were silly enough to go on a long backpacking and hosteling expedition.

This was his new purpose forming, the goal that he told nobody of for fear of censure or scorn. Yes, he might well agree with people that he was lost in his life right now; but in being waylaid, he was considering ideas that he would have dismissed as unreasonable and foolish only a few months previously. Had he not wanted to travel for a long time? Why not save up some money and go abroad? If he could do it, if he could manage it, why shouldn't he? There would always be the common drudgery of life, of work, upon his return.

He wasn't certain which countries he could go to or what towns and sites he would visit. All of it was still vague and hazy—except for one city. A full itinerary had been made for it last year, and Richard had every intention of beginning his travels in Paris; that much he knew. Paris—it was a city whose name was almost inseparable from thoughts of Augusta. Still, he longed to see the great museums and sights that he had traveled to in his imagination. Would it be different without her company?

Richard still craved her despite everything she had done. When was she getting married? Would she follow through with it, or would she stop before walking off the precipice and seek him out to beg for his forgiveness? A silly fantasy: Paris, she followed him there, sought him out, found him at a cafe, told him she was a fool, told him she loved him …

"Richard?"

The sound of his name pulled him from his fancies of a cafe at night sitting beside a woman with a mischievous smile. His vision returned to the bright bookstore and its aisles. The inquirer was just to his right; he turned. A young woman stood, uneasily, looking at him. It took him a moment to register her, here, in this place.

"Natalie," he said. Though he had spoken it aloud as if greeting her, it was more of a declaration to himself. His immediate thought was of disappointment. For a fleeting moment, there had been hope that the woman who called his name, who had summoned him from his musings, was the same one he was supposed to be with in that distant city.

"Yeah. Hi," she said. She smiled meekly, watching him closely with an air of trepidation. Her torso was turned to face him as if she wanted to linger, while her legs pointed down the aisle as if she might walk away at any moment. She was holding a cup of coffee in one hand, while her other hand carried a rain jacket with a book tucked under her arm.

He felt shame rush into him. Natalie had borne the brunt of his anger months ago—he had misdirected all his frustrations in a single text to this innocent bystander. He knew she had little to do with his ousting, but she was the only person he had lashed out at. Maybe because she had benefited from his demise, regardless of her part to play in it.

"What have you been up to?" Natalie asked. "I heard you were doing some general contracting stuff?"

"Pretty much. I work for my friend doing renovations."

She needed a few seconds to digest this, as if she was confirming something she never believed in the first place. "So, this isn't temporary? Like, it's full time?"

When he nodded in agreement, Natalie's face recorded surprise. "Oh," she said. And then "oh," again. "That's great," but her tone implied she was skeptical of how great this intelligence was. "So, you left tech completely?" She looked embarrassed and was striving to recover. She no longer appeared as if she might dash away and even moved closer to his chair.

"Tech kinda left me," Richard replied.

Though he tried to grin to let her know he was fine with how things were, Natalie's face fell. She tensed up. The book slid out from underneath her arm, hit the floor, and tumbled to land near the pile of European travel guides at his feet. He leaned over in his chair to pick her book up at the same time she knelt to retrieve it.

"*Managing Talent?*" he said, reading the title on the front cover as he handed it back to her. "Jeremy giving you grief?"

Natalie was frozen in position at eye level with him. He could smell her perfume, a deep and strong spice. She was dressed casually in blue jeans and a long-sleeve white shirt with flaring cuffs.

"No, just keeping up to date on stuff," she said, taking the book back from him. "I like this store. I'm glad you told me about it. Do you remember?" She didn't make an effort to stand back up but remained crouched near his chair.

"Yes ... I do. Still only business books, I see." Then, realizing what day it was, he said, "Hey, why are you in town on a Saturday?"

"I moved here in April, just over near the park," Natalie said.

"Far cry from Toronto."

"Definitely. A lot quieter. I'm getting familiar with the place now—it's pretty small."

"Does small and quiet mean boring?"

"It's different," she laughed. "I'm working too much to really enjoy anyplace, so maybe low key is just as well."

Seeing her now, outside of Enigma, was like beholding her for the first time. He became suddenly conscious of his own appearance. His shirt stuck together in some parts from wiping caulking on it and there were stains from paint, grease, and drywall mud covering his pants. He probably stank. There was a time when he would never have been out in public looking like this. There was a pang of embarrassment and insecurity that he tried to push away.

"You look really different as a handyman," she remarked.

"Looks can fool, because I'm not that handy."

She reached over and picked up some of the books he had assembled: Eastern Europe, France, Italy, Spain, Scandinavia, Germany.

"You seem a little undecided about where you're going for vacation," she remarked.

"I suppose I am. Just trying to do some planning. Research."

"I suggest picking a country first. No way you'll see all of this. How long are you going for?"

"However long my money lasts. Six months maybe, a year—who knows."

Natalie's head shot back. "Are you serious?"

Richard nodded. "I've often wanted to travel. Never did it, though. I think now is the time." That was the first time he had spoken of his idea to anyone, this silly plan that he was turning over and over in his thoughts. Now that he had given it voice, now that it had been heard by someone else's ears and lived in someone else's mind, it seemed more concrete. For too long, it had only charged up and down the wires of his brain in solitude and isolation.

Natalie shook her head. "Holy shit," she said at last. "You're like a new person. I don't think I ever pegged you as a free-spirited kinda guy—you were always a bit reserved. Now, you're doing construction and talking about traveling for a year. Are you the same Richard I knew in the Pit?"

He couldn't help but laugh at that. No, he was not the same. He was more lost now than he could ever recall. The future was a great mystery. And for once, that seemed all right.

He asked her if she had any suggestions. She shrugged her shoulders. "Never been anywhere overseas," she said. "I'm jealous."

"How are things at Enigma?" Richard inquired. The question was tucked into the pocket of his cheek for a while. He was interested to hear her take, especially after Jeremy's transformation.

"It's good, I guess," she said.

"You said you were busy at work. That's good, right?"

"Oh yes, too busy, I think. The product is a little more stable now. Easier to use too. I've worked with Jeremy a lot to get it to a point where we can sell it elsewhere as modules—and we have. We closed a deal with a small college, and I'm hopeful about a proposal we have in with one of the universities in Toronto. It will be a small project there to start, but it can grow. And Jeremy ..." Natalie stopped, as if catching herself saying something inappropriate. She looked away briefly. "We're busy, yeah, lots to do ..."

Richard had done his best to try to focus on looking pleased instead of disappointed, but something in his visage must have betrayed him. Maybe a downward turn in his lips, a flicker of irritation in his eye, he couldn't say, but it had compelled her to stop talking. He realized he hadn't fully moved on from the events last November—his anger was latent and could still be triggered.

"I'm glad things are going well," he remarked. But he wasn't—he heard the disappointment in his own voice while he tried to stay composed.

Natalie looked at her lap. "Xavier shouldn't have done what he did to you. I don't know what happened, but I know it was wrong. Please don't blame me. I never knew any of what he was planning. I swear I never would have gone along with it, and I don't feel right about it."

Evidently, Xavier had abstained from mentioning anything to her of Richard's relationship with Augusta. And Richard made no attempt to complete Natalie's understanding of events.

"It's not your problem, Natalie," he told her. "And I'm sorry about that text I sent. It wasn't meant for you. Wasn't thinking right."

Natalie closed her eyes and rubbed her temples for a moment. "No, I understand. We're good."

Richard was unsettled. Hearing about Enigma's success from Natalie made him wonder what his financial situation could have been had he stayed. Of course, he wouldn't be happy, but he would be content and financially secure. What would his world look like if he never met Augusta? There was the trigger—and the need to be alone.

Standing up, he began to restock the travel books back on the shelf except for two that he thought promising for his planning. "I realized I haven't eaten dinner. I should get home. But it was nice seeing you," he said.

Natalie frowned slightly then perked up. "I need dinner too. Want to grab something together?"

"I can't go out like this. I'm in my work clothes. And I need a shower!"

"I'll wait. I don't mind if you want to go home and change first," she said. She was chewing the inside of her lip, watching him.

Struck by her persistence, and at a loss to give an excuse for avoiding her or her offer, he conceded. He did owe her an apology of sorts, and maybe dinner would clean the slate. "Okay," he agreed, "but as long as we don't talk about Enigma."

"Deal," she remarked enthusiastically. "That suits me fine."

They agreed to meet at a pub just up the street at 7 p.m.

The thought he had while he was driving home to clean up was that he hadn't been out for dinner with a woman in months.

PART FIVE: COUPLING

CHAPTER 27

Another Spring Gathering (Natalie Mitchell, May 2005)

B ILL Spindrall was telling Sanjay the story of his "lucky wife." It was the second time Natalie had heard it tonight, and she noticed how practiced Bill was in the recital. He must have written a script, rehearsed it, and memorized it for occasions such as this. Unfortunately, it seemed to be the only script he had; fortunately, the times he could use it were few.

"She always steered me true, you know?" Bill was saying. "I wouldn't have been able to invest in Enigma without her. I had bought some goldmining stock in a company called Bre-X when it was still under a dollar. In less than two years, it was climbing well past $200. We'd just had our second child and were living in a two-bedroom apartment. Not the nicest place, but nice enough for the rent we were paying. But Margaret wanted a house. She told me, 'If you're going to work all day and night and leave me to raise the kids, the least you can do is get us a half-decent home.' I fought her; fought her tooth and nail. Said I would have to sell these stocks if I was to get her a house. And she told me to do it."

Sanjay looked at Bill with a calm face belying the impatience of his eyes. He no doubt would have preferred that Bill's much-practiced speech be shorter. But he probably felt obligated to listen out of politeness, since he knew Bill might be influential in bringing him business.

Xavier had made it a point to walk Sanjay over to Bill and Natalie. Sanjay was the VP of sales for a company that provided offshore developers and QA resources to companies. He was working with a few medium-sized organizations in the area and some larger ones in Toronto. Natalie was no fool; she knew Xavier had a specific purpose for inviting Sanjay to the gathering and facilitating this conversation.

"Lord, I fought her," Bill resumed, interpreting Sanjay's head nodding as abounding interest instead of a signal to get to the point. "Told her we would all regret it years later when the stocks climbed higher. 'I care about the family today,' she said, 'not about money in twenty years.' So, I sold it to appease her—at around $250 a share. Walked away and bought our house outright. And then a few months later, the whole Bre-X thing went bust! No gold to be had in Indonesia. The company went bankrupt—people lost everything! People even started dying. Some geologist who had lied about the gold samples jumped from a helicopter when it was flying over the Indonesian jungle; though there is a rumor that he might have been assisted with a push. The CEO moved to the Bahamas and died of an aneurism some years back—that was after his house was broken into and he was tied up by people demanding money. The whole business was cursed! But I made my money, thanks to lucky Marg! Then, when I was thinking about Enigma but was too scared to approach James Hardich, you know what she told me? 'Go and talk to him. What's the worst that can happen?' she said. And that's what I did. I got 'im. God rest his soul. Got James Hardich to invest. And, I have to say, Enigma's done quite well."

Natalie, sipping on her glass of wine, couldn't disagree with the last statement. Enigma's prospects were looking very good. In addition to landing their first client outside of their co-development university partners, all signs pointed to winning another contract with the University of Toronto. And Natalie was working on two more proposals for other educational institutions. Yes, things were looking up for Enigma.

Sanjay took the closing of Bill's story as an opportunity to start his own inquiries about the type of developers at Enigma and what their processes were. Bill, like a faucet just turned on, gushed information. Where Sanjay might have been disappointed in Bill's long-windedness before, he now seemed very pleased with the extensive details he was receiving. And Natalie was left to wish Bill didn't reveal so much—she hadn't bought into the outsourcing model and was worried about what Xavier was planning.

At least Bill was talking to someone else other than her. He had been clinging to her most of the night, and in so doing, had prevented her from socializing as she normally would. When she had first arrived at the party, she had been paraded about by Xavier and introduced to several guests before she saw Bill standing alone in the dining room with several groups of people talking around him, but never to him. He was in a black suit, the jacket slightly too long for his arms, and the pants too baggy at the break point. He looked like a boy dressed in his father's clothes. With hands in his pockets, he beamed with a smile and nodded at anyone standing near him or passing by him. Nobody, however, bothered to converse with him. Pitying him his ostracization, she went over to him and had been trapped since.

Though Bill was pleased to be at the gathering, he might have been dismayed to learn he was not entirely welcome. Natalie knew he wouldn't have been invited were it not for Elinor Hardich.

"Mother says I must invite him. Otherwise, it suggests I have bad manners. I suppose there's no harm in a court jester," Xavier had said to her scathingly at the office a week ago.

She began to sense that she, too, was an outcast as long as she was with Bill. Only Bart Miller had joined them for a short time to give his greetings to Natalie and ask after David. Bill, unable to read the situation, immediately started to belch out the story of his lucky wife. Though Bart listened, he kindly excused himself midway through the tale on the premise that he had just seen someone he needed to speak with immediately.

Natalie had to admit the Spring Gathering really was a splendid affair. The Hardiches spared no expense at this party. There was all manner of hors d'oeuvres and skewers of vegetables and chicken, as well as steak and noodle bowls. Someone had said that at 10:30 p.m., the spread would be taken down and replaced with desserts, including a chocolate fondue. She was looking forward to that.

The rooms on the main floor of the house were cozily filled with the well-to-do acquaintances of the Hardiches. She saw Jocelyn Miller across the room, looking gorgeous in a dress slightly risqué for a party of this respectability: a deep V-slit cut down the front to her navel. Xavier was beside her, talking to Derek Lam, his soon-to-be brother-in-law. She also saw a few people she had met only briefly and wanted to talk to. If she was going to break away from Bill for a bit, now was the time.

She was determining whom to approach when she heard her name. Even as she turned to see the owner of the voice, she felt disconcerted. She knew who it was; a point confirmed when she stared into the smiling face of Augusta Hardich.

"Hi! It's so nice to see you!" Natalie said, hoping she sounded genuine.

She was wary of Augusta; there was something not quite right with Xavier's sister. David had said he found the girl to be "too clever for anyone's good, including her own," and that she was "pleasant, but one was never sure what she was about." Natalie couldn't corroborate David's opinion, but she had her own assessment of Augusta. She had only met Augusta once, and what she took away from that encounter was a certain reticence from the woman.

"I'm so glad you came," Augusta said, surprising Natalie with a light kiss on the cheek. Then she linked arms with Natalie as if they had always been the best of friends.

"I hear you're engaged with a wedding coming up. Congratulations!" Natalie said, looking down at Augusta's arm intertwined around her own, confused by the display of affection. She saw the large diamond that now encircled one of Augusta's fingers. There was no doubt that rock cost a pretty penny.

Augusta shrugged as if dismissing the comment. "Come with me. Mother wants a word," she said.

"Oh," Natalie said. She had not seen Elinor since her last visit to the house. "Is everything okay?"

"No, she's upset that David isn't here," Augusta responded, pulling on Natalie to guide her away from Bill and Sanjay.

Bill, seeing Natalie being torn from him, looked alarmed, and he made a move to leave Sanjay. But Augusta abruptly turned to him, placed her hand gently on his breast over his heart, and drew close to him.

"No, no, Bill," she said tenderly. "You cannot come—this is women's business. I'll return her to you eventually." The smile she gave pacified him, and he submitted readily to her.

The rooms were full enough of guests that walking abreast was impossible, so Augusta led Natalie by the hand as they snaked through the partygoers. On occasion, Augusta would chirp into a conversation she overhead as they passed a group of people and make some comment or other.

Together, they moved through the kitchen and into another room.

"You clearly needed saving," Augusta remarked turning her head as they walked. "You'll not meet many people standing with Bill all night."

"He seemed lonely, and nobody else was talking to him."

"Of course not; he's lucky money," Augusta said stopping so quickly and turning around that Natalie almost bumped into her. Augusta's cheek was nearly touching Natalie's; she brought her mouth close to Natalie's ear and gently spoke. "The snobs here don't like people who make it by a fluke. It disrupts the ideals of 'good old capitalism,' where hard work and intelligence are the things that get rewarded. Bill's viewed as a bit of a lottery winner. He's done it to himself, really. If he had just said he made his money by investing in the market, it would have been acceptable. But all the talk of his lucky wife grates on folks."

"Are you one of the folks?" Natalie inquired. The question was more abrupt than she had intended, but she was feeling a certain uncomfortable injustice on behalf of Bill.

Augusta laughed, and her eyes danced alive as she pulled her face back to look at Natalie. "We live in the West—we've all won the lottery. And everyone in this house is luckier than most. The system has its hypocrisy, and we must go along with it." She turned and clutched Natalie's hand again to guide her through the crowd once more. They entered a room with a sitting area and a door to the side, where several sandals were laid out.

Elinor Hardich was on a loveseat with Cassandra Martin beside her. As soon as the two young women entered, Cassandra stood and greeted Natalie like a relative she hadn't seen in years.

"You're so lovely. Isn't she, Elinor? You and Augusta standing together are absolute visions! You should have seen all the men looking at you two when you were coming over here. Their expressions … oh, it was very interesting!" Cassandra placed her hands on Natalie's shoulders and kissed her cheeks.

In her peripheral vision, Natalie thought she saw Augusta smirk at the display. Even Elinor's brow wrinkled slightly.

"I wonder if Derek or Xavier have any friends for this girl," Cassandra continued. "She's a catch! Now that Augusta is ineligible and off market—and taken a fine bachelor with her—we must make Natalie our new project!"

Augusta's arms were crossed. "I'm sure she'll do well enough without our assistance," she haughtily commented.

"Really?" Cassandra asked. "Really?"

"Really," Augusta chimed back dismissively.

"Where is David?" Elinor enquired of Natalie, a touch of concern in her voice.

"He won't be able to make it, I'm afraid. He's sick, but he sends his best," Natalie lied. That was what David had told her to say. What would this woman think if she knew her picture had been on David's bedside table for decades? And how would she feel to know it had been broken and disposed of?

Cassandra's hand went to her heart. "David too ill to come? Interesting! He always comes. Doesn't he, Elinor? He's never missed a Spring Gathering. Am I right?"

Elinor received Natalie's intelligence with a frown. "How long has he been ill?"

"A few days," Natalie lied again. "Seems to be the flu, and he didn't want to spread it." She felt uncomfortable deceiving Elinor, a person who had only shown her kindness. She seemed to always be lying for the man.

"The flu? In spring? Interesting," Cassandra remarked. "I didn't know that was going around. Perhaps it's the start."

"He's never missed a gathering. Always been here," Elinor said, echoing Cassandra. Then to Natalie, she asked, "Has he been to the doctor?"

"Not yet, no."

"He's missed a couple of my events too. Did you know that? Did he say why? It's not the same without him."

"He didn't mention it," Natalie said.

"Has he said anything about us, about me?" Elinor queried.

"Mother," Augusta interrupted soothingly, "Natalie is our guest, not an informer."

Elinor shook her head in apology. "Yes, forgive me."

The women of the group chatted on, although Natalie seemed to be the primary topic, for she had to answer several questions. How was she getting on in Waterloo? How were her grandparents? Did she have many friends yet? Was Xavier working her too hard? Why didn't she come by to visit at the house? Wouldn't it be nice if she went out with Augusta sometime?

Throughout the Natalie-centric conversation, Augusta was quiet. She was listening intently, however, as if scrutinizing Natalie's answers.

At last, Augusta seemed to grow weary of Cassandra's fawning praise and interest in Natalie. But instead of leaving the women, she declared that Natalie needed some respite; after all, Natalie had come to the party to socialize with everyone. Once again, Augusta took Natalie by the hand and said, "Come outside with me. We'll see who's there."

Natalie was instructed to put on a pair of rubber sandals, and they stepped out onto the veranda. Heat lamps had been set up at intervals to provide warmth to those outside, mostly smokers. The night was cool, but when Augusta positioned the two of them under one of the lamps, Natalie felt quite comfortable. Thankfully, there was no breeze.

Augusta pulled out a pack of cigarettes and offered Natalie one, but she declined. Augusta smiled and lit it for herself.

"Are you having a good time?" Augusta queried. "You can be honest."

"Wonderful, thank you. It's quite a party."

"Did Burlow send you on his behalf?"

"No, like I said he hasn't been feeling …"

"We both know that's not true. He's been avoiding my mother." She took a drag of the cigarette and watched Natalie's face. "My mother knows it too."

Natalie stared at her shoes, feeling uncomfortable. Lying to Augusta was pointless. Not only could Augusta decipher truth, she was bold enough to call out the lies.

Augusta nodded in satisfaction. "Did he tell you why? Is it because Mama moved the money away from him?"

Natalie shook her head. "I don't know. He never said anything to me about money."

What money was Augusta referring to? And why did she defend Natalie against her mother's interrogation only to fish for answers herself? She had left Elinor's frying pan to jump into Augusta's fire.

"Burlow made no mention of it? Well, we all have our secrets, I suppose," Augusta remarked with an amused smile. "Are you fond of Burlow?"

The question seemed strange. Of course, she was. "Yes," Natalie replied, surprised. "He's been very kind to me and my family."

"Indeed, he has," Augusta said. "Why do you suppose that is?"

"My mother and David—"

"No, no," Augusta interrupted. "Not that version. Come on, Natalie, we need to be on better terms. You can tell me the truth. I want us to move past the story you and David are telling everyone. You can trust me."

Natalie's heart quickened. She felt a trap closing. Something in Augusta's manner was insidious. She was not fishing for possibilities or shooting arrows into the sky to see where they landed.

"Trust you with what? I don't understand," Natalie said.

There was a small turn in Augusta's manner. Her amusement was still there, but it had a tinge of annoyance or irritation in it. Or was that malice? "Do I need to spell it out, Natalie? We're talking about you and Burlow and what you're playing at." She lowered her voice, but it was more taut than usual. "We're talking about who we both know your father is. Which is the reason you're here after all, isn't it? What's the endgame with this charade?"

"You know, then? How?" Natalie whispered, surprised.

Augusta answered by spluttering smoke out of her lips in a breathy laugh. "Does it matter?"

"Who told you?"

Augusta only smiled. "Just be honest with me," she said.

Now, Natalie understood David's comments about Augusta; she did know more than everyone else. How had she found out? Surely, it was not by David. And what was she going to do with this information? With the truth? All Natalie could do now was convince Augusta that she shouldn't say anything to anyone.

"There's no game. He's just not ready to tell people yet," Natalie said. "Maybe he never will be. I don't want to be the source of scandal for him. Please respect that. Although I've always known, he only admitted it to me a few months ago when he gave me this," she said, holding up her hand to show the simple gold band on her finger. "It was his mother's wedding ring. If he wants to tell people what I am to him, he'll do it when the time is right and when it suits him. Please. Please say nothing to anyone."

Augusta stared at her, a confused expression on her face. She reached out and touched Natalie's hand, touched the ring that David had given her. At last, digesting the news, she asked, "He gave you his mother's ring? What did he say?"

"That it should stay in the family."

Augusta's brow was furrowed. Then, running her finger along the simple smooth surface of the band, she nodded. "I never thought him sentimental enough to keep such things. Never thought him a man to want such things," she said thoughtfully while she looked at Natalie.

"You can't say anything. Please. Do you promise?" Natalie was desperate to obtain a sworn silence.

"Of course. I'll say nothing." Augusta gently squeezed, then released, Natalie's hand. "Send my regards to old Burlow. He's a good man."

Natalie wondered if she was being played by Augusta, the same way she had watched Augusta play Bill Spindrall earlier. A touch, a soothing remark …

Augusta stood smoking in silence for a time, lost in her own thoughts. Then she casually just switched the conversation. "I knew someone who worked at Enigma once. He was at this very gathering last year. Richard, I think his name was. Did you know him?"

Natalie couldn't understand why Augusta would flit to another topic so quickly. Perhaps she was trying to push away the intimacy of the secret they had just shared. "Yes, he doesn't work with us anymore," she responded.

"Oh?" Augusta took another drag of the cigarette. "He didn't like it, then?"

"I don't know exactly what happened, but there was a disagreement between your brother and Richard. You should ask Xavier."

Augusta smiled. "Well, Xavier is a disagreeable sort of man. I'm not surprised. There may be a cautionary tale for you there." She chuckled. "Do you know what happened to Richard? Where he went?"

Odd that Natalie would now be questioned on this topic after only seeing Richard a couple of weeks ago. But she offered up the information she knew readily. "You'd have to know him well enough to understand how crazy this sounds, but he's doing renovation work. He's left IT altogether. Traded in the suit for steel-toed boots."

"You still talk to him then?" Augusta asked.

"From time to time. We had dinner a couple of weeks back," Natalie said. She did not tell Augusta that she had seen Richard about five times since meeting him in the bookstore.

"I see. I wonder if he remembers me. Last year I was trying to keep my foul smoking habit discreet. He was kind enough to give me cigarettes, and I thought him entertaining. He's well, then?"

"As far as I can tell," Natalie answered. "He's saving money, and he plans to do some backpacking odyssey across Europe."

Richard had never mentioned that he knew Augusta. But then again, it was one brief night; perhaps he had forgotten. Though, how one could forget an interaction with Augusta Hardich was beyond Natalie.

Augusta's reaction was odd. Digesting this news, she winced, as if in pain. She looked away. Then, with a long inhale of her cigarette and a pronounced exhale of smoke, she threw her cigarette on the veranda and vigorously twisted the toe of her heeled shoe onto the sparkling end.

"Yes," she said softly. "I remember him wanting to go to Paris. He told me that. Sounds like he's doing what he wants. I'm happy for him." She crossed her arms and huddled in on herself as if she were suddenly cold, despite the warmth of the heat lamp. "We should get in; Bill will be beside himself in your absence."

Augusta put her arm around Natalie's waist and guided her to the door. But before they went inside, Augusta paused, saying, "I'd like us to talk more and be friends. We should meet up for coffee."

Natalie smiled and nodded to her escort. But she felt little inclination to be Augusta's friend. No, there was something about Augusta that she couldn't understand. David was right: who knew to what end Augusta applied her knowledge?

How had she found out about David and her?

CHAPTER 28

Pacts *(David Burlow, June 2005)*

THE early June night was unusually warm. David remained inside the house, taking comfort in the air conditioning. He wished Natalie was with him. He was becoming increasingly fond of her presence and conversation. Her appearances at the house were more regular now, even if only for short visits. But today, she had left to visit her grandparents in Toronto after work, something she tried to do every few weekends.

Natalie had stopped in for a drink earlier in the week, and they'd sat on his porch for over an hour, talking. She was worried about Xavier's scheming with an outsourcing company. In a strange irony, David found himself defending Xavier's investigations. "Why not outsource? If it's a commodity service and you can save money—do it," he told her. She didn't want to hear that reasoning. She continued to argue about local jobs and the importance of having the team close at hand. He found she could be remarkably idealistic at times, a trait that was good for humanity and employees but bad for business.

Now, David poured himself a scotch and sat in his leather chair in the living room to read. He wasn't at it long, however, when there was a knock at the front door. He looked at his watch. It was 9:30 p.m., too late for a solicitation or unplanned visit.

Both irritated and curious, he stood up, walked to the door, and opened it. The sun had set, but the afterglow of twilight still lingered in the park across the street. Darkness did not hide the figure before him, though he still peered at it for a long time to make sure his eyes weren't playing tricks on him. For a fleeting moment, he saw Elinor's young face from decades ago at an Oktoberfest hall.

But this was not Elinor. Rather, it was her daughter, Augusta.

Augusta was wearing a black pencil skirt and a white blouse with ornate cuffs flipped backward. Her red-brown hair was pulled upward in a bun, but wisps of bangs dangled on either side of her face. A thin leather purse strap crossed over her chest. She was slimmer than Elinor would have been at that age, and she didn't have her mother's soft eyes. David always found Augusta's eyes inquisitive, searching, prying.

"Is everything all right?" he asked nervously. Had something happened to Elinor?

"Yes, fine," she said, a smile playing across her face.

When he made no movement and only stared at her, she advanced to be so close that he felt compelled to retreat a step back into the house.

"Are you going to invite me in, or do I have to throw my weight around?"

He stepped aside quietly to make room for her to enter.

"I hope I'm not interrupting anything," Augusta said, walking in and removing her shoes, presuming a welcome before he extended it. She rightly guessed there was nobody there other than him. She looked into the living room and strode in as if the place was familiar to her.

"Why are you here?" David queried. He was searching his memory—had she ever been here before? Yes, once he recalled, when she was young. She had come with her dad.

She laughed. "We'll get to that. Plenty to talk about." Augusta picked up David's drink on the side table, held it to her nose, and winced. "Do you have anything other than scotch?"

He stared at her for a good while before answering, amazed at her impertinence. "Wine," he answered. "Will you really be staying that long?"

"A wine then," Augusta responded, ignoring his question.

Perturbed, David went to the kitchen to open a bottle. He half liked this woman and half distrusted her. It was the half that distrusted her that caused an agitation in him, a discomfort in his stomach, a foreboding.

Natalie had told him of what transpired at the Spring Gathering with Augusta. He had feigned shock when Natalie confusedly described Augusta's seeming omniscience. But he knew Augusta was merely poking at Natalie with one of the rumors that had been in circulation for almost a year about their relationship. The details of the rumors varied, but they all had the same outcome: Natalie was David's child from some clandestine affair. Where before he would have been appalled at the story and what Elinor might think, he was now pleased that this is what people were inclined to believe.

But what had brought Augusta to him tonight? He doubted it was to get more details relating to Natalie's paternity. If this had been a preoccupation of Augusta's, she would have shown up much sooner. So, what then?

Like everyone else, he had a hard time deciphering Augusta's behavior. James and Elinor used to say that Augusta leaned toward rebellion and revolt against any established order, and, indeed, social norms themselves. She had plenty of episodes that supported such a description of her. The political and social views she sometimes espoused were socialist enough to be shocking to her parents' conservative friends. And her boyfriends, before Derek, seemed to be selected by her only for their ability to deliver maximum shock value. They were spiritual or anarchistic waifs that made asses of themselves at Spring Gatherings or family occasions. James had once remarked that Augusta was intent on antagonizing the whole family with her fashionable Marxist education and friends.

But David did not subscribe to such a simple reasoning away of Augusta's motivations. For his part, he believed there was some deeper meaning behind Augusta's behavior, as if she was trying to prove a point. It's just that nobody understood what it was.

Was tonight one of her points?

He returned to the living room and saw Augusta was at the wall unit. The ornate vine-carved doors were open, and she was holding the picture of Natalie and her mother. Why had she picked that image of all the pictures? Did she want to know something, or did she know something?

When Augusta heard him place the bottle of wine and glass on the table in the sitting area, she put the picture gently back on the shelf and closed the cabinet doors.

"I'm beginning to think you don't like us anymore," she said casually as she went to the couch to sit down on the spot Natalie normally occupied. "You missed a Spring Gathering—a cardinal sin. Everyone noticed."

David did not sit. He stood behind his chair with his hands resting on the leather back, as if putting a protective object between himself and Augusta. "I was sick."

"Of course, you were."

"It's unfortunate. I missed the opportunity to congratulate you and Derek," David said. "I'm happy for your engagement. By all accounts, Derek's quite a capital match."

"Isn't he?" she said. "I believe there are many people secretly frustrated by our pending union. They wonder how a Commie like me, with nothing but contempt for the privileges of my station, managed to accomplish it."

David pondered her self-reflection. Yes, there would be many in the Hardich circle confused by the attraction of these opposites. "Doesn't matter what they say. I know your father liked him and would have been pleased," he said.

"Well, at least my family's fond of him," she said.

He saw it, a flickering smirk, then the smile back in all its finery.

"But you're right," she resumed. "Like Xavier, my father probably saw an opportunity in Derek. Access to a network of money or something. My family is good at finding people to use, to ride out— or ride up, as it were. You know all about that, don't you?"

He paused before answering. "I don't understand your meaning," he returned, wondering what she was stabbing at.

Augusta studied him, as if waiting for him to confess something freely, and then she gave a brief, airy laugh. She reached into her purse, rummaged inside it, and produced a pack of cigarettes. She took one out and rested it between her lips. "May I smoke in here?"

David didn't know she had acquired this habit. Was it new? But he chuckled as he watched her, for, in her usual way, she asked questions out of politeness and assumed an answer always to her taste. The lighter's flame was already dancing inches from the end of the cigarette protruding from her mouth. Her eyes were on him, waiting for the faintest nod of assent, which he gave. He grabbed a seldom-used ashtray from a cupboard in the wall unit and handed it to her.

"You know, for a long time I've contemplated how people use each other," she said, exhaling smoke into the air. "It seems like such an innate quality we all have, to be so completely selfish as to seek benefits at another's expense. I don't speak as one who is innocent of the allegation I level at humanity; I may even be the worst culprit." She paused, staring at the smoke as it broke apart before her. "Exploiting others seems to weave its way into everything about us; it weaves its way into our loves, and our friendships. I suppose it's at the root of our political, economic, and social systems. How could it not be? These systems are created by self-absorbed people like me. Like you."

David huffed in wonder at her. "Did you stop by tonight to discuss these musings? This sounds like bar talk for academics."

Augusta grinned. "We cleaned out my father's office this year. Xavier has claimed it. Did you know that? No? Well, it's his. The room was once the seat of my father's power. Now it's occupied by a pretender. You don't need to say anything—I know you agree. But I had some epiphanies while we purged the history of that room," she said.

David took a drink of his scotch. His fingers were squeezing the leather of the chair.

"My father printed many of his emails. He seems to have held a

242

suspicion about the permanence of digital things. And he was a very meticulous filer, as it turns out. He kept everything. I never took much interest in his affairs, I'll admit, but when we were cleaning, it got to a point where I realized we were just shredding up all your little orders and instructions to him. You always told him exactly what he needed to do. In a sense, we were cleaning out *your* things, not his. I'd have to be a fool not to see that you were the one running the show all these years."

David snorted, his wariness subsiding and replaced with relief. Is that what this was about? These epiphanies he could deal with. "Even if what you say is true, it means nothing. There's no one who would care to hear it," he said.

"There's no one who would care to believe it." She sipped her wine. "Except me," she added.

"And why do you care?"

"Helps me understand things, understand you," Augusta said. "What would motivate a person to do that? To give another man all the glory of his accomplishments. You must see how that's puzzling. And you let everyone believe you were my father's pitiable servant. You know I'm being diplomatic—people have said much more disparaging than that."

"I don't care what people say," David growled.

She raised her head slightly at his anger, one side of her mouth curling into a smirk. She seemed pleased to have struck a nerve in him. "But you do care a little, I think. I can't make out what you got in return for propping up my father all these years. You're too smart to get nothing."

David was considering how to answer her. He never thought anyone would learn of this, and in a strange way, he relished the truth being discovered, even if only by one person. That it was Augusta Hardich, of all people, who saw what nobody else did, should not be surprising. But why was she bringing this up? So many years had gone by—it was all irrelevant.

She was looking at him expectantly with her amused smile. She even beckoned for him to sit down. She had a commanding presence in her demeanor for someone so slight. What was the source of her power? What in her made people succumb to her will—to her presumption? It wasn't charisma, it wasn't compassion—it was something entirely different. That's what always intrigued him about her. She was certainly striking like her mother, but that gave her no authority. No, there was a force of character in her, mixed with mystery, and a quick intellect that made people defer to her. And she expected that deference.

David took a seat in his old leather chair opposite her. If she understood that he was the prime gear in the partnership between him and her father, then why not tell her she was right? There was no harm in it; she could share it with nobody. Besides, the sooner he gave her some tidbits of information, the sooner she would leave. He was still confounded by this visit of hers.

"You don't give your father the credit he deserves," David said. "James had an invaluable gift—he was loved by everyone. That's important when you're trying to raise money to start a venture. People don't love me. I don't have the charms of you Hardiches. And where doors were shut to me because of my look or manner, James could blow them clean off."

"So, he was just your salesman?" Augusta asked dismissively.

"Just? You underestimate that skill," David said. "Let me tell you, for a year I tried to get my own capital to start my business. I had everything planned out. I worked out how I would capture market share with exquisite detail: the types of niche parts I would make, their costs and sales prices, the labor force required to make the parts, the logistical shipping network for transport and the material providers. Everything was ready—except the money to start it. Try as I might, I couldn't secure the financing. I could never sell my idea to the banks or investors. In a way, I guess I was above selling myself or my ideas—I had a crude pride then. If people couldn't see the value of me or my business proposition, then they were fools."

"But the fools had all the money," she chimed in.

"It's an insufferable fact that they do. So, your father was my front man, my filter to distill information down to the ignorant. Everything I did, the opportunities I saw, the facts and data I knew to be true, never stood on their own merit. To bring them to fruition, I needed a translator, a proxy, to communicate it all in embellished terms to people who didn't believe in truth or facts, but in the person who was speaking them. Your father was the person they always believed, the one they wanted to go to dinner with after the presentations. He was the man they would give their money to."

"Still," Augusta said, "you made him quite the man as a reward for his little service. You gave him most of the money and a glorious reputation at your expense. Surely, that was too much."

David shrugged. Maybe it was. He had thought about this before and always landed on the same point. "He was my friend," he said. "He was the only person who ever tried to help me, the only person who believed in me, and the only person who really liked me. In the end, I'm glad it was him that I chose to partner with. I didn't mind giving him the majority of the spoils. He needed it more than I did. He had your mother to look after."

"Ah, of course; he had Elinor, didn't he?" Augusta snickered, butting out her cigarette. "I was trying to figure out the depth of his hold on you, and now I see it." She shook her head. "You poor man; you'd do anything for my mother, wouldn't you? What I really wonder is what secrets you would keep for her happiness."

David glared at her. Had she come to taunt him? "I think you got all the answers you came for tonight," he said.

"The background, perhaps, but not all the answers," she said quietly. She reached into her purse again. This time she produced a carefully folded piece of paper with a clip in one of the corners. "From the time I met your Natalie, I found her intriguing. There was something about her. A familiarity. Something I had seen before but could never place." She handed the paper to David. "Until this."

David reluctantly took the paper from her and unfolded it. His heart nearly stopped. His stomach knotted instantly. He could hardly focus on the contents of the package, his hand was shaking so violently.

The paper clip attached a small, faded Polaroid photograph, but the subjects were still clear. In the photo, A young and smiling James Hardich was sitting at a table. A woman was on his lap with her arms tightly clasped around his neck and her face nuzzled right up against his cheeks. Written below in the white edging of the photo was the caption *James and Ayisha, The Riverboat, 1975*, followed by a small, drawn black heart.

For a long time, David stared at the picture of Ayisha and James. Then he flipped the picture back to see what was on the paper.

It was a photocopy of Ayisha Mitchell's obituary from a newspaper. He knew it well, for he was in possession of a similar clipping.

So, James had thought about Ayisha, had known about her death. He had even stored little fragments of her in the files of his office, not just in the recesses of his mind. *A foolish thing to keep*, David thought. After the lies and the sacrifices that David had made to keep it a secret, James should have had the decency to dispose of any incriminating evidence. And where was James now? Dead. Protected in death. James never had to deal with any of this—he never did.

David could feel Augusta's eyes on him—felt them trying to pry into him. He refused to look up at her. Everything was slipping away, all the order he had tried to maintain. All the facades and histories were unraveling. He sat there, wishing Augusta away. He could hear the flick of her lighter as she lit another cigarette, and the long, deep inhales and exhales of Augusta's breath, followed by the creation of the cloudy smoke between them.

"Natalie knows none of this," Augusta went on. "I only realized that at the Spring Gathering. You gave her your mother's ring. Come, David, are you really leading her on like that? Making her believe you're her father?"

David shook his head, partially in answer, but partially in disbelief. Why had James kept anything? His mind was filling with smoke, and his thoughts were becoming clouded. This was her trap; this was why she had come—it was her point. And he could hardly deny it; she had the evidence and the understanding. Augusta merely wanted to fill in the holes of her knowledge. *Goddamn it, James! Why would you keep this?* But then, he too was guilty of breaking the pact he had made with James.

No, David could not fault James for having kept evidence of an old secret. For David had done worse: he had brought the secret home to roost. And this was his day of judgment, of reckoning.

"Quite a web of secrets, then," Augusta said. "When I discovered the picture, I spent a long time contemplating your motives. Were you going to sow discontent in our family? Were you going to reveal Natalie to us, to the world, to muddy my father's name? And why now? But then, there was no reason for you to wait so long if your mission was slander and vengeance. You could have done it years ago, even when my father was alive. So, it comes back to my mother again, doesn't it? You—"

"Enough!" David snapped.

He was trying to get a handle on his breathing, trying to stop his shaking, trying to make the weird sensation in his head go away, so he could pull thoughts together, pull himself together. Fear and anger were competing for prominence inside him. When he looked up from the obituary on his lap, he could see Augusta's composed face.

"What do you want from this?" David challenged. He was desperately trying to take control of the situation. He could demand she leave, but what would that do? She knew enough—too much. What was she going to do? He needed to convince her to be silent. But what would she charge for that silence?

Augusta leaned forward, still composed. "Just information, David. Just the truth. Then we can determine our course."

What did she mean by that? There was only one course. Only one. Elinor was never to know; Natalie was never to know. There were no alternatives. Augusta needed to understand this.

Augusta was sitting comfortably across from him, holding her wine elegantly, with one leg crossed over the other, appearing at ease, as if she were the master of the house. Maybe, right now, she was. She was telling him to dig into the dirt and dust off events from decades ago.

Augusta prodded him. "Did you know her? This ... Ayisha?"

There it was, she was striking at him now, David knew. "No."

"Yet, you found out about her. How? Did my father tell you?"

He resisted. *Say nothing, do nothing,* he thought. *Be silent and she'll tire of this,* he told himself.

But she didn't. She was still there, waiting. "David? Tell me. How did you learn about her?"

Finally, he understood she would not relent. He would need to tell her. She would give him no peace until she was appeased, until she could fit all the pieces together. And she was holding all the cards.

He rubbed the leather armrests of the chair slowly and firmly. He poured himself another scotch and drank it quickly to grease the gears of his mind and have it clink into operation. The engine of memory started, reversing into the past to explain the present.

"Late one night, many months before the wedding of your parents, your father came to the apartment I had in downtown Kitchener," David said. "He was distraught, beside himself. Never saw him like that. For such a confident man, to see him in near tears was a strange thing."

David didn't mention how scared he had been that night when he feared something had happened to Elinor.

"I had to give him a half a bottle of rum before he would tell me what was wrong," David went on. "When James finally blurted out that 'she' was pregnant, I wasn't much alarmed. I assumed he was talking about Elinor. Although eyebrows would be raised, it wouldn't be the first time a wedding was moved up and done away with quickly to keep everything in moral order. You may laugh now, but in those days, these trifles mattered.

"But the woman he was referring to wasn't your mother; it was Ayisha Mitchell. That's when I learned of her. She was a waitress at the Riverboat. James had met her on one of his many weekend outings to Toronto, and they had started some relationship, it seemed."

Augusta kinked her head sideways a little. "You knew of his indiscretion even before he married Mom? You covered for him."

David snorted. "Wasn't the first time. There were a few wayward confessions he made to me when he was dating your mother. He had the occasional relapse into his old philandering habits, a one-night stand with some woman or other. Your father was a different sort of man then. He had many natural qualities that made him desirable to women, and he damn well exploited them for his enjoyment.

"It was the strange nature of our relationship that when this happened, he sought forgiveness from Elinor through me, as if I were her proxy. He could clean his conscience, be absolved, and feel as if he had been above board with everything. But he had sworn to me that once he had proposed to your mother, he was done with these antics. And never had his past transgressions resulted in something as calamitous as this."

Augusta shook her head and leaned back on the couch. "That makes no sense. If you loved my mom, why would you protect him? All you had to do was tell her, and you'd have ruined my father's chance with her."

"I seriously considered it," he said. He was finding a strange rhythm in his story, in the ordering of his recollections. There was now so little reservation as he talked. Like a hole in the side of a rugged mountain that spews out a waterfall, his mouth gave breath to something that he never thought he would share with anyone, but that sought release. "I wondered how I might capitalize on your father's fall—for might your mother not turn her eye on me in light of this news? But try as I might, I couldn't bring myself to do it.

"You're still shaking your head. No! You have no idea how much your mother loved him; how much she adored him. I realized that to play the snitch would put me no further ahead. In fact, I'd likely lose the only two things I had: my only friend and the woman I wanted so desperately to make happy. It would all be too much for Elinor. The fact is, that to undo your father was to undo your mother. I forgave him, as I always did. And because he loved your mother, and I did too, I had to become James's co-conspirator to spare her."

The wine bottle was tipped again as Augusta filled her glass. She was quiet for a long time. Then she said, "So, the two of you swept it under the rug. Did *Papa*,"—she pronounced it in a pompous French accent—"pay her off? Make her go away?"

David didn't like this part: what he would say, what he would have to admit to. This was his transgression. "No," he said. "We didn't decide anything. I did." He took a large gulp of scotch—no savoring. There was no joy in this.

"Christ, your father sobbed a hell of a lot that night," he said. "He drank every drop of alcohol I had. And do you know what he asked me? 'What should I do?' He kept on me with that question. Wanted me to tell him how to get out of the mess. I didn't know what to advise. Finally, he passed out, and I had time to think. All night, I considered every angle while I watched over James spread out on my couch."

David grunted, thinking back in bafflement. "James had everything and was on the verge of throwing it all away. And yet, he could sleep. Even when he was on the cliff edge, he could sleep." He paused, building up his courage. "By the time your father awoke in the morning, I had the answer to his question. I told him what to do. I said, 'You will never see this Ayisha woman again. And you will never utter her name.' I made him swear. He was torn by this, even suggesting she was waiting for some word or guidance from him back in Toronto, but because I was so firm and angry, he relented. And that was it. He married your mother and moved on. It really was as if nothing had ever happened."

David wasn't looking at Augusta anymore; he didn't want to know if she was revolted by him. "Now you see, I would not only sacrifice myself for your mother's happiness, but also a woman I had never met. I have wasted more than one life for your mother's sake."

There was a long silence. "Yet, my sister is here, in Waterloo," Augusta said.

"She is," David said quietly. "That's my doing, but it wasn't supposed to be this way. Your father and I never spoke of Ayisha to one another. Taboo, I suppose. But I thought of Ayisha. Over the years, as I watched the arrival of your brother and you, Ayisha's name lingered in my mind. I began to feel guilt and shame. Had I damned a woman and her child in some way because of my counsel to James? Was this woman alive? Did she keep her child? I suppose I thought of a young pregnant girl waiting—waiting for your father to return to tell her what they would do. But he never did, because of me."

David sighed and rubbed has hands together. "I warred with that guilt for years, but I think I was finally moved to action after a speech your father gave at an awards banquet for the Chamber of Commerce; 1980 or so, I think. By that time, our business was doing well, and your father and I were making a name for ourselves. Well, I suppose your father was, at least.

"James talked mostly about the need for business leaders to not only create jobs for residents but to give back to the community and public institutions. But what I remember most were his closing remarks, his challenge to all of us present. They were something to the effect of encouraging us to look after each other's children—that we all had a responsibility to do it in the community. 'Look after your own children, look after mine, and I will do likewise,' or something like that.

"I wonder if he was talking to me that day—reminding me of Ayisha. I don't know. Maybe it was just a speech. But his words seemed like an instruction to do something. It was an order to make amends—perhaps for both your father and me. The following week, I visited Bart Miller to devise the means by which I could answer your father's call. I told Miller of my intent to help someone in Toronto but gave him little context as to my reasons. Giving him Ayisha's name and the date of her last known place of work, we employed men whose trade it is to find people for a variety of reasons. Over the course of a couple of months, Miller was able to locate Ayisha and her nearly five-year-old daughter, Natalie."

Augusta got up and started walking about the room. Another cigarette lit. "But you said you never met Ayisha," she said. "Why go through the trouble to find out where she was if you were never going to see her?"

"So I could create a trust fund for Natalie, to be used at her mother's discretion," David said. Augusta was behind him. He could hear her open the cabinet again. He didn't need to turn around to know she was pulling out the picture of Natalie and Ayisha again. "It was to exist until Natalie turned twenty-one. There were two conditions on it, however, the violation of which could prohibit access to the money. The first was that periodic updates needed to be sent to the trust on the health and welfare of the child. The second was that Ayisha must not know, nor attempt to discover by any means, the person that had set up the fund. That second clause was more to protect your father rather than me. I didn't want to have to explain to the Mitchells why I had set up the trust, and since I needed to hide your father's identity, I likewise needed to protect mine, since we were so closely associated in all our dealings. I couldn't risk people connecting dots, even though it would have been hard back then with no computers and all. Miller and I setup an anonymous PO box address to receive the communications."

Augusta gave a short laugh. "Always in the background, working secret deals. I'm becoming very fond of you. Even Bart Miller is one of your chess pieces. You sent him to propose the terms to Ayisha, and she accepted?"

"Yes," David agreed. "I can't say exactly what transpired when Bart went to the Mitchells, but he said that Ayisha tried to understand who the benefactor was and the reason behind the generosity. However, with the encouragement of her parents, she let the matter drop, and the deal was made. The family was not well off, and the money would be a boon in many respects.

"What happened after was unexpected. I assumed I would receive only general updates about Natalie's health and welfare—simple statements that the child was well, that another grade was passed. I was surprised, then, at the letters that came. They were long and descriptive, giving insight into not just Natalie but Ayisha. Two and three times a year these letters would come, sometimes containing pictures. From the child's schooling to riding a bike, from acting in a school play to dance classes, I accessed, through words, this family—these people. I became an active observer. I felt like I knew them as well as I knew the people in my own life. And as Natalie grew, these communications never abated. Boyfriends, driver's license, a poor semester in grade eleven after falling in with the wrong crowd, I was told everything about Natalie. I looked forward to receiving those letters. They were like a diary."

The door of the cabinet behind him closed. There was silence, and then there was a hand on his shoulder. He felt Augusta's touch. Is that what Elinor's would feel like?

"Ayisha thought you were James," Augusta's voice from above him said.

There was a slight stinging in David's eyes. His vision was blurred. When was the last time he had felt the sensation of tears? Was it the memory of mistaken identity or the touch of a hand on him? Augusta's hand—a relation to Elinor.

"Yes, she did," he said. "I had my own suspicion this was the case. But it was confirmed when Ayisha became sick and was dying. She sent a letter to the trust, begging me to continue to support Natalie after her death. In her note, she said she knew it was 'me.' She also said she was grateful for the assistance but never understood why I would have no interest in meeting 'our' daughter. She implored me to see the woman Natalie had become.

"Of course, I had Miller draft the documents so that Natalie could get the money until she turned twenty-one. It was just an administrative exercise—a signature on some forms and some basic personal information. Miller filled out everything to keep it as simple for Natalie as possible, and I sent the papers for her to execute."

David looked down at the obituary in his hands. "But Ayisha died, though I didn't know this until later. For a full two months I waited, but the documents were never returned. I was on the verge of deploying Bart Miller to investigate the delay, when a letter came, at last, to the trust PO box. It was from Natalie. She said she'd rather know me than receive money from me—isn't that strange? Nobody ever wanted to know me."

The hand on his shoulder was removed, and Augusta appeared in front of him as she sat on the couch again.

"You could have ended it there," Augusta remarked quietly. "You did more than enough. You had done what my father should have."

"Yes, it would have been a clean break, but my curiosity got the better of me," David replied. "I don't think I was ready for this story to come to such an abrupt end. I'd grown attached to Natalie over the years by her mother's letters. To abandon this now was akin to having the power go out while watching a good movie on television— the movie still plays on, somewhere, just not for me.

"I concluded I would see her, but on my terms. If the meeting went poorly, I could disappear. I wanted to understand where I stood. Would she be hostile to me? What had Ayisha told her of me—or rather, your father? I had to glean the answers to these questions. We arranged to meet in High Park in Toronto. A good meeting, I thought. We walked on trails and talked. I told her my name, my real name, and she seemed to accept this without surprise. That suggested Ayisha had never told her much.

"At one point, Natalie asked me if 'I was him.' I knew what she meant. I had anticipated the question and contemplated it for the entire drive to Toronto. Why wouldn't she ask that?

"So, I told her something vague. I told her I was 'like a father,' but that I didn't deserve the title; it wasn't mine to claim. I guess I knew, even then, how she would interpret those words. She would think that was my shame coming through. The fact is, I could tell her nothing, correct none of her suppositions. I couldn't tell her the truth. There was too much risk. What would she do if she knew the facts? Would she sever ties with me? Would she demand to know her true father? Would she piece it all together through some research and show up on your doorstep, demanding an audience with James? You mustn't forget, your father knew nothing of what I had done. I figured he had moved on and wouldn't want to know. He *had* moved on. His life was as it ought to be—perfect."

Augusta was leaning forward, her elbows on her knees, her hands rubbing her temples. She was looking straight down at the floor. "But that changed. Now you've told Natalie something else, and it's not very vague at all."

David's throat was dry again. He took a long gulp of his scotch. This confession was draining, but it was also a magnificent release. There was so much buried in his heart that he had never shared with anyone. Was this the liberation that James had become addicted to whenever he confessed his indiscretions to David?

"Why should I be vague?" David demanded. "She already believes it to be true. If she has mistakenly put too much stock in who I am, in what I am, could I not rise to the occasion for both our sakes? She wants to love me. What a thing is that? Old Burlow loved by someone. That can change a man. I can be what she thinks I am."

"It's a lie."

"The truth has never been kind to me," David retorted. "Besides, if you want to preach that gospel, will you tell your mother what you now know? Will you break your mother with honesty?"

"Will you?" Augusta rejoined.

David sat back in his chair, sighing heavily. "No. I almost did. At a dinner before Christmas. Thought I would use the truth to topple the pedestal your father occupied in her mind. But I couldn't. And I renewed the conclusion I had arrived at many years earlier—Elinor would only hate me for telling her. Your mother will never love me, not in the way I've hoped. I don't blame her. I blame myself for my delusion. Years, wasted …"

Augusta shook her head. "Think of what you're doing. You're

using Natalie. She's just a new vessel for you to pour your feelings into," Augusta said.

David felt anger rising in him. "I will know a little of family. I will know a little of being needed—of love. By my means, your parents lived a fabled life. Even your father's success was by my hand. And still, I have nothing. No family I speak with, few friends beyond your parents, and a reputation as the pitiable jester of you Hardiches. Am I not entitled to pursue my own happiness?"

"Jesus, David," Augusta said. She rubbed her temples again, and he watched as her jaw clenched and an invisible hook pulled one corner of her mouth down into a frown. They were quiet again—just silence between them, eventually broken by Augusta's sudden light, breathy laugh. "Well, she's quite perfect, your Natalie. I think she's the only Hardich that turned out well." There was a crack in her voice, faint but there. Then she seemed to move off into her thoughts.

He was waiting for her to announce her intentions with the information he had shared. But Augusta only smoked and sipped her wine. What was she thinking? He was a man waiting for the verdict of a jury that would determine his fate. Or maybe he was waiting for her to name the price of her silence.

When he could no longer conceal his agitation, he addressed her. "I've asked nothing of you Hardiches. Ever. But I ask this of you now. Keep this between us. You mustn't say anything to anyone," David said. Then he softened and added, "Please."

He thought he saw compassion in Augusta's eyes. Again, a long silence before she nodded slowly and smiled. "I'll play along with you, David. I'll be your co-conspirator. Just like you with my father."

He took a deep breath. In his relief, he whispered a prayer of thanks, either to God or Augusta, maybe both.

"I don't want to go home tonight," she said quietly. "I'll sleep here on the couch. I don't need you to wait on me. You can go to bed."

He was surprised at first. There was her commanding presumption again, dismissing him from his own living room. But then he considered all she had heard. Yes, Augusta needed time to take this in too, her own time to reflect. He fetched her a pillow and blanket, which she took without acknowledging him.

Leaving her, he made his way slowly upstairs to bed. Despite the drowsiness that the scotch made him feel, his pulse was running, and his mind was swimming in spirits and the past. Sleep was fleeting, and he spent most of his night lying on the bed thinking about Natalie, about James, about Elinor, and about Augusta. He was grateful to Augusta, as James must have once been grateful to him.

Their lives and histories were all intersecting in secrets and deceits; it seemed to have the hand of destiny in it. He prayed to this unforeseen hand for forgiveness for what he was doing with Natalie, but also thanked it for the opportunity to be happy, to be needed, to be loved, and to give love. When the first rays of light came through his window, he went downstairs and peeked into the living room.

Augusta was awake, sitting on the couch, looking weary, her eyes bloodshot and her hair wispy. He wondered if she had slept at all. The stench of smoke was strong, and the ashtray was near full. She must have smoked her entire pack of cigarettes. It would take him days to air the place out. The bottle of wine was empty, as was the bottle of scotch, which was now near the couch, within arm's reach of her. She had finished that too when the wine ran out.

She gave him a weak smile when she saw him and asked for Advil. Her manner was casual, as if there was nothing different this morning from any other morning. David brought her the painkillers and a glass of water. She had two or three other bottles of pills out at the ready. Medication? He returned to the kitchen to make coffee.

As he stood over the percolating machine, watching the pot fill, he heard Augusta come into the kitchen. They waited until there was enough coffee for two mugs.

"My mom told me about what happened—at that dinner before Christmas you mentioned," Augusta said. "I know you've been avoiding her, and she does too. She's upset and hurt. How long will you be angry with her?"

"I'm not angry. I just won't pretend to be her friend when I've always wanted something else. The problem is, before she was ignorant of my feelings. Now she knows them, and that has changed everything."

"Is it possible to just cut it off? Cut it out? To just end love—stop it from hurting?" Augusta asked with intensity.

David was caught off guard by her question. Something important seemed to hinge on the answer. And he knew that her question had nothing to do with Derek. Was there someone else? A person she actually cared for?

He felt oddly comfortable with her after what he had told her last night. There was nothing more to hide. If she chose to undo him, to speak out against him to her mother or Natalie, he was powerless. So, he told her exactly what he felt. "Not that I know of. I'd have done it long ago if it was possible."

His response brought frustration to Augusta. Her face contorted, and there was her frown again. And pain.

She took a sip of her coffee. "In another time, David, we'd have been a perfect couple," she said, laughing mournfully. "Reminds me—I had a favor to ask you about my upcoming wedding. Would you walk me down the aisle?"

David felt a sudden thrill at the honor. "Me? I'd be honored, but why me? There must be—"

"You didn't think Xavier was going to do it, did you?"

"No," he said, "I suppose not." But he was reminded of her remark last night, and even the question she had asked him this morning. "Will I be walking you down the aisle to a life you don't want?"

Augusta said nothing. Her red fingernail just tapped the glass of her mug, counting seconds.

"Why are you marrying him?"

A smile from her. Amusement. "Safety … greed … justice, punishment … hatred. It doesn't matter, David. It's fitting." She took a last swig of coffee and dumped the rest in his sink. "I should get going. Thanks for letting me stay over." She came close to him and rested her hand on his breast over his heart. Then she leaned forward, her lips rested on his cheek, and she kissed him.

He froze. *Elinor. Elinor. Elinor.*

She pulled back and turned to leave but suddenly stopped. Her back was to him, but her head was turned so he could see the side of her face. "I'm sorry to do this to you, but I expect you to resume relations with my mother again. Soon."

There was no denying her. He sensed an implied threat in her instruction to him, and he knew this was more than a preference of hers; she expected compliance. The old Augusta was back as she walked out of the house.

CHAPTER 29

Particle Collision *(Natalie Mitchell, July 2005)*

EVEN on a Sunday in July, a day of supposed rest, Natalie was up early. While the sun streamed into the living room of her apartment, which overlooked Waterloo Park, she sat on her couch and worked away. There was plenty to get done before she met Richard for brunch at a cafe a short walk from her place.

When she heard her phone buzzing, she assumed it was Richard, but then she saw the name appear on her screen—Augusta.

Since shortly after the Spring Gathering, Augusta had sent Natalie repeated invitations to meet for coffee or dinner. To these texts and phone calls, Natalie had said she was swamped with work or too busy. She was busy, it was true, but her avoidance was because she found Augusta unnerving.

She was thinking of letting it ring through to voicemail, but she had done that the last time. She picked up the phone, smiled widely, hoping that would make her sound happy and amicable when she talked, and flipped the phone shell up.

"Augusta, how are you?"

"Wonderful," Augusta said. "But I'm just getting ready to leave the house. I'll be up at the school today. Meet me for coffee in the afternoon."

Natalie tried to sound regretful, like she just discovered she was missing out on a great opportunity. "That would have been so nice, but I can't. Meeting a friend for a picnic in the park."

"After that, then?"

"We're going to be together all day," Natalie said. Why did she feel she had to explain this to Augusta? It's like she couldn't just say no; she had to have an excuse. "I'm sorry, it just won't work today. Another time?"

When they ended the call, Natalie thought she could hear Augusta laughing.

* * *

Natalie and Richard walked on a well-trod trail that encircled a large pond called Silver Lake, which formed one of the boundaries of Waterloo Park. She was glad they had chosen to walk in the park today—the trees seemed drunk with life, having swallowed up the several days of rain the city received last week.

They were coming up on the Perimeter Institute for Theoretical Physics. The black facade of the building was punctured with glass windows of varying sizes and with no uniformity or consistency, as if they had appeared by chance.

The Institute had opened the previous year on the edge of the park. It was a testament to public-private partnerships, having been funded heavily by the philanthropic founders of Research in Motion.

The building was not aesthetically beautiful in Natalie's eye, but it inspired contemplation, and that was likely its intent. Because of the irregularity of the window placements and shapes, Natalie found herself lightly musing about the concepts of randomness and spontaneity. Were meetings in book shops just coincidence, or did they only seem so because she did not understand a system that operated beyond her comprehension?

Beside her, Richard was also looking at the building. His hands were tucked into his pockets, and a backpack slung over his shoulder occasionally clinked and clanked with empty containers and cutlery from their picnic lunch.

Natalie reached out and squeezed his forearm. "What are you thinking?" she asked.

He looked at her with a blank expression that turned into a smile. She found he did that often; whenever she touched him or pulled him out of his introspection, it was as if he was re-recognizing her.

"If I said theoretical physics, would you believe me?"

"Not from an arts grad."

Richard grinned. "You'd be right. So, I must be enjoying the day, I guess," he said.

They met regularly now since their encounter in the bookstore. Usually, it was for a coffee or drink in the evening, but there were also dinners in there too. Recently, on the nights they didn't see each other, they would have some text conversations.

She was being cautious with him, and he seemed to be likewise with her. Maybe he was confused by her intentions. She couldn't blame him; after all, she was too. She wasn't sure she wanted a boyfriend right now, but she enjoyed her outings with him. He grew on her a little more each time they met. At times, she wished Richard would be more assertive or give some indication of what he wanted this to be. He seemed to be in the back seat. At the very least, he was in neutral.

Perhaps it was his relationship that turned sour last year. Richard had confided to her one night over a drink that he had gone through a tough breakup, but he didn't say more than that. She was glad; she hardly wanted to be involved with someone who complained about his past girlfriends.

Or perhaps his caution in advancing anything with her was his way of keeping ends loose because he was going away soon. He planned to leave on his little odyssey in the late fall.

Something was different about him since he had worked at

Enigma. He seemed to have a greater presence and purpose—a quiet strength, a conviction she hadn't noticed before. He even walked with more certainty. Was this transformation the product of his plan to go away next year? Was it the new job?

"Oh, I forgot to ask," Richard said. "Did anything happen at the Enigma pub night last week?"

The Enigma employees had been taken out by Xavier in celebration of another company victory—this one at a university in the United States. The whole deal had been quite an achievement. Enigma beat out a much larger and more established firm called LearnTech. LearnTech was one of the market leaders in the US and seemed sure to win. But Natalie had sold the university hard, and her pitch was flawless. Against the odds, Enigma triumphed.

She seldom talked about work with Richard, though—only if he asked. She didn't want to aggravate any old wounds.

"The party was good. Everyone came, even Bill. I was happy about that, since he doesn't like to be around Xavier at all. By 10 p.m., the university crowd showed up and things got rambunctious. Jeremy and the team got pretty trashed. Some kid, who was nineteen, tried to pick me up, though."

"Really?"

"Yeah! I was surprised to learn that guys in Waterloo would be interested in a plain girl like me," Natalie said. She liked giving him little openings to say something complimentary. He didn't volunteer much flirtation with her, so she had to test his interest in her own way.

"There's nothing plain about you," Richard said, looking at her briefly before turning away.

Natalie reached over and took the inside of his arm with her hand. She felt like doing that just now, and she wasn't going to overthink it. He didn't move away or flinch.

"Xavier's girlfriend showed up. The Pit may think Xavier's useless, but they sure enjoyed ogling Jocelyn the whole time. They were clamoring over one another to talk to her and get pictures with her.

God, she's so beautiful, it's sickening. You've seen her, right? The one who does that morning show?"

"Yeah, she's not really my type, I guess," he said indifferently.

"What? You're not into the supermodel look?"

He shrugged his shoulders and smiled.

"Xavier's friend Derek popped in too," Natalie went on. "I spent some time talking to him. Or rather, he was talking to me, trying to get me to invest with him. Said he'd make an exception and take me on if I could get half a million. As if I've got that floating around. He's the one getting married to Augusta. Did you know? He's taking her to Bora Bora for their honeymoon after the wedding in June next year. He must be doing well."

"I'm sure."

They continued walking around the water. Richard began to talk about a book he was reading on European history during the Enlightenment. He was gobbling up texts on the destinations he wanted to visit and was always happy to discuss the different cultural and philosophical movements he learned about. She didn't follow politics or care much for history, but she liked it when he filled her in on the things he discovered: bite-sized lectures she would not otherwise learn about on her own.

Eventually, they merged onto another trail that went through the park toward the University of Waterloo. Just up the path was a small petting zoo, if it could be called as much, with only a few llamas, miniature horses, rabbits, and pigs. The park was busiest here with many families, everyone wanting to get out after being cooped up indoors from the rain. Richard made a motion to turn around, suggesting they head back the way they had come, but Natalie shook her head.

"Come on, let's see the animals," she said, grabbing his hand in a dramatic show to pull him toward the zoo.

He rolled his eyes but gave in with a laugh.

On their way to the animals, they passed a vendor selling ice cream, doing a booming business; a steady line of parents with young kids waited eagerly for a chance to grab refreshment on the hot day. The scene reminded Natalie of High Park back in Toronto, although everything here was on a smaller scale.

Just as they were nearing the first animal enclosure, Natalie saw her.

Even amid the various bodies running, walking, and playing in the park around Natalie, she couldn't miss the figure coming the opposing way. The woman's attire seemed out of place for a casual stroll in the park; it was more appropriate for a yacht on the Mediterranean or some exotic and luxurious location. She was walking on the path toward them, wearing black sunglasses and a wide-brimmed black sunhat tilted to the side. A beautiful white dress that exposed a pale neck clung to her slim body. The bottom of the dress was simple but elegant, with a black hem that hung just above the knee, waving back and forth. She carried a large purse by the handle. The whole outfit was captivating.

Too late, Natalie realized who it was. She wished she had let Richard steer them the other way. Had Augusta been in wait for her? Keeping an eye out for her?

Augusta's sunglasses were focused on them. Natalie knew it.

As Augusta drew near, she removed her glasses. Her face struck Natalie as unusually pale.

"Natalie, it's nice to see you," Augusta said enthusiastically. Her eyes, however, hardly stayed on Natalie. They were looking elsewhere. They were looking at Richard.

She remembered, then, the conversation from the party a couple of months back when Augusta asked after him.

"Yes, and you. You decided to come for a walk in the park too?" Natalie asked, irritated. Augusta knew they would be here. Why was Augusta so interested in her and what she was doing?

"Coming back from the university. I'm going to Derek's," Augusta replied. "I remember you telling me you met up with Richard for dinner a while ago—I suppose this is a bit more of a regular thing?" She smiled and pointed at something between them.

It was their hands. Natalie was still holding Richard's hand.

Natalie tried to say something, but she was speechless. She could feel Richard turn stonelike. His hand was releasing hers.

"I hear you're going on a long trip, Richard." Augusta directed the question to where her eyes were focused most.

Richard nodded, saying nothing. Natalie felt there were things passing around her, through her, that she didn't understand. Would he be upset that she had told Augusta he was going away?

"We must have dinner sometime," Augusta said, turning to Natalie. A faint smile played across her lips. "You can't ignore me forever. Seems like we have plenty to catch up on."

"Yes, let's," Natalie said, fumbling slightly for something else to say. "I'm sorry, time is just short right now," she added.

"I can see you've got plenty to do. I'll let you two continue," she said and bid them goodbye before resuming her walk.

The day seemed off after that. Richard retreated inward and was distant. She tried to lure him out with conversation, but he was only half-engaged. Something about the run-in with Augusta had disrupted the flow they had between them.

"I forgot to tell you she asked about you at the Spring Gathering," Natalie said as they finished circling the park and entered Waterloo's downtown to poke into the shops. "She remembered you from the party last year, apparently. I told her you were going away. I didn't think that would be a problem. Are you upset?"

Richard shook his head. "No, it's fine." But he didn't sound himself. "Are you really going for dinner with her?"

"I don't want to. But I feel as though I should play nice with her. She's trying really hard to connect with me." Natalie shook her head. "There is something about her ... She just ... makes me uneasy."

"I know what you mean," Richard said.

CHAPTER 30

An Opportunity *(Xavier Hardich, September 2005)*

XAVIER hung up the phone and leaned back in his chair so quickly that he rolled away from the desk. He resisted the urge to call Derek immediately; he wanted to assemble his thoughts before pulling his friend into this. A rare energy was surging through him—a mix between a thrill and anxiety, as if he were standing at the top of a cliff with clear turquoise water below, preparing for a jump.

He got up, paced around his desk, then went to the front window. Looking outside, a pleasantly warm fall day greeted his eyes. Some leaves were starting to line the lawns and street, but many of the trees in the neighborhood retained a full foliage of vibrant red, yellow, and orange colors. Xavier couldn't help but wonder at some broader plan in the universe today. He even pondered the possibility of his father's spirit being in the office with him, bequeathing good fortune.

The call he had just made was as glorious as the sunshine outside, as wondrous as the changing leaves. The makings of destiny were in it. This was the beginning of Xavier's rise, the making of his name, and the continuation of the Hardich legacy.

He could hear his mother in the kitchen. Earlier, she had barged into the office during his phone conversation to ask if he wanted brunch. In his irritation, he pointed to the phone at his ear, and shooed her away with a wave of his hand. She had left offended at his discourtesy, and he knew he owed her an apology and explanation. But it was an important call!

He was hungry now. Brunch would be good before he reached out to Derek.

Walking down the hall from the office to the kitchen, he was surprised to learn it was not his mother that was the source of the noise there, but Augusta. She was at one end of the island counter, pecking at a fruit salad. Beside her bowl, she had a large textbook open, and she was scribbling in the margins. At the other end of the counter was a lone plate with eggs and sausages. His mother must have made it for him.

Walking up to it, he poked the food with his finger—it was cold now. "Where's Mom?" he asked.

"Upstairs," Augusta responded, turning to look over at him, her face unreadable. "You were quite rude to her, apparently."

He grimaced. So, his mother *was* upset at him. "I had an important business call," he said defensively.

"Really? Something I should know about Enigma?"

Xavier shook his head. "Nothing you'd understand or care about."

"Of course not," she laughed. "Only you and my fiancé can speak of Enigma. I just own a third of it."

Xavier pulled a fork and knife out from the cutlery drawer and returned to his end of the island. He tried to ignore her. He could feel her watching him, as if wanting a response to her statement.

"The only time you took an interest in Enigma was when you were screwing one of its employees," he said calmly, biting a piece of dry, cold toast.

She sneered at him but said nothing.

"I sometimes wonder if I should have kept your secret," he continued, speaking quietly so as not to arouse their mother upstairs. The siblings were never alone together, and he was overcome by the desire to express things he had too long kept inside. "I abetted your betrayal with my silence, so you didn't throw away a good thing. And I worry I've damned Derek to a marriage with a miserable bitch because of it. He could have done a lot better than you. A lot better. Do you keep yourself medicated enough to be pleasant for him?"

The smile that he despised played across her mouth. "Don't worry, Xavier. I'm a good girl for now. But I wonder—are you getting what you need? Has he invited you into any business dealings? Are you in on any of his rental properties in Toronto? Has he ever offered to invest the little money that you have? Maybe just given you one stock tip? I don't think he's done anything for you. I wonder why. Is it him? Or is it you?"

Xavier glared at Augusta. He swallowed his food, which seemed dryer now, less flavorful.

"You think that because he has me, you have a hook in him," Augusta said, closing her textbook. "You don't. Just because you talk to him like he's your business partner doesn't mean he's going to share what he has. He's not. He's shrewder than you think. You won't be able to ride his coattails."

Augusta picked up her book, left the kitchen, and went upstairs. He stood at the counter alone, cutting up cold eggs he no longer wanted. An anxious feeling spread in him.

Why didn't Derek ask him to join in on investment properties? Why was he hearing about this for the first time from Augusta? Had he not shown Derek every courtesy already? He talked to Derek like he was a partner at Enigma, and he helped ensure that all his mother's money moved over to his friend. And still, Derek offered nothing in return. Not yet, anyway. Clearly, waiting for Derek to broach the subject wasn't working.

Returning to the office, Xavier sat down at the desk. He ignored the spiteful words of Augusta; the woman was a poison. He wondered again, as he had on many occasions, what Derek saw in her. But he believed he knew the answer as soon as he asked the question. Augusta had a strange gift: the ability to mask who she truly was around others. She seemed charming and pleasant to everyone but him. Only Xavier saw her for what she was. Would Derek eventually scrape through her veneer?

Composing himself, Xavier grabbed his mobile phone and dialed his friend. As soon as Derek picked up, Xavier jumped into the meat of his call.

"Nobody knows what I'm going to tell you," Xavier said, "but I had the craziest call a half-hour ago. Hal Jennings, president of a company called LearnTech in the US, pinged me. You remember them? We've beaten them on a couple of bids. Guess we got their attention. Hal wants to fly up here and meet me next month to have a talk about partnership and how our companies can work together. His executive team has been studying Enigma, and they're impressed by what I've accomplished. He thinks our two companies have some synergies."

Derek was quiet at first, only asking a few questions, but his voice became enthusiastic as he understood the full scale of the opportunity and what it could mean for Enigma. "We'll take him out for the best dinner he's ever had," Derek declared. "Are you gonna show him that hole-in-the-wall office of yours?"

"Well, he's going to want to see Enigma and meet some of the people," Xavier said. "When Hal's done at the office, you and I can spend the evening with him." He paused and added, "We're like partners in this, you know? I want to include you in my success."

"Yeah, yeah," Derek dismissively agreed. He remained fixated on the meeting next month. "You gotta give him presentations and stuff at the office. Pull Natalie in for those. Have her talk. She'll rock it. Everyone loves her. But she'll need to speak positively about the off-shore development. She needs to say it's going well, however much of a shit-show it is. Make sure she knows that!"

Xavier bit his tongue. Did Derek think he couldn't manage this on his own? He had made Enigma what it was. Ever since he took it over, Enigma was thriving.

"And Xavier," Derek added. "Don't underestimate this opportunity. There's a bigger play here. LearnTech may be talking partnership, but this is the dating round for something more. You know what I mean?"

"You think he wants to buy Enigma?"

"I think it's possible. If it was just partnership, Hal wouldn't fly up—he'd send a minion."

They planned out more of the content they would present to Hal when he was in town. Derek suggested they even bring Hal to Toronto and all stay at Derek's condo there for a night. A Toronto Maple Leafs game would provide some additional schmoozing time.

As the call started to wind down, Xavier took the opportunity to prod Derek. "So, what are you chasing in Toronto right now anyway?"

"The usual. Meeting some investors and getting more of their money." He laughed.

"Oh, nice. I wasn't sure if you were looking at property. I thought I heard Augusta mention something like that to my mom."

"Got that on the go too," Derek said. "Busy, busy."

Xavier wanted to make sure Derek understood his position. "I'm interested in property, you know? If you're looking for another partner to pony up some cash, I'm in."

"Sorry man, one sec," Derek said. He began talking to someone else. He was ordering—surf and turf. "What were you saying?"

"I was saying I'm good to invest with you on some property ventures if you're looking to partner with someone," Xavier said.

"Oh! For sure. I always keep you in mind," Derek replied. "I think I'm good on this one. But maybe next time," he said reassuringly. "Anyway, when I'm back home later this week, we'll plan some more for Hal. Gotta go."

CHAPTER 31

Acceptance (*Richard Earning, October 2005*)

THOUGH the October days were warmer than usual, the evening temperature dropped so that light jackets and sweaters were needed. But even in the nighttime coolness, the Waterloo downtown patios continued to do a roaring business. After seeing a movie at a popular art-house cinema called The Princess, Richard and Natalie walked to a bar overlooking the main street and were just in time to secure a small table outside. After they took their seats, a large group of patio-goers had shown up at the same place and jockeyed every stray table and chair together to accommodate most of their party. The few of the group left standing kept a watchful eye on the other tables, waiting to pounce the moment something was vacated.

Richard felt Natalie's easygoing manner was subdued tonight.

From the moment they met at her place to walk the five minutes to the theater, Richard felt as if he were driving the conversation, and he was struggling to initiate any meaningful exchange with her. Even at the movie, he noticed a chasm between them despite being separated only by an armrest. Her casual touches and affections were absent. Usually, she would link her arm around his if they were walking, or gently swing her leg repeatedly to playfully kick him if they were sitting beside or across from one another.

But all these displays that he had grown accustomed to were missing or withheld tonight. And he wanted them because they were gone—because he found them comforting. Was she sending him a message? Had he done something?

This craving for Natalie's touch was new to him.

He had never been blind to her subtle flirtations; they had been going on for months now. Initially, Richard received them with an emotional and physical austerity. For Augusta's branding of him still stung, made him wary. Some part of him was loyal to the remnants of that relationship, loyal to the intensity of feeling that he had with her, loyal to what she had shown him about himself. To move on so carelessly, so quickly, to something new would be a betrayal, not to Augusta, but to himself and what he had experienced. For as long as he could, he wanted to preserve the residue of the feeling he had with her.

He knew the wedding would be in the spring next year. And he secretly wondered if Augusta would go through with it. He imagined various scenarios in which the ceremony never came to pass. In one of them, on the eve of the nuptials, everything ended in scandal when Augusta fled town to live a life of solitude. Richard would interpret such an event as a tipping of her hat to him, an apology of sorts, her own homage to the relationship that the two of them had once shared.

An absurd thought, with no grounding in reality, he knew.

But throughout August and into the fall, however, Richard had become more stoic to the memory of Augusta. He still loved her;

he still hated her. But he was functioning; he was moving. He had planned his new path. He only needed to buy a ticket, to commit. He was supposed to leave this month for Europe, yet he delayed. Maybe next month.

Now, everything seemed a little more tolerable—there was no urgent need to rush headlong into completing his ambition. In those first four months after Augusta, he wanted to be away from here, from everyone and everything, to start anew. Lately, he found he was calmer, less restless. And much of this change had come about by Natalie's companionship. She was soothing for him; she distracted him.

Natalie was not without her own charms. Her beauty was subtle, but her personality was a playful force. She was always upbeat and had an inexhaustible source of energy. She pulled him out to plays, movies, and little festivals around town. He attended more cultural events in Kitchener-Waterloo with her in a few months than he had in his entire life living in the area.

Tonight, however, as Natalie sat across from him on the patio, none of those attributes he had come to rely on, had fed off, could be seen or felt. In her present manner, she was the embodiment of the very coolness in the night air. Yet, he had detected nothing wrong in her voice two days ago when they made their plans to see the movie. What had changed?

She looked slightly comical wearing a toque that concealed her thick curls. This was in addition to her windbreaker jacket and a fleece underneath zipped right up to her chin. Between the sips of her scotch—a taste she had acquired from David Burlow—she kept her hands tucked into the pockets of her jacket. They were speaking of the movie, and although she demonstrated some brief bursts of animation, she slid back into a brooding state.

"You're off tonight," Richard remarked at last, feeling he couldn't avoid what was bothering her any longer. He couldn't stay out late; he had to be on the jobsite at seven thirty in the morning to start on a basement renovation. Even now at 9:30 p.m., he was stifling yawns.

"Tough day at work," she said.

"What happened? Xavier still trying to outsource everything, or is he on to some new scheme?" he inquired, trying to draw her out and shift her mood.

Natalie remained stone faced. She took a sip of her scotch. "Something like that."

A long quiet followed. The table beside theirs let out a unified cackle of laughter.

Richard was at a loss as to how to draw her out. They wouldn't see each other this weekend since she was going to Toronto to stay at her grandparents'. He needed to resuscitate a connection with her now and understand what triggered this unusual mood. While mulling a new approach, he reached into his jeans pocket for his cigarettes.

"Are you really going to have a smoke?"

"We're on the last days of patio season—why wouldn't I?" he responded defensively. "It's never bothered you before."

"It always bothers me. I just never say anything," she said.

He could have put the cigarette away; he could have made a concession. But for some reason, he saw this as a battle of wills. And it was the only thing that seemed to stir her into conversation. He lit the cigarette, the flavor of burning tobacco mixed in with the bitterness of the beer taste in his mouth, and he gave a long exhale.

She shook her head. "Thanks for giving a shit."

"What? I need something to do with my hands and mouth," he quipped back. He had chosen his words deliberately. It was exactly the type of statement Natalie would usually catch and use to make some witty and flirtatious retort like "I'll give you something to do with your hands." He wanted her to say something.

Tonight, she didn't use his fodder. She only looked away at the table beside them longingly, as if everyone was having more fun than she was. When a small tendril of smoke wafted toward her from his cigarette, she dramatically waved it away with her hand and whispered something under her breath.

"What's with you? If something's wrong, can you just tell me?" Richard asked, frustrated.

"Yes, let's talk about this," she said, taking another sip of her drink. "I went out last night."

"Oh? By yourself?"

"No."

"With whom then?"

"Augusta Hardich. I couldn't avoid her anymore. She's been badgering me. So, we grabbed a coffee," Natalie said. "Maybe I should have invited you."

"Hmm," Richard grunted, trying to sound unfazed. But inwardly, he was stunned. Now it was coming out. What had Augusta told her?

"She's the girl. From last year. Isn't she?" Natalie assumptively asked.

He was looking for words to deflect her—something clever. Yet, in the brief moment when he needed to respond, to deny it, he couldn't. His silence was incrimination. He took a long drag of his cigarette while Natalie scrutinized him.

"What did she tell you?" he asked at last. Was Augusta trying to sabotage his next relationship? Was she not content with the hurt she had already caused?

"She didn't tell me anything," Natalie said. "I just began to piece it together. I usually can't read that girl. But last night, I understood everything: every facial gesture, every intonation in her voice, and every question. The way she asked about us ... about you especially... And I felt her jealousy. Saw it in her slight little frowns, the narrowing of her eyes. When you and I met her in the park in July, I saw how she looked at you. Something was up, but I had no idea what."

"That's classic Augusta," he said. "She's just playing with you."

Natalie shook her head. "No, I don't think so. Why is she trying to keep tabs on you? Is she trying to befriend me because of you?"

"Why are you asking me? I haven't talked to her since we ended things."

"You should have told me it was her. That she's the one you were with."

"Does it matter who my ex was?"

"Yeah, it does!" Natalie's voice rose as she sat up in her chair. "I thought this whole time I was responsible for you getting pushed out of Enigma. You let me believe that. Your little dalliance is what cost you your job—not me."

"So, you think it was right that son of a bitch fired me?"

Natalie grimaced and gave an exasperated breath. She grabbed her purse from underneath her chair and began rifling through it. She slammed a twenty-dollar bill on the table.

"I'm going home," she said, standing up and slinging her purse over her shoulder. "Get home and get some sleep."

In his confusion, he said nothing; he didn't move as she walked briskly away from the table and toward the patio exit onto the street. A young man tried to slow her down and made a comment about her toque in an attempt to engage her in conversation, but she didn't stop. She marched on, stormed on. Richard followed her with his eyes until she rounded the corner of the building, disappearing from sight.

When the waitress came by, Richard requested the bill and paid up. As the surprise and shock of Natalie's abrupt departure subsided, he internalized the error of his judgment. Guilt gnawed at him. Yes, Natalie was right to be upset.

On a busy patio, he sat alone, reflecting on his own stupidity.

Why didn't he tell Natalie about Augusta? That was a fair question. The fact was, he couldn't answer it. Was it shame? Was it humiliation? Or was it for Augusta he had kept everything quiet? He didn't know. But he never felt right talking about that relationship with anyone. Even his friend Robbie only knew there had been a woman—there were no names, no connections.

He was only half-aware of the assent he gave to someone who asked to take Natalie's vacated chair. The grinding and scraping of the chair feet on the patio stone as the person dragged it to another table snapped him out of his thoughts. He took a last quaff of beer, stood up, and walked out onto the street. Passing a couple of other bars, he continued to walk until he reached an apartment building nestled in among trees on the edge of Waterloo Park. His car was here in the visitors section, but he didn't go to it.

Instead, he went into the empty lobby and used the intercom to dial Natalie's apartment.

"Hello?"

"Natalie. Can I come up?"

There was a pause in which no answer issued from the speaker, but there was a buzz and the sound of the lobby door clicking before it slowly opened, permitting entrance. He went to the third floor and came to Natalie's unit. Knocking, he waited.

Natalie opened the door holding a tumbler filled with a yellow-ish-gold liquid. Her fleece was still on, but she had changed into some flannel pajama bottoms. She stood defensively in the center of the doorframe.

"I don't want to leave off like that," he said. "Please let me come in."

Studying him, she at last stepped aside. He entered her well-orga-nized space. His own place, when he lived on his own, never looked so perfect. She had a knack for decoration. Large black-and-white photographs of Waterloo Park in all four seasons hung on the living room wall. A white couch in front of the TV was simple, but the flanking white lamps with large shades on either side added a modern accent. In the corner of the living room was a small desk with her computer on it and a picture of her mother.

He had only been up here a few times, and even then, only to col-lect Natalie before they walked somewhere. Then, as now, he always felt like he had just stepped into a furniture showroom—everything was ordered and uncluttered; everything went together, fit together.

He followed her to the couch. She sat down, bringing her legs up to her chest. Sitting down beside her, he could still detect anger radiating from her, but he mostly felt her disappointment.

Richard had to take a few breaths before starting. He rubbed his hands on his knees, then squeezing the muscles of his thighs, he finally found his voice, as if he needed to press the thoughts out of his own body.

"I'm sorry about tonight," he said. His voice was low and gruff to his own ear. "You were right—I shouldn't have made you feel the way that I did. I should have told you about Augusta. I guess it's not something I like to talk about." He paused, looking at the floor. "Whatever she and I had hurt ... I guess I'm ... I'm still moving on from it."

She looked away, but she nodded in what he hoped was understanding.

"I know I'm slow getting over her," Richard continued. "But I'm doing it. And I don't want to lose anything we have. I like being with you. I mean, I really like it."

After a long silence, she asked him a question that caught him by surprise. "Do you wish you were still with her?"

"No," he answered. Was that a lie? He went on. "I know we're done. And it can't come back; it shouldn't come back. But it all ended so weirdly. It wasn't done right. Sometimes, I wish horrible things for her. At other times, I just wish she admitted she used me."

Natalie moved into a cross-legged position, resting her elbows on her knees. "Does knowing she still thinks about you make you feel good?"

He hadn't considered this point at all. "No," he stated again, confidently, but he wasn't entirely sure that's what he felt. Why did Augusta think about him?

"Good, because she doesn't deserve your loyalty, Richard," Natalie said. "The grass isn't growing under her feet."

"I know."

They fell into another awkward silence. He poked her, smiled, and asked, "Now that you don't feel responsible for me getting the axe from Enigma, I guess you don't pity me much anymore."

Natalie snorted. "You're still pretty pitiable." There was a faint trace of a grin.

"Pitiable enough to keep seeing me?"

"I guess so. It's not like I know anyone else around here other than the guys from the Pit," she quipped. Natalie took a sip of her scotch. "We've been dancing around this 'thing' we have for a few months now. I guess I'm starting to think we're dating, that we're together, but I'm not sure. I'm at the stage where I need a little clarity."

"I've been trying to figure it out too," he admitted. "I was getting over my stuff and doing all this planning for when I go away. I was supposed to be gone by now. I'm gonna leave and don't want to string you along. I don't know how far we can take this," he confessed.

"We don't have to be all crazy and serious. We're not talking about marriage," she said, smiling.

He was struck by how appealing Natalie looked to him then. He craved her touch again. He craved something else. Her thick, black curls were tied up high, showing her elegant face and her slender neck disappearing into the fleece of her sweater. Her light-brown skin was flawless.

Whatever he was feeling must have been rousing in her too. For she deftly moved from her cross-legged pose to sit on his lap, her knees on either side of his thighs. She looked down at him skeptically from her vantage point, one hand on his shoulder, the other still holding her scotch. The fleece revealed only the faint outlines of her breasts, level with his eyes. His hands, without his control, without guidance, were suddenly resting on her waist. Compulsion made him crane his neck upward to try and taste her lips. When he was just about to make contact, Natalie arched back, away.

"Do you want to try my scotch?" Natalie asked mischievously.

When he agreed, she told him to close his eyes, so he could focus entirely on the flavor. He was expecting her to hold the tumbler up to his lips, and was waiting to feel the glass rim, but instead, he felt her lips. As his mouth opened, the warm liquid she was holding in her mouth trickled into his, filling it. As he swallowed it, there was a subdued bite in this throat. Then her kiss began.

When she pulled her mouth away, she looked down at him. "Are you ready for this?" she asked.

His hands moved up from her waist to the center of her back and pulled her nearer, and again his lips quested for her mouth and made contact.

"Ready," he said. He became entirely present to Natalie, the warmth of her body, the taste of her mouth, and the feel of her skin, as she slipped her fleece off. For the first time in a year, he let himself go.

For a moment, a fleeting second, was there a blip of disruption in his desire. He snuffed it out as soon as it bubbled into consciousness: was Augusta really jealous?

CHAPTER 32

Dangling Carrots *(Natalie Mitchell, December 2005)*

NATALIE arrived at Enigma Solutions at ten thirty on Monday morning. She went immediately to Xavier's office, but he wasn't in yet.

Bill was sitting at his desk in his own office, and he hailed her. "Natalie. Welcome back. How was Boston last week?"

"Good. But I hate to be gone that long," she said. "Lots to get done before I go back next week with Jeremy."

"Now Jeremy's going down too?" Bill asked, shaking his head in dismay. "LearnTech is happy, I hope. They seem to be taking all our people away from running our business here."

"What are you working on?"

Bill shook his head and then ran his hand through his hair. "Xavier wants a full spreadsheet of all our financials for the year. Up to date and accurate, he says."

"Did he say why?"

"Who knows. Maybe something to do with LearnTech and our partnership to crack the US market. All hail the partnership!"

Natalie knew that would probably be Xavier's line. He was betting big on this partnership. But at what cost? It was becoming Xavier's obsession. Bill had no say in it and was becoming increasingly bitter. She went back to her cubicle.

Someone had set up a medium-sized Christmas tree in the corner of the Pit. The lights wound about the tree were of different sizes, types, and colors. Some were blinking, and some were a constant glow, but the ultimate effect was chaos. The decorations, too, were a mess: figurines of Charlie Brown and The Grinch mixed with Star Wars action toys and candy canes. Even though the tree was plastic, it still had the air of dying slowly with its decided lean to the left side. Its branches were bent, and a whole bunch of fake pine needles littered the floor around it. Not even plastic survived in the Pit basement, as it turned out.

Still, it was a nice touch and brought a smile, if not a little cheer, to Natalie. It was good to be back, even though she was still tired from Boston. Last week, her days had been filled pitching Enigma's products into LearnTech's accounts, and the nights were booked up dining with prospects or with LearnTech executives. On two occasions, she had been out very late with the president and the CFO of LearnTech.

The big difference between this trip and her other two trips was that Xavier had not accompanied her. It was a relief, since when he was there, he wanted to do hours of post-meeting debriefs with Natalie, particularly after every interaction with a LearnTech executive. He would want to know her opinion about everything: who said what, how they said it, whether it was good or bad, and what they might have meant. It was exhausting for her.

Not having Xavier there gave her time to reflect on the speed of the partnership, and she was beginning to feel uncomfortable. She needed to talk to him. Since the first meeting with Hal when he came up to Enigma in October, there was an inexplicable pressure for the companies to cosign deals together.

In the Pit, she caught up with everyone and got a status of the projects, but it was Jeremy she locked in on to prepare for the next trip to Boston.

"You'll need new jeans or a pair of dress pants," Natalie told him. "And at least two more sports shirts. We should actually get you a blazer."

To the clothing list, Jeremy slouched in his chair. "Why do I need all that?"

"Because you're not wearing the one and only shirt I bought you for four days straight."

"I haven't got the money. Besides, I don't know what to buy when it comes to this stuff."

"You've got the money. I know what you make, and I'm not buying any more of your clothes. If you want, Richard and I can go with you to the mall to pick out some outfits. Has to be tomorrow night. We'll need time to get the pants hemmed if they need shortening."

Jeremy made no complaint about her offer of help, but he still appeared bothered by something. "Do you agree with what they are having me do down in Boston?" he asked.

"You're meeting people. You're the CTO; it's not unusual."

"No, Xavier is having me go through the technology of our product with LearnTech's team. He even wants me to show the code. I don't understand. If this is about integrating the product with theirs, I don't need to show code. I just need to explain our webservice and APIs."

This was the first Natalie had heard of this other purpose to the trip, and it concerned her more.

When Xavier ducked his head into the Pit and asked Natalie to come to his office for a regroup meeting, she was eager to get some time with him. This would be a good opportunity to discuss her uneasiness about Enigma and LearnTech.

When she approached Xavier's office, the door was open, so she went right in. Xavier was there, sitting behind his desk. But occupying one of the two chairs opposite him was Derek Lam.

Derek stood to greet her and pulled the chair out beside him, indicating Natalie should sit. When he went to the door, she assumed he was leaving, but instead he closed it and retook his seat.

"Great to have you back," Xavier said. "Hal Jennings told us you were amazing. He loves you. We want to hear your take on everything."

"We?" she asked, still eyeing Derek, wondering why he was a part of the conversation.

"Relax, Natalie," Xavier said. "Derek is just helping us as we forge this new and vital partnership for Enigma." He then asked her again about the details of her visit.

Natalie provided a summary of the presentations she had done, the prospects she had met, and where she saw opportunities. To this report, Xavier and Derek listened without interrupting. But when she talked of her evenings, her discussions with LearnTech executives, the two men became more attentive and demanded specific details on questions that Hal Jennings or anyone else asked about Enigma, and how she responded.

"When they asked you again about the throughput on offshoring, what did you say? Exactly?" Derek queried.

"What Xavier and I agreed. I stretched the truth and said our offshore efficiency factor was estimated to be eighty percent." It was one of the many *truths* she was feeling slimy about; less of a stretch and more of a torture. The offshore efficiency was probably a quarter of that.

"And the relationship between Bill and me?" Xavier jumped in. "What about that? We are on great terms, no problem in us finding agreement. You said that, right?"

"Yes," Natalie said. She was becoming agitated by the interrogation. And she was still deeply confused as to why Derek was present for the conversation. "To be honest, I didn't like many of their questions. I thought they were beyond reasonable. Hal also presumed I would be sharing details about the opportunities we are chasing here. Even more alarming, he started asking detailed financials questions over dinner."

Derek shook his head. "He shouldn't have asked that of you." Then to Xavier, he said, "Hal's baiting us to see if there are inconsistencies. He knows we're sending over stuff. Probably wants to know if there is anything he should doubt."

"Leave that to us," Xavier said to Natalie. "Hal's playing."

"What are you sending over?" Natalie asked, leaning forward, remembering what Bill was preparing. "Not our financials, I hope. Our internal financials."

"LearnTech doesn't just partner with anyone—they have a ton of clients," Xavier said, holding up his hands, as if he were not responsible for the message he was delivering. "If they are going to bring us in, they want to know we're viable."

Natalie had worked with partners in the past, and never was such a request appropriate. "I don't understand why we're doing that," she said. "In fact, I don't understand why we are offering up half as much as we are. If this is what LearnTech wants, it's almost invasive. Didn't they call you? We're the ones that are beating them right now, not the other way around. You've had me present our entire strategy for how we are hitting the market, and next week, Jeremy is flying down with me to Boston to explain how our technology is built at a code level? Why should they be privy to any of that? What are they giving us?"

Derek and Xavier exchanged a glance. Whatever message floated between them, Xavier took the lead in answering. "I've been wanting to talk to you about this, Natalie. Now's the time, but we should keep our voices down. You know the grouch next door," he said, pointing to the wall that separated them from Bill's office. "The next few months are very important for Enigma. They will define Enigma. You understand?"

"I understand you're banking on LearnTech. But we don't need them."

Derek smiled and crossed his arms. "Come on, Natalie. You're not thinking big enough. They have a strong foothold in the US and can get us into all their accounts."

"Who says we couldn't get into their accounts on our own?" she asked. Why did Derek Lam think he understood any of this?

"I've been privy to partnership discussions in my experience with private equity," Derek said. "This is Enigma's ticket to exponential growth. You'd be slogging it out for a long time with uncertain re-sults to get to the level that they can bring you in a year."

"The point is," Xavier jumped back in, "we need you to really shine. Everything needs to be perfect next week. You need to prop Jeremy up."

"Jeremy will be fine," she said.

"You know what I mean," Xavier said. "He needs to be … less un-couth. Lots depends on it. For both of you."

"What does that mean?"

Xavier sat forward and put his arms on the desk. "I know this is a lot of work for you. But it's worth your while."

"More equity in the company is worth your while, right?" Derek chimed in.

Natalie caught her breath. This was a new proposition. Xavier had always been protective of equity in Enigma. She had been wanting to up her position for some time, even if it meant buying in. She believed so fully in Enigma, and in the Pit, that she would readily have used her own money to get a greater share. But on the one or two occasions she mentioned it to Xavier, he had been evasive.

She crossed her legs, trying to appear composed, even nonchalant. She ignored Derek and looked directly at Xavier. "So, is that what's on the table? Voting shares?"

"All things are up for discussion," Xavier said, pulling back from the desk. "But we need to make sure the next couple of months are done perfectly."

Derek held up his hand in a caveat-like manner. "Now, obviously Bill needs to agree to it all too. We'll sell it to him when the time is right."

"But I don't think he'll question that you are really driving this for us," Xavier said.

She bit her tongue. Again, Derek with the answers, like he was Xavier's mouthpiece. When did he become such an intricate part of Enigma? If Bill could hear this through the wall, he would be irate.

Xavier rested his hands on the armrest of his chair. "And when you're there next week, I need you to review our opportunities with LearnTech. Brief them on who we're talking to up here. Figure out a way to pull them into our sales cycles, sell their stuff. We need to show them that the partnership isn't all one-way, you know what I mean?"

She nodded, somewhat grudgingly.

"What would make you happier about everything?" Xavier asked. "I need you on your top game. So how do we get you motivated?"

There, he had given his olive branch, and she would certainly take it. "I need to know that LearnTech will do nothing malicious with the confidential information we are giving. What if, after everything we share, they decide they don't want us? Can they copy everything?"

Derek laughed. "Oh, trust me," he said. "There is more than an NDA, and we are very well protected. We had a lawyer do this one. No templates grabbed from the internet, if that's what you're worried about."

"Can I see it?"

"Yes," Xavier said after a pause. "But there are some other matters in there that are for the voting shareholders only. So, we'll have to remove those. When you've read it, and you see everything is in order, you'll kick ass next week, right?"

"Absolutely," Natalie said.

* * *

On Wednesday evening, Natalie came home from work and quickly began tidying the apartment. Richard would be over in an hour with groceries. They would cook dinner together and relax. Richard said he would pop by the movie store and rent a film for them. She hoped it would be something other than an action movie.

Richard was still here, and for that she was grateful. She felt he was slightly less sure of his plan to go away. For months, he had been convinced he would leave in the fall, and now it was winter. She felt that he might well be staying for her. She suffered no guilt from his delay, and she hoped more and more that he would lose his resolve entirely. She was bringing him to Toronto at Christmas to meet her grandparents, a big occasion, indeed, since she had only ever brought home one or two boys to meet them.

As Natalie cleaned her counters, she saw she hadn't put away the mail she brought up when she passed her box in the lobby. Flipping through it, most of it was junk and advertisements, but there was also one bill, and, surprisingly, one envelope addressed in handwriting to her. There was no return address, but judging by a certain thickness of the envelope, she already had an inkling of what it was.

She opened it, and her thoughts were confirmed. Inside was an invitation to the wedding of Augusta Hardich and Derek Lam on June 24, 2006. She already knew the details of it from David, who was quite keen to attend now, in his honored position of walking Augusta down the aisle. The usual envelope enclosed with an RSVP card was there, but so was a small slip of folded paper. Opening it, she saw an elegant handwritten note.

Dear Natalie,

I know that the last few times I called, you were busy. If you believe it, I thought it easier to rely on a letter to speak with you. I do hope we'll see you at the upcoming Christmas Ball that my mother is putting on for charity. I know David will be going, and I trust you'll be accompanying him. Nice to see my mother and David on speaking terms again, don't you think?

Regarding the wedding invite, I know it's a bit early, but we wanted to ensure that our mandatory favorites knew the date and would reserve it in their calendars accordingly. I always assumed you would be coming. You are welcome to bring a guest. We Hardiches and our circle can be a tedious bunch, so it's best to bring your own entertainment and company. I wish I could tell you that Derek's side would liven things up, but I fear he's rather light on the guest list all around. And the people he is inviting are, I can attest, a bit boring.

I hope you are well and that you are tolerating my brother. I very much enjoyed our last meeting and wish we could see more of each other. Do reach out when you can.

Augusta

When Natalie inspected the RSVP card, she noticed Augusta had already taken liberties. Two names were filled in—*Ms. Natalie*

Mitchell, and Mr. Richard Earning—with a checkmark in the box *Accept(s) with pleasure.*

Natalie slammed the invitation down on the kitchen counter and went in search of a pen.

No, she would not bring Mr. Richard Earning to the wedding. She wouldn't have Xavier and Richard in the same room. But more importantly, she didn't want Richard in the same room as Augusta.

There was a reason Natalie shirked appointments with Augusta. What was her game? Was Augusta wanting to rub salt into the old wounds of her former lover? Was she trying to humiliate Natalie?

When she had her pen, Natalie put a line through Richard's name and wrote her own little note on the RSVP to mail back.

Thank you, but Richard can't make it. David and I are looking forward to your special day.
   Natalie

CHAPTER 33

Decision *(Richard Earning, February 2006)*

THE February temperature was cold, especially for Natalie, who swore that Waterloo had more snow and was colder than Toronto had ever been. But it was winter, and this was all to be expected. With the right clothes, everything could be managed. That was the thought when Richard and Natalie planned a weekend getaway at Blue Mountain Ski Resort on Georgian Bay. Natalie had an old school friend who worked in the hospitality business and put her on to a weekend deal at a new hotel called The Westin Trillium House.

On a Friday afternoon, they got into Richard's Honda Civic and drove north for two hours. They went up through the small towns and hamlets of Grey County, where the *Welcome* signs and the *Thanks for Visiting* signs were almost beside one another. Though it was dark out on the country highways, the roads were free of snow and ice.

This was the first real time they had spent together in weeks. Since November, Natalie had been traveling back and forth to Boston. Even when she was at home, she would be too exhausted to do much of anything other than sleep or watch a few movies. Often enough, she was on her phone late into the night, communicating with Enigma's offshore development partner in India, which was posing more problems than benefits.

Even today, she fell asleep for a nap shortly into their journey. When she awoke, they would talk about news, and Natalie would sometimes slip into some musings about Enigma. Richard was more comfortable discussing Enigma now; he didn't feel any of the anger or frustration he used to.

"I keep having this thought about something," Natalie said, lowering the volume of a country song playing on the radio. "What if you were to work for Enigma on a contract?"

Richard gave an exasperated laugh. "I'm sure Xavier would love that."

"He wouldn't need to know."

"How?"

"You register a business, and I could hire your company. You wouldn't have to come to the office. Nobody would know it's you. I'm swamped, Richard. Honestly. I could really use you," she said. She was smiling at him from the passenger seat. "We could work together a bit. Besides, you do all that product stuff better than me. It could be ten or fifteen hours a week."

"I have a job, Nat."

She turned and stared at the road for a while. "You could be doing so much more. You're just killing time working for Robbie. How much longer are you gonna do it?"

"I like my job," he said. But he felt the twinge of doubt inside him that had been stirring. He felt it and knew where it was pushing him.

"Maybe it's not Enigma," she said. "Maybe it's another company.

But come on, you can't do what you're doing forever. You can't be one of those people who doesn't try."

"Doesn't try?" he echoed her. "Try at what?"

"Everything. Life, work, success. All of it. You're not using your talents."

Richard went quiet.

Her words were colder than she likely intended, frosty like the temperature outside. Even her hand resting atop his on the gearshift didn't change that. This was not the first time she had alluded to his situation, his peculiar purgatory. Though she often talked now like he wasn't going away anymore, this was the first time she had been so explicit as to say he was wasting time or, rather, *not trying*.

Natalie must have sensed his distance. "I didn't mean it in a bad way. I'm sorry if I hurt you."

"No, no. It's fine."

Richard wasn't angry. He had his own doubts, his own fears that were needling him. Was he doing the right thing? Time made him second-guess himself and the plans he had been so fervent about last year. He began to fear the failure of his enterprise, his journey. What if he couldn't write? What if his dream was only meant to be just that—a dream? It would be wasted time and money.

In a moment of rash decision making, he had done something last week, made a bold move to confront this fear.

But he had not told Natalie yet. And he was beginning to think he might be setting her up to be disappointed.

They arrived at the Blue Mountain Resort around 7 p.m. The Village, like its ski mountain, was on a much smaller scale than its siblings in Mont Tremblant and Whistler-Blackcomb. Its manicured pristineness and orderly layout thwarted any attempt at being an authentic alpine experience. It had mostly been built in the last decade. But it had its own romantic appeal as thick fluffy snow alighted the brown, green, and blue angled rooves of the condo-chalets and shops. As darkness descended, the lights of pedestrian walks glowed with the illusion of warmth, while restaurants and bars beckoned through windows with candlelit tables and the occasional fireplace. In the middle of the village, families and couples skated on a frozen pond.

They checked into their hotel room at the foot of the ski hill and grabbed a late dinner. Much later than Richard would have liked, since Natalie had booked them in for a ski lesson first thing in the morning.

Back in their hotel room, Richard turned on the gas fireplace, and Natalie fell asleep when she hit the pillow. Richard pulled out a notebook and stayed up for some time watching the flames dance while writing.

> *The longer he stayed here, with her, the more he wondered if he would leave. She was reordering him, pulling him into the reality he rejected but found comfort in … found sense in.*
>
> *She was at odds with another force, a fire burning inside him that he concealed and protected within his cloak. He was not yet ready to let it go out. The lick of those flames on his spirit was chaos and bliss, ruin and happiness …*

He wondered when he would tell her his news.

* * *

Richard's skis stayed together in a triangle as he traversed the hill. When he finished his arc, he adjusted his weight to the other ski to begin another turn.

"Good! Good!" yelled Luke, a red ski-suit-clad instructor. Richard closed in on him and the small group of skiers waiting on the side of the hill. "Now, turn up the hill, up, more until you stop. Good."

With his turn done, he clumsily jockeyed his way to stand beside a middle-aged couple from Toronto who were also taking part in the ski lesson. As it turned out, they were staying at the same hotel as Natalie and Richard. Natalie had already made plans with them to meet up later for a drink in the lobby bar.

Luke raised his ski pole high in the air to signal the next person in the group of three standing further up the hill. A figure in a beige snowsuit with a scarf covering her face and a toque with a few stray wisps of hair poking out began her descent.

Natalie's turns were too small; her arcs were not wide S shapes, but a narrow, squiggly line. Her speed was picking up.

"Wider. Go wider! Bigger S. Do a big S" Luke yelled.

Whether Natalie chose not to listen, or couldn't hear the instructor because of her insulated head, she must have realized her predicament. For she did one final turn that aimed herself at Luke's class, at the couple she was to dine with that very night, and at Richard.

"Slow down, make your plow wider. Big pizza slice!" Luke bellowed.

But Natalie wouldn't or couldn't. And as she approached Richard, he heard panic in her voice as she called out his name. He tried to get out of the way, but his own ineptness on skis meant that he flailed about without making any meaningful movement. At the last moment, Natalie managed to slow down a little, though not enough to prevent the collision.

Richard could only brace for impact as she dropped her poles, opened her arms wide as if she might hug him, and shout out "I'm sorry!" before plowing into him and toppling them both over.

He didn't feel much in the way of pain; rather a shock and a winding, followed by a cold bite on his wrist where snow had somehow worked its way into his mitt. Gathering his senses, he immediately thought of Natalie and panicked. Was she hurt? He could feel her on top of him, wrapped around him, their skis tangled together.

Before he could sit up and say her name, Natalie's face, with her scarf pulled away from her mouth, came into vision.

"Richard! Oh my God. Are you okay?"

"Yes," he answered. "Are you?" Richard gave her a smile to assure her he was fine.

And then he felt her head on his chest, and a convulsing of her body, a steady shake. Only when he heard the sound of her laughter did he link it with the spasms he could feel through his jacket. Luke was studying them and asking if anyone was hurt. He looked relieved when they both said they were fine.

Since Natalie was on top of him, she tried to get up first. It began with trying to twist this way and that, to roll to a side, but her skis were always preventing her. And his too seemed to be in the way.

"I swear," Natalie said, "I am trying to get off of you, but I can't." And she would laugh again uncontrollably.

Finally, Luke felt his expertise was needed, and he unclipped Natalie's bindings so that her skis came off and she could angle her legs unimpeded. As she pulled herself off Richard with Luke's assistance, Richard felt a tinge of regret—this was what it felt like to be filled, to be content. When he was with her, he was at peace. He would even say he was happy.

Later that night, as they ate dinner at a restaurant. Natalie reached her arm across the table and touched his hand.

"You see, you don't need to go away," she said. "There's plenty for us to do here. Canada's a big place." She laughed and added, "But maybe we'll go south next time. Cuz it's still really cold here."

He smiled, listening. No, he couldn't say anything to her tonight. Why spoil it?

After more than a few drinks with the couple from Toronto, Richard and Natalie returned to their room. Before he had even taken off his shoes, she pulled his face to hers and began kissing him. Her clothes didn't stay on her long, and neither did his.

* * *

They walked around an outdoor skating rink on Sunday afternoon. Families and couples of all ages glided and carved up the ice, some with grace, some with brute determination. Richard had bought them coffees earlier, which they carried. The weather, though still cold, was warmer today than it had been on Friday or Saturday.

"There's something I haven't told you," Natalie said. "About someone we know."

He didn't need to ask who. Her tone, her manner, told him exactly who it was. Augusta was still never very far from his thoughts. She was there, lurking. "Oh? Who's that?"

Natalie stared out at the skaters on the ice. "I had an invite for Augusta's wedding. When she sent it to me, she invited you too."

"Really? Can't see how that would work."

"Neither do I. So, I declined for you. But I feel guilty for deciding on your behalf. I'd love for you to be there with me, but ... I don't know," she trailed off and took a sip of her latte.

"When is it? End of June I think, right?"

"Yeah. The last weekend."

"I can't go," Richard said.

"You don't want to?"

He reached for her mitted hand through his own. "I don't think I want to, but even if I did, I can't." It was hard to feel her hand through all the layers of the mitt. All he could do was clamp the end of her mitt where he faintly felt her fingers. Her hand, however, seemed lifeless. She knew what was coming next.

"I bought an open-ended plane ticket," he said. "I leave in April."

She was quiet for a long time as they walked. The sounds of blades scraping the ice and shouts and laughter surrounded them. "Maybe you'll only go a couple of weeks and come back," Natalie said, not looking at him. She sounded hopeful.

"Maybe," Richard said, not wanting to eliminate the possibility for her.

The first leg of his odyssey was already well planned, and he knew it would take him over three months to accomplish it. He intended to travel from France to Spain and Portugal, then cross the Mediterranean to Morocco, cut over to Tunisia and cross up into Italy. From there, he would decide his next path.

"Rightly or wrongly, sounds like you've made up your mind," Natalie said.

There was no question of her disappointment. They walked a little further apart now than when they had begun.

That night in bed, he felt her distance; she could have been in a different room, not lying beside him as she was.

On the long drive home Monday, Richard thought Natalie put on a brave face. She would ask him about the cities or destinations he wanted to see, and she tried to sound curious. But he could tell her interest was tepid.

He was certain he had let her down.

CHAPTER 34

The Money Man (David Burlow, March 2006)

DAVID filled two tumblers with scotch and passed one to Natalie. She had come over after work to have dinner with him. Now, they were sitting in his living room with a warm fire that he sometimes stirred with the poker. Richard wasn't with her tonight. She sometimes brought him over, and though David didn't mind the boy, he also liked his alone time with Natalie.

"So, he's off in April," she was saying. "He thinks he could easily hold out a half year, maybe longer."

A boy on the run, that's all David could think about it. "He's actually doing it, eh? A silly business," he said.

Natalie frowned a little. "It's what he's wanted to do for a long time, I think. I should be happy for him, more supportive ... I *am* happy for him."

David snorted. "If you want to be supportive, tell him he's a fool. Grow up already. If he goes, that's it—he's turned his back on you. You tell him you're not waiting for him to go find himself." He didn't understand Richard's state of mind at all; it's not like he was going off to start a new business. Rather, he was off to live like a gypsy and try and write a book that nobody would ever read.

Natalie put her hand to her mouth to keep her scotch in while she laughed. She was able to swallow it.

"What's so funny?" he demanded.

"You. You're a tough talker. We both know you've never turned your back on the people you care about."

He snorted again in response, which brought on another giggle from her.

Natalie stared into the fire. "I think I might go over with him for a couple of weeks when he leaves. I've never been to Europe, and I need a real vacation."

David had never been anywhere outside of Ontario and had no desire to travel. The world was a dangerous place, as the newspapers reminded him every day. In November, France had featured prominently in the international headlines with protests and riots where cars burned, and some people had been seriously injured or killed. When he remarked this to Natalie, she shrugged her shoulders.

"There's always something happening somewhere," she replied. "Can't let it stop you. Who knows what could happen in Boston next time I'm down there?"

"Are you going again next week?"

She shook her head. "No. Hal Jennings and some of the LearnTech team are coming up here. Going to meet our university partners," she said and took another sip of scotch. "Xavier and Derek are planning an outing to Toronto with them after the meetings. I'm not invited—boys' club."

The fire received a good poke from David now, and a whirl of sparks followed. Something didn't seem right at Enigma. He had told Natalie as much before, but the more he considered the information being exchanged between Enigma and LearnTech, the more troubled he became. There was something odd. Maybe a merger?

He had taken some liberties and called Bill Spindrall to see if he could shine a light on the peculiar interactions between the companies, but Bill gave him the same line as Natalie: a "deep partnership" was forming. Though Bill speculated they would each be the exclusive representative of each other's products in their respective countries.

"Has anyone said why Derek Lam is involved?" David asked.

"Nope. But Xavier treats him like more of a partner than he does Bill."

David nodded. Maybe that was the key. "Bill's definitely angry about that."

"He should be. Derek shouldn't know anything about us."

He was caught by her use of the word *us*. She really did take her small slice of ownership to heart. "What's going on isn't normal, and Bill's in the dark too."

Natalie bit the inside of her cheek and leaned back to think.

David couldn't help but be reminded of Augusta. Strange that she had these little gestures that seemed almost hereditary, in the blood. For Natalie never would have learned them from her real family; she never had the opportunity to. But these little tells of her ancestry would only be known to Augusta and him. So far, Augusta had kept her word. There had been no disclosure of secrets, of truths.

He was reminded of an upcoming appointment he had. "Bart Miller asked to meet on Friday. Said he would come over for a visit in the afternoon, but I told him I would go to his office. Assured me it was entirely personal. But I wanted to ask if you knew of anything."

"No," she said. "Nothing to do with me."

* * *

David sat patiently in a boardroom in Bart Miller's law office.

When Bart came in, he greeted David kindly and sat opposite him at the table. He had a folder with him containing some papers.

"I fear this all seems like a bigger production than I wanted it to be," Bart said. "It was merely a social call. That's why I was happy to come by your place."

"You've never called socially," David retorted.

Bart laughed and seemed embarrassed. "Not because I didn't want to. But I hope I can put your mind at ease, this has nothing to do with you or our dealings. It's everything to do with me. I wanted your advice."

"Oh?" David grunted. Never before had his lawyer asked him for guidance on any matter. "What on?"

"When we were at Elinor's Christmas gala, I spoke for some time with Derek Lam," Bart said, sliding the folder over. "What do you make of him? His investments?"

David opened the folder. Inside were some marketing sheets on Derek Lam and why he was the best at managing the money of high-net-worth individuals. It was all the usual stuff: years of experience at some heavy-hitting firms, a unique perspective for seeing things nobody else saw, a discipline in diversification to minimize risk.

He closed the folder with a bit of a chuckle. "Nothing. I make nothing of him or his fund."

Bart looked at him expectantly. He was waiting for more, and when he realized he wasn't getting anything else, he seemed flummoxed. "I know that the Hardiches moved all their money to him."

"Yes."

"And he's been getting more clients. People we know. When the Hardiches handed over their money to him, it was a bit of a stamp of approval."

"I don't know why," David said curtly. "It's not like Elinor understands what she's doing."

Miller grinned. "True. But Xavier?"

"He certainly doesn't know what he's doing."

They sat staring at one another. Bart wavered and broke the silence. "I won't beat around the bush. Derek says he can really accelerate my wealth generation. I'd be a fool not to consider it. I was thinking of investing a rather large sum. The returns in his fund are exceptional. He says this would be a great time to get in."

David grunted. "It's always a great time to get in."

Bart Miller fidgeted with his tie, seemingly frustrated at the progress of the conversation. "Do you have an opinion as to whether or not I should do business with him?"

A strange question to ask, David thought. He had only ever looked after his own money and that of the Hardiches until Elinor moved it away from him. He couldn't imagine someone else minding his investments. How many people had no idea what they were doing and gave their savings over to other people who barely knew what they were doing?

"If you want to know what I think, I wonder why you'd bother risking it," David responded. "You're doing well enough. What do you need Derek for?"

Bart looked at him in disbelief. "For better returns, for more," he said.

"Do you trust him?"

"Shouldn't I?"

David grunted. "You want me to tell you it's a good choice. Seems like you've made up your mind; you just want an assurance."

Bart gave a frown and then a chuckle. "You might be right. These things are never for sure. Would have been nice to know that a cautious man like you approved of our money man."

"A cautious man like me doesn't trust my money with other people."

"True, but that means you are missing out."

"I have enough. I don't want more," David said. "And as a man who I respect, I'd advise you to stay away from things that you don't understand. That's what I can tell you."

He could tell Miller would have preferred a different answer.

When David left, he asked to keep Derek Lam's marketing literature. As he drove home, he began to think more of Derek and his rise to prominence in the Hardich circle. For a man whose supposed pedigree was from some of the most reputable boutique wealth firms in America, it seemed strange that Derek would set up camp in a sleepy town like Waterloo.

Now Lam appeared to have his fingers everywhere. Though they seemed to touch unrelated subjects, they had one common theme: all the subjects were people David cared about or, at least, in the case of Bart Miller, were acquaintances. Whether it was Elinor and her money, Augusta and her marriage, Enigma and Natalie's ambitions, and now Bart Miller chasing more returns, Derek Lam was becoming a bit of a lurking specter in the background.

What was this man about? Who was he? The fact was, David knew very little about Derek Lam. And he decided it was time that Derek fall under a little more scrutiny than he had in the past.

CHAPTER 35

An Offer *(Xavier Hardich, March 2006)*

THE door was unlocked, and Xavier stepped into Derek Lam's condo at the Seagram Lofts, a former whiskey distillery warehouse converted into condos in the late nineties. The unit was large and spacious. Light poured in from floor-to-ceiling windows that led out to a large terrace overlooking the small downtown city center of Waterloo. In the living area, Derek lounged on a couch, reviewing some documents, with his feet resting on a glass coffee table.

Derek looked up and gave Xavier a grin, followed by a thumbs-up. "Did you see it?" he asked knowingly.

Xavier nodded.

"Stepping into the big league," Derek said.

As much as he wanted to feel more celebratory, Xavier was perturbed. He was having a hard time matching Derek's optimism and good mood. He sat down on the couch opposite his friend.

Derek, seemingly sensing his inner discord, gave him a confused look. "What's the matter? You should be ecstatic."

Xavier crossed his arms. "I don't know ... I guess I thought ..." He didn't know how to say it because a part of him was feeling guilty for his own disappointment. Under Derek's scrutiny, he finally confessed, "It feels low."

"Low?" Derek scoffed. "What do you mean? This is a great offer. A couple of years ago, you took over a company that had shit revenue, and now you're flipping it for a solid return. What's wrong with that?" Then he added more forcefully, "What's wrong with you?"

Was there something wrong? Xavier had wanted to shake the frustrated sensation since the letter of intent from Hal Jennings had landed in his inbox. Derek had been CCed, so he knew all about it. The LOI covered the key terms of the acquisition of Enigma by LearnTech—one of them being the offer price. "I feel Hal should offer more," Xavier said. "Enigma has some great potential. I don't know that his valuation is accurate."

Derek shook his head. "Enigma's potential can be gone tomorrow. Or the next day. We've discussed this. You know how these things work, especially in tech. You gotta seize an opportunity when you can." He removed his legs from the table and sat forward on the couch. "Look at it from Hal's perspective; he's buying your company to accelerate his own product development. If he has to pay too much for it, he'll just build it himself, and Enigma will be crushed. You don't have something he can't do or figure out in-house; you just have something that will save him time compared to doing it on his own. For both sides, there's a window of opportunity. If you let it shut, you're fucked. LearnTech will gobble you up later for less. Or even worse, Hal will just starve you out of the market."

Xavier listened to Derek's reasoning. He understood it, even agreed with it, but still, something in him resisted. "But Enigma has a great product. It's just taking off. I've researched standard valuations, and this—"

Derek double-slapped his palm on the coffee table. "Stop," he said. He breathed in slowly and exhaled as if trying to contain his agitation. When he spoke again, it was a with a deliberate, even pacing of his words. "You're doing it. Do you know what it is? Overvaluing your company. I've seen people ruined by that mistake. It's foolish greed. Now listen." Derek looked Xavier right in the eyes. "This is why I asked you a while back about your exit timeline. You said a year. It's been over a year and a half. You're emotionally sucked into your business and getting more sucked in by the day. There's no emotion here. Your balance sheet and revenues are what they are; they don't factor in the maybe or the possibility. The last time possibility in tech was factored in was 2000, and everybody lost a lot of money when the bubble burst. Because *maybe* and *possibility* can change. You need to stay committed. Get out when there is money to be made. Got it?"

Whether it was the confidence with which Derek spoke or the fear he instilled, Xavier began to be swayed. Hal Jennings and Learn-Tech did have the resources to build a competing solution within their own product. How long did Xavier and Enigma have? Maybe a couple of years at best? Derek was right—why would Hal pay top dollar for something he could make on his own?

As Xavier began to nod in agreement, Derek struck home. "You're going to be an amazing success story, following in the footsteps of your father. You took a little fledgling startup and set it up for acquisition by the big player. You'll be on the local lecture circuit—invited to business conferences and panel interviews ... all that stuff. And when I'm done doubling your money in few years, you'll be laughing that you even had this conversation today."

"I look forward to laughing, then," Xavier said, feeling more optimistic. "Now we just need to make sure Bill falls in line."

"He'll have to," Derek said, sitting back again and clasping his hands behind his head. "Because he won't like the alternatives. But we should sweeten the deal a bit for him. You know, an extra bonus on top of his equity payout for going along with everything. Don't worry, he'll be in our camp. And you'll be the next generation of savvy Hardiches."

When Derek got up to fetch them a beer from the fridge, Xavier was starting to feel the pride of what he had accomplished.

PART SIX: LOYALTIES

CHAPTER 36

A City of Light and Death *(Richard Earning, April 2006)*

H IS pen frantically jotted in his notebook, staining the page with a memory.

A woman passed by holding the hand of a young boy. She was encouraging the child to keep moving, pulling him gently along while also restraining him from jumping into the shallow puddles on the sidewalk. In her preoccupation with her charge, she was oblivious to the moped weaving leisurely from side to side coming up beside her, its helmetless rider slowing down to eye her figure from behind and then peek at her face as he passed, accelerating off down the street.

The boy had noticed. The cafe server sweeping the sidewalk had noticed; he shook his head in disapproval before returning to his short, heavy pendulum strokes that appeared to sand the pavement more than clear unwanted debris.

And Richard had noticed. He noticed all of them.

These mundane sights, and many more, Richard surveyed from his chair outside the cafe near the Grands Boulevards in Paris on a late Saturday morning. He sipped his espresso, thinking it a good one, though he was by no means a coffee connoisseur.

The city was beautiful, and Richard felt the enchantment that is only known to the traveler, the visitor, the guest. Removed from his familiar surroundings, he found pleasure in the everyday of a new place. People and their interactions were all accentuated against the backdrop of five-story nineteenth-century buildings, old churches, and cafe-lined streets. The cars were different, the air was different, the sounds of speech were different. He was watching, smelling, and hearing it all. Wondering. Thinking. Analyzing.

Still, he was troubled. For despite the hand of a muse that exposed him to all this newness and placed before him these scenes to interpret, to write down, to make a story of, Richard was behind a glass wall—a barrier. Something was blocking him. He could see inspiration, but he could not touch it, internalize it. Why? What was he missing that stopped him from crossing the threshold to become one with the scenes around him?

Something was off, something didn't fit. Was it him?

His contemplation was interrupted by a figure that seated herself beside him with two large shopping bags.

"I hope that's still your first," Natalie said, pointing to his espresso.

He shrugged uncertainly to suggest he wasn't sure, which meant it sure wasn't. Natalie shook her head and smiled. She reached over and slid his notebook out from under his hand and flipped through some pages.

"Lots of beginnings and middles," she said.

"I gotta start somewhere," he said. He had told her he wanted to start a book, write a journal of his travels, and maybe even get a travel blog up, which were becoming popular on the internet. But he was still writing scraps. Snippets of nothing. Richard deflected the conversation by pointing at her bags. "I see you have been more successful than me."

"It's impossible to fail at the Galeries Lafayette," she declared, opening one of her bags and proceeding to hold up various purchases of clothing and accessories. The Galeries Lafayette was an infamous place where any person with money and the slightest sense of fashion was obliged to pay homage. Natalie had come from giving her tithe and was, if not spiritually rejuvenated, content and fulfilled in the material renewal of her wardrobe.

They returned to their hotel to drop Natalie's bags off before embarking on their sightseeing. Their modest accommodation was a few minutes from the cafe, down the narrow one-way street of Cité Bergère. Initially, Natalie wanted more elegant lodging on the trendy Champs-Élysées or in St Germain, and only grudgingly accepted Richard's budget-hotel pick. However, she eventually conceded, after a few days, that it was the right choice. The two were only in their room to sleep. They were constantly in motion from one museum to another, strolling through various neighborhoods on their way to sights, and dining out in restaurants all over the city until late at night.

The hotel had only one minor inconvenience. Although their room was on the fourth floor, they took the stairs up and down every day for fear of the tiny, slow, shaky elevator. The lift moved between levels with such uncertainty, and its single sliding door hesitated in opening for so long, that Natalie was inclined to boycott it. The assurances of the hotel manager that no guest had been trapped in it "this year" did nothing to quell their doubts in the machine. The same manager suggested that the unfortunate incident last year was entirely the fault of some guests. "You cannot pile into an elevator here—it will reject you," he said. "And the guests were much larger than the elevator was designed to accommodate—a problem I have seen from people of … certain nations."

But this was a minor irritant, usually only noticed at the end of a full day of walking when their legs were weary and gelatinous. What did some extra stairs matter? After all, Richard was in Paris, the legendary city of history, romance, and beauty—the starting point of his travels planned for nearly a year.

And Natalie was with him—a gift, a blessing. He was glad of her company and that she had joined him. Six days had passed with lightning speed, and soon she would be gone, returning home. He wanted to slow it all down, slow the pace at which time moved, so that they might be together just a little longer. In fact, in moments of self-reflection, when he was completely honest with himself, he admitted he was beginning to worry about her imminent departure. Soon, he would be alone, traveling for months on end, writing and experiencing foreign countries. Is that still what he wanted? This is the journey he had planned for so long, yet doubts were starting to surface. Can dreams change? Do they have dependencies on people? What did he want?

Natalie, too, seemed to sense that time was running out. She became more affectionate with each passing day, searching for his hand regularly when they walked around the city, and searching for his mouth with her lips when they sat beside one another at dinner. Still, they did not speak of the months ahead, of the future.

This afternoon, Richard had chosen a destination that thoroughly puzzled Natalie. As they rode the subway to Père Lachaise, Richard knew she was indulging him. She made no specific protest against visiting the illustrious cemetery, but noted it was a rather morbid place for a couple to visit.

"I'm on vacation in the City of Light, and you're taking me to a place whose inhabitants have had their light snuffed out," she said, as the subway cars shuffled in the underground tunnels of the Metro. "You're really upping the romance on this one."

"It's supposed to be quite beautiful," he said. "And some historical figures are buried there." He had to admit, it was hard to sell hundreds of years of consolidated death. He put his hand on her leg. "Okay, fine. I really want to see this. It's weird, I know. But I'm glad you're up for it."

She smiled at that and rested her head on his shoulder. Her thick curls puffed right into the side of his face, but instead of brushing them away, he let them stay.

Arriving at the cemetery, they entered through the main gate, wandering into lives past, expired. The rain was at bay, though the sky remained overcast; its grayness added to the dreary silence of the place. Mausoleums stood on either side of the walking avenues, like perfect little houses in a quaint community. Some residents had well-kept structures with fresh flowers decorating their iron gates, while others had come upon hard times and their dwellings were dilapidated, almost appearing abandoned by the dead and the living. Behind the more illustrious houses were the numerous open-air residences—the tombstones. Richard and Natalie walked up and down avenues, peering into the dark houses, reading the dates of life and brief inscriptions.

"This place can humble anyone. Makes you think of how much time you have left," she said somberly, drawing nearer to Richard.

He agreed; it was humbling. Even the great tombstones of Molière, Chopin, Marcel Proust, and Honoré de Balzac inspired not fascination but reflection. The clock was ticking, always—on today, on his time with Natalie, on dreams, on life. Path after path, they wandered, living souls forced into uneasy contemplations amid the quiet and peace of the deceased.

Richard became increasingly introspective as he surveyed his own life and what he had done with it—not very much. What was it he needed to accomplish so that he might be a meaningful memory to someone before his final rest? Why was it important to accomplish something, anything? And what was it he should contribute to this world? The answers were elusive, and it made him uneasy. For many who dwelt here, the answers were a mystery as well. For the famous graves were surrounded by the unknown, the obscure, the forgotten, those who were dead to all. The outcasts of memory received only a passing bout of curiosity, if anything.

An image birthed in his mind so quickly, so without warning, that he became stiff—Augusta. Where did that come from? In the presence of the dead, a memory was resurrected. He was supposed to come here with her. But that was an old plan, an old dream.

"You cold?" Natalie asked, looking at him, surprised. They were both wearing sporty light rain jackets.

"No," Richard said trying to conceal his inner shock at the

haunting memory while pointing down another avenue for them to journey down.

At length, they came upon a small group of tourists congregating around a large vertical slab of stone some ten feet tall. Richard recognized it immediately from his guidebooks—the resting place of Oscar Wilde. An angel, donning an Egyptian-like headdress, was hewn into the side of the tomb, but instead of ascending to the heavens, the angel appeared to be in some horizontal flight just above the ground. Her posture was neither free nor graceful; rather, she was prostrate, the weight of her rectangular stone wings forced her into an uncomfortable submission. That which was to give her flight upward damned her to the earth.

The base of the grave was where Wilde's congregation practiced their art of worship. Hundreds of red lip impressions adorned the smooth stone of the monument. Lipstick vandals had kissed it in a strange form of homage and respect to the great writer and poet. Other admirers chose a less invasive adoration, leaving folded pieces of paper with rock paperweights atop them on the ground at the foot of the tomb. Richard's guidebook had told him that these papers were a mixture of private letters, personal reflections, poems, stories, and sometimes even pseudo-prayers. The devotees of Oscar Wilde were many, their rituals varied, but they were all inspired by him: writers, readers, lovers, and the downtrodden.

The visitors today were of all ages. One woman, to the amusement of the small crowd gathered, rolled red-lipstick over her lips and pinned them to the tombstone while her friends took photos. Pulling her mouth away, she left her fresh mark to join the countless others placed there earlier in the day, from yesterday, and from the innumerable days before that had not been washed off or faded by rain.

"The mood here is so different. It's cheerful," Natalie commented.

She was right. There was light here. Somberness and despondency flittered away. This was the first spot in Pere Lachaise where people gathered out of happiness, as if wanting to feed on the energy of the living for a few minutes before moving on. Groups and couples asked each other to take pictures, and quick greetings and conversations were exchanged.

Richard and Natalie waited patiently until another photo was done before approaching the front of the tomb to read the inscription below the angel.

And alien tears will fill for him / Pity's long-broken urn, For his mourners will be outcast men, / And outcasts always mourn.

"He died poor, you know—a bit of an outcast himself. Likely thought nobody would remember him," Richard said.

"He's certainly embraced by more than outcasts," Natalie noted, looking around before linking her arm in his. "You're the Wilde fan. You should pay your respects. Do you want some of my lipstick?"

"Nope, I'm fine," he said. He was a fan, yes. But most of that had been driven by Augusta—again, her memory struck him hard. People jockeyed to get a photo opportunity in front of the stone angel.

"You're not going to kiss the stone then?" Natalie pursued him. "You're here—don't be so uptight!"

"Not today," he responded, shaking his head. A part of him wanted to do it. He just didn't like to make a spectacle of himself in front of the onlookers.

Natalie let out an exasperated sigh. "Okay. Then let's just get a picture of us with the tomb in the background. Hurry! Stand here or someone will sneak in behind us and mess the picture up." Natalie looked around and set her sights on an older couple admiring the grave from a short distance away. Approaching them, she exchanged some words that Richard couldn't hear, gave them her camera, and returned, smiling, while producing some lipstick from her purse.

The woman nominated to be the photographer seemed unusually enthusiastic about her appointment.

Natalie rolled the tube over her lips making them a fresh bright red before leaning in close to Richard's shoulder.

Richard faced the eager photographer and gave his best fake smile.

Painfully long seconds passed. At last, the camerawoman signaled that the photo would be taken in "One, two," (was that a click of the shutter?) "and ..." *click*, "three!"

Somewhere between the second and third click, his head was abruptly pulled to the side and Natalie's lips were planted squarely on his cheek. He froze in surprise and turned to see the giggling Natalie clutching his arm. Other onlookers laughed at the ruse that had been played on him.

"You need to keep those beautiful lip prints on your cheek all day," their photographer said, returning the camera to Natalie. "She has claimed you."

"I agree!" Natalie declared. "Promise me you will!"

"I'll do my best," Richard mumbled, but he knew he was only half-committing.

They set out along another avenue. He could feel the place where Natalie's lips had pressed against his cheek; feel the branding of her lipstick. He had to continually resist the urge to wipe it away. If they came across other tourists, he would try to conceal his cheek by tilting his head and burying it in his shoulder.

On one of the paths that was empty of travelers, Natalie gently tugged his arm to have him stop underneath a tree.

"When I leave ..." she began, and then paused and stopped. She laughed awkwardly as she fumbled to find the rest of her sentence. "When I leave, what will it mean for us?"

Richard exhaled deeply. The question was not a surprise. He had been thinking about this over the last month, as well, more so over the last few days. They had avoided talking about their looming separation.

"I'm not interested in pushing you into anything," Natalie went on, speaking quickly. "I just want to know ... you know, make sure we're on the same page."

"I wouldn't ask you to wait for me," he said. "I'll be gone for a while."

"Yeah, and there's plenty of Eurosluts to be had, I suppose," Natalie said with obvious sarcasm, but he thought he heard a slight uncertainty in her jest.

He chuckled. "Don't be like that."

"If I try to keep something going with you, would you try?"

"Yes," he said. There was no thought to his reply. It was instantaneous. And he believed it.

Amid the tombstones of the forgotten, surrounded by monuments to the great, in a place filled with decay, her face was alight with expectation, energy, and life. She kissed him on the lips and placed her forehead against his. "Good," she said, smiling. Richard felt the pull of her on his soul. She was quite remarkable, beautiful.

Yet, still, another woman hid behind trees, crouched behind mausoleums peering at him; he felt her, felt Augusta—would she ever leave him? It had been so long. And still she was there, lurking.

When they left Pere Lachaise mid-afternoon, they proceeded to the Metro to catch a subway to Notre Dame. No longer protected by the deathly quiet of the cemetery, the noise of cars, of people, and of the bustle of the city, sounded deafening to Richard's ears. Life—movement and motion—blurred about him.

Only after a few odd looks by some passerby did Richard remember he still had Natalie's lip print upon his cheek. Embarrassed, he went to remove her red brand, but she stopped him.

"No!" she shouted with mock anger while grabbing his hand. "You said you would keep it on."

"I said I'd do my best."

"Keep it on until we get to the cathedral. Please?" she pleaded, laughing. "I'll do anything you want if you do!" she added, with a certain grin that implied she would make it worth his while.

Richard capitulated, keeping the red lips on his cheek for the whole underground ride.

* * *

Later that day, Natalie rented a scooter in the St. Germain neighborhood. It was an impulsive decision when they happened upon a rental shop while walking along the south bank of the Seine River.

He never, in all his life, thought he would be sitting behind Natalie on a Vespa, clasping onto her waist and praying to a God he hadn't spoken to in years.

Around streets, through thin alleys, and over bridges they drove, only occasionally beeped at for their recklessness. Stopping for a coffee and snack, she insisted they switch spots and that he take a turn driving. By then, he was interested in trying it. Starting out unsteady, he got the basics down, and his confidence grew as he zipped around the Marais and Bastille neighborhoods before weaving up to Montmartre. Once, he risked a quick turnaround to look at his passenger. Natalie was laughing while Sacré Coeur disappeared behind some buildings.

In the evening, they had dinner on the Champs Elysees, a beautifully lit wide avenue teeming with the traffic of people and cars. Afterward, they chose a night walk down the Champs to the Place de la Concorde with its obelisk and fountains. This was once a place where guillotines were erected, a reminder that the City of Light and the energy of its citizens could sometimes rage, flow, and spew blood when its populace rebelled. But tonight, all was calm as they meandered through the Jardin des Tuileries under the watchful eye of its many classically inspired statues before they came to stand at the glass pyramid entrance of the Louvre.

Fatigue was taking hold of them. Though they were stimulated by the sites and their all-day rambles, they were weary and opted to head back to the hotel. Four flights of stairs needed to be climbed yet!

They took the Metro to the Grands Boulevards and walked down the street to their hotel. Upon entering, the manager greeted them from behind the desk.

"Ah, *c'est les Canadiens*. You're Natalie, yes?" he enquired, although he seemed confident in the answer.

Natalie nodded.

"There is a message. A gentleman called for you some two hours ago. Asked to be put through to your room. I'm not sure if he left something on the answering machine, but he called back and told me to give you a message in person."

"Who's it from?" Richard asked, surprised.

"A minute," the manager said, rummaging through his pockets and pulling out little slips of paper. Then he found the piece he sought. "Here. David Burlow. He said everybody's good, but it's very important you call him." He handed Natalie the paper. "I wrote down the numbers on the paper you'll need to dial for an international call."

Natalie thanked him, taking the note. Richard was puzzled as they climbed the stairs to the fourth floor. Burlow might say everyone was fine, but then why had he bothered to call? Richard could tell Natalie was anxious; she moved quickly and with purpose.

"Everybody's fine," Richard repeated as they entered their room, trying to reassure her.

Natalie didn't seem to hear him. She immediately sat on the bed, unfolded the paper, and called David. It would only be six o'clock back in Kitchener-Waterloo.

Her conversation with Burlow was short. Burlow must have asked her about her time, for she briefly described some of their adventures, but didn't go into details. She was eager to learn the purpose of his call. Eventually, she became quiet; her face darkened. "What? No! How?" she finally yelled in a short burst. "And the Pit? Goddamn it. Not again!" And she hunched over on the edge of the bed, resting her forehead despondently in her left hand. Just before she hung up the phone, she said, "I'm coming home. I'll be on the next flight."

She started to run about the room in a flurry, grabbing articles of clothing and wildly throwing them in her suitcase. Richard stood to the side, watching her, calmly saying her name. She continued to ignore him, to not look at him, to brush past him as if he wasn't there.

"Natalie!" he shouted, no longer able to endure the mystery of her actions or silence.

She stopped in the doorway to the bathroom where she had just been gathering her toiletries. She put her hands on her head.

"I'm sorry, Richard. I'm so sorry. I have to get back. They're selling Enigma."

CHAPTER 37

A Last Resort *(David Burlow, April 2006)*

ON Sunday afternoon, David Burlow watched the staggered procession of travelers arriving through the gate at Toronto International Airport. She should be through soon. He had seen from the arrivals board that Natalie's flight had landed about thirty minutes ago.

He knew he had done the right thing by calling her when he found out what Xavier was up to. Unfortunately, the bearers of bad news, even when they have no hand in its making, suffer guilt from delivering it. He anticipated putting a cloud on her vacation, but what he hadn't anticipated was that she would end it midway through and return home immediately.

Why? What was the point? There was nothing she could change—it was all beyond her control. He should not have mentioned to her on the phone that Bill Spindrall was not pleased with the sale either—even felt like his hand had been forced. Had Natalie received false hope from that information?

David saw her come through the gate pulling her luggage and waved to her. His largeness and the fact that most people gave him a wide berth would make him easy to spot. When she saw him, she gave a smile of relief, despite the fatigue on her face. She was happy to see him, and that made David feel like a great man. He immediately walked toward her to help with the suitcase. She embraced him and thanked him for coming to the airport to pick her up.

On the way to the parking garage, he asked questions about the flight and the trip. Her answers were terse; she was distracted. He decided to leave her the peace and silence she sought.

They got in the car and began to drive west to Waterloo. He would glance over at her from time to time. She stared straight ahead. Sometimes she would close her eyes and breathe deeply, but the constant fidgeting of her legs or the rolling tap of her nails on the passenger door armrest suggested these were all calming tactics. As much as she needed sleep, she was probably too wound up for any repose.

The traffic was moving well on the sunny Sunday afternoon. Under other circumstances, the ride would have been almost enjoyable with the sun hitting the green treetops and fields on either side of the highway. Spring was here, new beginnings for nature. New beginnings too, for his passenger, but not ones she had hoped for.

"I can't believe it," she said, shaking her head. "It's happening all over again! I didn't miss the signs; I just chose to ignore them. I'm a fool."

David tried to console her. "Nobody could have predicted this."

"I could have. I should have," Natalie countered. "For a plain old partnership with LearnTech, we were always giving away too much. It's so obvious what was happening, now. There I was, embellishing on our outsourced development throughput efficiencies. Everything's great. Partners are great! I was helping sell Enigma to LearnTech, thinking I was just promoting it. All the work I did for that equity was bullshit. Xavier and Derek were lying."

David listened to her venting. She had every right to be upset. Xavier really had duped her. And worst of all, he tried to do the whole thing behind her back when she was away. He tried to console her with some good news. "Bill says that LearnTech will probably keep you on. They are very impressed by you."

He knew it was hollow encouragement. Judging by her grimace, Natalie thought so too. More minutes passed with only the sound of the tires rolling on the road.

"Does anyone know I've come home?" Natalie asked.

"I didn't tell anyone."

"Not even Bill?"

"I haven't spoken to Bill since he called me yesterday."

"We need to go to his house."

David looked at her. It was an odd request. "Why?"

"I need to talk to him," Natalie said, as if the answer was evident.

"No. It's Sunday and he's probably with his family. I'm not driving you there so you can start tearing a strip off him. You need to let it go."

"David, please. Only talking. I'm not going there to fight."

He wasn't going to be a blind chauffeur without understanding her motives. At last, he asked the question that had been on his mind since Natalie had told him to meet her at the airport. "Why did you come home early? There's nothing you can do other than yell at people. What's the point of all this?"

She was looking out the car window as she spoke. "You said last night on the phone that the formal offer to buy is coming tomorrow. Then they will meet Wednesday night at Xavier's to vote on the deal. Is that still true?"

"Yes," David agreed. "But everyone knows what's in the offer. Bill already has a preliminary copy. Wednesday is a formality. A kangaroo vote and signing."

"They all need to agree to the sale. You told me that. They can't sell unless Bill, Xavier, and Augusta all vote in favor. That's in the partnership agreement. Has anything changed?"

"No."

"If I can talk Bill out of it, we can save the company. He's my last resort."

David impulsively laughed in disbelief. He forced himself to look at the road instead of at Natalie. *She is fatigued*, he told himself; *she hasn't slept.*

"The company doesn't need saving, Natalie," he said at last. "It's business. I know that you've been deceived, but that doesn't change the facts. Xavier is cashing out. It's all good for him—he never invested a dime. Bill may not like the price and think he's getting ripped off, but he is still going to make good money. At the end of the day, it's not your company—it's theirs."

"It's our company! The only thing Xavier did was walk around and tell everyone to keep working hard and we'll all make a ton of money!" When she turned to him, her bloodshot eyes welled with water and fury. "We've succeeded despite him! We made Enigma what it is. And he lied. Xavier lied."

David shook his head. Now he understood. Had she told him of her wild intentions beforehand, he would have advised her to stay in Paris. In fact, had he known that this would be her reaction, he would never have called her at all. David knew this Natalie; he had seen this will of hers play out before, admittedly with positive results. This was the Natalie who had challenged him so many years ago when she refused the trust; the same Natalie who persevered under his cold rebukes until, finally, he showed her the love she deserved.

But this was different. There were some things her perseverance couldn't alter. Not all obstacles could be overcome by determination alone. She could not always triumph. He needed to brace her for the inevitable defeat. There was an odd feeling in his stomach, a knotting, when he considered how painful the blow would be to her when she understood the futility of her actions.

"You used to understand that when you're an employee, you don't get a say," he stated. "A maid can do a great job cleaning a house, doesn't mean she's consulted when the homeowners want to sell. You had your own business where you were in charge. And you left that for Enigma. I cautioned you against it. I told you not to trust Xavier."

"Is this an 'I told you so' moment?" Natalie snapped. She powered the passenger window. The noise of rushing air filled the car as if she could release David's lecture outside to the wind like a trapped bug.

David checked his frustration and focused on the road. Her petulant behavior made him wonder if this is what parents must suffer all the time from their children.

After a few minutes, the window went up. "I'm sorry," she said, reaching over to touch his arm. "I know you think it's crazy, but I need to stop this from going through. I've given way too much to Enigma. I believed in it! And now what? LearnTech buys us, takes the code and they'll do all the product development out of Boston and India? And what of the Pit? These guys have been blowing their brains out working nights and weekends to make the product what it is. They'll almost all be turfed the moment their knowledge is transferred. I can't let that happen. And we are just getting started—my vision for Enigma is a lot more."

David sighed and felt a strange sensation when she touched him. She was wearing his mother's wedding ring. He felt her kindness, her trust, her love. He wanted to help her, to protect her, but how could he make her see this was the way of Fortune? She looked tired, and he knew that only a misplaced hope was keeping her awake.

"Please," she implored. "Will you take me to Bill's?"

Resisting, fighting, would only agitate her. *Best to get this over with*, he thought. He would be her accomplice in this act of desperation. Maybe this was his role today—to be the one to console her when her plan unraveled.

* * *

In a pleasant neighborhood just to the west of the University of Waterloo, David parked on the road across from Bill Spindrall's place. Bill had an unpretentious gray-bricked 1980s-style bungalow with a long porch. Bill's car was in the driveway and, judging by the manner it hugged the grass lawn on one side, David assumed a second car was absent.

Before the engine was off, Natalie was out the door. "I know you think this is crazy. You can wait here." She shut the door and crossed the street to walk up the driveway.

Though he didn't think he could render her much help, David got out of the car to follow her. Natalie was halfway up the driveway when she must have heard his car door shut. She turned and, seeing he was coming, stopped, giving him a grim smile. She was impatient, wanted movement and action, but she waited for him as he lumbered up the driveway to her. Together, they went to the front door and rang the doorbell.

David had hoped against Natalie's hope, secretly wishing that nobody would be home, thereby sparing them a fruitless meeting. He snorted when he heard light thuds and bounces of feet issuing from within the house. The universal powers must have favored Natalie's will over his own. The door was whipped open, and a young, lanky boy of some twelve years stood behind the screen. He was wearing blue jeans and a black shirt with the imprint of a fluorescent green beaker on it. His facial expression was one of confusion and awe as he stared at the visitors. They must have looked an odd couple: David, with his great mass and thinning hair, accompanied by a slender young stick of a woman with a head of dark curls.

"You must be Jack," Natalie said through the screen door bending over slightly. "Your dad talks about you a lot." She received a rather emphatic nod from the boy and continued, "I was in the area and wanted to say hello to your dad. I work with him. Is he home?"

Jack said no more and did not invite them in. He merely turned around and ran down the hallway of the house, shouting, "Dad, somebody's here!"

After a moment, Bill appeared. As he approached the door, his face animated surprise.

"Natalie? Burlow?" Bill queried as he opened the screen door. "What are you doing here?" Then to Natalie, "You're on vacation."

"Bill," Natalie said, "we need to talk." Her voice was low and soft; she was bottling up her anxiousness.

Despite a flash of alarm that crossed Bill's features, he invited them into a sitting room just off the front entrance hallway. David and Natalie stepped over a few action figures on the floor and took a seat on a couch. Bill remained standing. He fidgeted, constantly pushing his bangs back before they had a chance to fall on his forehead.

"I know what's happening," Natalie told him directly.

Bill began to pace, and his face flushed. "I don't like how it's all going down. That's why I called Burlow," he said. "I'm sorry, but it wasn't my decision."

"You can stop it," Natalie reminded him.

"I think you'll do okay, Natalie. This Hal Jennings seems to love you," Bill said. "You'll get money for your equity buyout, and probably an opportunity to work for LearnTech. This could be really good for you."

Bill was trying to sound confident, like this was a great thing, but David heard the uncertainty in Bill's voice. Natalie was slowly moving her head from side to side.

"Don't do it, Bill. This isn't what you want, and you don't need to do it," she said in a firm tone. "Remember we talked about your vision for Enigma? Remember how you told me what you wanted Enigma to be? We can do it—we have done it. The company is just getting to the right spot—a great team and some great clients. You wanted to grow an amazing little company. And you can. You own it! Don't let someone else come in and change it. Don't let them come in and destroy what we've made."

Bill sat down in a chair opposite Natalie. He couldn't look at her anymore, and his gaze fell somewhere at her feet. "That's what I wanted. It's different now, though—"

"Then we can change it so it's what you want," Natalie interrupted.

Bill held up his hands, as if in defeat. "You know I can't. Things got messed up when Xavier came on. I try to put on a good face with him, but you know him and I are oil and water. We aren't partners. I know he wants to get rid of me, and I can't go on like this. What I wanted for Enigma ended when James Hardich died."

"I can make it what you want, but I need time." Natalie's voice rose passionately. "Trust me. After everything I've done for Enigma, you know you can. I'll figure it out."

Bill winced. "I'm sorry, Natalie. I do trust you, but not Xavier. If I use my vote to block the sale, I'll be damning myself. You must know that. Xavier will oust me if I reject this; that Derek Lam had words with me saying just that. And then what? I'll either get less when he buys me out or have to risk keeping my money in Enigma in the hopes he doesn't do something stupid." Bill let out a long sigh. "The deal's bad all around. It grossly undervalues Enigma's future prospects, but I'm done with it. Getting out is the best course for me. Besides, I was given an extra payment above my equity to play nice and help with the transition. The offer from LearnTech is the best I can make of a bad ending."

Natalie's hands were clenched on her lap. "What about the rest of us?" she said in an almost whimper. "What about the Pit? We've worked so hard. We were on to something." Her face began to fall as she must have sensed the first possibility of defeat.

Bill nodded. "It's true, but I can't look at that. I have my own problems. I need to look out for my family. I'm sure if you asked David here about the opinions or well-being of his employees when he sold his companies, he'd tell you he didn't much consider them. It's business."

David clenched his jaw but said nothing. He understood Bill's position, and in Bill's shoes, he would likely do the same—he would sell. His professional opinion did not side with Natalie in the least.

Natalie glanced at him expectantly. As she slowly understood that he would deliver no judgment that contradicted Bill, her head began to hang down toward her chest.

"Things change, Natalie," Bill said sympathetically. "I'm sorry. It's not ideal. But even my lucky wife said it's time to get out. She knows that always being under Xavier's thumb has been hard on me. If she says we sell, we sell."

That was the end of Natalie's plea. She was visibly deflated and defeated as Bill walked them out to the porch.

"You're young and talented," Bill said to Natalie, trying to sound encouraging. "I think there's plenty for you at LearnTech. If not, there will be more opportunities for someone like you."

She walked down to the car while Bill and David remained on the porch, watching her.

"You shouldn't have brought her here. You know my hands are tied," Bill said.

"I couldn't talk her out of it," David replied.

Bill gave a knowing smile. "She's a fighter. Big things for her ahead." He extended his hand. "No hard feelings, I hope?"

David shook Bill's hand. He had no grudge against the man. Bill had received his own share of lumps from Xavier and Enigma.

Fortune was giving Bill a chance to make a modest return, and he wasn't going to sacrifice it on an unwinnable fight.

"No hard feelings," David said. "Best not to mention this to anyone. If Xavier finds out she was on about blocking the sale, he might retaliate or something."

Bill agreed and David walked to the car. Natalie was already in the passenger seat, looking as dazed and lethargic as a drugged patient. Her head was resting on the window. The conviction, the faith, the strength to fight against all odds was being expelled from her like air from a balloon. She was fading fast.

"Take me home. Please," she told him softly.

As they drove to her apartment, David wanted to say something, but struggled to find any meaningful phrase of consolation. All he might have said felt preposterous and inadequate. When they pulled into Natalie's apartment parking lot, he suggested she come home with him. "I don't know if you should be alone right now," he remarked.

"Thanks, but I have a ton of laundry to do, and I just want to be alone," she said somberly. "I need to lie down in my bed." She politely refused help with getting her bags upstairs and told David she would call him tomorrow.

He watched as she walked into the apartment building with a plodding gait and without looking back.

It was nearly seven o'clock in the evening when David got home. He was not hungry and spent most of the night pondering Natalie's emotional connection to Enigma. He couldn't understand it, but he saw what it meant to her, saw how much it was hurting her to lose what she had invested so much energy and effort into.

There was nothing he or anyone else could do. Or was there? No, this would be a good lesson for Natalie. Some things cannot be changed; they must be endured. She would learn.

He went to bed.

He tossed all night. The nerves in his body, the neurons in his brain, fired endlessly until he felt as if he were on fire. As dawn broke on Monday, he could not ignore the idea that had seeded in his mind overnight. As much as he tried to push it away, it grew within. Without fertilizer or nourishment, a small, preposterous fancy turned to something large and possible.

David got up earlier than usual, washed, put on a suit and light overcoat, and walked in the park across from his house. The temperature was cool, and although the clouds were thick, crepuscular rays beamed down from gaps in the heavens. The park was still empty at this early hour, save for the occasional morning jogger. He was so preoccupied that he didn't feel his usual envy for the rhythmically moving bodies covering distance with speed—an experience he had not known since he was a young man. He reached the park pavilion on the little island and mulled the ludicrous idea more.

He didn't like it—not one bit. It was a desperate action and would probably yield nothing. For a man who had spent his life predicting returns, it was risky, a gamble. Yet, it was the only thing he could think of doing if he was sincere in assuaging Natalie's despondency. But if he were to pursue it, Natalie would need to be involved. That worried him.

Returning to the house, he waited until the hour when he thought it appropriate to make a phone call.

CHAPTER 38

Rivals *(Natalie Mitchell, April 2006)*

ON Tuesday, David told Natalie she needed to come over, that it was important. Despite her fatigue—a result of the unfortunate events surrounding Enigma as much as jet lag—Natalie was going to his house for an early supper. She was not particularly in the mood to see anyone and would have preferred to wallow in sorrow, but in the end, she thought some human interaction might be good for her psyche. If nothing else, it gave her some small purpose and motivation to shower and eat something.

Since David had dropped her off at her apartment Sunday night, she'd slept off and on and lived almost entirely in her head. She had stomped about the living room and bedroom, rehearsing the verbal lashing she would deliver to Xavier when she saw him. The speech was perfected now, but it neither mollified her anger nor made the betrayal easier to stomach. In fact, it might even have fueled her rage further.

She resisted calling Richard. She didn't want a long-distance crying session; that would be the result if she was given the chance to talk to him. A vacation had been forfeited, time with Richard lost, and all for no benefit. She sent him a quick email apologizing for her silence and informed him of her intention to go to David's tonight and would call him at the hotel on Wednesday night. Not for the first time since her return, she wished Richard was with her. There would have been comfort in his company.

At 5 p.m., Natalie arrived at David's. The food was, of course, ordered in from a well-known Indian restaurant. The two ate a solemn meal together in the dining room. David tried to stimulate conversation, but Natalie struggled to give more than monosyllabic bland responses. She found she just didn't have the heart. She couldn't find or arouse any energy within her. At another time, she would have found humor in his awkward attempts to lure her out of her defeated introspection.

Somewhere between a mouthful of butter chicken and a sip of water, David fired his salvo.

"Augusta Hardich will be popping in shortly to talk with us," he said, while moving food around on his plate.

Even in her physical and mental fatigue, Natalie reacted as if she had been electrocuted. "What! Why?"

"She's the only one who can help you."

"With what?"

"Enigma," David replied looking up. "She's the only one who can stop the sale."

Natalie was bewildered. "I don't want her help. I don't even think I like her. You know that."

David smirked. "This is business. I shouldn't have to tell you that. It doesn't matter if you love her or hate her. She has something you need—a vote. Get her to vote against the sale."

"And why would she do that for me? We're hardly friends."

David opened his mouth as if to say something, paused, and seemed to change tack. "There is no love between Xavier and Augusta. That's a start. It may amount to nothing, but I thought you would want to explore every avenue."

"You should have talked to me about this first," Natalie said, almost sulkily.

"Do you want me to call her and tell her not to come?"

She didn't answer but pushed her chair back from the table and got up. She began pacing between the dining room and the kitchen. Perhaps this stone needed to be turned over, but she was so certain of the emptiness underneath it that it seemed pointless. That Augusta, of all people, was her last hope, made her nauseous.

How solid was a plan predicated on exacerbating the wedge between the siblings? It didn't seem much to bank on, especially since Natalie had never told David how Richard factored into all of this. She had always been put off by Augusta's manner, but what truly prohibited any relationship between them was Richard. In some strange way, Augusta still coveted Richard, and once Natalie understood this, she never knew how to interpret any of Augusta's overtures of friendship.

"Does Augusta know what I want?" she asked.

"She knows the subject but not the details. And nobody knows her or her thoughts," David mused. "I don't like it either. But it's the last idea I had. At least, if this doesn't work out, you can say you tried everything."

David seemed to have low expectations of the meeting too. Though he likely would have preferred Natalie move on from all this drama surrounding Enigma, he had arranged this meeting for her peace of mind. Naturally, he had done it covertly, since she would have refused it if he asked her first.

Natalie walked behind David, who was still seated at the table. She rested her hands on his large, bulky shoulders. "Thank you," she said. "You're right, it may amount to nothing, but it's worth a try."

David rested his fork on the side of his plate—his dinner was only half-eaten, and he didn't appear to want more. Unusual for him. Maybe his own nervousness about the meeting was curbing his appetite. He got up to make coffee while Natalie carried the dishes in from the dining room. They bantered about inconsequential things, both of them trying to relieve their trepidation about the visit that would soon be upon them.

When the doorbell rang at 6:30 p.m., both of them froze and looked at one another. David's face was resolute as he gave a grim smile and indicated they should go to the front door. In the entranceway, David clutched the handle, paused giving Natalie one last look, and opened the door.

Augusta Hardich stood on the porch. She had sunglasses on and was wearing a slim-fitting black designer suit with the sleeves rolled up. Underneath the suit jacket was a deep-blue shirt with a white collar that complemented the thin white belt running around her slacks. Her expression was stoic as she looked past David to Natalie.

"Thank you for coming," David said, finally drawing her gaze to him. "Please," he added, waving his hand to invite her in.

She gave David a fleeting smile before stepping into the house.

"It's nice to see you again," Natalie said. She was trying hard to sound sincere, but listening to her own voice, she doubted whether it passed the test. She extended her hand.

Augusta moved forward, past David, past Natalie's hand and into Natalie herself, giving her a light embrace. Her airy perfume filled Natalie's nostrils.

"Is it, though?" Augusta asked quietly in Natalie's ear.

Natalie stood stone still before her arms, out of some reactive compulsion, weakly enveloped Augusta. "Of course, it is," Natalie said, summoning some feigned charm. She looked at David over Augusta's shoulder.

David grimaced and shook his head, as if to say, *"Who knows why she behaves this way?"*

When Augusta arched back to look at Natalie's face, she had an unnerving smile. There was something in it Natalie couldn't pinpoint—was it a touch of sadness or something menacing?

David suggested the women move into his office, and he would get some wine for them. Natalie declined the alcohol but requested a glass of water. She didn't need anything that would subdue her or cloud her mind.

Inside the office, Natalie took a seat in one of the two chairs in front of the large wooden desk. She thought Augusta would sit beside her, but Augusta went behind the desk and sat in David's large leather chair. She now opposed Natalie. Was she trying to make Natalie feel the instability of her position? Was Natalie to be made to feel like a supplicant in this affair?

When David returned carrying drinks, he paused, frowning, when he saw Augusta behind the desk. He then resumed his journey, delivering the beverages before pulling out the chair beside Natalie to sit down.

But Augusta shook her head. "I don't think you need to be here, Burlow," she said. "This conversation is really between Natalie and me—women's business."

A flash of anger crossed David's face, and he scowled. In return, she merely looked at him with calm indifference. David turned to Natalie with a questioning look.

Natalie wanted him there, especially given Augusta's demeanor this evening. Augusta was always an unpredictable force, but more so than usual right now. The woman understood her leverage, and she was enjoying the exercise of it. And if Augusta wanted the meeting to be private, there was little anyone could do.

After an encouraging smile at David, Natalie said, "Don't worry. I can handle this; we'll be fine."

"She's perfectly safe, Burlow," Augusta chimed in with a grin. "It's just an amicable chat, almost sisterly. I'm not going to tell her any dark secrets about you."

Again, David gave another glare but said nothing while he left and shut the door behind him.

The room was filled only with the sound of Augusta tapping her manicured fingernails on the large desk.

"He's quite protective of you, it seems," Augusta remarked. "He hasn't come out of the closet to say you are his yet."

Natalie shrugged her shoulders to indicate disinterest in the conversation. Augusta laughed, a joke playing out that only she found humor in.

Not wanting to give Augusta any more latitude in selecting the topics of conversation, Natalie steered them to what mattered now. This was, after all, not a social visit. "I'm grateful you came. I want to talk about Enigma and the upcoming vote."

Augusta ignored her. "David mentioned you rushed back from a vacation. Where were you?"

Natalie took in a breath, trying to conceal her irritation. "I was in Europe."

"Where?"

"France."

"A beautiful place. Were you traveling there alone, or did you go with someone?"

Natalie could no longer repress her rising frustration. "Is that why you came over tonight? If you want to ask about Richard, then just ask," she said curtly. She now wondered if Augusta had any interest in discussing Enigma—this whole visit might well be an intelligence-gathering exercise about her and Richard.

Augusta narrowed her eyes, looking suddenly petulant. She stared into the depths of the red liquid in her glass. "You were in Paris, I assume."

"Yeah," Natalie responded coolly.

"Did he come home with you?"

"No, he stayed. He has his own path."

"Good, he needs to do that," Augusta said, mulling over the information. "And what does that mean for the two of you?"

"What does it matter to you?" Natalie demanded. She must have spoken with some vehemence, as Augusta stopped the tapping of her nails on the desk, her eyes widening in surprise.

Augusta sipped her wine, swished it in her mouth, swallowed, and then spoke. "You've rebuffed my overtures of friendship. Every time I reached out, you had an excuse for not meeting up. You were too busy. Even now, you're not terribly friendly, are you?"

"Your friendship has always been suspect," Natalie said. It appeared Enigma was off the table for discussion. "Your interest in me was because of Richard. I know about you two. Richard told me after I confronted him. I saw the way you looked at him that day we met in the park—do you remember?"

"I remember."

"And then the way you continued to steer the conversation to him when we met for coffee? You concealed your relationship with him from me. Even at your family party, you pretended not to know him. Why would I be keen to have a friendship with you, given all that?"

"I was curious about your intentions with him."

"My intentions?" Natalie queried. "My intentions were purer than yours. In fact, I'm entirely confused as to why you continue to take an interest in him at all. You discarded him, if I am to understand correctly. I believe at one time he was quite attached to you—but he was one of your passing amusements, in the same way that we all are I suppose."

Natalie would have continued, but she was distracted by the doorbell ringing. The short chiming sound broke her train of thought, and she fell into silence, studying the woman across the desk.

Augusta was pressing her teeth together hard; her jaw was flexing in her cheeks, and her lips were firmly together, screwing her face up as if she had swallowed something sour. "You don't understand why I did what I did. And you certainly don't understand what we had."

"I think you're right."

"Do you love him? I mean, do you really love him?"

Natalie didn't answer. Why should she? She just stared back at

Augusta, overcome with the feeling that this woman was beyond analysis, she might even be slightly crazed.

Minutes passed. Natalie considered this the end of their conversation. She was about to get up when Augusta spoke again.

"So, despite all this resentment and distrust, you somehow thought it appropriate to ask me for a significant favor," Augusta said amused. "I know why I'm here. Old Burlow didn't need to say it. It's the old story—when you need something from someone, you'll set aside your scruples. You'd use me."

"This wasn't my idea," Natalie retorted. "It was David's. I only found out a short time ago you were coming over and that he had orchestrated this meeting. I think he was optimistic and thought we were on better terms. Maybe he erroneously presumed some affection existed between us and we'd find some common purpose regarding Enigma and you'd vote against the sale tomorrow. I don't think I ever thought it viable."

"But if I gave you my vote, would you take it, despite your dislike of me?" Augusta asked, leaning forward.

Natalie crossed her arms and was going to answer. There was a "no" working its way up through her throat, an impulsive answer divorced from reason and utility, an answer born from not wanting to be indebted to Augusta Hardich. But she never had a chance to give it utterance; she was interrupted by a firm knock at the door.

And Richard Earning walked into the office.

CHAPTER 39

Early Return *(Richard Earning, April 2006)*

FOR two more days, Richard had stayed in Paris and its environs. On Sunday morning of the first day, he had accompanied Natalie to the airport, where they had a coffee together before she moved through the security gate.

"I'll try to call you in a couple of days when I know what's happening," she said, as they lingered under the eyes of well-armed officers at the security point where only ticketed passengers could proceed. "But if I miss you while you're in Paris, get to an internet cafe and check your email. I might be out of a job soon. Maybe I'll come back for longer and tour with you," she joked. It fell flat with both of them; there was too much strain and anger in her voice to carry it off.

He told her everything would be all right, but she looked away. They both knew there was nothing he could say that would calm her or reduce her anxiety. He saw in Natalie's eyes that she wanted him to come home with her; heard it in her half-started sentences that trailed off with a feeble smile and a shaking of her head. Before she went through the gate, she kissed him fully on the lips. And then she was gone.

Returning to the city center, Richard walked about the streets, alleys, and boulevards, retracing some of the steps the two of them had walked together. He would come upon a church or museum, venture in and explore, but his mystical bewitchment of the City of Light seemed to have dissipated along with Natalie's hasty departure. He was frustrated by the events that precipitated the removal of her companionship. He passed the night at the cafe close to the hotel, trying to write something of significance, of meaning and clarity, but his notebook pages stared at him blankly.

On his second day, Richard boarded a train for the short ride out to the Palace of Versailles. He hoped, there, to rekindle a perspective that he had when he had first arrived in Paris: the ethereal feeling that imbued everything from buildings to landscapes with beauty. At Versailles, he moved through the palace with a throng of tourists, only half-listening to his audio guide that told him of the kings who had held court at the palace, and their audacious extravagance.

It was when he came upon the gardens that he experienced his revelations.

Standing on the large terrace behind the palace, he peered down over ordered nature—fountains, shrubs, and trees placed with precision in an Eden that no God created, but that men who had aspired to be godlike had made. At the end of the gardens, rowboats moved lazily upon a manmade lake that marked the boundary of the palace lawns.

The French aristocracy had once leisurely passed their time here enjoying theatrical performances and grand parties. These innocuous events masked the dangerous intrigues of the privileged as they jockeyed for royal favor, influence, and advancement. Their titles, their livelihoods, even their lives, all depended on playing a great game that consumed them. Nevertheless, however perilous their struggles seemed to be, they were oblivious to the true poverty and starvation that existed for most of the country's population living in the squalor of cities or countryside farms. There, in the houses of commoners and peasants, destitution and suffering were so pervasive and familiar that seats were reserved for them at dinner tables.

These thoughts occupied his mind while he wandered the grounds and came across elaborately concealed fountains. At some point, he journeyed down a path through a mazelike grove that deposited him in front of a circular fountain. Water jetted up into the sky almost as high as the linden trees that formed a perimeter of the area. He was alone in the space—a rare event, given the thousands of visitors on the Palace grounds—and he took a seat on a bench where he could rest.

He listened to the heavy thudding of the water as it fell back into the fountain basin on its descent from the sky. In this solitude, he asked why he had felt compelled to travel in the first place. What was the allure of "going away"? What was the strange comfort it afforded? Richard knew of the history that had preceded him; people in a time of personal hardship or crisis go off into the unknown. Even characters in novels would disappear to travel, fight in foreign wars, and return home with wealth, wisdom, or both.

When he had first planned this journey, he had believed in the possibility of such gifts being bestowed upon him. He thought that his travels would show him something about himself, would make him stronger, would inspire him to write, and conquer the rudderless feeling in his heart that had existed after Augusta's betrayal. Only now was he comprehending his error.

This trip, this journey, had been forged not by him alone. No, Augusta had been intrinsic to its creation. She had inspired him, had led him to believe that he could fulfill his impractical desires. And when he fell under that spell, when he committed himself to the course she offered, she had forsaken him. In folly, he continued to pursue the dream in absence of her—and he only now understood the futility of doing so. This great adventure was unnavigable without her. Augusta was the barrier, the film that covered his vision, preventing him from fully embracing this quest. She hovered about him, hiding behind lampposts, columns in churches, and tombstones in graveyards, reminding him that she was the missing link.

Everything seemed so foolish now, pointless. He was throwing drenched kindling on scorched logs. Augusta was gone. That dream was over. The fire was out. He, a writer? He, a traveler? Preposterous! He was fleeing reality, running from life and responsibility in some premature midlife crisis. He was running from someone who was good for him, cared about him: Natalie.

The more time they spent together, the more he felt that she was right for him. He appreciated her, respected her, and now, sitting in a grove in Versailles, knew that he loved her. It was a functional love, a manageable love—one that didn't throw him into great highs and depressing lows. Their relationship was normal, comforting, and tempered—very different from what he had experienced with Augusta. He could make sense of his feelings for Natalie, reason them out, explain them, and accept them fully.

Yet, here he was on another continent, pursuing some meaningless quest, the remnants of a nostalgic purpose that had grown stale, while, back home, Natalie needed him. Yes, he could continue his travels for months; he might well enjoy himself, but he would never attain or become the person he thought he foolishly imagined he was supposed to be. Finally, he felt that.

Returning to Paris from Versailles in the late afternoon, he went immediately to an internet cafe and checked his email. There was nothing from Natalie. Likewise, when he went to the hotel, there were no phone messages. It didn't matter. He knew what he needed to do. He called the airline and booked his ticket home for the following morning.

Perhaps, at the very least, wisdom had been granted to him after all.

* * *

By the time Richard walked into the office, he had been fully briefed on what was happening by a jumbled and restless Burlow. All the same, the knowledge of events did not prepare him for the shock, the mayhem of emotions, that washed over him when he stood before the two women.

Natalie's face registered complete surprise. She stood up.

"Richard, what are you doing here?" she asked in a frenzy. She gave him the reaction he had expected, that he had envisioned while sitting on the plane.

"I was worried. I came to see if I could help with anything," he said. That wasn't what he had imagined he would say at their reunion. He was supposed to utter something more romantic, something about missing her, about nothing being right after she left, about wanting to be with her. He felt all of it, but he was feeling something else too, some competing desire. He didn't want to look at the other woman; he even told himself not to. But he glanced past Natalie.

Richard hadn't seen Augusta for some time—not since he ran into her at the park when walking with Natalie. He had never encountered her at any bar or cafe, never pulled up beside her while driving. It was a peculiarity that a person could disappear even in the small cities of Kitchener and Waterloo.

His glance was brief, measured in milliseconds, but he took Augusta all in. She wasn't moving from her seat, and her mouth was slightly open in her own shock. But it was her eyes that caught him most; they were not amused, they were not cold, they were smoldering with anger.

Natalie stepped quickly to him, put her arms around his neck, and kissed him.

"Jesus! How? When did you get home?" Natalie blurted out questions, but then remembering who else was in the room, she suddenly stopped and looked at Augusta. Her hand fumbled for Richard's and, when she found it, she clasped it tight.

"It appears our little visit is done," Augusta said, standing up. She produced a smile that looked forced.

"No, there's no need to go yet," Richard said to her. "Can you just give us a moment?" He didn't wait for Augusta to answer but pulled Natalie's hand and guided her out of the office. He could feel her resistance, her protest. Stepping outside the office into the hallway, he shut the door.

Burlow was pacing in the living room and immediately came over to them.

"Is she going to vote against the sale?" Richard asked lowly.

Natalie shook her head. "I don't want favors from her."

"Did you ask her?" David piped in.

"No," Natalie said.

"No?" David stared in disbelief. "What have the two of you been talking about?"

Natalie looked at Richard. "Nothing."

David threw up his hands in exasperation and seemed on the point of lecturing Natalie until Richard beckoned for calm.

"Are you going to ask her?" Richard inquired.

"I don't know … No … I don't want her help," Natalie said. "I can't bring myself to be indebted to her, of all people."

"This is Enigma, Natalie—you might be able to stop the sale. This is the whole reason you came home early. Remember? You need to ask her!" Richard forcefully whispered. Was she blinded by some irrational pride?

"Not this way," she said, looking down at the ground with fists clenched at her side.

He could see she was going through an internal battle. She wanted to ask for Augusta's help, knew she should, but there was a block that was overpowering her. He couldn't understand it, but he could help her. "Then I'll ask," he told her. Even while he said it, he turned and opened the office door.

"Richard!" Natalie hissed and reached out to clutch his arm. "No! Don't! I don't trust her."

"Then trust me," he said. "I'm not saying she'll do anything, but I'll ask—for you." He pulled away from her and went into the office. As he closed the door, he saw Natalie and David staring at him from the living room. David was nodding his head encouragingly, likely pleased that someone was seizing this slim opportunity and acting upon it. Natalie, however, frowned; she looked as if she were going to speak, but no words were offered up.

Once sequestered in the room with Augusta, Richard didn't turn to face her—yet. In fact, some part of him must have wanted to flee, for his hand remained on the door handle. He breathed in deeply.

"It's been a while," Augusta said from behind him.

He thought he could hear a strain in her voice. At last, he turned to look at her. She was standing now, leaning against the desk, a near-empty glass of wine in her hand.

"Yes," he responded formally, moving to the center of the room. He wanted to sound officious, even indifferent, whatever his feelings were. Richard wondered if he would always be compelled to respond sensually to her allure, even after her duplicity and what she had done. Despite his anger at her, despite the weariness from the flight, despite the hopes and expectations from Natalie just on the other side of the door, Richard's mind wandered to a time, not so long ago, when he had shared experiences with this woman: a bed, a drink, a dream—the last had turned out to be an illusion.

Augusta watched him closely. "So, you came home for her? You put an end to your travels for her? She must be special indeed," Augusta said quietly with irritation.

"She is," he avowed.

"Then you're a fool," she snapped. "You were finally pursuing the things that mattered, and now you've gone and thrown them away, for what? The misguided belief that you can help her save Enigma? What does Enigma matter to you? Jesus, Richard!"

He was surprised at her anger. How could she possibly be livid with him? "Natalie matters to me. That's why I came back," he said.

Augusta took the last sip of her wine and put the glass down on the table. "You're giving up on yourself for her? You were so close to doing what you wanted—"

"Things have changed for me," he interrupted. He couldn't explain that those plans he had tried to pursue were now meaningless in Augusta's absence. He had never known until a day ago that one's aspirations can alter depending on who he or she is with—a point that was still perplexing to him. "But we're not here to talk about me," he continued, finding the strength to force his purpose. "You can stop the sale. Are you going to?"

She smiled at him, crossing her arms. "I suppose you would like me to thwart Xavier in the midst of his success, wouldn't you?"

"It wasn't his success. Natalie is the one who kept Enigma going. If it weren't for her, Xavier probably would have pissed away your inheritance. He can't run the place," Richard said. "Give her more time, and she'll give you a bigger return."

"What do I care about returns? I'm marrying money," she reminded him matter-of-factly. "Have you considered what voting against everyone else would do to me? To my family? Quite a bit of trouble all for your Natalie."

Augusta walked over from the desk to where he stood. She was so close to him, her eyes level with his, her airy perfume intoxicating. There was a carnal stirring in him. She could arouse him still.

"Strange that you would want to use me this way," she said softly. "For someone else's benefit—not even your own."

"I'm not using you. It's in your own interests to—"

"Her interests," Augusta corrected. "Not mine. If this is what you want, then ask it—from you."

Richard shook his head. "I won't ask you to do what's right. And I won't let you say I'm using you."

She leaned in closer, her hand lightly resting on his chest, her face inches from his own and her mouth slightly open. "If I let you use me this way, would I get anything?" she asked softly.

When she kissed him, it was not unexpected, but it still felt like a lightning strike. He didn't pull away.

He had yearned for that mouth often enough. Augusta caressed his unseparated lips with her own and tried to slither her tongue into a mouth that remained firmly closed. In those few moments, he was overcome with desire for her, but his loyalty to Natalie prevailed. He did not return her kiss, his body tightening rigidly when it should have loosened and melded with Augusta's form. He boiled on the inside, but he outwardly remained unmoved. Feeling his resistance, Augusta pulled back, her lips pressed together in the cynical smile he knew so well.

"Shall I interpret that as nothing?" she asked. She was trying to sound amused, but he saw the storm in her eyes.

"I suppose appealing to altruism is a wasted effort with you," Richard retorted in frustrated desire and with a touch of indignation. "Sacrifice hasn't been your strong suit in the past."

He could never have anticipated her reaction. The hand that was resting on him recoiled before both of her fists hammered into his chest with such a violent shove that he was forced to take two steps back.

"Fuck you!" she whimpered in anguish. In her rage, she looked as if she might say something else, but instead stormed to the door of the office and flung it open with such force that it slammed the wall.

Richard followed her into the hallway, keeping a few paces back. Her behavior was unpredictable—he had never seen her express anger physically.

338

Burlow and Natalie, who had been sitting in the living room, rushed over in alarm.

"What's going on?" Natalie asked.

Augusta stood up straight and looked at Natalie. Her face was still contorted in anger, but her voice was restrained. "I guess you were the best of the litter," she said. "Congratulations."

She opened the front door, but before she left, she said to Richard, "One more chance—ask me!"

Richard said nothing.

"You're a coward. In everything. You're too scared to live your own life. You should have stayed in Europe." Then, she turned and went outside.

Everyone watched while she got into her car and drove off.

"What the hell happened in there?" Natalie demanded.

"I don't know," Richard answered.

Both Natalie and David still looked disoriented. But it was Burlow who asked the question on their minds. "So, she's not voting against the sale?"

"I think that's safe to assume," Richard said.

Natalie took his hand.

CHAPTER 40

A Feast *(Xavier Hardich, April 2006)*

XAVIER inspected the table in the Hardich dining room with a mixture of pride and spiritual solemnity. He could feel his father with him tonight, watching over the coming transaction. James's ghost was proud and at peace as he circulated between the dining area and the living room where the small group of guests had gathered. There was a little more pomp to this occasion than might have been necessary, but Xavier felt the event was worthy of some formal excess. The imminent sale of Enigma was a big deal, and Xavier insisted on celebrating it with a catered dinner for the equity holders.

This was a great day for Xavier Hardich; he was building on the legacy of his father. He would show society that wise and profitable business decisions continued into another generation. Under Xavier's guidance, his father's investment in Enigma had made a sizeable return.

Elinor and Jocelyn fed off Xavier's enthusiasm and were helping him curate a memorable experience. Small place cards had been written in his mother's elegant hand for each of the guests, to indicate where they should sit. Jocelyn had helped him print, copy, and bind the proposal of purchase from LearnTech. These were inserted into Enigma-branded folders that lay on the dining room table in front of the plates of each shareholder. Of course, everyone had read the digital copies of the proposal already, and Bill and Derek had both given their verbal support. The folders were just a little flourish, a memento of this glorious day that Xavier had steered them all toward over the last year.

Xavier's folder had an additional document—the agreement of sale that he, Bill, and Augusta would all need to sign. He would have the other two shareholders put their signatures on paper after dinner—just before dessert.

He touched the breast of his suit jacket to make sure his father's Montblanc pen was there. It was, ready and primed.

The table was set for six: Xavier was to be at the head on one end, mirrored at the other end by Bill Spindrall. Derek and Augusta would be seated on one side of the table to Xavier's right, while Elinor and Jocelyn would be seated to his left. Although Bill's wife was supposed to come, she had declined late last night. Bill said her migraines had acted up and she was bedridden.

"Mr. Hardich," a voice behind him said. It belonged to Adam, the chef. "I'm ready to serve the dinner."

Odd to be called Mr. Hardich tonight. That was how his father had always been addressed. And now it was his name—Xavier Hardich,

Mr. Hardich. Tonight, for the first time, Xavier felt worthy of it. He would be worthy, too, of admiration at the next Spring Gathering. By then, everyone would know what he had accomplished.

Xavier glanced at Adam. The man was tall and lanky with a graying black beard and long hair tied back into a ponytail. His white chef's uniform was spotless despite his being in the Hardich kitchen all afternoon chopping, dicing, cooking, and frying food for tonight's festivity. Adam owned the Indonesian-inspired restaurant that Xavier was fond of. At no small expense, Xavier had secured Adam's services for this private party. Along with one of his assistants, the chef had assembled a multicourse meal. When the guests arrived, the assistant changed into some black dress pants with a white dress shirt and walked around with platters of hors d'oeuvres while Adam put the finishing touches on the meals.

With everything ready, Xavier gathered his guests in the adjoining room and ushered them to their respective seats. Glasses of wine were topped up, and food began to fill every open space on the table. As each dish was placed down, Adam or his assistant would describe its contents: ribs lathered in hoisin-spiced sauce, duck magret with fried egg noodles in a chiang mai curry, monkeyfish and lobster simmered in a lemongrass curry, beef tenderloin and lamb lathered in coconut and kukui sauces and other spices. Xavier couldn't remember half of what had been said, but he could smell the fragrances drifting and mixing in the room. He looked at his mother, at Jocelyn, at Derek, and saw what he had hoped he would: delighted awe. This would be a night they would all remember. Though Bill was reserved and could have been more jubilant, it was Augusta who was causing Xavier frustration. Sitting on the other side of Derek, she seemed unmoved; her plate remained empty, her wine glass full.

Augusta looked tired. Black lines were under her eyes, and her face was pale. Her mood was subdued; she hardly seemed to have energy to engage in her usual passive mockery of him or anyone else. Xavier had socialized with everyone before dinner except her. Tonight, he wished they could set aside their enmity for one another.

"Does the food not agree with you, Augusta?" he asked, eyeing her.

"I'm afraid I feel unwell," she responded, not looking at him.

"Augusta didn't sleep at all last night," Derek piped in. "Hope she's not coming down with something."

Elinor inquired what could be wrong, while Jocelyn expressed dismay at Augusta's mysterious ailment.

Augusta only shook her head.

Xavier could feel an anger growing inside him. This was his night, and she was focusing everything and everyone on her. He understood what she was doing now. In her jealousy of his success, she wanted to dampen this celebration. How often had she insinuated he would fail? The cause of her ailment was clear to Xavier: it was the venom of resentment flowing through her. In her perverse world, she would rather have seen him flop and lose her inheritance than have him triumphant. Even if it meant she made money.

Xavier decided to put an end to all this concern for Augusta. "What will you do with the money from the sale, Bill?"

Bill took a moment to shift his mind to the question. "My lucky wife and I are still deciding," he said at last. "She doesn't want to move from where we are, so I guess we're not getting a new house. The only thing she's said for certain is that we will take a nice family vacation."

"A woman after my own heart," Jocelyn affirmed. "Xavier has sworn to whisk me away to a tropical paradise. Did you know, Derek, that he promised to take me to Bora Bora too? We're inspired by all of your honeymoon planning. You'll have to share all you know."

Derek gladly ingratiated Jocelyn with all his research had revealed about French Polynesia. Xavier was pleased the subject had now turned to something more positive and joyous. They were gathered to celebrate Enigma's sale, not bemoan Augusta's indisposition.

Talk floated in pockets among his guests as they continued to eat. Derek even took the opportunity to remind everyone that all those who came into this money would be wise to invest with him. "After all, nobody is giving a return like my fund," he told them, particularly Bill.

Xavier maintained a certain abstraction from everyone. It was as if he was looking down on the gathering out of his body. Jittery, with anticipation for the grand finale of the night, he began to mentally run through his victory speech, rehearsed over the last two days. As the plates and leftover food were cleared from the table, he gave a nod to Adam. That nod had been explained in an earlier conversation: stay in the kitchen and allow the dining room some privacy.

Xavier took a long sip of his wine and then stood up and waited for quiet.

"I am thankful to have you all here with me tonight. This is a great day for us. A great day for Enigma Solutions. Since I assumed control of my father's investment, I have worked tirelessly to grow it, to make it a successful venture. I haven't always done what's right, as Bill can attest to, but I think Bill would also agree that our differences and disagreements were always about the best direction to take Enigma."

Xavier looked to Bill and received the nod he expected before continuing.

"We both cared about Enigma and wanted it to succeed. Partnerships aren't always easy; like any relationship, they can make us angry and cause frustrations. But they can also bring some great blessings and happiness. Today, we see the culmination of that partnership journey as we accept a splendid offer from LearnTech. Bill, I know you didn't get to choose me as a partner, but I hope you can see it paid off.

"Jocelyn, thank you for being with me and supporting me," he said reaching out to hold her hand. "Even when I was dead tired and stressed out, you found a way to be in good spirits and cheer me up."

He began to tear up slightly. "Mother, thank you for everything." His voice was quivering. "You know how important it is for me to follow in Dad's footsteps. We are continuing his legacy here tonight."

Elinor had her hand on her mouth, and there were tears coming down her cheeks. But she was smiling with pride. Jocelyn embraced Elinor, and it took Xavier a full minute to collect himself. He cleared his throat to continue. "And there will be greater things on the horizon for us, Mom. You were a rock for Dad, and you've been a rock for me. Thank you.

"Derek, you have been a steady adviser since I took the risk of joining Enigma full time. We've bounced ideas around, and you've always been there to help whenever you could. I consider you a partner in this business, along with my sister, as I know you would consider me a partner in your endeavors." He bowed his head to Derek briefly, wanting Derek to understand that his counsel was appreciated but also that there were implied expectations. Derek had been welcomed into the Hardich fold; it was time for reciprocity.

"Augusta," he continued. This part had always been challenging for Xavier, so he opted for diplomacy. "I know you've kept your distance from Enigma. We all know your passions lie elsewhere. Thank you for trusting me with your portion of the inheritance; I hope I have not disappointed you."

He had never seen the expression on her face that she now displayed, and he didn't know what it meant. Was she flustered by the kind words?

"A toast then," he said, raising his glass. "To us, the beneficiaries of Enigma. We all deserve this, each in our way. And I am honored to be a part of bringing this wealth to you. My father would have expected nothing less of me. Cheers to you all!"

There was clapping—as he expected there would be—and everyone stood, even Augusta, as the glasses started to clink. With that, and many handshakes, Xavier opened the Enigma folder in front of him and removed a document to place it on the table. He flipped to the signature page while Jocelyn fetched the camera.

"It's time to sign the deal, so we can enjoy our just desserts," he said confidently. He removed his father's pen from his breast pocket and signed the document above his typed name with a flourish amid the camera flash. A thrill surged through him as he finished writing the last letter of his signature. Pausing, and staring down at the paper, he was overcome with pride and satisfaction.

Xavier then looked up to Bill and asked him to come around the table to sign. They shook hands, and Bill took the pen to write his name. Another flash. Bill turned to Augusta and held the pen up. He made space for her to come around and sign.

But she remained standing where she was, holding her glass of wine.

"Come on, Augusta," Derek encouraged her. "You're the last one!"

Augusta didn't look at Bill or Derek; she looked straight at Xavier. It was then he felt unsettled. Was she feeling sick? Did she look even more pale than before? Even when Derek grabbed her arm and started to gently usher her toward the contract, toward the pen, her steps were short and uncertain.

When Bill handed the pen to Augusta, she received it with a tremoring hand. Derek appeared to be holding her up as he positioned her between Bill and Xavier. There was another flash of light.

Augusta stared at the pen, as if it were a foreign object. The contract was before her on the table, awaiting formal closure—just a signature. But the Montblanc never moved closer to the paper to deposit.

"Augusta, sign it," Xavier told her firmly. "Just sign it," he repeated, trying to restrain the anger and fear that he could feel knotting his stomach. There was heat all over him, all over his body. His face must have been red, for it felt so hot. She would not thwart him this way, would she?

When Augusta turned to him, he realized all his anxieties were justified. He saw the crushing defeat she would deliver him, heard the words before she spoke them. He knew, when he saw her distracted and glazed-over eyes suddenly jump to life and become determined, that a resolution had been made that would undo him.

"I'm sorry, Xavier," she said as if reporting a casual fact, "I cannot."

Despite his emotions having recognized that her look portended his humiliation, to hear her say the words still stunned him.

"What do you mean you can't!" Derek bellowed incredulously.

"Augusta!" Elinor pronounced in her own confused disbelief.

"I'm not selling," she repeated, more firmly.

Xavier could feel his fists clenching, shock being replaced with rage. He was at an explosion point. He reached out and grabbed her arm at the bicep and forcibly whirled her around to bring her face to face with him.

"What are you doing? Sign it!" he growled. He could feel his hand compressing around her arm, feel her skin folding below his grip, feel her slight muscles as he continued to close his fingers together so that they might meet, encircling her limb.

She stared back at him levelly, but she was wincing. He could see her eyes watering. "Let go of me." Her voice was rising. There was pain in it, and panic.

He relaxed his grip, but only because he needed space to maneuver. The rage in him demanded release. While letting go of her arm, he pushed her back slightly to give his other arm maximum time and space to swing. He struck her, fist closed, with such force that she was sent spinning up and onto the dining room table. As soon as the violence was done, he knew he had gone too far. The astonished shouts of everyone in the room, the screaming of his mother, only reinforced what he felt an instant too late.

Bill urgently hoisted Augusta off the table and practically carried her to the other room and put her on couch. Jocelyn brought serviettes over and held one up to Augusta's face. Xavier could see the white cloths quickly staining red. Elinor ran over to them, wringing her hands, uncertain what to do other than call her daughter's name repeatedly.

Only Derek remained standing in the dining room, looking shocked and confused, as if he could understand nothing that transpired in the past few minutes.

Xavier was the same. Afterward, the events of the night just moved around him in a great fog, and he couldn't order them. Augusta went upstairs, accompanied by Elinor. Everyone else in the house left, and Xavier retreated to his office with a bottle of wine and slammed the door. He was still bitterly angry, and now he was ashamed and humiliated.

Did nobody understand what Augusta had done? Did nobody see that she was ruining him? And yet, in one irrational moment, he was now the object of blame. And with this thought, he became all the angrier.

Xavier's phone rang. He looked at the name displayed on the screen and ignored it. It was Hal Jennings, giving him the congratulation call. Xavier had no idea what to say to him. Everything was a disaster.

Then, sometime later in the night, the quiet of the house around him was broken by some swish of slippers on wood floors coming to the office. When the door opened, his mother stood there with a gym bag and dropped it on the floor.

"Leave," she said. "I don't want you here when she gets up."

CHAPTER 41

Debts *(Natalie Mitchell, April 2006)*

EARLY Thursday morning, Natalie was in bed staring at the ceiling after a late night talking to Richard. Technically on vacation, she had no intention of going in to work. Richard lay beside her, still sleeping. He too wasn't going into work; he was jobless and not even supposed to be in the country. When her phone screen lit up with Bill's name at 7 a.m., she assumed he was going to formalize the news.

"Did you have a hand in this?" Bill asked when she answered the phone.

"A hand in what?" she shot back, having no idea what he was referencing.

"You don't have to say if you don't want to," he said. "I won't badger you about it. Strange if you managed to convince that woman to take your cause. Stranger still if you didn't."

"What do you mean?"

"The deal didn't go through. At least not yet. Augusta refused to sign."

Stunned, Natalie was at first silent, then could only say, "Oh my God! What? Oh my God!" in a rising crescendo of excited disbelief. She had given up hope.

Richard stirred beside her. His eyes fluttered, and he rubbed them. He eyed her with a mixture of confusion and sleepy irritation.

She whispered empathically to him, "It's Bill. Enigma—the sale didn't go through!"

Richard woke instantly and sat bolt upright. He was attentive, waiting for more information.

Natalie realized then that Bill might not look with the same favor on events as she did. He was looking forward to a rather sizeable payout. "Are you angry?" she asked him. "I know there was a lot of money for you."

"Not really. I guess things turn out the way they're supposed to," Bill said. "When I told the lucky wife about your visit to me, she really started to wring her hands about the sale. Never seen her like that—she's usually pretty certain about things—no waffling when she's made her mind up. Margaret has always heard how wonderful you are. She was so angry with Xavier she couldn't even go to his little party. It's a good thing she didn't, given all that happened."

"I can only imagine. Xavier must have been furious. Did he expect her to sign?"

There was a pause on Bill's end. "I've left out a big part. It was bad. I wish … I wish I wasn't there," he fumbled for words. "I didn't even tell Margaret the whole thing. Hard to talk about."

When Bill told Natalie the extent of Xavier's fury, how it had turned to violence, a shock ran through her body.

The joy she had felt from the initial message vanished. "What do you mean? Hit her how?" Her mind was running off. She was trying to clarify what Bill meant by *hit*, as if it mattered. But it seemed important—was it slap on the arm, a shove? She was mindful that Richard was there, still staring at her, waiting for information, more snippets of her conversation to make sense of what was happening. He looked alarmed now.

Bill spoke. "He punched her, Natalie. In the face. Full strength. It probably would have knocked me right out. I don't know how she was still conscious."

Natale breathed in and out. Deep, full breaths. "Okay," she whispered, to try to calm herself. "Shit. Okay." Nothing was okay. But she needed to regain some control so she could think. Had Augusta done this for *her*? "Shit." Should she go to Augusta? Should she check in on her?

Bill interrupted her thoughts. "I'm going into the office, but I'm not sure what I'll do."

Natalie thought for a moment but then gave her advice. "Business as usual for now. Don't say anything to anyone. Call me later, especially if Xavier shows up."

"God, I hope not," Bill responded before ending the call.

As soon as Natalie pulled the phone away from her ear, Richard was released from his prison of silence.

"What happened?" he demanded. "What the hell is happening?"

Natalie put her hands on his chest. "Augusta came through for us, but she was punished for it."

When she recounted Bill's story, she didn't know what to expect. Would he jump up in a rage? Would he yell something out?

For a time, Richard remained still. But when she put her arms around him to hug him, she felt tremors running through him, and the hands that hugged her back were twitching against her spine. She knew he was enraged and trying to contain it.

He was furious on behalf of Augusta.

Despite everything Augusta had done, despite the pain she must be going through, Natalie felt the rush of jealousy and resentment running through her blood. And in that selfish instant, she was filled with shame. She clutched Richard tighter, kissed his cheeks, and placed her forehead against his while she admonished those dark emotions and thoughts.

* * *

They ate breakfast together in her apartment. Natalie talked of what might happen next. Would Xavier show up for work? Was there the possibility of Augusta going to the police? Her conversation was all speculative, filled with *could* and *might* and *if*. Richard chimed in here and there, but Natalie was doing most of the talking. She could see he was preoccupied. Again, she subdued her frustration with Augusta and focused on the gratitude she should have to the woman.

Richard decided he would take a shower after breakfast and then leave to surprise his parents with a visit. He had stayed at Natalie's for the last two nights and hadn't even told his parents he had re-turned. As far as they knew, he was still in Europe. She said she would happily drive him.

"I hope so," he remarked, "because you're coming in with me. Oth-erwise, they'll assume something went horribly wrong."

As soon as Richard was in the bathroom, Natalie called David. When he answered, she skipped all the pleasantries. "Did you hear what happened?"

"Yes. Yes, I did," David said slowly. "Augusta called me an hour ago and asked me to come over to the house. I'm leaving shortly."

"Do you think I should come with you? After what she's done, I feel I should … I should do something."

"No. Not yet," David said without hesitation. "I'll reach out to you later. Let me get the lay of the land."

* * *

Natalie spent most of the day with Richard at his parents'. Richard had rightly intuited the reception he would receive when he first strode into the house. There was shock at first, then alarm and worry, followed by a certain restrained joy.

That joy, that contentedness, that sense that all was right in the world emanated from Richard's parents as they all sat around the kitchen table eating lunch together. Mr. and Mrs. Earning listened to some of the brief stories of the couple in Paris with interest, but their smiles hinted that it was all well and good it was done.

"So, now what's your plan?" Richard's father asked.

Richard wobbled his head from side to side. "I'll ping Robbie and see if I can get some work with him again until I find something more in my field."

"You mean you're going back to the office? To computer stuff?"

"Yeah," Richard said.

And Richard's father sat back in his chair and nodded. "Good man."

Here, Richard's mother leaned close to Natalie. "I knew if anyone could set him right, it would be you," she whispered.

This small reunion—a celebration for the return of a prodigal son before he had gambled all his time and money away on a silly dream—served as a respite from the tempest over the last few days. But Enigma was never far from Natalie's thoughts. And when David called her telling her to come by his house at 4 p.m., the peaceful distraction was over. Business needed to be done. She left Richard with his parents to meet David.

She parked on the street and ran up to the door. Knocking three times, she didn't wait for an answer but walked in. David's voice beckoned from his office, "We're in here."

Entering the office, Natalie saw David was sitting at his desk. But in one of the two chairs facing him was Bill Spindrall. She sat down beside him and looked at David.

"How are they?" she asked. "Did you see Augusta?"

David's face immediately turned to a gloomy, sour expression, making his jowls more pronounced. "When I left there, Elinor was taking Augusta to the doctor," he said. "There is some fear she may have some fractured bones in her face."

Bill gave out a loud audible breath, shaking his head. He said to Natalie, "I was telling David that Xavier emailed me around noon. He's taking a few days off in light of everything."

"Should go to hell is what he should do," David thundered.

"He can't still be at the house," Natalie remarked.

"No, he's been banished to a hotel for now," David said. "Elinor is thinking it might be time to toss him out for a while. Wants him to rent an apartment. We both agree he shouldn't be near Augusta."

Natalie bit the inside of her lip. If Augusta was going to the doctor, Bill must not be exaggerating about the force of Xavier's blow. Natalie's victory had come at a cost.

"I should go to her," Natalie said.

David scoffed. "No. Augusta's not seeing anyone, not even Derek. He called a couple of times today while I was there, but she wouldn't talk to him."

"She saw and talked to you."

David's usual look of affection for her was replaced with a piercing stare. "That's different. I think the ship of friendship has sailed between you two. Besides, I have my charge from her. It's why you're both here." David turned his attention to Bill. "The fact is, decisions need to be made about Enigma. It's still possible the sale to LearnTech could be salvaged if we act quickly."

"What?" Natalie stood up in panic. "Why on earth would we sell now? Everything that's been done over the past week was to prevent it!"

David was breathing loudly through his nose as if he were trying to calm himself. "Natalie, this is not your decision. You don't own the equity. It's Bill's. Now sit down."

She hadn't seen this side of David before, this commanding and domineering behavior. Her initial inclination was to resist any authority imposed on her, but she was confused by it. Was this how he was when he wanted to get business done? Or had being with the Hardiches all day and seeing Augusta frayed his nerves? Whatever the case, she sat back down, a little hurt by his tone with her.

"Bill, what do you want?" David asked. "The money or the company?"

Bill was motionless for a full minute, as if processing the weight of the question. Then he pushed his bangs back frantically four or five times. "I want the company ..." here he turned to Natalie, "and I think we could do some great things. But I just don't know how this can work with Xavier."

Natalie had been avoiding this line of inquiry in her own mind all day—resisting it. What was going to happen if the company didn't sell? Xavier and Bill were still at odds. She could never trust Xavier again after the deceit about the equity. What was the next step?

"If Xavier were not a factor, would you choose Enigma?" David asked.

"Of course, I would," Bill returned.

"Then that's the end of it," David said. "Sale is off the table."

"And Xavier?" Natalie asked.

"Augusta has given me the responsibility of representing her interests. I'm her proxy." He held up a folder that presumably had documents that would support this claim and dropped them on the desk in front of Bill. He went on. "I have advised her that if Bill does not wish to sell the company, Xavier's employment must be terminated. It's the only thing to do to ensure the proper running of Enigma. She has agreed. The termination is effective immediately, but Xavier will be given a severance. Unfortunately, there is little we can do right now about his equity. If you agree with this course ..." here David pulled out a piece of paper from the folder and handed it to Bill, "you should sign this."

Bill took the document and read it—at least twice, judging by how long it took him to say something. "We're really firing him?"

David snorted. "Indeed, we are. And if I can find more screws to put in him, I will. To say nothing of his friend, Derek. Which reminds me, I want to make sure—neither of you have given money to him, have you?"

Bill shook his head. "To Derek—no."

Natalie followed suit. "No. Why?"

"Nothing for you to worry about yet," Bill said. "I have some inquiries to learn more about him, but I don't like my feeling on this one." He picked up a pen and offered it to Bill. "Will you sign?"

When Bill looked at Natalie, she smiled encouragingly at him. Bill took the pen from David and signed the paper.

Natalie was feeling a renewed sense of hope. But there was something nagging her that checked her from relishing too much in all this news.

Her debts to Augusta were piling up.

CHAPTER 42

Folly (*Richard Earning, April 2006*)

RICHARD was driving. The closer he got to his intended destination, the more he second-guessed himself. At one point, he pulled into the parking lot of a Tim Hortons coffee shop to just sit and think.

What was he doing? Why? He could turn around. He could abort, go back to his parents' house. Was it the fatigue that was making him irrational? Was it his nerves that had been overstimulated yet repressed for an entire twenty-four hours?

He had been up all night—slept not a wink. The tumultuous events of yesterday had eaten him from the inside. But he couldn't let it show, not to anyone, especially not to Natalie. When he had heard of Augusta's plight, he had raged on the inside. He wanted to find Xavier and bash his face in; he wanted to go into an uninhabited forest and scream for hours. But he could do none of this. Richard had to remain composed, had to put on a mask of mild concern and shock, and pretend that he was bothered—but not too bothered, no, not the berserk bothered—by the revelations of what Augusta had endured.

"Turn around," Richard said aloud to himself in the parking lot. His hands were on the steering wheel, trying to remain steady—but they wouldn't. And he couldn't turn around. He had to go forward.

He had to see her.

* * *

Richard rang the doorbell and heard the fall and rise of the chimes from within. It had been almost two years since he had heard that sound, but he remembered it clearly, knew on which chime it would cease. The only thing he didn't know was if the woman who had met him on the night of the Spring Gathering would be there to greet him now.

As he waited, a car pulled into the driveway. It was a taxi.

When the house door opened, Elinor Hardich stood before him with a coat on, ready to go out. Her face was neutral at first, as if she thought he might be a knife salesman—or maybe an extra courteous cab driver letting her know he was there—but then there was some brief recognition followed by curiosity.

"Yes?" she inquired.

"Mrs. Hardich, it's Richard. Is Augusta home?"

Elinor didn't move. She glanced over at the taxi in the driveway. "She is, but she doesn't want to see anyone. She's sick. And I'm afraid I'm going out. I'm sorry."

"Can you check? Please?" he implored. *Thank God she's home*, he thought. "Please tell her it's me."

Elinor glanced between him and the cab before letting out an exasperated breath. She invited him in. "I'll check. But if she doesn't want to see you, you'll leave. You understand?"

Richard agreed.

He waited in the entrance hallway while Mrs. Hardich climbed the stairs to the upper regions of the house. He looked about him at the wood benches and then down the corridor into the kitchen. He imagined the house filled with people, with conversation, and with Augusta moving about, littering her persiflage on proud men and women who became timid in her presence.

When Elinor came back downstairs, she seemed surprised at the words she spoke. "She said she'll be down shortly." She opened the French doors into the large sitting area. "You can wait here. I'm sorry, but I have to go, otherwise I would offer you something."

Richard went into the sitting room and thanked her. He paced about while Elinor stepped out the front door and locked it behind her. From the window overlooking the front of the house, he saw her get into the taxi and drive off.

He was alone. Waiting. But she was here. He paced in a circle, listening for sounds, but all was quiet. What was Augusta doing? How long would she keep him in this purgatory? He was tempted to venture upstairs, but he resisted. He sat down on a loveseat and fidgeted—he was shaking.

At last, he heard some faint creaks on the stairs, ripples of a light weight on old boards coming down. The sounds came slowly, almost tentatively. He nearly got up to meet the noise, to see her come down the stairs, but he contained himself. He needed to be on his guard. He still felt her mouth from a kiss a few nights ago. He was here to check on her, to thank her, not to run to her. He viciously rubbed his hands on his knees.

When Augusta came into the room, he stood up and gasped. He might even have let out a moan of despair. From her left eye to her chin, Augusta bore the mark of Xavier's fury—red, black, and swollen. The contrast of her disfigured side with the pristine perfection of the other side of her face could not have been greater.

Despite being in flannel pants and a sweatshirt, she looked at him with a casual haughtiness, her chin held high as if to dare him to see her in any other way than her glory.

"You'll forgive me," Augusta said. "I didn't have time to make myself up. Wasn't expecting anyone today." There was a slight smile, but it only showed on the right side of her face. She walked over and seated herself on a couch opposite him. "I certainly didn't expect to see you."

She was so far from him. Richard wished she had sat beside him.

"I heard what happened ... I heard about what you did," Richard fumbled. Even in that outfit that could make anyone look like a rag, she was beautiful. "I'm sorry, I never knew it would be like this. That Xavier would do this."

She gave a breathy laugh. "I never knew he could swing that hard." Silence.

"I'm grateful," he said standing up and stepping toward her. "What you did for Natalie was—"

"Don't insult me," she said vehemently, a sudden storm in her eyes. "It wasn't just for her." Her chin was raised now, and she peered down at him, though he was the one standing up.

He feared those words and took another few steps closer. "Who else then?"

But Richard knew the answer. Knew by the way she was clenching her jaw.

"You," she said. A single word that never needed utterance, but once spoken, dispelled all uncertainty.

Since hearing of what had happened to her, Richard had been desperately hoping her decision to go against Xavier had been out of self-interest, a realization that Natalie was the better steward of Enigma and her equity. Or maybe he hoped Augusta's decision was for the sheer amusement of spiting her brother. These reasons might have consoled him, might have made seeing her bruised grace more tolerable, might have made seeing her less resistible. At least then he could distance himself from her pain, her disfigurement, her sacrifice.

He knew now why she had done it. And wasn't that why he had come today? To know?

The truth was simultaneously unbearable and glorious. Not only because he was directly implicated and responsible in her suffering, but because he was overjoyed by it. Had he not dreamed months ago of some sign of her loyalty, some tipping of the hat to him to show that what they had together was more meaningful than the nothingness she had once suggested it was? In that single solitary word, "you," she made her motive clear: she had taken a blow for him, against her nature—or at least the nature she believed to possess.

Richard knelt before Augusta. He could feel a watering in his eyes. And in hers, there was a softening; her stormy defiance was replaced with a wariness, a confusion. He reached up with his hand to the swollen black-and-red skin, slowly, as if he was tending to a wounded and dangerous animal. He wanted to avoid any abrupt movements that might cause fear or retaliation. When his fingertips touched her cheek, just below her eye, Augusta flinched and pulled her face away. But he persisted, delicately, until she let his tips linger, until he could cup her face with his hand. If she felt pain, she was normalizing to it. He leaned his head forward, and upward, until his lips touched the bruise. He kissed it tenderly.

"No," Augusta said in a cracked voice, pulling her face away. But Richard would not relent. He continued kissing the hideous mark; perhaps enough caring caresses would banish it. Augusta tried hard to keep her composure, but he could taste her tears as they ran down her cheek—he felt her shaking, and her breathing came in irregular pants. Even now, she fought to appear indifferent to what happened to her, to treat it as just another joke, but the tears were a much-needed release for her.

When their lips touched, it was not she who sought out that treacherous physical connection; it was Richard. He hardly knew what he was doing. First, he had meant to thank her, then had meant to touch her to show affectionate gratitude. He only meant to kiss her once on that blemished cheek. But as he crossed each boundary from concern to loving intimacy, he found his soul was fast achieving an objective his mind had not yet been briefed on. And what was worse was that as each boundary was crossed, a bridge was burned and there was no retreat, no undoing, no going back.

When his tongue sought out hers, her toothy portcullis denied him entry, just as he had denied hers three nights ago in Burlow's office. Under his gentle nudging, however, some insider in her, some traitor, sacrificed the keep and accepted defeat.

The moment he tasted her mouth, he prayed he would be appeased. But this boundary, too, proved to be fluid, and he was spurred on. His arms were around her, feeling the frame of her body, of her bones that had always aroused him: the blades of her shoulder—yes, her spine—yes, her hips—yes. When she embraced him, caressed his face, he wanted more, and her clothing became a veil concealing the treasure he yearned for.

He gently pushed her down on the couch and pulled up her sweatshirt. Her small breasts concealed by her bra tempted him, and he reached behind her to unfasten it. But the clasp was unrelenting to his shaky hands and fingers, so he gave up. He just pulled the cups of the bra down to lick her firm, pinkish nipples.

His other hand clasped her waist and grabbed at the band of her flannel bottoms, pulling them down without any need to untie the drawstring. Clutching one of her thighs, his hand could feel warm embers emanating between her legs. Her panties, slightly damp in one area, were viciously removed. Now his own pants were in the way, and he unbuttoned and unzipped them to free his erection, which had been causing him pain in its confinement.

While his lower body moved into position between her legs, his mouth worked its way up from her breasts to where Augusta's neck met her shoulder. And that's when he paused. His mind, which had been nonplussed until now by passion, began a revolt. What was he doing? Stop! Vivid images of Natalie filled his vision.

Had he not arched up then to look at Augusta underneath him, perhaps he would have found the resolve to fight off his desire. He should have lingered a little while longer at her neck, thinking only of Natalie, of reason, of morality, of loyalty. But the moment he pulled away to gaze on Augusta, her glorious face that he saw no flaws in, her breasts pinched upward with nipples exposed by the bra he had been unable to remove, her legs spread, revealing her bare womanhood concealed only by a thin strip of hair, he was forced to submit to his intimate need for her. Just as he leaned down to kiss her, she craned up to meet him halfway. They were in sync, in rhythm, and choreographed by the goddess Aphrodite. He gently inserted himself in her, and only after one or two thrusts, his shaft was completely enveloped by her.

Sex and love with Augusta had always been ecstasy. But this time, it was divine. It was a dream to be with her, to feel her; a nightmare that lasts forever.

* * *

Richard's eyes opened. Confusion.

He was on his side in a comfortable bed, staring at a window unfamiliar to him. There was quiet, stillness—peace. A small cloud of cigarette smoke passed over him. His mind was active again, out of a numbing slumber, his senses gathering.

Augusta's room—he had carried her up here after their lovemaking ...

He sat up quickly in a panic. Augusta was beside him. She was under the sheets, propped up by two pillows, and a coffee mug was resting on her stomach that she held her cigarette over.

"How long have I been sleeping?" he asked urgently.

"Fifteen, maybe twenty minutes," she said.

He dropped his head back down on the pillow. Only that long? He felt he had rested for hours. But judging by the light outside, Augusta's statement was true. There had been no obvious change in its texture from when they were downstairs.

Richard too was under the sheets. He could feel the warmth of Augusta's body only an inch or two away from him. He could reach out; he could touch her. A part of him wanted to, while another part was taking in what had happened downstairs with clarity, with guilt.

Natalie. Betrayal. What had he done?

Augusta exhaled another cloud of smoke and then dangled her cigarette in front of him as an offer.

He declined. "Are you allowed to smoke in the house?"

Augusta laughed. "No, but these are strange days. Between my brother's battering ram to my face and the probability of my wedding being called off, I'm relying on the leniency afforded by pity."

In the limbo state between breaths, neither inhaling nor exhaling, Richard's body, his life-functioning organs, froze. Did she just say the wedding would likely not go through? So many prayers from a year ago answered. No wedding—Augusta free. But the thrill was equally matched by a downward spiraling panic—anger, sadness, frustration, and again, guilt.

He heard the cigarette drop into the mug with a *ssst* sound. From the corner of his eye, he could see she was studying him.

"That's new," she said, rolling over so her face, pristine on one side, and bruised on the other, hovered directly above him.

"What?" he whispered.

"Your eyes. I only use to see myself in them. But now I see her too."

Strange to hear Natalie alluded to. She was there with them now.

"I don't know what I'm doing anymore," he said. "I'm lost."

"You were lost when you came home. And now you love her. But it's different than our love."

Richard wanted to protest. He opened his mouth to, but nothing came out. Had he not disgraced Natalie enough today? He wouldn't deny his feelings for her on top of his infidelity.

A tear formed in the corner of Augusta's eye and streaked across her face and then dropped down onto his cheek.

"And you should love her. She's perfect for you," she said. Then her lips pressed together in their smile. "I want to tell you something about your Natalie so that you know why I did it—and why I have given her to you," Augusta said. She started to draw little intricate patterns on his face with her fingers, as if painting him. "It's a story about how my blood is in her, and hers is in mine. How she's one of us, but so different ..."

CHAPTER 43

Helping Hand *(Xavier Hardich, May 2006)*

XAVIER pushed a sequence of numerical buttons on the intercom panel and waited while it rang. A connection was made.

"Yeah?" a clipped voice queried from the speaker.

"It's me," Xavier said.

Nothing else was spoken through the intercom; there was only a buzz indicating that the door to the lobby was open. Xavier entered and caught the elevator to the top floor. He had been here before on multiple occasions and knew exactly where to go.

Once outside the thick door of the suite, he knocked. The same voice that had granted him admittance to the building yelled for him to "Come in." He entered.

As Xavier moved from the entrance hallway to the main living area, he saw Derek standing in the chef's kitchen, watching a shot pour from a Nespresso machine.

"Coffee?" Derek asked, never turning around.

"No," Xavier said sliding himself onto a bar stool. "Thanks for seeing me."

Derek stirred the contents of his cup before turning around. "Didn't know I had a choice. You've called me two times a day this past week; not to mention the texts."

There was a coldness in Derek's tone. Did that mean Derek was against him too? If so, at least Derek was talking to him. For two weeks now, Xavier had been devoid of most social contact. Only his mother would talk to him from time to time, but it was strained. To everyone else, he was a pariah.

"I mean it," Xavier said. "It's good of you to see me. I wanted to apologize for my behavior. For what I did. I can't explain what came over me that night. I was just so angry ... for what she did. But I never knew I ... I can't believe I did that ... God."

Derek had come to stand at the island across from Xavier. "That was a real fuckin' hit, man. You spared her nothing."

Xavier put his hands on his head and stared down at the granite countertop.

"Did you really get pushed out at Enigma? Did they actually fire you?" Derek asked.

Xavier nodded.

"They needed her to do that, you know?" Derek reminded him.

As if Xavier didn't know that. The documents came by way of David Burlow and Bill Spindrall, but Augusta would have agreed, there was no doubt.

"It's bad, but we can fix it," Xavier said, looking up. "We can still figure this out, you and me. What do we need to do to get everything back to normal? I bet LearnTech will still be interested if we can hook them again fast. Maybe you get Augusta to talk to me. I can tell her how sorry I am, I can give her something else—"

Derek let out a laugh and his head shook in disbelief. "That ship has sailed, man. And what? You think I can convince Augusta of something? She won't even see me."

Now it was Xavier who was confused. "You're not talking to her?"

"We've talked on the phone a couple of times. Short, stupid conversations—like the weather."

"What about the wedding? It's at the end of next month." Xavier was stunned.

Derek crossed his arms and smirked. "I don't know what the hell she's thinking." Then in a bitter tone, he added, "Your family is proving to be a big disappointment."

The change in Derek's demeanor was sudden, and Xavier took a moment to find his ground. Was this why Derek had invited him over—to unleash his own frustration and anger at how things had gone?

"Tell me, do you think Hal Jennings at LearnTech just contacted you out of the blue?" Derek asked. "Do you really think that? I set it up. I pretty much sold your company before you ever talked to Hal. I told him what he needed to know and what he needed to offer."

Xavier was stunned. "Why? Why didn't you tell me you were doing that?"

"I wanted to help you," Derek said. "I like you. Wanted you to be the big hero—follow in your father's footsteps and all that shit." He turned around and rummaged through a kitchen drawer, producing another pod for his Nespresso machine. "You were always trying to get in on my action. I saw that. So, I gave you the means to get capital and play in the big league with me." He gave a wry laugh as he brewed another cup of coffee. "But you couldn't rein your sister in. All you had to do was guide her hand to paper with a pen, but you couldn't. Shit, it should have been a slam dunk."

Xavier was still reeling from the information. Derek had gone behind his back to orchestrate the sale? Naively, Xavier had believed he was the one including Derek on the deal. He had desperately wanted to impress his near brother-in-law, show him that he could negotiate, could sell, could make money. But it was Derek that had brought Xavier along for the ride?

Derek loomed over the island counter close to Xavier. "You want to know what the worst of all this is? Your family keeps kicking me. I've tried to help you; I've helped your mother with her money; I was ready to marry your sister; and you Hardiches just keep fucking me over." Now Derek's voice rose sharply. "You can't control anyone, your sister is acting like a lunatic, and now I've learned that your mother's jilted lover—yes, David bloody Burlow—is spreading lies about me, trying to turn my clients against me. Do you know how insulting that is? You know that in my line of work, all I have is my credibility?"

Xavier's anger was dissipating and replaced with surprise. "What did he do?"

"Bart Miller called me saying Burlow had told him that I misrepresented my work history—that I didn't have the positions at the firms that I said I did. David told him I was never an investor! Now Miller wants to have a meeting next week so I can explain myself, and if he's not satisfied, he'll pull his money."

"Just tell him Burlow's lying."

"It doesn't fuckin' work like that! When you start getting bad press in this business, what's true doesn't matter. Nobody gives their money to someone with a question mark on their head."

The cost to Derek was not just Bart Miller, it was the cascading effect on all his clients. Now it was becoming clear just why Derek was feeling so wronged by the Hardiches. Sadly, he didn't even know it all. Xavier had wronged him too. He had never told Derek of his sister's relationship with Richard Earning. Information had been withheld—the crime of omission.

"How can I help?" Xavier asked. He wanted to make amends, to be helpful in some way.

"I don't think there's much now. Well, maybe tell Burlow to back the fuck off," Derek said, shaking his head. He relaxed his stance and seemed to have regained his self-composure. "I'm going away. I need some time to think."

"Where? How long?"

"Bahamas for a week. Couple of my clients live there and want to give me more capital to invest. Some people know I'm good for them, believe in me."

Xavier was quiet, trying to process everything. "I'll talk with my mom and find out what the hell Burlow's doing. And I'll get her to talk to Augusta too. I'm sure my sister is just not thinking right. It's because she's angry at me—it's messing her judgment up. We can still sort this out. I know we can," he said.

Derek paced about the kitchen for a bit. Then he walked into the bedroom and returned with a pair of keys.

"Look," Derek said, "you're the one in front of me, so you're taking the brunt of my problems. But of everyone, I know you're trying. I know you're a friend. That's why I was thinking you could stay here while I'm gone, maybe even until you get a place to rent. Get out of that hotel. Think you'll be able to find a rental for next month?"

Xavier almost laughed with happiness. Gratitude filled him. He hadn't experienced an act of kindness in nearly two weeks. "Yes, I've got my eye on a place for June. But would be great to stay here until then."

Derek handed him the keys. "I leave tomorrow. Come then, and we'll talk when I get back."

"Thanks," Xavier said. And again, "Thanks, really."

He would talk to his mother. He would talk to Augusta. He would sort this out for Derek by the time he returned. It was the least he could do.

* * *

Three days after Derek left to visit his clients, Xavier met his mother at a noisy cafe at the north end of Cambridge. Even though he had offered to pick her up, she was adamant she would take a cab and meet him, so determined was she to avoid him being near the house or Augusta.

"You must see she's upsetting him," Xavier said to Elinor. "Why won't she see him? He's starting to think the whole wedding will be called off."

"I don't think it will come to that," his mother said. But she frowned, as if uncertain of her own conviction. "She's in one of her states. Very bad. She needs time. What you did was just shocking to her ... to all of us."

"I know," Xavier said. He had been over this ground a hundred times. Every conversation they had always had one reference to the horrific event. "But I'm trying to help her now. Think of it from Derek's perspective. His future wife refuses to see him."

Elinor turned the coffee cup around in her hand, pondering. Finally, she nodded. "I'll speak with her."

Xavier was relieved. "Now there's another thing that is upsetting Derek. Burlow is up to some tricks. Did you know he's spreading rumors? I don't care how upset Burlow is about the money being transferred away from him, he can't lie to damage someone's reputation—especially your son-in-law's."

Elinor took a deep breath. "Who else did he tell these things to?"

"What do you mean, who else? You know he's doing it? Did he tell you?"

Elinor grimaced. "Of course, he told me something about Derek. About his past companies. David's got some suspicions about him. Wants me to move the money out."

"I bet he does," Xavier growled. "No doubt wants it all back in his pockets." When Elinor said nothing, Xavier added, "You've rightly not listened to him."

366

"I have enough preoccupying me right now than to start this battle with Derek or David," Elinor snapped, slamming her coffee cup down forcefully enough that a few people looked over from other tables. "My children are driving me mad."

"I'm sorry, Mom. Just tell him to stop and cool it for now. There's too much that's a mess with Derek and Augusta, and me and Augusta. He can tell us his concerns later."

She was evidently irritated by his latter request. "I don't just call people and tell them what to do. I'll ask him."

They finished their coffees, and once again, Elinor rejected any idea of a meeting between Xavier and his sister. "Give it another week," she said.

As they were leaving the coffee shop and he was walking Elinor to the car, his mother asked, "Have you seen Jocelyn lately?"

"On TV."

"What does that mean?"

He didn't answer.

She shook her head then put her arms around him. "Oh, Xavier, I'm sorry. I wish I could undo things for you. Maybe she just needs some time too."

It was good to feel her love and caring. He didn't know that touch could be so comforting, and he felt a small lump in his throat. As he drove back to Derek's, he felt things were turning around.

* * *

The day Derek was supposed to come home, he didn't. There were no phone calls, no texts, no emails—just a missing person.

When he didn't come home the next day, or the day after that, Xavier tried calling his friend repeatedly. But Derek's phone always went through to a full voicemail and disconnected.

On the fourth day, Xavier contacted the police to report a peculiar absence. There was the usual notetaking and a promise to look into it, though a speedy response was never committed to, as the missing person was, after all, out of country. And as the official taking down the report put it, one could easily justify spending some extra time in the Bahamas, could they not?

On day five of his friend's continued absence, Xavier sat in the living room filling out a short-term lease agreement for a condo he viewed earlier that day. Though the form was simple, it was taking him time to focus and fill it out because of the constant wondering about Derek. Like a persistent irritating sliver in his brain, the question mark around Derek's whereabouts distracted him.

And when the front door banged loudly, he jumped right off the couch, half in surprise and half in eagerness. It must be Derek. Had he lost his keys?

But when he opened the door to greet his friend, it was not Derek. There was a man and woman peering at him suspiciously.

"Derek Lam?" the woman asked.

"No."

The two eyed each other. Then the man spoke. "Is he at home?"

"No," Xavier said. "Who are you?"

"We're with the Waterloo Regional Police, fraud unit," the woman said. "We'd like to speak to Mr. Lam. Do you know where he is?"

It seemed many people wanted to speak to Derek Lam.

PART SEVEN: LEGACY

CHAPTER 44

Old Flames *(David Burlow, June 2006)*

DAVID spent more time getting ready this morning than usual. After his walk in the park to the pavilion in the wet, windy morning, he returned home to shower, donned a newly dry-cleaned charcoal suit, a white shirt, and even put on a black tie. Despite all this effort, he knew he would not look flattering. Yet, some old impulse in him, some hardwired routine, instinctively compelled him to put his best foot forward for the visitor who would be arriving.

He now sat in his favorite chair in the living room, reading the newspaper, thick fingers turning the light, thin pages. Grim articles abounded. Over the course of the last two weeks, the headlines had changed, but they all referenced the same story. The incident in Waterloo was getting national attention. A scheme that had stolen the wealth of the hardworking affluent and rendered their magnificent dreams mediocre was news anywhere.

Over seventy million dollars had vanished. It would take years to track down the money, if it could ever be found. The authorities would first have to locate the man who knew where it was. The perpetrator, like the money, had disappeared. Some speculated he went to Indonesia or Brunei, others Thailand or Vietnam, and still others Russia or China. The diverse range of opinions suggested nobody had a clue, but that didn't stop a multitude of op-eds outlining why he would choose one country over another. Whatever the whereabouts of Derek Lam, the real story to David was the wave of misery and despair that had swept over the duped investors. Many people that David called acquaintances had lost small fortunes.

And one family in particular had been a significant casualty—a point that troubled David greatly and given him sleepless nights. Too late had he pulled the fire alarm. Too late had he told Elinor to pull her money out.

By being on the board of various companies, David knew some men of finance on Bay Street in Toronto. He made a copy of Derek's marketing brochure and prospectus and emailed it over for them to do a little digging. Though the news took some time to come back, once it did, David immediately wished he had done it earlier.

Derek Lam's impeccable pedigree at the illustrious boutique US firms proved to be a half-truth. He did work at them, but as an operations manager, not as the Midas touch investor he advertised. Derek's role was to support advisers and fund managers with reporting and compliance. He had never made a trade for anyone, but he had apparently learned how to create all manner of reports to meet regulatory and compliance requirements.

David didn't need to know more to believe that Derek was up to something. He just needed time to prove it. But he had enough information to sound the alarm to both Elinor and Bart Miller. He requested Elinor's financial statements from Derek's fund from the previous year. And in the middle of his sifting through it, Derek fled. Unfortunately, Bart Miller panicked and tripped the wire that alerted Derek. Miller wanted to believe there was an explanation and gave Derek an opportunity to clarify things. Wrong call, as it turned out, for it warned Derek that his Ponzi scheme was up. Law enforcement would later discover he had never invested any money; he just kept depositing it into a single bank account. He'd pay out when he needed to by using the money in the pot to satisfy a withdrawal from a client who requested some money. But mostly, investors were content to keep their money in "the fund," watching it grow on quarterly and annual reports, even though the reports had no bearing in reality.

What was most impressive about Derek Lam was how well he was prepared for the house of cards to crumble. He knew the day of reckoning would come, whether by someone like David or just the long-term impossibility of being able to fake returns, fudge the paperwork to investors, and keep the regulators at bay. The speed at which money transferred over borders into a chain of shell companies and foreign accounts using middlemen of high position and low repute astonished regulators and police services alike. And Derek quickly followed the money, vanishing. His last known whereabouts were London, England, not the Bahamas as was initially reported.

And back here, in Kitchener-Waterloo and in Cambridge, duped investors were left to wonder if they would ever see their money again. Some people's lives might well be dramatically altered, others possibly ruined.

When the doorbell rang to announce his visitor, David straightened his suit jacket, pinched the dimple of his tie, and went to the front door. Opening it, he greeted the woman who had, for so long, electrified his desire.

Elinor Hardich stood on the porch, clasping the collar of a spring coat tightly at her throat, as if the damp breeze would slither into every exposed opening of her clothing and freeze her. She appeared so small, so petite and light that the wind might transport her right off his porch. The taxi that had dropped her off pulled away behind her.

"Thank you for seeing me," she said.

He ushered her into the house. "I would have come to you," he said. "Why didn't you let me?"

She said nothing while he took her coat.

Elinor looked weary and drained; her face was unusually pale, pronouncing dark rings enveloping her eyes. Still, she looked beautiful to him. She always would.

David's heart went out to her. The last two months had made

this woman wretched beyond belief. Her family was fractured, the much-anticipated wedding of her daughter had been hastily called off; but above all else, the scandal surrounding Lam Investments now threatened the financial security she was once assured of.

He guided Elinor to the living room and sat her on the couch while he went into the kitchen to fetch the tea he had made. "Here's something to warm you," he said, bringing in the pot and a cup.

Elinor's eyes were darting around the room, surveying it. Her tremoring hand reached out and took the cup from him. "You keep a very nice place, David," she said.

David sat down opposite her. This was her first time here. She would never know that in his fantasies from bygone days, she had inhabited this house, walked around it, made it her home, gone to bed with him at night and risen with him at dawn.

Being close to her, alone with her, caused an old, sad yearning to surface. It was not so much a fresh wave of desire, but rather the memory of desire, the shadow of it ingrained in him. The knowledge that he would never be with her was still hurtful, but now it was mixed with shame. He regretted that he had exposed himself to her, exposed his heart, and in so doing, had indelibly altered their friendship.

For things would always be different between them. Though he attended a few of her events last year, gone were the times when they would stand beside one another and talk while the whole world moved on around them. Her hands no longer touched his arm with innocent affection. Now, in their interactions, an uncomfortable space existed, an awkwardness, a no man's land that neither of them could cross. The night she rejected his confession of adoration, the dreamscape canvas he had created for decades in his mind was smeared and blotted like a rained-on painting. Despite its destruction, its end, he could never truly change his heart. He could never become indifferent to Elinor, but he managed to view his yearning for her with abstraction. It was like the unattainable infatuation one has for a celebrity: real but lined with the knowledge of implausibility.

"I miss our old talks," she said, staring into the empty fireplace as if she were reading words etched into the soot stains there. "I miss the days when you used to advise me."

"We can talk whenever you like," he replied. "I'm always here. Have you had any news?"

Elinor closed her eyes momentarily and took a deep breath. "They were over again this week, the RCMP, and some others. They reiterated what they told me before, you know, that they are searching for the money, searching for Derek. That these things take time. But one of them, a woman, said to me ... I should ... I should prepare ... for the worst." Elinor's hand began shaking and she placed her teacup down.

David felt the weight of Elinor's words. It confirmed a suspicion that had dogged him for some time. A part of him had hoped that the Hardich money was safe, that perhaps Derek had left it alone out of some courtesy to Augusta or Xavier. But it was a foolish wish. Nobody was spared.

He leaned forward in his chair. "I know these are trying times," he said softly, "and I'm very sorry." What other words could he say? He would be remiss to encourage her in any other belief, If the police were skeptical in their ability to resolve the crime, who was he to challenge them? There was anguish in Elinor's face, but he resisted the urge to reach out and touch her.

"I'm ruined, David. Ruined. I've been a fool! It's all gone. All of it. Gone as if it never existed." Elinor's tone became bitter as she sobbed. "Stolen, swindled, by that conman. We trusted Derek with everything! The shame he's brought on us all!"

After a moment of tears, she pulled out some tissues to dab her eyes. "I should have kept it with you," she went on. "That's what James would have done. It's what he would have wanted. It's what I wanted, but ... I'm sorry David. I'm sorry."

David couldn't resist anymore. He reached out and gently took her hand. Elinor flinched. He thought she might pull away, but then she relaxed, accepting the comfort he offered. "You couldn't have known; it's not your fault," he said. If only he had raised more questions about Derek when he had transferred the money over to him. But those were the dark weeks of his desolation, when he felt the sting of Elinor's rejection, and he had willfully executed her instructions without a thought so he could hide from her and the world.

"I don't care for myself. I don't," Elinor said. "I can live modestly. It's the fact that I've lost everything James set aside for us. I'll have nothing to leave my children or even my grandchildren." She shook her head. "I need your counsel, David. I need to know what to do to keep what little I have left safe. Will you? Will you help me?"

"Of course, I will," David said confidently. For in truth, he had a suspicion of why she had come today and had already been planning on how to help her. He would do his utmost to minimize the hardship for her, so unwavering was his commitment to Elinor. He was even ready to contribute to her finances, to ensure she was reasonably looked after. "I am pleased that you came to ask for my assistance."

An immense release of emotion, a mixture of tears and gratitude followed from Elinor. She clutched his hand tightly. "You have always been our truest friend," she repeated time and time again. "I only trust you; I will only trust you."

At one time, Elinor's words would have ignited a fiery bliss inside him, would have spurred him to a rapture, keeping his spirits soaring for days. He would have imbued those words with a meaning that corresponded to his fantasies. But now, he only heard the truth, unalloyed with his biased desires. Elinor requested friendship and help—she insinuated nothing more. The sadness crept up inside David again; he would always serve her, and she would never understand how happy he could have made her, and she him.

Elinor regained her composure, relief restoring her spirits, and she slowly decoupled her hand from his. "This family owes you so much—I do."

"How is Augusta holding up?" he asked. Augusta was an enigma to him, but whatever her demons, whatever her motives in life, she had sacrificed much for Natalie, and, in a way, for him.

Elinor was quiet for a moment. "I don't know. I wish I could say. We barely talk about anything meaningful. She's retreating from me, keeps to herself. She's decided to take the summer semester off from school. This family is suffering, David. My poor children. I know you and Xavier have never been close, but he's dealing with so much too. His setbacks at Enigma, and now the catastrophe with Lam Investments ... he's a broken man. I fear for him. He trusted Derek—they were friends!"

David snorted. The mention of Xavier's name immediately gnawed at his nerves. His devotion to Elinor did not extend to her son. "I must ask, where is he in all of this? What is he doing to help you? What is he doing at all?"

"He's hardly in a state to help," Elinor said solemnly. "He's living in a sublet condo until the end of summer. Augusta has agreed he can come home then. It will be a long road to healing us. A long road."

"I have said I will help you," David replied. "And I will. But for me to do that, Xavier needs to be a part of the conversation. I have expectations of him. And you should as well. He has responsibility for the situation you now find yourself in."

Elinor made no excuse or defense for her son.

"You must make him come here to see me. Will you do that?" David said.

"He has no choice. Neither one of us does."

When Elinor left that day, David contemplated the demise of this great family. For so long, they had been a source of envy for him and others. But now, Fortune had turned against them. In fact, Fortune was tearing them apart.

Only one member of the family had managed to come out ahead in all of this disorder and confusion. Though she had all the disadvantages at the beginning, she proved to be more resilient and determined than the purebloods. Natalie's prospects were rising. And David felt there was a certain amount of justice in it all, of equity. He had begun to doubt in Fate and Destiny. But he had to admit, he thought he could glimpse some divine plan at play.

The equity of Enigma was now where David's mind turned. For he saw how he might press an advantage and solve a problem for Natalie that had previously eluded both him and her.

Although Elinor would always have a pull on him, it was Natalie whom he now fixed his hopes and affections upon.

David Burlow was emboldened to strive and be something to his new daughter that he had never thought would be his lot to experience: a parent, a guardian. At last, he was loved, unconditionally. He would love and be loved—he deserved that.

His intent was pure, and that was all that mattered.

CHAPTER 45

Selling *(Xavier Hardich, July 2006)*

XAVIER sat in his living room, eating pizza and having a beer— his third. He was alone, as had been all too customary over the past month and a half. He was thinking about his meeting tomorrow at Enigma, about what it represented for him, and for his family.

When his phone rang, he looked down at the number, and his heart was filled with gladness. It was not one of the detectives, nor his suffering mother. Jocelyn. It had been almost two months since they had broken up.

Xavier answered. "Hey. This is a really nice surprise," he said gently. It would be nice to hear her voice, talk to her. Sometimes, he would get up to watch her on the news, to admire her.

"How could you not know?" Jocelyn's angry voice answered back. "You. Your sister. How?"

"Know what?" Xavier demanded, his own anger rising to meet hers. This was not a kind check-in call or reconsideration of a breakup— this was an ambush.

"What do you think I'm talking about? Your friend stealing everyone's money. My father's money!"

"He stole our money too!"

"We all wonder about that. You sure it's not sitting somewhere waiting to be collected?" Jocelyn asked, her words venomous. "Maybe you get everything back in cash plus a referral fee? Should I ask Augusta? She's in the know, that's for sure! Wedding postponed until the superyacht comes in?"

"Oh, fuck you! You're not the only people on the planet, you know!" He hung up.

However angry Jocelyn was, he was now furious. To accuse him of knowing about the fraud was disgusting. How would he ever have known? His own family had been robbed blind. He bit his knuckles viciously. It was a new habit he acquired to try and disperse his rage, his shame. His fingers sometimes bled as they did now.

But he knew Jocelyn was not the only one to express this opinion. That was making it all the worse for him. The good Hardich name was taking a beating, becoming soiled by the mud society slung at it. Xavier's mother had called him one night, weeping. She had just learned that the charity groups she had raised millions of dollars for over the years were excluding her from their fundraising activities. How could Elinor be the orchestrator of events, soliciting money from families who lost untold wealth at the hands of her almost son-in-law?

The Hardiches were now forever associated with Derek Lam. And society needed someone still around to blame, even if the someone suffered the same fate as everyone else.

What had become of them? His family? What had become of him? He was falling apart. Every dream he once had for himself, his wonderful prospects, his good name, seemed to have left along with Derek Lam and the millions.

All that remained was his equity in Enigma Solutions. But David Burlow was making short work of that.

* * *

Shortly after 6 p.m. on a warm summer evening, Xavier sat inside his car in the Enigma parking lot. The meeting would begin soon. He would rather wait outside until the last moment than be forced into some small talk with people he didn't like—with people who reminded him of how far he had fallen.

In his rearview mirror, he saw a car coming toward the parking lot where he was. He knew the shape of VW Golf lights—of her Golf. Concealed behind his tinted windows, he watched as the car came closer, turned, and parked on the other side of a car some five spaces from his own. Then Augusta appeared and walked to the metal entrance door of Enigma. He thought he saw her pause to peer at his BMW before going in. Did she know he was inside it?

So, Augusta had decided to come in person instead of sending her proxy, David. Xavier hadn't laid eyes on her since the night he struck her—almost three months.

He had been thinking a lot about her recently, trying to get into her head, to understand her. But she had always eluded him, and probably everyone else. Did Augusta care that the family's fortunes were destroyed? She had long seemed to pretend she was indifferent to the family legacy, almost dismissive of it. She certainly had no regard for Xavier's own fortune and prospects when she had rejected the sale of Enigma.

Perhaps that was the greatest irony in all of this. When Augusta stopped Enigma's sale, she protected the only asset the two of them now had left at their disposal. For had the company sold, Xavier would have handed over the money to Derek Lam for safekeeping and good returns until he could figure out his next venture. It would have vanished along with his mother's money, and the millions from other investors all duped by Derek. In many respects, Augusta had saved Xavier by thwarting him, He should be grateful to her. And maybe he was.

Xavier could feel the fit coming on, the shaking of his hands caused by bottled-up anger and angst. There was so much shame in him, so much disappointment, so much frustration with nowhere to direct it, no target except himself. He bit his fingers hard to feel the pain that gave some relief, a temporary release of the tension and discord thrashing in his mind.

Looking at the clock on his phone, he saw it was almost 6:30 p.m. It was time. Getting out of the car, he walked over to the brown metal door. The simple plaque to the right of the door was still the same: "Enigma Solutions: Innovating Education, Suite B." When he had first seen the sign, it had filled him with pride and excitement— he was going to put this little company on the map. Now, he didn't know what to feel. Opening the door, he descended the stairs. At the bottom, he heard voices coming from the boardroom at the end of the hall. But before he went there, he peeked into the Pit.

A young woman, likely fresh out of university judging by her youth, was sitting at a desk just inside the Pit entrance. She was typing on her computer and looked up at Xavier.

"Hi!" she said enthusiastically. "Can I help you?"

"I'm here for the shareholders meeting. Who are you?" Xavier asked. The desk she sat in wasn't there when he had left. There had been a reconfiguration of the cubicles to make this space for her.

"I'm Carly, Natalie's assistant," she said. "And you are?"

"Xavier Hardich."

The moment he said his name, he saw the flicker of surprise across Carly's face and a faint *ah* escape from under her breath. She had heard of him; he knew that much. Everyone had heard of him. He likely had a reputation here that was not at all favorable.

"The boardroom is—"

"I know where it is," he said, and turned his back on her to walk down the hall. Passing by his old office, he saw a new nametag on the door: *Natalie Mitchell, President*. He strode past Bill's office, until he stood in the doorway to the boardroom.

His arrival silenced the small group gathered there. The faces all turned to look at him. He felt uneasy under the stares and fidgeted with the button of his suit jacket. At one time, his tailored suits used to make him feel powerful and confident, but now he felt like an imposter in them. The old magic of his clothing was no more; the charms seemed to have run out. The fabric that used to mold to the shape of his body was trying to slide off him and run away. He had lost weight, and neither the jacket nor the pants fit him as well as they ought to. He had hoped that by wearing one of his best suits today, he could try to revive that feeling of success and respectability. These people had once respected him, hadn't they?

"Good to see you, Xavier," Bill said nervously, pushing his bangs off his forehead. "Grab a seat; we were just going to start."

Xavier glanced at the walls that still had the motivational posters on them. At the front of the room, a PowerPoint presentation projected a title slide reading *Enigma Solutions: 2006 Mid-Year Review*. Avoiding further eye contact, he slowly pulled out one of the chairs and sat down. He was alone at the end of the table with an empty seat on either side of him. Bill slid him a file folder with papers in it and a bound presentation.

Natalie gave a faint formal nod of greeting to him. She then started the meeting and presented Enigma's financial position for the first six months of the year. The whole fiasco with LearnTech was downplayed under Natalie's statement that, "A partnership venture, which redeployed most of Enigma's resources away from development, has been put on hold." Everyone in the room knew what had happened, and no details were required—the first half of the year was a bit of a wash.

But then Natalie switched to some sweeping changes and plans she had for the latter half of 2006. She spoke confidently and positively about the revenue she expected to achieve by way of refocusing on the product, hiring more people, terminating the Indian outsourcing contract, and exploring new office space. Bill provided some additional commentary here and there, and the shareholders were encouraged to look at the supporting information in the bound booklet in front of them.

Xavier had read the documents circulated by email beforehand, so it came as no surprise to him. Even if he didn't agree with Natalie's direction, fighting it was pointless. He would be outvoted by Bill and Augusta. He merely sat, quiet in his isolation, trying to keep his gaze fixed on the presentation.

But however hard he tried, he inevitably stole quick glances at Augusta sitting beside Natalie. Augusta was stone-faced; her eyes would flit between the speakers, the presentation projecting on the wall, or rest on the paperwork in front of her.

What was she thinking? Did she care about any of this?

Augusta looked well, he had to admit. She was perfectly healthy: there was no trace of worry, stress, or fatigue on her face.

Her face—he imagined the imprint of his fist on it and immediately felt sick.

Once, Augusta looked his way, her expression unreadable as she stared intently at him. Xavier was the one to avert his eyes. What had he seen? Anger? Hate? Disappointment? Revulsion? Nothing … everything …

"There is some other business to close out today, as I know you are all aware," Natalie was saying, looking slightly uncomfortable.

The statement triggered a smile from Augusta, and she sat forward to flip open the folder of papers that she had in front of her.

"The documents in front of you also contain the changes to the shareholder's agreement, as well as the package for the sale of equity," Natalie went on, nodding at Augusta's folder. She glanced at Xavier briefly too. "When everyone signs the documents, I will ensure each of you receives an executed copy."

Xavier opened the folder and looked at his copies. Again, no surprises. He had already agreed to everything. This was the bargain with his mother and David Burlow. His hand had been forced; it was no secret the Hardiches needed money.

His mother refused to give up the house. Elinor insisted she would live in it until the day she died. It was the only thing she had left of James Hardich's labor and toils over the years. Despite the points Xavier had made about the proceeds from a house sale being sufficient to provide for her—and him—Elinor remained steadfast in her desire to keep the singular asset. She heeded her son not one bit, and he couldn't fault her. Had Xavier's advice not led to the family's much-reduced circumstances?

If Burlow was to help Elinor, he needed capital to invest. And the only available money outside of the house was the equity Xavier held in Enigma. Elinor demanded that Xavier sell his stake to give her the lifeline she needed. Whether Burlow had whispered this solution in Elinor's ear privately or whether it truly was the only way, Xavier didn't know. But the result was that he was obliged to notify the shareholders he was interested in selling his equity.

No surprise that Natalie was keen to relieve him of it. She was likely backed by Burlow. His father's old dog was getting the last laugh at Xavier's demise. Like so many other things lately, Xavier was seeing Fortune's grand conspiracy against him, and he could do nothing but let her spin him dizzy on her wheel while she hurled daggers at him.

Bill and Augusta both approved of the sale, but not before Augusta did something peculiar. She notified everyone that she would also sell some of her equity. In the end, this meant that each of the Hardich siblings kept a 10 percent stake in Enigma for a total of 20 percent—a far cry from the 60 percent they had once controlled between them. Natalie was set to purchase 30 percent of it, in addition to her nonvoting shares, but that still left 10 percent unaccounted for, or at least repurchased back by the corporation. Was Natalie thinking of extending the employee equity plan or was she going to offer it to someone specific? Xavier puzzled it over and kept landing on the same name—Richard Earning. If anyone was to get in on the bandwagon of Xavier's disgrace, it would be Richard.

Xavier signed his documents in the silence of the room. In addition, he signed, with a bitter chuckle, the papers relating to a change in the shareholder agreement. Under the amended terms, a fifty-plus-one vote from shareholders could trigger the sale of the company and its equity. It had been that small and powerful detail that had prevented him three months ago from being successful.

The folders and documents moved around the room in a flurry of signings and witnessing. On more than one occasion, everyone glanced at Augusta suspiciously. She acknowledged this when she gave an amused laugh. "I have quite a reputation, it seems. Don't worry, I'm signing," she said. But instinctively, in the middle of her joke, she touched her face. That memory would never leave her.

When it was all done, the meeting was adjourned. Xavier thought Natalie looked relieved, even a little breathless. She likely hadn't dared to believe that everything that transpired in the boardroom tonight would happen. Bill went around the table to shake Natalie's hand with a beaming smile.

When Natalie went to shake Augusta's hand, Augusta leaned in and embraced her.

"Congratulations," she said to Natalie.

Xavier knew his sister, knew the subtle tones that alluded to other meanings. He heard another layer of depth in her words. What was this strange affection for Natalie and what did those intonations mean? Judging by Natalie's startled expression, she didn't know either.

Augusta waited for no response but grabbed her purse and walked out of the boardroom and down the hall. Xavier grabbed his papers and pursued her.

"Augusta," he said firmly, following her.

She didn't look behind her but continued onward, up the stairs, through the metal door, and into the parking lot with Xavier in pursuit.

"Augusta," he said again, stopping his advance as he walked outside into the warm air. He desperately wanted her to look at him.

Only when she was halfway to her car did she abruptly halt. She turned around, her fists clenched and her stance defensive as if she were ready for a physical altercation.

Now that he had her attention, he realized he had too much to say.

"I don't ... I understand ..." He was trying to ask questions and make statements at the same time. "Why did you sell some of yours too? I was ready to sell all of mine to make sure Mom was looked after."

"She's my mom too. I wanted to help," she said without emotion. Her hands unclenched as she interpreted this was not to be a violent exchange.

The door opened behind him, and Bill stepped out. "Everything all right?" he asked, looking at Augusta.

She nodded, telling him, "It's okay." Bill lingered a moment longer and then went back inside, but not before giving Xavier a suspicious, even threatening look.

Xavier was filled with another bout of shame, knowing what everyone thought of him, thought of what he might do, thought of what he was capable of.

He didn't know what to say next but knew if he waited too long, she would turn and leave. "I hope that when I return home, we can get past what happened."

"I doubt it," Augusta said, smiling.

"I can't give you any good reason for what I did. For what I've done. I'm sorry."

"I believe you. But I still dislike you. Let's face it, Xavier, we've never been very good siblings to each other. I've had my part in that too."

Xavier wanted to tell her that wasn't always the case. They had never been close, but they had never been this far apart either. There was a time in Europe, on a family vacation, when they might even have been friends.

"Don't take it too hard," she added, seeing him at a loss for words. "If it's any consolation, I can't stand myself either."

He was ever at a loss to understand her. Her words revealed something dark, but the lightness of her tone suggested she was detached from it.

"Why did you come tonight?" he inquired. Had she wanted to see him?

"It's a bit of a celebration—an occasion. We passed on a part of what we didn't deserve to someone who did."

"Why do you say that? What is it with you and Natalie?"

She didn't answer but turned to go. "Goodbye, Xavier." Just before getting in her car, she paused. "Good luck with your new job."

He stood, frozen, as she drove away.

So, she had heard about his new opportunity, if it could be called that. Under Elinor's pleadings, Burlow had grudgingly used his network to place Xavier at a company. It was a manager position, one which, just a few months ago, Xavier would have felt was beneath him. But now, he was filled with anxiety about it. What if he failed? It would be yet another humiliation.

Though the night was warm, Xavier began to shake, and he bit his calloused and blistered knuckles until they bled again.

CHAPTER 46

Deal Making *(Natalie Mitchell, July 2006)*

NATALIE sat in the waiting area at reception first thing in the morning. She was thirty minutes early for her meeting—she was taking no chances with time today. Though she had little sleep, she was alert, ready. She had bought a new suit for this, a pale, bluish-gray jacket with matching skirt cut just above the knee. It looked great on her, and she felt great in it.

As the light but steady stream of people passed through reception on their way to meetings and offices, Natalie recognized some of them, and they her. Initially, they glanced at her without acknowledgment as they strolled past, still under the veil of zombie commutes or organizing thoughts for another meeting. After a few steps, however, they would halt, finally aware of her. "Natalie? What are you doing here?" they asked amid smiles, handshakes, and the occasional hug. But she remained tight-lipped on her purpose.

At 9 a.m., she was escorted through doors and down hallways to a large office with a grand desk on one end and a seating area composed of four cushy chairs around a coffee table. Natalie opted to sit at the coffee table and declined offers of water and coffee. Left alone, she looked around and noticed that the art on the wall had changed. Where once there was an abstract piece, it was replaced with a photograph of a red-bricked gothic building with steepled towers and one thick tower rising up from the middle. She knew from tourism brochures at the airport it was a building on the Harvard campus.

She rubbed her hands together to try to manage the excitement and anticipation running through her. She pulled her laptop out of her carry-on bag and made sure it had plenty of power and that her presentation was open and ready to go.

When Hal Jennings, the CEO of LearnTech, stepped into his office, his face was stoic at first, all business. But as soon as Natalie offered her hand, Hal cracked a grudging smile.

In his early forties, Hal looked older. His hair was thinning, and when he undid his suit jacket to sit down opposite Natalie, the buttons near his stomach strained and pulled to keep flesh inside his shirt. Perhaps Hal was unaware his body had changed over the years; the paisley tie he wore might have been the right length when his stomach was flatter, but now it barely dangled down to the middle of his belly.

"Thought we were doing a call," Hal said.

"Thought I'd surprise you," Natalie rejoined. "I flew in last night from Toronto."

"Quite a gamble. My schedule changes on a whim. You might have been sitting here in Boston doing a phone call with me while I was in New York."

"Maybe. But big gambles can pay off."

Hal laughed. "Always liked you, Nat," he said. "It was a messy business with your friends. I'm still pissed about them jerking my chain. I had to get board approval for that purchase, and I looked like an idiot when it didn't go through."

"I don't think anyone could have foreseen those complications."

"Complications? Does Xavier know his sister or not?"

Natalie resisted the urge to tell Hal that nobody knew Augusta. Instead, she said, "There have been some developments."

Hal gave her a level look. "Shit, Nat. I hope they didn't send you up here to kickstart the sale talks again. Please tell me that's not why you've come."

"No. I actually wanted—"

"Wanted to talk about leaving those clowns? That would be good. You know you're liked here. I couldn't walk down the hall without everyone telling me you were in the building. You're like Elvis or something."

"It's kind of you to say so," Natalie said. "And maybe that's something I'll explore in the future if things don't go as planned." She sat back in her chair and smiled. She felt a bit of redness in her cheeks. This was going well. She hadn't known how Hal would react when he saw her. Would he blame her for the Enigma affair? Fortunately, he didn't seem to be harboring any grudges against her. Now, it was time to strike. "Right now, I need to make sure the company I run, and own over a third of, is exploring all its options."

Hal stared at her. "Enigma? You own a third of Enigma?"

"I do."

Natalie proceeded to tell him all that happened over the last few months. And though Hal was not one to feign shock, he had his moments of keen interest when he learned more of Augusta, and disbelief when informed how Derek Lam had swindled the money from the Hardiches and several of their acquaintances. The news of the financial theft might be big in Canada, but in the States, it hadn't featured on page ten, let alone a headline.

"God. I liked that Derek guy more than Xavier. Always knew he was a bit greedy, though. I suspect he never told anyone he was getting a few hundred grand payment if the sale went through—for services rendered and all that. But he turned out to be real scum," Hal said. For some time, he looked at Natalie, as if sizing her up. "But Xavier's fall has been your gain. You've done well by it."

Natalie agreed. "I have a proposition for you. One that doesn't let all that work we did together go to waste. I mean, when we think about it, Enigma's products really do complement LearnTech's, and vice versa."

Hal put his hands behind the back of his head and took a deep breath. "Here it comes."

"Why not take a 10 percent stake in Enigma?" Natalie said. "That way, partnering makes sense for everyone." And she opened her laptop to start her presentation.

* * *

After her meeting with Hal, Natalie immediately boarded a plane and flew back to Toronto's Pearson International. She cleared customs and wheeled her carry-on case out through the sliding doors of the secure section into the public arrivals area. When she saw him, she stopped and laughed.

There, in the midst of people milling about and waiting for travelers, was Richard, holding a *Welcome home* sign with her name on it and some half-dozen balloons. He had taken the afternoon off to pick her up.

She put her hand up to her eyes, pretending to avoid seeing him. But she couldn't keep her own joke up and went to him.

"It's so good to see you," Richard said dramatically. "How long has it been?"

"Not even twenty-four hours."

His hands enveloped her in a hug, and he gave her a kiss.

There was a change in him over the last few months. Was it since Paris? Before, he would never have conducted such a public display of affection. He might have held hands, given a discreet peck here and there, but never anything as brazen as this to call attention to himself. He was extra attentive to her, and she loved it. For so long, she had been the one chasing him. Now he seemed to fully accept her and what she was to him.

Once in the car and beginning their drive back to Kitchener-Waterloo, Richard asked the big question. "So, who won the bet? You or David?"

"I did. Hal will buy 10 percent of Enigma. He'll need board approval, but he knows he can get it."

"Really? Hal Jennings is playing ball then?"

"Absolutely."

"Great news! David will think he's taught you too much; you're outdoing him now."

David had a pessimistic view of any meeting with LearnTech; he didn't think Hal would touch Enigma with a ten-foot pole after the whole fiasco of the sale falling through. But Natalie believed Hal could be persuaded—and she was right.

"Any caveats?" Richard asked.

"The ones we expected. LearnTech will want to be treated like a reseller, so they get money on every license of Enigma they sell. We're also responsible for all commission payments to LearnTech sales reps if they close an Enigma deal. And we still need to integrate our product fully into LearnTech's suite. All worthwhile for access to the US market and a sales team."

Staring out the window, Natalie reflected on the last few months—a complete whirlwind. Only in April, she had driven down this highway with David Burlow after being picked up from the airport. But that had been under anxious circumstances. Enigma was being sold; she had been duped again, and Richard looked like he was gone for a year. Now everything was different; fortunes had reversed.

In fact, she thought, forget a few months, look at the last couple of years. Who knew that meeting David Burlow in High Park one spring day to ask for help would bring about so many changes? She had a new relationship with a man who had been a mystery for many years, and she owned a significant part of a company. Not bad.

Then there was Richard, another wonderful positive in all this. And that was where her mind turned to most right now, because she needed his help, and she felt he needed hers, though he didn't know it.

"You know, things are going to get busy for me," Natalie said, her eyes lifting from the blurring buildings, trees, and fields they passed. "I'm gonna need help. Hal even said that. I need someone I can trust."

"You can trust Jeremy," Richard said, not taking his eyes off the road. He raised his thumb from the steering wheel and checked his speed.

"No, it's not his role. I need someone to head up product. Who already knows it and can ramp in a week. And someone that can steer the Pit. I can't do it all. There's too much." She reached over and rested her hand on his leg.

He knew what she was angling at. "We've talked about this, Nat. I'm not sure it's a good idea. Dating and working together … you know? Might be awkward for other people too."

"That's ridiculous," Natalie said. "Everyone loves you there. Everyone wants you back. Especially me." She paused now. She didn't want what she said next to come out the wrong way, like she was holding him hostage, but she needed to tell him what she saw. "You promised me and your dad that you were going to get work back in your field. I know you said you finished your résumé, but what else have you done? You're still with Robbie, making a fraction of what you should be. Why? What aren't you telling me?"

Richard stared at the road. He didn't want to answer, Natalie could see that. But she was patient. He would have to talk eventually.

When he finally did speak, he sounded a bit melancholy. "I just know that once I get back into it, I won't have time for other stuff. I've really enjoyed all the reading and writing I've done. Whether I go somewhere else or to Enigma, maybe especially Enigma, you know the hours I'll be working are crazy."

Natalie kept her hand on his leg. "If it's really important to you, you'll make time. You can do it on the side," she said. "It's time, Richard. You have to come back now. You need to do the work that you're good at, that pays you well."

He chuckled. "Are you saying I'm a bad writer that won't make any money?"

"Richard," she said, giving him a stern look, "I don't mean that. But then again, I wouldn't know—you never show me anything you've written. Anyway, what I'm saying is that it's time to get serious again."

"Sounds like you're saying I have responsibilities and gotta think about my future," he grumbled.

"You said it …"

They drove down the highway for over ten minutes without a word being spoken. Richard was preoccupied, lost in his own thoughts. Then he asked, "You really think it's right for me at Enigma still?"

"I do."

"If I come back and you don't feel it's working, you have to tell me."

"I will, but I won't have to," she said.

Another pause. "I'll give Robbie my notice tomorrow," he said.

Although Natalie was happy, she knew this was hard for him. But it was also necessary. The longer he stayed in limbo, the harder it would be to get back in the game.

She undid her seatbelt and leaned over to kiss him on the cheek. "I can't wait," she said. "I've got so much work for you!"

He smiled. "Wow, I love you too."

Laughing, she looked out the window again. It was a beautiful hot day, and the sun shone brightly on the trees and fields on either side of the highway. Everything was perfect. Everything had turned out so well.

And yet, there was one note of discord, a lurking fact that was closeted away in some hidden recess of her mind. But she knew it was there. She could hide things in that small room, but she could not hide the room itself, its existence.

What was hidden there? A form of a ghost. Or maybe a ghostly form—the feeling of a person. Augusta Hardich. And that name, that face, would jump into Natalie's thoughts at the most peculiar times and infest them. Why had Augusta helped her? And why did Natalie continue to feel guilt for never trying to be Augusta's friend?

Would it have killed Natalie to be a little kinder to this woman who had been instrumental in her good fortune?

* * *

The nagging questions around Augusta were such a frequent preoccupation with Natalie that one day after work, she could no longer resist action. When everyone had left the Pit and she was alone in her office, she pulled out her cell phone and found Augusta in her contacts. Her thumb hovered over the dial button for some time but then committed to her original purpose. The button was pushed followed by the sound of the digital ring.

Augusta answered. "A peculiar thing—you calling me," she said. "I think it might be the first time."

"Yes. It is," Natalie said. "I'm sorry. I haven't been on this. I mean, on calling you. I wasn't good at finding time for us to meet. Thought maybe we could get something in the calendars now."

A breath of silent laughter from Augusta. "You don't need to make nice. You're doing this because you think it's right, given what's happened. But you don't owe me anything."

"How about we meet for coffee? At least give me a chance to redeem myself."

"I don't think it will work anymore, Natalie. At one time, I really did wish we could have been friends. But I think that time has passed."

Natalie winced. "Oh. I see." Far from being a call that relieved Natalie of guilt, she was feeling more ashamed. "I'm sorry," she said. She could feel her face blushing. Something inside her still resisted gratitude and debt to Augusta. "Thank you for what you've done. For helping me."

"Don't thank me, Natalie," Augusta said, her voice suddenly strained, like she was repressing something. "It takes all my strength not to turn on you."

Natalie was shaken out of her submissive appreciation. There was danger here, but also an opening, an opportunity to ask the question.

"If I frustrate you so much, why did you do it? Why have you been kind to me? Why did you try to befriend me?"

Silence on the other end—a long one. "I hope you do well, Natalie. I still have some equity in the company that I'm entrusting you to grow. Isn't that what Richard promised me? Good night."

Augusta ended the call. Natalie sat alone at the office trying to understand the woman.

CHAPTER 47

Old Time's Sake (*Richard Earning, August 2006*)

RICHARD pushed the rotating blade down and sawed through a piece of MDF. When the cut was done, he quickly inspected the angle. Then, with nail gun in hand, he mounted the stepladder and held the piece in place while joining it to the wall by shooting the nails straight through it.

When Robbie strode into the room holding coffees, he glanced up at the ceiling. "You're nearly done with the crown in this room. Looks good."

"Yeah, another hour, tops."

"Counting hours now, eh?" Robbie said, handing Richard one of the coffees. "Your last week. You sure you want to go back to boring old office life?"

"It is boring. But the money's a hell of a lot better."

Robbie gave a laugh and shrugged. "I'm gonna help Danny in the other room. Take five if you want."

Richard stepped outside of the air-conditioning onto a deck in the backyard. It was a hot day, over thirty degrees Celsius—almost too hot for the coffee that Robbie brought him. But it was better to be outside than in. He lit a cigarette and took a big inhale. He was thinking he might need to give the habit up when he started back at Enigma. Natalie was becoming increasingly intolerant of it.

He reached into his pocket to pull out his phone, remembering he felt a vibration an hour ago when he was working. There was a text from a number not in his contacts. It didn't need to be. He knew it by heart.

Knew it was Augusta.

Meet me for coffee Saturday at 10 am. Melville's Café in Cambridge. For old time's sake, the text read. Though it was short and simple, he must have reread it four times.

Since the complete collapse of his reason and moral judgement when he had been with Augusta back in April, he had neither seen nor communicated in any way with her. Guilt wracked him for what he had done to Natalie. Especially because he knew if he could redo that day, he would have made the exact same choices.

Now he practiced deprivation. He punished himself through the abstinence of Augusta, and by the doubling of his attentions on Natalie. He hoped this would purify him, compensate.

But this text from Augusta showed him that he was only steadfast in his righteous resolutions when he functioned alone, in isolation. Each time he read her words, her boldness and impertinence, he became more certain he would go and meet her. All despite the loathing he had for himself for doing it.

* * *

Melville Café was located downtown Galt, overlooking the river, a mere fifteen-minute walk from the Hardich house. The café was at the north end of the University of Waterloo's School of Architecture building, which a couple of years earlier had moved to Cambridge from the main Waterloo Campus.

The morning was pleasantly warm, so Richard parked his car at the south end of the school and casually walked the length of it to the café. Red-bricked and three stories, with a solid industrial feel, the structure had once been a silk mill built in the early twentieth century. The outside might be what it was a hundred years ago, but the inside was entirely modernized. Peering into the windows, Richard could see classrooms, drafting tables, small computer rooms, and libraries, and what must have been student projects featuring miniature model buildings and landscapes.

When he arrived at the café, he saw her. Augusta was sitting at a table on the patio in a flowing white sundress, with sunglasses resting atop her head as a sort of band to keep her hair from falling around her face.

A wave of bliss, yearning, and anger combined to halt him and render him immovable. He watched her stare off to somewhere, maybe a building or church across the street, or maybe she was looking inward to her own thoughts. Dangerous to meet her, he knew. She would always set him alight, and he would always feel guilty for this primitive and uncontrollable reaction to her appearance and presence.

He moved out of his rooted state and approached the table. Her face was pristine again, no mark upon her cheek.

She looked up and gave him her amused smile when she saw him. But there was something different about her eyes—they were more piercing and seemed to study him anew.

"I'm glad you came," she said as he sat down. She had already placed his order, for she pushed a to-go cup of coffee over to him. "I hope I didn't interrupt any of your plans for the day."

"Nothing. No. I only have some things on this afternoon," Richard replied. He would be with Natalie, though he never mentioned that part. "It's my last free weekend before I start back at Enigma."

Augusta looked at him with a blank expression, then gave one brief shake of her head. "So, that's it. Back to where you started." She took a sip from her cup. "How's the writing coming?"

"Here and there," he said. He had been trying—the scribbles were coming consistently now.

"I wish you'd given it more of a try when you had the chance. I know it's important to you," she said.

A sudden irritation stirred in him. Was she prodding him? Was she reminding him that he had failed to pursue his dream? If so, should he tell her she was partially to blame for that?

Augusta seemed oblivious to his frustration. "I wonder if you'll ever write about this," she said, gesturing to the space between them. "Our little rendezvous. Our secrets. I'd like to read it, to see what you make of it. Do you suppose you'd capture the role reversal?"

"Role reversal?"

"Once, you were the other man, banished to secrecy. Now it's me playing the other woman. Surely, you can appreciate a good joke."

He remembered too well what it was to be the one in the shadows, slinking about. The anger, the fury at having to share someone he loved with another person. And in Augusta's case, the other person was her half-sister. Had she invited him here to tell him she felt like an ignored secret lover? That she was upset he had never reached out to her in the last few months? Did she consider herself his lover? If so, then she underestimated everything—she was so much more than that.

"I don't think the joke's funny," was all Richard said.

"Well, it's certainly not serious. It would only be serious if I told you to leave her," she said, her lips pursing together.

Disarmed, Richard was forced into silence. He couldn't tell what she was about today. Certainly, her confidence had returned in full. That bruised and vulnerable woman he had made fierce and passionate love to a few months ago was closeted away again behind playful, mysterious meanings and jabs.

"Why did you ask me to come, Augusta? We agreed it was the last time in your bedroom. I was willing to honor that. But you know I can't resist you. I can't stop ... Don't play with me."

She was quiet and looked about the patio, at people walking in and out of the café. "We're paid up. Let's walk along the river."

They grabbed their coffees and began to amble along the trail atop the floodwall of the Grand River. Below, the slow-moving brown waters flowed south. Eventually the wall became a steep embankment covered by trees and shrubbery. Augusta walked only a foot or so away from him, and he wanted to reach out for her hand, but he didn't know how she would react. Richard lit a cigarette and offered her one, but she refused with a wave of her hand, saying she'd quit. They didn't talk too much, only making the occasional comment on the growing warmth of the day or about some young boys fishing on the opposing bank of the river.

"I'm sorry about what happened to your family," Richard said. "I can't believe Derek … what he did … It's just crazy."

She shrugged and sipped her latte. "He turned out to be a bit of dick, didn't he? I'll admit I'm a little frustrated with myself. I should have seen we were being played. It hurts to be out-used."

All Richard could do was smile in disbelief. Even as Augusta's life was changing around her, likely for the worst, she couldn't help but find some strange humor in it.

"Does it affect you?" he asked. "I mean, I suppose you'll do what you were always planning. Finish your PhD. But then what?"

They came to the shade of a tree and a park bench. She stopped and sat down.

"I'm taking a break from my PhD," she said. "Last couple of years have been a bit of a challenge. I'm distracted."

He sat down beside her. "What will you do?"

"It's why I wanted to see you today. I know what our bargain was. But I wanted one last time. I'm going to India. I leave at the end of the month—last day of August. Before Xavier moves back."

"India?" Richard felt a sense of panic, and his heart skipped. "On vacation?"

"Not really." She paused as if she was unsure of what she was about to say. "I'm going to do some volunteer teaching in a village for a year. And then I'll travel around a bit after that. Who knows, maybe a couple of years." She gave him an earnest look and then quietly laughed. "Maybe I'll never come back."

Richard was trying to absorb the news. Was she toying with him? Leaving for India as a volunteer? Augusta, a volunteer? She, herself, would have scoffed at the idea only a year ago. Had the events surrounding her family—or maybe even him—changed something in her?

"Are you going with someone? Is it through the university?" he inquired.

"No," she said adamantly, and then seemed to doubt her answer. "Oh, I see. Yes, it's a team of volunteers. Obviously, I wouldn't go by myself. Can you imagine a privileged girl like me, all alone there?"

"Alone or with others, I'm still shocked. And for so long …"

"Yes, it's a bit silly, isn't it? White girl traveling to the Far East to make recompense for the grotesque world order. Sad, I know. Maybe when I'm back, I'll open a high-end yoga studio and charge exorbitant sums, teaching people how to achieve serenity in the modern world. That'll wrap up the cliché nicely, don't you think?"

Richard looked out at the water, trying to think of what to say.

He felt her hand rest on top of his. He closed his eyes and sighed. Immediately, he felt peace at her nearness, and the tension of her sex. "I don't know what to say," he said. "I'm happy for you, but I'm not. It sounds ridiculous. As soon as I'm with you, I'm messed up."

Augusta's hand moved behind his head and then she gently pulled his face toward her. "Don't return it if you don't want to, but don't deny me this," she said before kissing him. Her tongue licked his lips before moving into his mouth.

He did not deny her. He let her in willingly, tasting her breath, her warm milky tongue, and hoping she remained inside him for as long as she could. He went to slide his hand around her waist, but she seemed to know what his limbs were doing and checked them by grabbing both his hands. Her clutch was firm, but he felt a tremor from her.

When she pulled her tongue back, then her lips, then her face, she studied him again with her piercing eyes. She stood up. Richard did too.

"Let's not do a long goodbye," she said. "I'm grateful for this brief outing with you. Thank you."

Richard was not content to be parted from her. He wanted to

touch her more, kiss her more. "Let's walk around. Then we can grab lunch."

"Will that make this easier?"

"No, but it's better than just … ending."

"It has to end, Richard."

He saw a flicker of something pass over her face: fear, uncertainty. Her breathing quickened.

"Would you … do you want to …" Augusta's mouth worked and paused, while her eyes met his. "Could you see yourself coming with me?"

He stared speechless back at her, marveling at her question. He was filled with both excitement and dread. He looked away.

"I'm sorry," she said while she backed away from him. "I never should have asked that. I didn't mean to. Don't answer."

"Augusta."

Augusta smiled. "Goodbye, Richard." She turned away to walk down the path from where they had come.

Richard stood, motionless, watching her leave. As Augusta took each step away from him, his yearning for her increased—and his anger. What was she doing to him? He wanted to follow, but Natalie's face hovered in his mind, and guilt was stirring again. Natalie.

"Why did you tell me about Natalie? About her being your half-sister?" he called out after her.

Augusta stopped and turned to face him. "Because. I might let her have you, but I'll make sure you think of me whenever you're with her. When you look into her eyes, you'll find me too." She gave him one last smile, abruptly turned, and walked down the path in the direction of her house.

Richard watched her go, fighting his instinct to chase her. This needed to end. Or he would never be sane; he would never do what was right.

* * *

Richard couldn't deny that returning to Enigma felt good.

On his first day, he walked into the old cubicle where he had worked endless long days and weekends. The Pit had decorated it with some toilet paper streamers, and all his old trinkets were still intact. Jeremy brought coffees for everyone, and for the rest of the morning, the Pit gathered around him to chat. There was a year and a half of catching up to do.

Yes, it had been that long ago on a November evening in 2004 when Xavier had summoned him after work. Much had changed since then. Xavier was gone, and Natalie now occupied his office.

Bill was especially happy to see him when he popped by Richard's desk. "I think all my dreams came true," he said, leaning against the cubicle wall. "You and Natalie both here. Dynamic duo."

"Let's hope I still work as hard as I used to," Richard said. "You sound like you have expectations."

"I do, but I'm not worried. Besides, you'll have to answer to Natalie if you mess up."

There were a few days of adjustment. Getting back into the product, remembering the complexity of the modules and how they interacted with one another, all took time. But by the fourth day, he knew he could do it; he could return to this life, this job. He fell in stride with the rhythm of Enigma Solutions, and the long hours began anew.

But the rhythm was different from what it had been.

He remarked on this new vibration at Enigma when pressed by Natalie on Friday night. They were at a casual bar just a few minutes' drive from the office, to celebrate the completion of his first week. He didn't much feel like talking about work, but when she asked him if there was anything different about the Pit, he was obliged to answer.

"Well, there's the obvious," he said. "Jeremy doesn't wear Bob Marley shirts or tattered jeans anymore. And what faces are not completely clean shaven have tidy beards. But I guess it's the energy that's different. More ambition. More urgency. It's still a startup feel, but it's different. More drive."

"You feel that too? Good. I wanted to make sure it wasn't just me," Natalie said. "I think the Pit knows we're gonna grow, that their work is going to go everywhere. We will have North America, Richard. It's ours." Her hands were starting to gesture rapidly, but she probably saw that Richard was exhausted with this topic, so she took a breath to calm her excitement. "Sorry, you know I just can't stop talking about it."

"I know. And it's fine."

"No, it's not. You have your boundaries and that's good. I need to have them too." She leaned back in her bench seat. "Especially given what I've been thinking about."

"What's that?"

"Well, no rush or anything," Natalie looked away and around the bar, "but I thought we'd look for a place together. We could rent a bigger apartment or a condo."

"You want to move in together?"

"Don't you? Because if you think it's better to live with your parents than with me, then we are not doing well."

Richard smiled. There was some truth to her statement. Why shouldn't he take this leap with her? "I think it will be good," he said. "I've never done it before, but I'll try it with you."

Natalie got off her chair and came to sit on his lap. She put her arms around his neck and kissed him.

He was so grateful for her. But as he stared into her eyes, he thought of someone else.

In less than two weeks, Augusta would be gone. For what seemed like—ever.

* * *

Maybe he had hoped that work at Enigma would distract him from the knowledge of Augusta's looming departure. There was something about her going away to the other side of the world, the length of time, the finality of it all, that was driving Richard mad. As each day of the month passed, he wanted to see her again—one last time. This would be the ending.

Richard had let her go so easily and with minimal objection when they had last met. And he knew why. Because a part of him at that meeting knew he would rest his eyes at least once more upon her. She was not gone.

With seven days left to go before her departure, he sent a text asking how she was. She never responded.

With four days left, he sent another text asking to see her. Still no response.

She was being stronger than him, ignoring him. He should have respected her wishes and his conscience. But he couldn't. Her pull was upon him. On a Tuesday night, when there were only two days remaining in the month, he got in his car after work and drove. This was not like the last time he drove to the Hardiches a few months ago; this was not blind confusion. Richard's head was clear.

He parked around the corner from the house. It was a glorious evening, and the thrill of seeing her awakened his senses to it. At a park just across the street from the Hardiches', he heard the symphonic melody of summer—laughter, joyful screams, and barking dogs—all melding together. The great trees on the lawns seemed to languidly recline on their trunks, enjoying these hours when the light had all its vibrant brightness but not as much of its heat.

He reached the walk to the Hardiches'. Augusta's car was in the driveway, but the curtains in her bedroom window were closed. In fact, all the curtains and blinds in all the windows were closed, giving the home an almost abandoned feel. Approaching the door, and for the third time in his life, he rang the doorbell. He hoped it would be Augusta who answered and not her mother. He was wary that some passing remark might be made by Elinor to David Burlow.

But his hopes were dashed when, as the bell still rising in its crescendo of announcement, the door opened to Elinor's weary face. She appeared disheveled in a nightgown despite the relatively early hour of 7 p.m. There was no trace of the elegance that she previously possessed on the other occasions he met her. Elinor Hardich looked frail and dejected.

"You again," Elinor said, with neither mirth nor accusation. Just a statement of fact.

"I'm sorry, did I wake you?"

"No, I rarely sleep now," she said with a wave of her hand. "I know why you're here. Just a moment."

She stepped away from the door but didn't invite him in. He watched as she disappeared for a minute or two. Richard expected Augusta to emerge from somewhere, but instead it was Elinor that returned to the door, carrying a small, wrapped package.

Elinor held it out to him. "She said you'd come by."

"She's not home?" Richard inquired skeptically, taking the package.

"No. She left weeks ago."

"Left? For India? Already?"

"India? Good heavens. No, not India. But gone."

Confusion muddled Richard's mind. Augusta wasn't going to India? She had lied and left weeks ago? Why? Yet she had left something for him, knowing he would come by?

"Where did she go?" he asked, feeling his heart racing.

Elinor gave him a stern look. "That's not for me to say or you to know. She's gone."

Still reeling, Richard verbally stumbled as he pleaded for something more. "You have to tell me where. How long?"

"I do not," Elinor Hardich said firmly, seemingly irritated at his persistence. "This family has had enough of public shame. We'll not be a spectacle anymore. I'm not sure what your relationship is with Augusta, but she needs time alone now. And if she wanted you to know something, she'd have told you."

With that, Elinor Hardich ducked back inside the house and closed the door.

Left alone, Richard tried to reconcile what had happened. Augusta was gone.

Looking down at the package, he saw that his name was written on the plain beige paper in Augusta's elegant handwriting—decisive but feminine lines. He could tell already by the package's weight and dimensions that it was a hardcover book. He walked out to the street and looked up at the windows again. Augusta wouldn't be up there watching him, would she? He kept a close eye for any signal that she was trying to communicate to him as he slowly strode away.

As soon as he reached his car, he got inside and immediately tore the paper wrapping off. Revealed were *The Complete Works of Oscar Wilde*. He only briefly glanced at the cover before opening it to see if she had left an inscription for him. No, she had done better; here was a letter folded over three times with his name on it.

This must be the explanation he needed—the answer to all the questions he had. Unfolding the pages, he began to read.

My dear Richard,

If you are reading this, then it means you came by the house looking for me after I've left. You see how well I know you?

My departure is earlier than you expected. As I write this, I have only just returned from our walk along the river together. I leave tomorrow.

Honestly, Richard … India? Does that sound anything like me? Can you imagine me trudging around in some village with the poor and destitute to find myself? God, the whole thing would be a macabre rendition of that "Eat, Pray, Love" book. What a dreadful thought: me surrounded by those bubbly do-gooders getting in their volunteer experience though budget travel philanthropy. I'd go mad. And again, I must ask, India? I hope you didn't believe that.

But still away, and to a destination I cannot disclose. But I will take a very circuitous route there. For I must make a stop at a place that has been preoccupying me for a long time and want to see again. We were supposed to be there together. Yes, it's Paris. You were there recently, and I hope you saw the beauty of it. You were with her. I never wanted to know if you loved it without me. My regret is that I was not able to show it to you myself and have you experience it as I do.

I hope you can hear me in your head as you read this. I hope you can see me laughing. And if you do envision me as I wish, can I be holding your hand? Can I be lying on the bed talking to you as I once did? We share something special—the connection we had, and the one we will have, is rare. You must know we were never supposed to be this. You were to be a diversion and fizzle away. But a misfit from a Hardich Spring Gathering proved to be my nemesis.

I think you were the first man I ever 'made love' with. I cringe at using those words; they are such a preposterously gentrified term for a carnal activity. Yet, with you, it fits. You were always tender, loving, and reverential with me. And I fell in love with you. And when that happened, it was over. It couldn't work; it can't work—not with me.

There is something in me that I conceal from everyone, but especially you. I'm ashamed to tell you more about it, just know that some days can be unbearable for me. Sometimes, it takes all my strength, and plenty of pills, to keep it at bay, to stop the descent into dark places.

It has poisoned me, and it would poison us. However much you think you love me, it will seep into what we have, into our interactions. If I were with you in earnest, fully and completely, I swear I'd smother you with a blanket of regret and ruin.

You'll tell me I'm wrong, but I'm not. I know myself. I would never taint those moments we had together. I will keep them pure, always. Everything I have done since we became lovers, I have done for you.

You must promise me you will not fight this ending. I should never have proposed what I did to you at the river—that was a moment of weakness. You know that Natalie is right for you, that what she can give you is tenfold better than what I can. She may be my tormentor, but I am grateful that she cares for you, that she loves you.

The fact is, I confuse you—and you me. And I fear I'm pulling you off the path, away from someone who loves you and can bring you happiness. You have taught me what it is to want something entirely for someone else, to love someone so much that you will undo your happiness for them. I didn't know that altruism was possible until you, and for that, I will always be grateful.

Goodbye, Richard. You will forever have a part of me with you, and I a part of you.

Augusta

P.S. Enjoy the book. Fond memories of Wilde and our readings together. I'll visit his tomb when I'm in Paris. Perhaps his work will inspire you. Writing is one thing you mustn't give up on. For me, please finish at least one thing—a short story, a novel, anything. Your eyes were always so magical when you talked about traveling and writing. I've read enough of your scraps to see your potential. Find a grand story to apply your talents to. But remember—be kind to your characters.

Be kind to me.

When he finished reading the page, he folded it up and took a deep breath. He felt confused and miserable, grateful and furious. Richard lit a cigarette and just sat in his car staring at the book on his lap. That's when he noticed a slip of paper peeking out just above the pages like a bookmark that had slid too far down. He opened Wilde's works at the marker.

It was at the title page of a play called *A Woman of No Importance*. Curious in itself, but only when he studied the slip of paper to see if it was another note to him did he freeze. His heart skipped several beats, and he became numb.

There, on the paper were black-and-white images, half-shapes, inside an inverted cone.

An ultrasound image.

EPILOGUE

Paris, 2010

WE arrived by train in Paris two nights ago, after traveling through the Netherlands, Belgium, and Luxembourg. All too quickly—for me at least—we are nearing the end of our second week of vacation.

Natalie enjoyed it, but I can see she is churched and museumed out. She misses home, or rather, she is eager to return to Enigma. The Blackberry is pulled out of her pocket more when we sit at cafes and amble about the streets and neighborhoods. I have heard her reference the many things that need to be done when she returns home. Her mind is already leaving here to go there, as if it caught a flight yesterday and her body just needs to follow.

I could spend longer here: months, years even. But that chance has passed me by. Years ago, I forsook the bohemian life to plod along in the world I know. For though I may dislike it, I understand it, it makes sense to me. The rules and expectations are clear.

Natalie leaves tomorrow, but I'm staying on a few days to wander alone. Though she's known this since we booked the trip, she continues to ask me why. I only say that it's important to me; that there are things I need to ponder and resolve. Of course, she is confused, and wonders if she should stay, but I laugh and joke with her, so she knows there is nothing serious afoot. She smiles and shakes her head, cautioning me against the siren call of Europe. She playfully reminds me not to get any ideas of staying—we're engaged, after all, and have a wedding coming up.

I'll only be three or four days behind I remind her. And it's true.

There is an errand I must complete, and I pray I will have peace at its end.

* * *

I stroll down the pathway leisurely, stopping frequently to look inside the small, empty houses. There is only darkness and shadows in them, and occasionally, some decaying flowers. It is a little cool this morning, and a gray-black sky entombs the city, heralding a downpour that will soak the soil and make the bones of decomposed bodies swim in their caskets. For now, however, the rain is at bay, and the place is sparsely habited by the living. As the city and its tourists stir into action, the museums and indoor venues will be the focus today—not the places exposed to the elements.

Augusta has been on my mind this entire vacation. At home, I have fallen into a routine where I feel she is there, but I have learned to accept her persistent pull on me, to function. The closer I came to Paris, though, the more she seemed to demand my attention. This cemetery is her home for me; her signal is strongest here, though I suspect she is nowhere close.

On one of the quiet avenues, I break and lean against a tree to check my determination. The package is under my arm, paper in an envelope. This is my offering for the altar today.

Sadness washes over me, as if I just stepped out into a thick, muggy day from a cold, air-conditioned house. I don't know if I've made the right decisions anymore. They were all good decisions, they were all logical, but were they right? I suppose asking about the right decision is the wrong question. I've learned now that when we make decisions, they don't always result in simple good and bad outcomes—they just take us to a different place that's either further or closer to who we are.

Thunder rolls its deep drum in the sky, long overdue. In the near west, there are flickers of lightning. Rain begins to fall; light spatters at first, but a weight is gathering in the droplets. I have walked the various avenues and paths, gazed on centuries of eternal rest, but have avoided one place: a particular tomb. I spied it from afar, frequently, through trees and mausoleums, always beckoning to me.

Yet, I never came within more than a hundred feet of it. To that place, that edifice, I walk to now—to see it, to be with her.

Rain is drenching my hair and matting it to my face. I have no umbrella and don't bother to pull up the hood of my raincoat. I can see it, as I drew near: a prostrate angel crushed by the weight of its own wings. I stand under a tree just across from the tomb. Heavy drops are pelting the leaves above me with fury, and the ground is muddying around my feet.

I know the feeling of that crushing weight: love has it; secrets have it. And I have both. The root is Augusta Hardich.

Over the past few years, the Hardiches have become reclusive; there are no gatherings, there is almost nothing to report from them at all. Xavier moved back to the house and still works as a sales man-ager at a parts manufacturer—the job David got him. He apparently does well enough at it, but keeps a low profile. We never see him out at restaurants or bars. Elinor seldom leaves her bower, and few can say they've had any interaction with her, even by telephone. Only David Burlow sees her on occasion, but he tells me the visits are about once a year now, and painful for him. The great Hardich house, once pristinely maintained, shows signs of neglect: the paint flakes, the wood rots, and the lawn weeds.

As far as anyone knows, Augusta has never returned. She has seem-ingly made a new life somewhere else. Everyone remains mystified as to her whereabouts or what she is doing. Only I know why she left.

I reach into my envelope and pull a few inches of printed manu-script out. I scan the opening paragraph, and it brings me back to a different time, a simpler time—before Augusta.

Finally, something is finished: my grand story. I never imagined people I knew—and me—would form the basis for my first novel, and likely my last. The water droplets slam down onto the page, blot-ting out some of the typeface and rendering holes of transparency on the paper. I make no effort to protect it.

Stepping forward, my feet soak in a puddle. I approach the tomb and put my hand on the monument to steady myself. I move around to the back of it, careful not to step on the small pieces of paper covering the ground that could be love letters, poems, or petitions. My face slowly draws near to the grave, and I can feel it radiate a cold dampness.

As I lightly press my lips to it, and they overlay a thousand kisses from a thousand people, I feel the strangest sensation. A sadness and a connection with both the dead and the living stirs inside me, makes me shiver. I sense an eternal song of opposites: love and loss, hope and defeat, purpose and aimlessness, life and death. Pulling away, I shake as my soul is grabbed and twisted about in a whirlwind of chaos. And I pray, that ritual act that remains foreign to me but always seems the only thing to do when experiencing the mystical, the profound.

The rain is unforgiving while I lay the wet papers of my story at the foot of the angel. This is my sacrifice to her, to Augusta. At one time, she had encouraged me to pursue this writing, but I grew fearful when she was not by my side. And I have slid now into the old ways of doing things. Still, the task she set out for me is accomplished, the story is written, and who better to be the protagonist and the antagonist than she.

There is bitterness in me today. Like the sculpted angel, I am kneeling prostrate in the mud at the feet of the dead, while dead memories resurface of a time with her: at a coffeehouse, debating; at a bar in low candlelight, yearning; at my apartment, reading stories; in bed, awakening to her. Augusta always felt she was an outcast, and she believes she sacrificed herself to save me. But she has made me an outcast too, for I now live in limbo between loves and between lives. Blood is the only bridge.

My prayer is on my lips again. I pray for her to be safe; for my child to be safe. And I pray for peace to try to help me forget her. Yet, no matter how much I end the prayer on those words, there is more that my soul wishes to be included. It rebels against my abbreviated lines and adds a constant amendment, an additional closing parenthesis, an appendix I try to stymie with my mind while my heart inserts it.

I pray that we will meet again.

Made in the USA
Las Vegas, NV
19 November 2024

12145243R00246